# PARALLEL UNIVERSE

# PARALLEL UNIVERSE

## BERT ERNIE

iridium peach

Parallel Universe




Published by iridium peach
Melbourne, Australia


ISBN-13: 9780648551416

# Chapter 1



Max rode his bicycle through the morning chill and caught himself smiling. It was a strange reaction on what he'd privately decided might be his last day on Earth. He had never been particularly successful; he was always broke, lived a life that felt narrower than it should have been, and kept to himself apart from his aunt Céleste who gave him a place to stay. If the world ended today, he doubted anyone would miss him. Still, there was a certain thrill in pedalling towards something extraordinary. He was about to witness the first man-made black hole — and a white hole beside it — assuming the theories put forward by Dr Gaidon Ballerat and Daniel Mittermayer held up. If they were wrong, none of them would notice the mistake. They'd simply disappear inside an expanding event horizon under the fields of Prévessin-Moëns.

The laboratory sat thirty metres underground, like most of CERN's facilities. From the surface, the only sign of it was the large, weathered metal structure housing the lift. Max leaned his bike against the wall, scanned his access pass and descended into the quiet hum of the complex. A few minutes later, he joined the others in the control room.

The space resembled a windowless office more than a laboratory. Twenty tall racks of equipment occupied the rear wall, forming a compact supercomputer cooled by ducting that dropped from the ceiling. Cables thicker than his wrist snaked into the floor. The team worked along a ten-metre desk lined with displays and keyboards, each station tuned to a different slice of the system.

Gaidon Ballerat, the lead physicist, carried the weight of both reputation and responsibility. He was regarded as one of the finest quantum theoreticians in the world, the person with the old-school grounding and the original idea. Daniel Mittermayer, younger and sharper in a different way, brought the new world of quantum simulation to the table. Baset Theron, CERN's senior engineering manager, had been chosen because no one understood system integration better. Emerancie Favre oversaw the computer hardware and software, a role she occupied with the ease of someone who had long ago mastered both. Vincent Duke handled the electrical systems and had designed the rapid-firing pulse array that made the machine possible. And then there was Max — the mechanical engineer and draftsman who turned their requirements into detailed models. He still suspected he didn't belong here, but Gaidon had insisted he stay on for the final phase of testing. After that, his contract ended and he'd be back to searching for work.

The machine's purpose was deceptively simple: to transfer matter. Thousands of individual gold atoms per second were meant to fall into a controlled black hole inside the transmitter chamber. At the receiver, an inverse construct — the white hole — would emit the same atoms, allowing them to be detected. The team called the entire setup the Rapid Argon Compression Experiment. In practice, it relied on compressing a positively ionised argon sphere at one point and a negatively ionised sphere at another, both collapsing nearly instantaneously. The sequence linked the two points. Shut down the transmitting chamber at precisely the right moment and the atoms would only exist in the receiving chamber. If it worked, physics would take a step forward and Gaidon and Daniel would have their names etched into history.

When they'd applied for funding, they'd minimised the language of black holes and white holes. The proposal spoke instead of sub-atomic compression — argon squeezed to a scale smaller than a hydrogen atom — which sounded ambitious but palatable to a review panel. The real challenge was getting the ionised argon to collapse rapidly enough. To do that, they had built a spherical array of magnetic pulse injectors, each firing at a precise interval. Daniel had spent countless hours of supercomputer time iterating simulations; each run shaped the next until the solution emerged. The pattern resembled a fragment of sound — what the two men half-jokingly called the "argon song of containment" — a vibration lasting just five attoseconds. An attosecond sits to a second the way a second sits to thirty-odd billion years. Even thinking about it felt absurd.

At 10:10 a.m., the warm-up cycle ended. Gaidon entered the final command and the system launched into its 875-step sequence. When the countdown clock appeared with ten seconds to go, the room settled into a tense quiet. Everyone leaned towards the primary display.

Zero.

The world remained intact. No flash, no collapse. Instead, the control room filled with an alarm tone as data streamed across the monitors. Red and orange advisories flared across every screen. There was no gold-atom signature, no clear transfer data — only numbers that defied anything they had prepared for. Chairs dragged across the floor as the team leaned forward. Voices rose over one another as the confusion edged towards panic.

Gaidon stood.

"Enough."

The room went still.

"Baset — are we safe? Any breach, any radiation, anything unstable?"

Baset scanned his readouts again, tapping through diagnostics with increasing urgency.

"I think we're safe," he said, though it sounded more like hope than certainty. "But something's wrong. Very wrong. These numbers *shouldn't exist.*"

***

**Wednesday, 17th November 2010, 11:32 a.m.**
**Machine room, Laboratory 832, CERN, Prévessin-Moëns, France.**

All six members of the RACE team stood in front of the machine. It filled the room — seventeen metres across, ten metres high — two steel spheres surrounded by layers of hardware and shielding. It looked perfect, which only made the morning's failure feel stranger. The receiving chamber should have shown a clean stream of gold atoms. Instead, its sensors had thrown out incomprehensible data and its triple-redundant vacuum system had collapsed at the same moment. Nothing about that combination made sense.

"We'll have to do a manual purge," Baset said. "I'll pull one of the data probes. After that I'll need to take the accelerator out. It's not quick."

"Fine," Daniel replied. "I'll go through the readings again. Something might line up."

Ten minutes later, Baset was stretched across the top of the receiving sphere, moving between pulse guns, capacitors and lengths of pipework. He worked the puller into place, braced himself and forced the handle down. A violent rush of air tore through the room as the dead vacuum finally surrendered. The others fell silent, watching from below.

"Probe's out. Vacuum's gone," Baset called. "Now comes the fun part."

With Max and Vincent helping, they set up the lifting cradle. Bolts came free. The accelerator slid away from the sphere with a heavy groan as the crane took the weight and lowered it onto the cradle beside them.

Baset climbed back up, torch in hand, and eased himself towards the open chamber. One quick look was enough to stop him cold.

The interior that should have been polished to a mirror shine had turned dull and matte. Every surface carried a film of tan-coloured powder, thickest near the base where it had settled into a soft layer. He touched it, rubbed it between his fingers. No smell. No obvious texture. Nothing that fit with any part of the experiment.

He climbed down slowly, his face drained of colour.

"Well?" Gaidon asked.

"I found something," Baset said. His voice had lost its usual steadiness. "I can't tell you what it is. But whatever it is, it killed the experiment. You need to see it."

Gaidon didn't hesitate. He went up the ladder, took the torch and leaned into the sphere.

A long, tight silence followed.

Then the man who never raised his voice, never swore, never slipped from composure, said one crisp, unfiltered line:

"What the *fuck* is this shit?"

***

**Friday, 19th November 2010, 10:16 a.m.**
**Gaidon Ballerat's office, Laboratory 832, CERN, Prévessin-Moëns, France.**

Daniel Mittermayer looked as though he'd walked out of a fashion shoot and straight into a physics lab — gold-and-blue suit, sharp red shirt, hair styled to appear effortless. On most days it made him seem eccentric. Today it simply amplified how charged he was as he stepped toward Gaidon and Baset, who were hunched over the microscope.

"I know what went wrong," he said.

Both men turned. His certainty didn't match the week they'd had. Nothing in the data had lined up; nothing about the failure seemed logical. Yet Daniel looked as though he'd solved something fundamental.

Gaidon nodded toward the microscope. "You haven't even looked at the sample."

Daniel bent over the eyepiece, studied the powder for a few seconds, then straightened with a quiet, almost pleased confidence.

"I know what it is," he said. "And I know how it ended up inside the chamber."

Gaidon and Baset exchanged a brief look. They recognised that tone. Daniel only sounded like this when the pieces had finally locked into place.

He explained it without theatrics.

"The containment algorithm — the argon pattern — didn't hold the boundary at thirty-something picometres. Instead of stabilising, the black and white holes slipped past the limit. Then they rebounded."

"How far?" Gaidon asked.

"Roughly twenty *billion* times the intended scale."

Gaidon closed his eyes for a moment. A rebound at that magnitude meant a structure metres across instead of atomic. Nothing about that was a simple miscalculation.

"But that isn't the real result," Daniel said, his excitement settling into something steadier. "We aimed to transfer gold atoms across a shared space. And we did move matter. Just... not inside the same universe."

The room fell still.

Gaidon's voice was quiet. "Say that again."

"The transmitter stayed here," Daniel said. "But the receiving chamber formed in another universe. A single geometry stretched across two realities."

Baset let out a slow breath. "And the powder?"

Daniel nodded. "Debris from the other side. When the portal shell expanded, it tore through whatever occupied that space. And when the transmitter shut down first, the pressure imbalance dragged the material back through. That sample is dirt from a parallel Earth. Same coordinates. Same thirty metres of depth. Just not ours."

He stopped there, letting the conclusion settle between them.

For once, Daniel didn't pace or fidget. He didn't need to.

The discovery spoke loudly enough on its own.

***

# Chapter 2



**Wednesday, 1st December 2010, 10:00 a.m.**
**Fairfax Woods's office, CERN, Prévessin-Moëns, France.**

Gaidon and Daniel waited in the outer office of Fairfax Woods, chairman of scientific policy. Daniel paced a slow loop, already sketching ideas in the air with quick movements of his hands.

"The shells share the same structure," he said quietly. "Generated here, but one forms on the other side. Anything inside either shell is mirrored at once. When the transmitter shuts down first, whatever's left is dragged back to us. That's why we found the powder."

Gaidon nodded but kept his tone steady, trying to stop Daniel from spiralling into another torrent of possibilities. "And you still believe the shells are stable once formed?"

"Completely. They're sealed during expansion, then permeable once they reach full size. If we're precise with the modifications..." Daniel paused, eyes bright with the idea he'd been circling for days. "We could step into the shell here and walk out into the parallel universe."

Before Gaidon could interrupt, the door opened.

"Dr Ballerat," Fairfax Woods said, ushering him inside.

Fairfax carried the calm weight of someone used to deciding the future of expensive science. He sat behind his desk, folded his hands and waited.

"I understand you've completed your review of RACE."

Gaidon took a careful breath. "Yes. There's good news, and there's bad news."

"Start with the good," Fairfax said.

Gaidon shook his head. "The bad needs to come first."

Fairfax leaned back slightly. "Go ahead."

"The shutdown wasn't caused by a flaw in the machine. Being thirty metres underground, with dense matter on all sides, destabilised the formation of the controlled black and white holes. The safety systems triggered almost immediately."

"That's the bad news?"

"Yes."

"And the outcome of the experiment itself?"

"It worked, but not in the way we intended. We only had fourteen milliseconds before the shutdown. Far too little time to detect gold atoms."

Fairfax absorbed this without interruption.

"And the good news?"

"We've already produced a redesign. With the right changes, we think we're close to something far larger than the original aim. But we can't run it underground. The machine needs to be moved above ground."

Fairfax nodded, unsurprised. "You have costings?"

"Eighteen million euros for a new building. Twenty-six million for modifications."

Fairfax considered that for only a moment before his expression softened into a small, approving smile.

"Gaidon, too many people here treat fourteen milliseconds as failure. It isn't. It's the start of something we've never seen before. And as for funding..." He made a small, dismissive gesture. "Forty-four million euros is nothing compared to ATLAS or the LHC. Leave it with me. I'll get it approved."

***

**Monday, 7th February 2011, 10:04 a.m.**
**Gaidon Ballerat's office, Laboratory 832, CERN, Prévessin-Moëns, France.**

Max sat in the uncomfortable chair opposite Gaidon's desk, hands loosely clasped, still unsure why he'd agreed to take a day off for this meeting. The office was small and crowded, its walls covered with printouts and sketches that had been pinned up over months of thinking. It looked like the inside of a mind that rarely slowed.

Gaidon closed the door behind him, let out a long breath, and took his seat.

"Max... thank you for coming."

"You said it was important," Max replied.

"It is." Gaidon leaned forward, elbows resting on the desk. "Laboratory 888 has been approved. Full funding. Construction starts in May."

Max blinked. "That soon?"

"Yes. And I want you on the redesign from the start."

"Gaidon... I've only just started at Nexter. And the pay—"

"I know what it pays," Gaidon said, cutting him off with a brief, impatient wave of his hand. "But you're the only engineer who understands the original geometry of RACE. The shell tolerances, the injector patterns, the alignment work — no one else can adapt it without months of slow progress."

Max shifted in his seat. "Surely you could get other drafters in."

"And they'll need time to reach the place you're already at. I don't have that time." Gaidon held his gaze. "Not for this project."

The room settled into a quiet stretch that neither of them rushed.

"What exactly are you asking me to do?" Max finally said.

"Stay at Nexter," Gaidon replied. "Keep your job. But give me your evenings. Work from home — revisions, updated schematics, oversight on the redesign. Then come in on weekends once construction begins."

Max ran a hand across his jaw. "You're asking a lot."

"It's the only way forward," Gaidon said. "And if we get this right... Max, we're close to something extraordinary. I need you on this."

Max wanted to turn him down. After years of uncertainty, the steady routine at Nexter mattered more than he liked admitting. But the machine — the sheer complexity and challenge of it — had stayed with him long after the first run. Part of him still burned for that work.

He let out a slow breath. "Evenings from home. Weekends here. That's the deal?"

"Yes," Gaidon said. "I won't ask for more."

Max hesitated long enough for the choice to feel real, then gave a small nod.

"Alright. I'll do it."

Relief softened Gaidon's expression for a moment before his usual intensity returned.

"Good. Because the next six months will be demanding."

Max offered a faint smile. "Aren't they always?"

Gaidon didn't answer. He didn't have to.

They both understood exactly what they were stepping into.

***

**Tuesday, 15th May 2012, 10:05 a.m.**
**Control room, Laboratory 888, CERN, Prévessin-Moëns, France.**

Laboratory 888 wasn't so much a building as a structure built around a single purpose. Morning light filtered through the high roof panels, catching the steel and casting long, pale reflections across the interior. At the centre stood the twin spherical chambers, each suspended on a network of dark-green structural beams. Grated walkways wrapped around them like a narrow balcony, providing access to the injector clusters positioned in precise patterns across the surfaces. Above each chamber, the argon accelerators rose in tight helical arcs, polished enough that the light from the roof broke across them like moving lines.

Beneath the main platform, the lower level was all shadowed metal: beams, ladders, hydraulic lines and the six concealed rams capable of lifting all 290 tonnes of the machine by four metres. That movement was essential. Without it, they'd never be able to align the portal shell with the unknown ground plane on the other side.

The control room overlooked this steel expanse from behind reinforced glass. Inside, the team sat in the same worn chairs they had used in Laboratory 832 — evidence that the new budget had gone entirely into the machine, not the furniture.

Today was the first operational test.

RACE had been rebuilt from the ground up. The gold-injection system was gone. In its place was a design focused entirely on opening the shell, observing the parallel universe and preparing the way for controlled entry. The receiving chamber now held a movable steel platform, lifted and lowered on hydraulic rams so instruments could be placed directly inside the active shell. Anything unnecessary had been stripped away; anything essential had been reinforced.

Gaidon initiated the ten second countdown. The team members each had systems to monitor. They did so quietly.

On the main screen, the countdown reached zero.

"Machine is ready," Emerancie said, her voice steady.

Gaidon glanced around the room. "Clear?"

A round of quiet confirmations.

He clicked the mouse.

The chamber pressure stabilised. The magnetic injectors fired one after another, the sound softened by layers of shielding. Two seconds later, the cameras which were mounted in the chamber walls, extended into the shells.

No one spoke.

The monitors brightened.

Instead of the mirrored steel interior, the cameras showed the faint blue shimmer of the ionised argon boundary and, beyond it, another world. A clearing. Trees shifting in a light wind. Sun on compacted soil. A patch of ground that looked cultivated, edged by dense forest. The camera's position sat several metres above the ground on the other side, giving them a wide view across the space.

The control room held its breath.

Gaidon broke the silence. "Vincent? Chemical profile?"

"All readings normal."

"Baset? Mechanical tolerances?"

"Well within limits."

Gaidon gave a single nod. "Then we shut it down. First test complete."

He made the final clicks. The image disappeared. The shells collapsed. The camera views returned to showing the polished steel of the interior of the receiving chamber.

Two hours later, every parameter had been reviewed — injector timing, pressure curves, vacuum behaviour, thermal drift. Nothing out of place. Nothing dangerous.

Gaidon stood with his arms folded, looking through the glass at the machine.

"Tomorrow we begin ground-plane alignment. The footage puts the portal roughly three metres above the ground on the other side. We'll lower the machine in stages until both planes match."

No one said anything in response.

There was nothing to add.

Today, they had seen the other universe.

Tomorrow, they would begin preparing to reach it.

***

**Wednesday, 16th May 2012, 3:40 p.m.**
**Control room, Laboratory 888, CERN, Prévessin-Moëns, France.**

They had needed only three lowering tests. Each time the shells opened, the camera feeds dropped closer to the ground of the parallel world — first several metres above the clearing, then just above the ground plane, then close enough that individual blades of grass were clearly visible through the shimmer.

"Final adjustment," Baset said. "Down forty centimetres."

The hydraulic rams hissed beneath the platform, lowering the 290-tonne machine in a slow, controlled movement.

Readings stabilised.

Gaidon entered the command to initiate the portal opening.

The shells unfolded into existence and the cameras extended through the boundary. The blue haze dissolved.

This time the view sat steady above the ground, the camera's fixed mid-height catching the clearing from roughly two metres up.

Gaidon leaned closer. "Baset, alignment?"

"Twenty-three centimetres below the ground plane," Baset said, checking the depth maps. "Couldn't be cleaner."

"Shut it down," Gaidon said.

The portal collapsed with a tight flicker. Chamber pressure equalised. Readouts returned to baseline — and the receiving chamber remained empty.

No dirt. No dust. No debris.

Just the clean steel floor.

Exactly as the physics simulations promised.

They logged the results, archived the footage and moved on with the rest of the afternoon's schedules. By the time the final checks were due, the control room had settled into the quiet routine of late-day work.

An hour later, the team crossed to the machine. Baset lowered the internal platform and swung the inspection lights into place.

Nothing.

Perfectly clean.

Daniel broke the quiet with a grin. "So, Gaidon... no tan powder this time. Should we be disappointed you didn't swear?"

Gaidon gave him the same flat look he'd worn the first time he'd leaned into the chamber at Laboratory 832 and seen the impossible tan dust.

Baset chuckled. Emerancie hid a smile.

Gaidon sighed. "Let's not make my not swearing a measurement of success, Daniel."

But the small twitch at the corner of his mouth gave him away.

They had done it.

The ground plane was aligned.

The machine was ready.

***

**Friday 18th May 2012, 2:23 p.m.**
**Control room, Laboratory 888, CERN, Prévessin-Moëns, France.**

Adéhémar Baille stood at the end of the long desk, hands resting lightly on the custom-built control rig he'd designed for himself. At twenty-five he had the self-assurance of someone who knew his skill set was rare and valued. His heli-drone waited on its stand beside the machine: a one-metre carbon-fibre and titanium frame, four high-torque electric motors, a 1.4-kilogram sensor module assembled by Baset and Vincent, and a high-resolution video array that streamed directly into the control room. The unit had cost CERN one hundred and seventy-five thousand euros and looked every bit the purpose-built instrument it was.

Gaidon looked down the row of his team. "Ready?"

Adéhémar checked his laptop. "Drone powered and stable. All green."

"Then we begin."

Gaidon clicked through the initiation sequence. The two largest displays shifted: one filled with machine telemetry, the other showing twelve camera feeds — four from inside the receiving chamber, four from the laboratory, four from the drone.

Seven seconds later, the shells opened.

The receiving-chamber cameras filled with the now-familiar blue haze after the boundary had formed. Adéhémar launched the loading routine. On the wall display, one of the lab cameras showed the six-axis robot arm swing out from its parked position. Its gripper descended onto the humming drone, the rotors spinning just enough to keep it steady as the robot lifted it clear, rotated, and carried it to the underside of the receiving chamber.

Gaidon released the chamber platform. The hydraulic rams lowered the steel platform by two metres — a slow, deliberate movement — stopping level with the drone's position.

Only then did the robot arm move again, easing forward and placing the drone precisely at the centre of the lowered platform. Once the load sensors confirmed a stable contact, the arm withdrew and folded away.

Gaidon raised the platform and locked it into place.

"Emerancie? Vincent?" he asked.

"Systems good," Emerancie said.

"All clear," Vincent added.

Gaidon nodded. "Take her out, Adéhémar."

The drone lifted cleanly from the chamber floor, hovered for a moment, then moved forward through the shell boundary.

The instant it crossed, the video stabilised into sharp clarity. All four drone feeds showed the clearing exactly as before: the cultivated beds, the heater posts, the poles, the treeline. Sunlight. Wind making the nearby trees shift softly. A world that looked close enough to their own to unsettle in its familiarity.

One camera angled back and captured the experiment itself from the outside: a glass-smooth blue sphere, four and a half metres in diameter, hovering with it's lowest portion having just fractionally clipped the ground plane of the parallel world. Inside it were only the grooved chamber plate and the protruding camera housings.

The control room fell silent.

Gaidon spoke first. "Team?"

A round of quiet affirmations from the six other members of Gaidon's team.

"Adéhémar, take us up slowly. Let's see more."

The drone climbed — and the feed tore apart. Streaks of static. Blocks of digital noise.

"What's wrong?" Gaidon asked.

Adéhémar's hands moved quickly across the keyboard. The status lights on his rig flickered red. "Signal strength collapsing. Pulling it back."

The drone drifted toward the shell. At around twenty metres from the boundary, the image snapped clean again — sharp and stable, as though nothing had happened.

Adéhémar exhaled. "Interference. The transmitter isn't strong enough past twenty metres. I didn't anticipate how much extra signal strength would be needed to power through the portal shell environment."

"You're certain?" Gaidon said.

"Yes. Stronger transmitter, different band. I can fix it. Two days."

Gaidon nodded once. "Bring it in."

The drone slipped back through the boundary, settled on the chamber floor and powered down. Gaidon shut the machine down. The shells vanished. The harsh steel interior of the receiving chamber returned.

Gaidon moved to Adéhémar's station. "Good work. Let's upgrade the transmitter."

"I'll start tonight," Adéhémar said. "We'll have range by Monday."

The team didn't need to say anything more.

They all understood it now: they weren't standing at the threshold anymore.

They were already stepping through it.

***

# Chapter 3

**Saturday, 19th May 2012, 8:25 a.m.**
**Parallel Universe. Diderot farm, Prévessin-Moëns, France.**

Renato Diderot lived for three pleasures: cultivating magnificent produce, making devoted and frequent love to his wife, and presiding over the monthly gatherings — half party, half orgy — where their friends consumed drugs from his home-grown psychedelic garden and behaved accordingly. That final indulgence demanded the least from him these days. The private acre where he grew his mind-bending plants was buried deep within his eight-hundred-acre property, tended almost entirely by the automated watering, lighting, shading, and nutrient systems he'd built over the years.

He wouldn't normally be here this early. But over the last few days he'd heard a strange sound — a single, whip-like crack somewhere on the property. Not thunder, not machinery, and unsettling enough to stick under his skin. He barely slept. At dawn he gave up, dressed, and walked out to investigate.

He slipped through the narrow gap in the bushes that hid the entrance. The familiar scents — damp soil, the faint sweetness of certain leaves — wrapped around him. As he moved between the rows, he checked a few heaters, adjusted a plant monitor sensor, brushed a hand across a trellis. To an outsider the place would look like a chaotic jungle of alien crops; to him it was calm, ordered, alive.

Several minutes in, he turned toward his favourite section — the cannabis beds. Late spring meant a carpet of juvenile plants, none more than a metre high, neat, delicate, full of promise.

He stopped.

At the eastern edge of the plot, a perfectly smooth hollow had been pressed into the ground — a two-metre-wide bowl cut with impossible precision. The soil inside had been compacted into a dense, rock-hard surface, dropping roughly a foot below the normal ground level. Not dug. Not torn. Pressed.

Renato crouched and touched the surface. It was like concrete. He tried scraping at it with his fingernails; nothing shifted.

"This is... impossible," he said quietly.

He stood back, taking in the flawless curvature of the hollow. It looked as though someone had pushed a perfectly round, invisible weight into the soil and lifted it away again without disturbing anything around it. For a fleeting moment he wondered whether decades of chemically enhanced weekends had finally betrayed him.

No — the geometry was too clean, too exact.

And the timing... the single, sharp whip-crack over the last few days...

He ran a hand through his hair, unease tightening in his chest.

He wasn't telling his wife. Not yet. Not until he understood what he was looking at. Because whatever had done this hadn't just flattened a part of his crop.

It had left a mark on the land that felt like something — or someone — had reached through it.

***

**Monday, 21st May 2012, 8:35 a.m.**
**Control room, Laboratory 888, CERN, Prévessin-Moëns, France.**

"Ready with the drone, Adéhémar?"

"Yes. Firing her up now."

He flipped a switch. A sharp, rising whine filled the control room. On the lab camera feed the upgraded drone sat on its stand, its four miniature combustion engines shuddering as hot exhaust trembled the air above it. The electric motors were gone; the new transmitter weighed two kilos more, and combustion engines were the only way to maintain the lift they needed.

Gaidon began the shell-initiation sequence.

On the screens, the six-axis robot arm moved toward the humming drone, clamped onto its frame and lifted. The arm carried it to the receiving chamber. Gaidon lowered the chamber plate on its hydraulic rams. When it settled into position, Adéhémar tapped a key. The robot swung forward and set the drone neatly onto the lowered steel platform. Once the load sensors stabilised, the arm retracted. Gaidon raised and locked the plate.

"Go ahead," he said.

Adéhémar eased the drone into the air. It hovered briefly, then slid through the shell.

The video held steady — not flawless, but far better than before. The drone climbed to a hundred metres before thin streaks of static crept across the image. Still functional. Gaidon allowed a slow survey.

The view silenced the room. Geneva lay spread across the horizon — similar at first glance, but older in its architecture, with fewer suburbs, more forest, more farmland. Prévessin-Moëns looked preserved, almost as if a century of modern expansion had never come. Yet the cars on the roads were sleek and unfamiliar. A world adjacent, recognisable, but diverged.

After five minutes, fuel dropped to twenty percent.

"Bring her back," Gaidon said.

The drone returned through the shell without incident.

***

**Monday, 21st May 2012, 9:55 a.m.**
**Control room, Laboratory 888, CERN, Prévessin-Moëns, France.**

Adéhémar's transmitter modifications worked.

The second run streamed high-resolution video as the drone climbed past two hundred metres... three hundred... four hundred. The team of seven watched a group of children playing football on a field near Prévessin-Moëns — ordinary, harmless, astonishing.

Then Emerancie's voice cut through the quiet.

"We have a visitor. Camera two."

Every eye turned to the chamber feed.

A man — plainly dressed, clearly a farmer — was walking toward the shell. He moved carefully, stopping a metre from the boundary. He circled the sphere, appearing on different feeds as he moved around it, studying the wavering surface with growing confusion.

"Drone back. Now," Gaidon said.

Baset asked quietly, "What if he steps in?"

Gaidon didn't look away from the monitors. "Fuck, I don't know. Let's hope he doesn't."

The farmer eventually retreated toward the trees. Gaidon exhaled, tension easing by degrees.

The drone approached the clearing.

Emerancie checked camera two again. "Looks like he has a camera, he's trying to get it to work."

The drone slipped through the boundary.

Gaidon shut down the machine at once. The shells collapsed. The control room breathed.

***

**Monday, 21st May 2012, 9:55 a.m.**
**Parallel Universe. Diderot farm, Prévessin-Moëns, France.**

Renato Diderot was crossing a field on his tractor when a single, sharp whip-crack rolled across the land. He turned toward the clearing seven hundred metres away.

He pushed the tractor to full throttle.

Before he reached it, a strange buzzing made him glance up. A satin-black miniature helicopter burst above the treeline — four rotors, fast and deliberate — and shot off toward Geneva.

Renato's stomach dropped.

He quickly reached the hidden path and forced his way through the branches into the clearing. Two days before there had been only a perfect hollow pressed into the soil. Today something entirely different filled the space.

A blue sphere hung towards the edge of the clearing — semi-transparent, its surface rippling in slow waves. It emitted a low hum. Now and then a spark snapped across the shell.

Renato approached cautiously, heart thudding. At ten metres he stopped, scanning the treeline as though expecting a witness. He edged closer.

Inside the wavering blue surface he could make out a grooved metal plate at the base... and four small circular discs set into the mid-plane.

Cameras.

Two of them shifted focus.

Renato stepped back so sharply he almost lost his footing.

He retreated to the trees, fumbling for his small digital camera. He switched to video mode. The device beeped — memory full. Panic rising, he deleted dozens of files, most of them photos of him and his wife at their monthly gatherings.

The buzzing returned.

The four-engine drone reappeared above the trees.

Renato raised the camera and hit record.

The drone slowed, approached the sphere, and moved straight toward the blue surface. It passed through it — and the entire sphere vanished with a hard, collapsing thump of displaced air.

Renato stopped recording and checked the screen, desperate to see what he had captured.

The viewer froze.

Unable to process video — out of memory.

"FUCK!"

His voice echoed across the clearing.

***

**Sunday, 27th May 2012, 10:11 a.m.**
**Parallel Universe. Diderot farm, Prévessin-Moëns, France.**

The days since he had seen the blue sphere had worn Renato thin. Every day had swung between dread and forced dismissal — half of him convinced the thing had been real, the rest sure it was the accumulated price of decades of drugs and long nights. He hadn't told his wife. He couldn't. Not until he knew whether he was losing his grip.

Last night he had broken a twenty-two-year tradition. For the first time he'd refused to take part in the monthly feast and lovemaking circle they hosted. He'd muttered something about feeling unwell and gone to bed before sunset. His wife had watched him closely but hadn't pressed.

He woke early and fled to the tractor, hoping the routine weight of work might steady him. But a little after ten, the sound came again — a heavy crack rolling from the direction of the hidden crop. Not thunder. Not machinery. The same sound.

Renato swung the tractor around and pushed the throttle forward.

At roughly one hundred and fifty metres from the clearing, movement in the sky caught his attention. A satin-black four-rotor helicopter rose above the treeline — the same machine he had seen before — drifting toward Geneva.

He braked hard.

"Not this time," he said.

He reached behind the seat, took hold of the rifle already loaded, and climbed down from the cab. He flicked off the safety, steadied himself and fired. The drone wobbled in the air, struggled to correct itself. He fired again. On the third shot the machine faltered, spun and dropped into the grass.

Renato jogged toward the crash site, swearing under his breath — at the drone, at the unease eating at him, at the possibility that it was all another hallucination waiting to ambush him.

The black craft lay on its side, the central frame split by a bullet. Two rotors still spun weakly, slowing as he approached. They stopped.

He stepped closer to pick it up — then froze.

A small camera turret rotated toward him, the lens adjusting with a soft mechanical twitch.

Renato let out a raw, instinctive shout. "You bastard!"

He drove the butt of the rifle into the camera, smashing it cleanly.

***

**Sunday, 27th May 2012, 10:11 a.m.**
**Control room, Laboratory 888, CERN, Prévessin-Moëns, France.**

Gaidon had scheduled the test for Sunday morning, assuming fewer people would be outside in the parallel world. The team sat at their stations while the drone's second major survey streamed across the large display.

Geneva came into view again — familiar yet distinctly altered. Older architecture. Less urban sprawl. More open land. Prévessin-Moëns looked almost pastoral, though entirely modern in its own way. The differences fascinated everyone.

As the drone climbed above the clearing, Vincent leaned forward. "Field to the west... that's a tractor."

The camera zoomed.

Gaidon groaned. "For fuck's sake. The farmer again. Doesn't he take Sundays off?"

The tractor stopped. A figure climbed down, carrying something long in one hand.

Daniel frowned. "Is that a—?"

They got their answer immediately.

The man raised the rifle.

The drone feed lurched — muzzle flashes, recoil, bursts of static over the digital telemetry. Adéhémar's console lit red.

"Shit — I can't stabilise it," he said, fingers moving fast.

The drone pitched violently. Two camera feeds cut to black. A third froze on a jagged view of shattered carbon fibre. Only one lens remained, its angle low and skewed.

The drone hit the ground.

Adéhémar killed the engines remotely.

The final camera rotated, catching movement. A figure walked into frame. Adéhémar focused the lens just in time to see the man lift the rifle and shout something before smashing the camera. The feed dissolved into static.

There was no audio, yet the words still landed — written plainly in the shape of his mouth.

The control room went silent.

***

**Sunday, 27th May 2012, 4:34 p.m.**
**Gaidon Ballerat's office, Laboratory 888, CERN, Prévessin-Moëns, France.**

Gaidon sat hunched at his desk, shuffling through papers with an agitation Daniel had rarely seen from him. The drones destruction had unsettled him more than he cared to admit.

"There has to be a better way forward," Gaidon said. "Drones are too expensive to lose, and now we don't have one." He found the printout he was searching for and tapped it. "One hundred and seventy-five thousand euros. Straight into the dirt."

Daniel nodded. "We still have to move. This isn't just science anymore. And honestly, I don't trust any government to handle this discovery without ruining it."

"That's exactly the problem," Gaidon said quietly. "I'm thinking about suspending the experiment."

Daniel froze. "Why?"

"Because I'm worried. About several things." He leaned back, rubbing a hand across his face. "First question: can we even use the machine the way we originally intended — matter from point A to point B inside our universe? No parallel worlds. Just a transporter."

Daniel waited while Gaidon rifled through more papers, muttering under his breath — an uncharacteristic loss of composure.

Daniel set a stack of folders on the table and flipped through them quickly. "You asked for a review of both the new machine and the old RACE system," he said, tugging out a single thick file. "Here — this is the one you need to see."

Gaidon opened it. Red-highlighted values and handwritten notes covered the pages — curvature drift, temporal offsets, gravitational anomalies, and the harmonic distortions from the first test of the RACE machine in Laboratory 832.

For forty minutes Daniel walked him through the data: the misjudged shell size, the runaway containment, the unexpected gravitational coupling, and the resonance effect that had forced the receiving shell out of their universe entirely.

Gaidon listened in tense silence.

"Two issues," Daniel said. "One mechanical — simple to fix. But the other..." Daniel pointed to a particular graph. "This is the spatial misalignment issue. If we ever tried to open the receiving shell inside our own universe, controlling the exact position would take absurd precision. A deviation of even a few microns would send the shell expanding into whatever matter is nearby."

Gaidon understood at once. "Meaning the shell could intersect with something solid before it stabilises."

"Potentially." Daniel tapped another set of values. "And if the white-hole envelope inverted on contact, the shockfront could behave unpredictably. Worst case... yes, it could be bad. Very bad. But we don't know. Not without thousands of simulations."

Gaidon leaned back, jaw tight. "And those runs would take months of supercomputer time."

"At least," Daniel agreed. "And we can't even guarantee they'd converge. The boundary conditions are insane."

Gaidon rubbed a hand over his face. "So the machine might be usable within our own universe... or it might tear straight through whatever it touches."

Daniel nodded slowly. "We just don't know yet. Right now it's only a possibility — a dangerous one."

Gaidon closed his eyes and went still, running the numbers and theory in the silent space behind his eyelids. Daniel waited, saying nothing, watching the older physicist work through the problem in his head. After half a minute, Gaidon exhaled sharply and opened his eyes, fully present again.

Gaidon rose, went to the cabinet and returned with a bottle of Scotch and two glasses. He poured them both and pushed one across the desk.

Daniel eyed it. "What's this for?"

"There's something else." Gaidon took a swallow. "With the right algorithm we could open that enormous shell anywhere — on land, at street level, or thousands of metres in the air." He touched the folder. "And I don't want to do it. In the wrong hands this machine is a disaster waiting to happen."

Daniel had seen this look in Gaidon before — the hard, distant focus that surfaced whenever talk veered too close to militaries, especially the American one. More than once he'd heard the older physicist mutter about the Manhattan Project, about brilliant minds corralled into building something they couldn't later unbuild, about how easily cutting-edge science became a weapon the moment the wrong people understood it.

That same shadow crossed Gaidon's face now.

Daniel lifted the Scotch, took a sip, grimaced at the burn, and set the glass down.

"If the US military knew that," he said quietly, "the first question would be, 'Can you aim it?'"

"Exactly," Gaidon said. "And I do not want to learn what they'd do with that answer. That's why I'm thinking about walking away."

"That would end your career," Daniel said quietly.

"Yep."

Daniel drummed his fingers on the glass, thinking. "Alright. Options. We never mention the location-targeting idea. If anyone asks, we bury it. We tell them the truth - moving the portal inside our universe risks collapsing the Earth into a black hole. There's no budget for the endless hours to test it first on a supercomputer anyway."

He paused, rolling the Scotch gently in the bottom of the glass as though weighing the memory.

"We were lucky that it only took eight hundred or so runs on the CERN supercomputer before we got it right."

Gaidon gave a short, humourless grunt. "OK. We'll try to bury this idea, it's too dangerous, and expensive."

"And," Daniel said, "I have one more idea."

Gaidon lifted an eyebrow.

"Before the drone tests, we were worried about matter continuity through the shells," Daniel said. "Organic or inorganic damage. Structural tearing. Any of it."

"Yes."

"Well, we've now done multiple crossings. Not a single anomaly. Nothing affected. The shells don't harm anything passing through them." Daniel leaned forward. "I think a human could walk through."

Gaidon went still, head angled slightly — the first crack of possibility appearing.

Daniel continued, more measured. "And we're seeing some buildings exactly where they stand in our world, but everything else — culture, development, architecture — has diverged. The technology is modern but not our modern. Why? When? What caused the split? Why two universes at all?"

Gaidon stared at the desk, absorbing the scale of it.

"We could send a person across," Daniel said. "Someone who can walk into town, talk to people, observe, bring back real information."

The silence that followed was long and heavy.

"Not me," Gaidon said eventually. "I'm not going."

Daniel raised a hand. "Not me either. I'm not... socially subtle."

They both laughed — a brief, tired reaction more than amusement.

Gaidon sobered. "We can't send Baset. His wife is dying. And Emerancie — brilliant, but terrible with people. Did you know she once broke a man's teeth for grabbing her in a nightclub?"

Daniel blinked. "No. Jesus."

"Vincent is smart and personable," Gaidon said, "but I don't trust him. Ten years ago on the LHC project, I'm fairly sure he leaked information to the CIA. And Adéhémar is far too young."

Daniel leaned back. "Which leaves one."

Gaidon nodded slowly.

"Maximilien Rivette."

***

# Chapter 4

**Monday, 28th May 2012, 6:02 a.m.**
**Parallel Universe. Diderot farm, Prévessin-Moëns, France.**

Renato and Bibiane Diderot had been married nearly fifteen years, and in that time they had lived with a kind of fierce, joyful openness. Their celebrations — food, laughter, closeness, and whatever pleasures their guests brought with them — were known across the region. He was earthy pleasure; she was elegant fire. Together they were a force.

Until this last week.

Renato had moved through each day as though carrying a stone in his chest. He drifted away from Bibiane's touch. His eyes never seemed to settle on anything. He slept badly and woke worse. That morning, when she had curled against him and kissed his neck, he had flinched — then snapped at her, sharp and defensive:

"Stop it! Can't I have some peace!"

Bibiane had sat up at once, stunned, her dark eyes wide and searching. He had never spoken to her like that.

Now, as he fled the bedroom, she followed him barefoot down the hall, anger and hurt balanced in her expression.

"Are you having an affair?" she demanded.

"No! Of course not!"

"Then why won't you touch me? Why won't you even look at me? You've been acting..." She held herself tightly. "Strange."

Renato kept walking until she caught his arm and turned him. Her grip had none of her warmth; it was firm, deliberate.

"Enough," she said quietly. "Tell me the truth. I am your wife. I will hear it. What is happening to you?"

He stared at her, breath unsteady.

The fight drained out of him.

Her gaze — steady, intelligent, full of love and anger — left him nowhere to hide.

"It's... difficult," he said.

"Then try."

He swallowed, nodded once. "You need to see it. Two things."

He led her out to the barn. Even in the half-light, his whole frame looked drawn tight as wire. He pulled back a canvas sheet with a rough, embarrassed gesture.

The broken drone lay beneath it.

Bibiane's breath caught. Her expression shifted not to fear, but to sharp, perceptive focus.

"What is that?" she asked.

"I don't know," Renato said. His voice sounded raw. "I shot it down. Yesterday."

She walked around it slowly, studying its angles, its materials, its symmetry — as someone who understood people also understood how to read the intent behind machines. "Where did it come from?"

Renato hesitated, then rubbed a trembling hand across his face.

"That's what's been driving me mad. I can't explain it. It came from... a place..."

He faltered.

"...from a blue circle in the air."

He dropped the canvas over the wreckage as though the sight of it hurt him.

"Come. I'll show you."

They climbed onto the tractor. Renato drove without speaking, hunched over the wheel like a man bracing for judgment. Bibiane watched him and the land, her expression thoughtful, protective, stern.

At the clearing they stepped down and pushed through the bushes. The psychoactive crops swayed in the breeze, their scent rich and familiar.

Renato led her to the cannabis rows and pointed.

The circular gouge in the ground lay before them — two metres across, a foot deep, packed into a dense, impossible sphere of compressed earth.

Bibiane stared, her face going very still.

"How?" she whispered. "What?"

Renato stepped beside her, but looked only at her.

"I heard a loud bang. Twice in two weeks. A crack — nothing natural. I came here and... there was a big blue ball. Hanging in the air. And the flying machine came out of it."

She turned toward him sharply. "A... ball?"

For the next twenty minutes he told her everything: the hum, the sparks, the way the cameras followed him, the second appearance, the gunshots, the crash. He spoke like a man emptying himself of a burden he could no longer hold alone.

Bibiane listened in complete focus, absorbing every detail.

When he finished, exhausted, she took his hand — not gently, but with a firmness that grounded him.

"Renato," she said, "you are not mad. Something happened here. Something real."

He let out a long, shuddering breath.

She squeezed his hand again. "Now we go home," she said. "And we decide what we do next."

***

**Monday, 28th May 2012, 1:52 p.m.**
**Parallel Universe. Diderot farm, Prévessin-Moëns, France.**

The moment Renato and Bibiane returned to the house, she phoned the local policeman, Azemar Hennecart. The call unravelled almost immediately.

"A big blue what?" Azemar said, baffled. "Bibiane, come on. You two grow half the psychedelic plants in the département. You've probably just—"

She cut him off with a tone he had never heard from her — calm, cold and absolutely certain.

"Azemar. Listen to me. We are not hallucinating. You will come. You will look. And you will do it today."

Something in her voice made him sit straighter in his chair miles away. After a noticeable pause, he gave in.

"All right. I'll come this afternoon."

He hung up, sat back, collected himself, then immediately phoned his friend and senior officer in Geneva, Titbaut Cardone. He relayed the story, trying and failing to keep it neutral.

"A blue sphere... a perfect hole in the soil... a flying machine... she says they shot it down. I know how it sounds."

Titbaut didn't interrupt. He waited, listening.

Azemar added, quieter now, "I've known them ten years. Yes, they grow their drugs. Yes, they have their... gatherings. But they've never lied. Not once. They're straightforward people. Unconventional, but honest."

"Then we investigate," he said.

A few hours later, the two officers pulled up at the farmhouse. Bibiane opened the door, composed but resolute. Renato hovered behind her, arms folded, wearing the look of a man hoping to be believed but bracing for the opposite.

They sat at the kitchen table. Renato told the entire story again — the sphere, the hum, the drone, the gunshots — while Bibiane studied the policemen's faces, measuring every flicker of doubt.

When Renato finished, Titbaut closed his notebook. "Let's see the machine."

In the barn, Renato pulled back the canvas. The broken drone lay there like a wounded animal — a carbon-fibre frame sheared in half, tiny two-stroke engines dented and scorched, wiring exposed, the remaining camera smashed inward by Renato's rifle.

Azemar murmured, "Mon Dieu..."

Titbaut crouched, examining the wreckage. "These types of engines haven't been used commercially in decades." He ran a thumb along the fractured carbon. "This isn't homemade. Whoever built it knows advanced fabrication."

He stood. "Renato, I'd like to take this to Geneva."

Renato exhaled with something close to relief. "Take it. I don't want it near the house."

The officers carried the remains outside and settled them carefully in the boot of their car.

"Now," Titbaut said, "show us where this 'blue ball' appeared."

Minutes later they followed the tractor to the clearing and stepped through the thick bushes into the hidden acre. The officers exchanged a look as they moved past the rows of unfamiliar plants, the whole place laid out with the precision of a research station, not a farm, and followed Renato onward.

But the admiration vanished when they reached the cannabis beds.

The spherical cavity in the earth stopped them cold. Two metres across. About a foot deep. The soil compacted into something that resembled smooth stone.

Titbaut knelt without speaking. He pressed his fingertips to the surface.

"Harder than concrete."

He drew his pocket knife and forced the blade in. After firm pressure an inch-sized fragment broke free. He dropped it into an evidence bag, frowning at the geometry, the density, the sheer unnaturalness of the shape.

He stood and turned to Renato.

"Renato," he said quietly, "I'm sorry I doubted you. No one here could have made this. And that flying machine..." He shook his head. "It's going to take a full team in Geneva to understand what we're dealing with."

Renato nodded, a mix of relief and unease settling through him.

Bibiane slipped her arm through his — steady, protective, a presence stronger than the fear that had gnawed at him for days.

For the first time since this had started, he felt the weight lift.

His secret wasn't something he had to hide.

Others believed him, he wasn't going mad.

***

**Monday, 28th May 2012, 7:58 p.m.**
**Gaidon Ballerat's office, Laboratory 888, CERN, Prévessin-Moëns, France.**

Gaidon waited until the door had fully closed behind them, then drew a steady breath — the kind that meant he was about to ask for something he knew he shouldn't.

"Max," he said carefully, "I'd like to have you do one last job for me."

Max didn't sit. "What kind of job?"

Gaidon hesitated only a second.

That was all Max needed to sense trouble.

Then—

"No."

Max said it plainly, and the finality in his voice stopped Gaidon mid-sentence.

"Max, please. We need you."

"You always need me," Max replied — steady, tired. "But I've got a real job now. Nexter expect me back tomorrow morning. I took two weeks off because you insisted — and because I didn't want to let you down. But I can't just disappear on my employers."

Gaidon blinked, thrown. "I... didn't realise it was a problem."

"A *problem*?" Max gave a small, incredulous laugh. "They've bent over backwards for the last year letting me moonlight for you. I'm stretching their goodwill already."

He gestured vaguely around the office. "And you're only paying me a three-hundred-euro retainer. Three hundred. It barely covers fuel for the rental car I have to get every time I have to come to Prévessin-Moëns."

Gaidon winced. "I genuinely had no idea."

"Right," Max said. "Because no one ever asks. Everyone assumes I'm just floating around waiting to be used. I like working with you, I do — but I have a proper job now. A stable one. If I screw that up, it's not like there's another waiting for me."

Gaidon leaned forward. His voice tightened with urgency rather than irritation.

"Max, listen. You're simply not replaceable. You know the machine better than anyone. You shaped half of it. You solved things Daniel and I couldn't articulate."

Max shook his head. "And now what? I sit here and watch camera feeds with you? You don't need a draftsman for that. You need a physicist."

"No," Gaidon said quietly. "I need you."

Max frowned. "What are you actually asking?"

Gaidon swallowed.

"The drone is gone. We can't build another in time. And the problem is—" He hesitated, searching for the right words. "We've been looking through a keyhole. We see almost nothing. A few glimpses. A few shadows. It isn't enough."

Max waited.

Gaidon continued, voice low. "There are subtle differences between our universe and theirs — there are big differences when I think about it— and the drone can't explain any of them. Why Prévessin-Moëns looks like rural farmland instead of suburbs. Why Geneva's skyline is wrong. Why road layouts diverge. Why the cars are all different. These aren't physics questions. They're... human questions."

Max felt a slow, uneasy roll settle in his stomach.

"We need context," Gaidon said. "Real context. Not pixels. Not telemetry. A pair of eyes. Someone who can walk, observe, ask harmless questions, and come back with the kind of detail a machine can't gather."

Then, with a rueful sigh: "And ideally someone who knows how to avoid that angry farmer Baset nicknamed 'the angry bear.'"

Max let out a sharp exhale that wasn't quite humour.

"You're asking someone to go through."

"Yes."

"And you want that someone to be me."

"You'd spend twenty-four hours at most," Gaidon said softly. "You'd walk into Geneva, see what's different, talk to people if necessary — safely, discreetly. No contact with authorities. No heroics. Then you'd come home and tell us what we're dealing with. Just enough to know whether we're looking at a harmless mirror... or something much stranger."

Max looked away, jaw tight. "And why me?"

Gaidon's answer came instantly, without calculation.

"Because you're steady. You don't panic. You pay attention. You blend in. You're smart. You're sociable. We need that."

Max stood abruptly. "I can't just abandon my life for this. I have responsibilities."

Gaidon rose too, desperation surfacing. "If you walk out, I may have to shut the experiment down. I can't justify continuing blind."

Max froze.

"Shut it down?" he asked.

"Yes," Gaidon said. "Because right now we know just enough to be fascinated — and not enough to understand what we're touching. We need clarity, Max. And the drone can't give it to us."

There was a long silence.

Max walked to the door, rested his hand on the handle, and spoke without turning.

"Let me think about it."

Then he left.

***

**Thursday, 31st May 2012, 11:35 a.m.**
**Parallel Universe. Sauson Bourel's office, Geneva Security, Geneva, Switzerland.**

Auguste Besse's appearance at Geneva Security Headquarters halted the usual chatter. His presence alone was rare; the determination in his walk made it clear he wasn't here for routine business.

He stepped into Sauson Bourel's office and closed the door behind him without sitting.

"Sauson," he said, his voice clipped, "that flying machine? It was not made in Europe."

Sauson frowned. "Then where was it made?"

"We don't know." Auguste set a thick forensic folder on the desk and spread out several photographs. "We contacted every composite manufacturer from Lisbon to Warsaw. No one produces a carbon weave like this. The resin is an unknown formulation. Completely off the books."

Sauson exhaled through his nose. "When the report first came in, I assumed the farmer was hallucinating. Diderot has a reputation."

Auguste gave a short, humourless snort. "Hallucinations don't produce engineered materials and precision-machined housings."

He produced an evidence bag and set it on Sauson's desk — the compacted soil taken from the circular cavity in the cannabis bed.

"And this," Auguste said. "No industrial process can explain it. The soil is compressed to near-lithic density. A perfect spherical imprint on one side. And elevated argon levels."

Sauson tapped the bag with a knuckle. "What does argon indicate?"

"We don't know," Auguste said, sharper now. "That's the baffling part. But the compression suggests an instantaneous high-energy mechanical event. Nothing we can reproduce. Not with anything on this continent."

Sauson rubbed his temple. "So the hole is real. The flying machine is real. Everything the farmer described matches your analysis."

"It does," Auguste said. "Which is why I'm here."

Sauson braced himself. "Your recommendation?"

"For now? Caution." Auguste began closing the folder. "The farmer reported several incidents. Each time a sharp crack, then the appearance of this sphere." He tapped a photograph of the circular cavity. "We can't rule out that it could happen again."

"But you don't want a team on-site?"

"No," Auguste said firmly. "Not yet. We don't know what we're dealing with, and we don't know who else might be involved. If this is foreign technology, an aggressive response risks escalating something we don't understand."

Sauson nodded slowly. "So we wait."

"We wait," Auguste confirmed. "We analyse. We keep this contained. And if another incident occurs, we respond immediately — and discreetly."

He paused, gaze steady.

"Sauson... this machine didn't come from any manufacturer that we know of. Not as we understand it."

He let the words settle.

"When — not if — it happens again, you call me directly."

Then he left as abruptly as he had entered, the door shutting with a soft, decisive click.

***

# Chapter 5

**Friday, 8th June 2012, 9:37 p.m.**
**Céleste Guérard's apartment, Prévessin-Moëns, France.**

Max arrived just as the last of the light slipped behind the rooftops, worn out from five hours in the tiny Renault hire car. Céleste had dinner already waiting — roast chicken, vegetables, and a tart cooling on the counter.

When he'd phoned earlier to say he was coming back to Prévessin-Moëns for "just a few days," something in his voice had unsettled her.

Not fear.

Not reluctance.

Something quieter, heavier. A note he hadn't used in years.

Finality.

They ate mostly in silence. After dessert, Max took over the dishes, sleeves rolled up, steam rising from the sink. Céleste leaned back in her chair, studying him. She knew this posture all too well — the overly careful attention to mundane tasks, the way he focused on the plates instead of her. It was what he did when he was avoiding something.

Max made the first move toward conversation, but it was thin.

"It's just for a little while," he said, rinsing a plate. "Gaidon asked if I could help with one last thing."

Céleste's brow tightened. "One last thing? I thought you told me they barely needed you anymore — that you mostly just sat with the others watching a monitor. You said you were the least important member of the team."

He paused mid-motion, water running over his hands. A moment too long.

Then he set the plate gently in the rack.

"Yeah," he said. "That's... mostly true."

But his voice betrayed him — not with what he said, but with everything he didn't.

And she heard it.

"Céleste... I have to work a very long shift tomorrow. We're running a special experiment. I won't be home until Sunday afternoon."

She frowned.

"I thought you told me last time something had broken. That there wouldn't be more tests for weeks."

"Ah... we managed to fix it."

"Oh?" She raised an eyebrow. "And did you tell Gaidon you wanted out? You've been saying for months you're tired of being at his beck and call."

"Yes. We talked. He agreed. And... this is the last time I'm working on the project."

The reassurance didn't land.

Céleste had raised him, watched him carry himself through grief, watched him rebuild. She knew his evasive tone better than anyone alive.

"Max," she said quietly, "what exactly do they need you for? You never tell me anymore. I didn't realise CERN was this secretive."

Max froze, a wet plate in his hand.

"Ahh... it's just that—"

"Just what?"

The plate slipped and shattered on the tiles.

He muttered a curse and crouched to collect the shards. Céleste's expression tightened; she'd seen this pattern of avoidance too many times. This wasn't secrecy. This was fear.

"Something is going on," she said. "I can hear it in your voice."

"I can't say," Max replied, keeping his gaze low. "It's... top-secret."

"I'm your aunt, Max. Not a spy."

He shut his eyes. The lie he'd carried all week pressed heavily across his ribs.

"Fine," he said, exhaling. "But you have to promise not to tell anyone. Anyone."

They sat at the table again.

Max talked for half an hour.

He told her everything:

the machine,

the shells,

the clearing in the parallel world,

the fallen drone,

and the plan for tomorrow.

When he finished, Céleste stared at him for a long moment. The room was quiet enough that Max could hear the faint ticking of the cooling oven.

Then she spoke, barely above a whisper.

"I don't want you to go, Max. It's too dangerous."

"It's not. Truly. And this... this could make history. I could be—"

"Important?" Her voice sharpened. "Max, what if the air is radioactive? What if you step through and your heart stops? What if something comes back with you? You don't know it's safe."

"None of those things—"

"Stop." She pushed her chair back and stood, her voice caught between anger and fear.

"I have a bad feeling about this. And when I have a bad feeling, I'm never wrong."

Her eyes glistened, though she held her composure.

"I don't want you to go."

She turned away and walked toward the hallway.

"I'm going to bed."

She didn't look back.

Max stayed where he was, hands resting uselessly on the table, realising with sudden clarity that tomorrow he wouldn't just be stepping into another universe —

he'd be stepping away from the only person who had ever been there for him.

***

**Saturday, 9th June 2012, 8:30 a.m.**
**Prévessin-Moëns, France.**

Max had barely slept. By morning the world felt brittle — too bright in some places, too muted in others — as he wheeled his old bicycle out of Céleste's garage. Warm summer air settled around him while sunlight climbed over the rooftops.

He mounted the bike and set off through the familiar streets of Prévessin-Moëns. It was early enough that the village felt suspended, as if it hadn't quite decided to wake. No church bells yet. No movement behind the shutters. Just a stillness he rode straight through.

*How will history remember this?*

An underpaid draftsman, too broke to own a car, pedalling a battered bicycle toward a multi-billion-euro laboratory... to step into another universe.

The thought made him laugh under his breath. Absurd. Impossible. And somehow, inevitable.

The road opened into fields. Houses fell behind him. Long grass shifted in the morning breeze, and the pale outline of the Alps stretched along the horizon. He pictured the drone's footage — the parallel fields, the parallel sky — and felt a quiet pull in his chest.

A few minutes later he rode under the tall power pylons feeding CERN, their soft electrical hum drifting through the morning air. At the small security gate he swiped his badge, heard the lock release, and rolled through.

Laboratory 888 rose ahead — a stark grey block in the summer light.

He braked, stepped off, and leaned the bicycle against the outer wall. Another swipe of his pass, another heavy door, and he was inside.

Today was the day.

***

**Saturday, 9th June 2012, 9:53 a.m.**
**Machine Room, Laboratory 888, CERN. Prévessin-Moëns, France.**

The machine was already alive.

Both spherical chambers pulsed through their readiness sequence, each shift of light marking another system settling into place. From the control room above, Gaidon, Baset, Emerancie and Vincent had confirmed the all-clear.

Down on the grated walkway, it was only Daniel and Max.

They stood side by side, watching the faint vibrations tremble the receiving chamber.

Daniel broke the quiet.

"You nervous?"

"A little," Max said.

Daniel gave a small grin. "You're about to be the first human in history to walk into another universe. Nervous seems reasonable."

Max managed a thin smirk.

Before either could speak again, Gaidon's voice came through Daniel's radio.

"Are we good to go?"

Daniel pressed the button. "We're ready."

"Starting the shells."

Above them, a warning light shifted — orange to yellow, then finally to green. Locks released with a metallic clack. The chamber's hydraulic platform began its controlled descent. The walkway vibrated gently beneath their feet.

Max had seen the portal many times on the monitors.

Seeing it in person was something else entirely.

A sphere of shimmering blue light hung in the chamber, translucent and alive with faint crackles along its surface. It looked less like technology and more like an imposed geometry — a perfectly defined boundary that space itself had been forced to accommodate.

"Mon Dieu..." Daniel murmured. "It's incredible."

Max didn't respond. The sight gripped him too tightly for words.

The platform lowered to walkway height.

Gaidon's voice returned.

"All clear. Systems nominal."

Daniel gave Max a small nod. Half encouragement, half recognition of what this moment meant.

Max stepped onto the platform.

The rams lifted him with steady, deliberate motion toward the glowing shell. Light sharpened across his skin. His heart thudded hard against his ribs.

Then his head crossed the boundary and the world changed.

A clearing. Crops. Trees.

No pain. No jolt. Not even a shift in the air.

The platform settled with a muted thunk.

Familiar in outline, but wrong in all the quiet ways. This wasn't his world. This was the parallel one.

This was it.

He drew a breath, rocked back slightly on one leg, and made the small jump from the raised platform through the blue, transparent shell.

His boots struck soil with a solid, grounded thud. Max shifted his weight, the strap of his small backpack cutting lightly across his chest — his camera tucked inside it.

He straightened and looked upward.

A flawless sky.

Birdsong from the treeline.

The scent of warm leaves and cut grass drifting on the breeze.

A beautiful June morning in France — just not his France.

He had made the leap and become the first human to set foot in a parallel world.

Behind him, the portal shell collapsed with a soft *whump,* sealing shut until tomorrow morning.

***

# Chapter 6



**Saturday, 9th June 2012, 10:04 a.m.**
**Parallel Universe. Diderot farm, Prévessin-Moëns, France.**

Max pushed through the last ring of undergrowth and stepped out of the farmers hidden clearing. The humid smell of soil and flowering plants fell away behind him as he moved into open farmland. The air felt lighter here, touched by a faint breeze coming off the distant fields.

He checked the paper map the team had assembled from drone stills.

It was crude, stitched together from half-recognisable landmarks, and within minutes it proved useless. Paths angled away in the wrong directions. Hedgerows appeared where none existed on the photographs. Entire clearings were missing or shifted.

Max folded the map, sighed, and slipped it back into his backpack.

Prévessin-Moëns was familiar to him in his own world; he'd passed these fields countless times on his bicycle, often half-asleep in the early mornings. Here, though, the landscape had been rearranged just enough to disorient him. A path that should have run straight curved toward a stream. A gate that should have guarded a paddock opened onto nothing but a field of rye. Every familiar detail had been nudged sideways.

After half an hour spent threading between hedges and narrow tracks, he reached a thin, rutted dirt road and followed it, hoping it would lead somewhere recognisable.

Ten minutes later he heard the soft whir of a car.

It appeared over the rise — sleek, modern, elegant in a way that felt slightly foreign. The design language was clean to the point of austerity. It glided past him with an insect-like hum.

*Electric,* Max thought.

*But nothing I've ever seen.*

He kept walking.

The dirt road joined a paved one that stirred his memory. A bend he recognised, a rise in the ground at almost the right angle — and he realised he was roughly five hundred metres from where the town centre should be.

But the town itself...

It wasn't his Prévessin-Moëns.

In his universe the village had been swallowed by the sprawl of Geneva's outer ring — blocks of apartments, long rows of cul-de-sacs, commercial streets lined with franchises. Here it remained a village: quiet, sparse, almost rural. The air carried the smell of fresh bread instead of exhaust fumes.

He pulled out the small camera and took a few stills: shuttered stone houses, gravel driveways, old fences patched with care rather than replaced.

A woman swept her porch, her broom keeping an easy rhythm.

Children raced past on bicycles, laughing.

A man trimmed a hedge with patient, practised movements.

A couple walked by with t-shirts that bore no logos.

That was the detail that struck him.

No brands.

No ads.

No signage shouting for attention.

Not a single corporate mark anywhere he looked.

He walked on, reaching a side street near the church. A handful of small shops lined it — a bakery, a florist, a repair workshop of some kind. A café stood at the corner with outdoor tables and a dozen people sitting in the sun, drinking coffee, eating pastries, reading newspapers.

Max paused. His stomach growled with embarrassing clarity.

But he had no idea whether his fifty euros meant anything here.

Drawing attention to himself wasn't part of the plan.

He kept walking.

The church came next — a place he knew well in his world, though here it seemed left to fend for itself. The stone was discoloured, the doors unvarnished, and the grounds overgrown. No flowerbeds, no trimmed lawn. Just slow, steady neglect.

He took a few photos and wandered into the cemetery beside it.

If the church was shabby, the cemetery was worse.

Tall weeds crowded the headstones. Two mounds of earth lay untended. A bench had collapsed in the middle, its wooden slats broken. The iron gates were rusted to the hinge, barely holding together.

Max left through those gates and headed down the nearest road, keeping Geneva in mind as a vague direction rather than a certainty.

Thirty minutes later he stopped at a crossroads he didn't recognise.

He turned slowly, trying to align the landscape with anything familiar.

Nothing fit.

A cold tightening at the base of his stomach made him still.

He had crossed the boundary less than two hours ago — and already he understood how quickly a person could vanish here, swallowed by a world that looked almost like his own.

Almost.

But not enough.

***

**Saturday, 9th June 2012, 11:37 a.m.**
**Parallel Universe. Prévessin-Moëns, France.**

The cars continued to fascinate Max. Every one he'd seen was electric — silent, smooth, and edging toward futuristic. Their badges were worse: no familiar marques, no Renaults, Peugeots, Citroëns. Only sleek geometric icons and minimalist names he didn't recognise.

He was following a rural lane he hoped angled toward Geneva when he noticed a small hatchback parked crookedly on the verge. No other houses or people nearby. Out of habit, he slipped out the camera from his backpack and took a few quick photos — angles, wheels, lights, badge.

Then he froze.

The emblem on the tailgate was unmistakable.

Bugatti.

A Bugatti... hatchback.

In his own world Bugatti built hypercars worth more than houses. Here it was stamped on a modest light-blue runabout that looked like the sort of thing a teenager might drive to school. The absurdity hit him so fast he swore under his breath.

"What are you doing?"

Max spun.

A man had emerged from behind a small cluster of trees, zipping up after relieving himself. Broad-shouldered, middle-aged, and already irritated.

"Ah," Max said quickly, "just taking photos of your car."

"Why?"

"Because... it's a nice car. And it's a Bugatti."

"So? Why would you take photos of my car?"

Max grabbed the first excuse that flared up.

"Because it's... special."

The man narrowed his eyes as if Max had just confessed to being unwell.

"Bloody hell. I stop for a piss and end up with some lunatic photographing my car. Move."

He shoved past, got in, slammed the door, and the little Bugatti zipped away with a soft, insect-like whirr.

Max stood on the roadside, breath uneven.

Same sun. Same air. Same land.

But every small detail tugged slightly sideways, hinting at a deeper divergence he couldn't yet see.

He kept walking.

The road curved left under a canopy of trees, rising gently. When he reached the crest, he stopped dead.

Eighty metres ahead, under a patchwork awning, stood a small farmer's stall — bright paint, crates of vegetables, hand-lettered signs.

And sitting behind it on a low stool, slouched in the shade, was the angry farmer.

The man who had shot down the drone.

Max froze. His pulse thudded hard enough to feel in his throat.

He could turn back. Slip down the road, vanish into the network of lanes.

Or he could walk forward.

The farmer turned his head.

Their eyes met.

And Max realised — with a clean, sudden clarity — that the farmer had never seen *him*.

He had seen the drone, not the face behind it.

No rifle. No raised voice. Just a man selling produce at a roadside stall.

Max forced his legs to move.

He walked toward the farmers stall.

***

**Saturday, 9th June 2012, 11:44 a.m.**
**Parallel Universe. Diderot farm, Prévessin-Moëns, France.**

The farmer rose from his stool as Max approached.

"Bonjour, my friend. Looking for anything in particular?"

Max's eyes flicked over the stall. Two dozen cylindrical wooden bins, each painted by hand with vivid murals of whatever they contained — peaches, tomatoes, herbs, potatoes. Not crude decoration. These were pieces of art: layered colour, precise strokes, care poured into every surface.

"Just looking," Max said. "This is... honestly incredible."

"Yes," the farmer replied, pleased. "Grown here on the farm. With care. Try an apple."

Max picked one from the nearest bin, bit into it — and almost groaned. Crisp, cold, sweet, perfect.

While he chewed, the farmer studied him with quiet, assessing eyes. The foreign clothes. The anxious scanning. The strange red T-shirt with *Enjoy Coca-Cola* written across it in looping script.

He had been restless all morning. The *crack*—boom from the hidden clearing was still lodged under his skin like a thorn. Bibiane had called the local policeman ninety minutes ago, but the officer wouldn't arrive until late afternoon. He'd been told to stay away from the site. He obeyed — barely.

"You're not from around here," the farmer said. "We don't get many people walking this road. What brings you to our little town?"

Max hesitated.

Too long.

"I, uh... went nightclubbing in Geneva. Met a woman. Stayed at her place. And... well... snuck out this morning."

His delivery was awful. Even if the farmer didn't recognise the word *nightclubbing*, the lie was transparent.

Combined with the *crack*—boom earlier...

A single conclusion formed.

He came out of that thing.

"I'm trying to get back to Geneva," Max said, a little too fast. "I think I've taken a wrong turn somewhere."

The farmer gave him a polite smile — warm enough, but with a hint of appraisal behind it.

"Well, perhaps we can sort that out. But first, you should meet my wife."

He raised his voice toward the house.

"Bibiane! Could you come here a moment?"

Bibiane stepped out from the front door, moving with the easy confidence of someone who owned every inch of the place. The sun caught the thin straps of her dress, and Max's brain simply stalled.

"We've got a visitor," the farmer said. "Says he spent the night with a woman he met in Geneva and needs help getting back."

Max felt the blood drain from his face.

Bibiane approached, studying him with sharp, deliberate eyes.

"So," she said, "a mystery woman swept you off your feet. What was her name?"

Max's mind blanked. "Céleste."

Bibiane frowned slightly, head tilting. "There's no one by that name in this village. We know everyone."

Her gaze flicked to his shirt. "And what exactly does 'Enjoy Coca-Cola' mean?"

"It's... a drink," Max managed.

"A drink?" she repeated, genuinely puzzled.

"A soft drink. Sweet. Fizzy. Comes in a can."

She looked at him as if he'd just described sorcery.

That was when Max realised:

Electric Bugatti hatchbacks existed here.

But *soft drink* didn't.

Another fracture. Another quiet impossibility.

"I should get going," Max blurted. "My girlfriend will be furious if I don't get back soon."

Renato and Bibiane exchanged a brief look — the kind only two people with decades together can manage. A flicker of understanding passed between them. No discussion. Just a silent decision: don't let him wander off yet.

Bibiane stepped in closer, voice dropping into something soft and coaxing.

"Are you sure you need to rush? You could stay a little while. I could... show you a few things that might make you forget all about this girlfriend."

Her fingertip traced a line down the front of his shirt.

Max jerked backward so sharply he almost knocked over a crate of peaches.

He turned to Renato, expecting shock. Disapproval. Anything normal.

Instead, Renato gave him a broad, amused smile and a single, subtle nod — the kind of nod older men give when they think they're sharing in a harmless joke or offering friendly encouragement. His eyebrows lifted, as if to say, *Go on, son* — what's the harm?

Max felt his stomach twist. Too strange. Too sincere. Too wrong. "No," he sputtered. "Really, no. My girlfriend — she'd kill me. How much do I owe you for the apple?"

The farmer frowned. "Owe?"

"The cost. The price."

"Price?" he echoed, confused.

"Yes — the money."

"Money is illegal."

Max felt the blood drain from his face.

"Right. Of course. Obviously."

He backed away, waving awkwardly. "Thank you, but I should get going."

Then he turned and walked — fast — desperate to put distance between himself and the impossibly friendly couple living on a farm in a universe that should not exist.

***

**Saturday, 9th June 2012, 11:59 a.m.**
**Parallel Universe. Diderot farm, Prévessin-Moëns, France.**

"Try calling again."

Bibiane hit redial and lifted the little mobile to her ear.

A few seconds passed. She exhaled hard and lowered it.

"Straight to message service. Again."

"Putain..." Renato dragged both hands down his face, pacing beside the fruit stall. "I knew it. I fucking knew it. That man he came out of the blue sphere. You saw his eyes, his clothes, the way he talked. He's not from here."

His voice cracked under the pressure of the last few weeks:

the impossible blue sphere,

the broken drone,

the perfect gouge in the soil,

the maddening sense of witnessing something real while everyone treated him like a fool.

He stopped pacing and turned to her, almost pleading.

"You believe me, don't you?"

Bibiane stepped forward and pulled him into a tight, grounding embrace.

"Yes, Renato Diderot," she said into his shoulder, warm and fierce. "I believed you from the moment we found that hole in the ground. I believe you now."

He breathed against her collarbone, the trembling easing from his arms.

Then her phone rang.

She snapped it up instantly. "Azemar? Yes — listen."

She told him everything:

the *whip-like crack* from the clearing,

the stranger who had a made up story as to why he was in Prévessin-Moëns,

his nervous evasions,

his bizarre shirt for something that he called a soft drink,

the mention of money and not knowing it was illegal,

and the way he'd bolted the moment they started asking questions.

A pause. Bibiane nodded slowly.

"Yes... yes, that's right. All right. Understood."

She hung up.

Renato hovered at her side, tight with worry. "What did he say?"

"He's calling Titbaut Cardone now," she said. "He wants us to stay put. They'll be here soon."

Renato looked at the road where Max had disappeared, jaw tight, chewing his lip.

Bibiane touched his arm.

"Don't worry," she said softly. "They're taking this seriously now."

Renato nodded, though his eyes never left the empty stretch of country road — the place the stranger had vanished, and the place from which, at last, answers might come.

***

**Saturday, 9th June 2012, 12:27 p.m.**
**Parallel Universe. Prévessin-Moëns, France.**

Max had been given what sounded—on paper—like the easiest job in history:

Walk around. Talk to a few people. Gather some discreet intel about another universe.

Simple.

Except it wasn't. Not even remotely.

Every step he took in this world made it clearer: this place wasn't just a quirky mirror of home. It was familiar enough to lull him, but different enough to trip him, again and again, like a badly laid carpet.

The cars were the first clue. Every single one he'd seen was electric—sleek, modern, humming softly past like props from a near-future film. Even more surreal was the badge on that hatchback Bugatti. A brand reserved for the wealthiest handful of people on Earth back home... reduced here to an everyday runabout.

But nothing compared to the farmer's words.

*"Money is illegal!"*

Max kept replaying that in his head, trying to hang some logic on it. Was it literal? A cultural metaphor? A simple misunderstanding?

No. The farmer had said it plainly, as if it were the most obvious, natural thing in the world.

Max tried to imagine how a society without money could possibly function.

Trading apples for cars? Oranges for houses? Tomatoes for electricity bills?

Ludicrous. Impossible. And yet... clearly real here.

He felt suddenly exposed, like a man who had walked into an exam for the wrong subject.

If he was going to survive the next twenty-four hours, he realised he needed to stop assuming anything about this place. He'd have to watch what he said, watch how people reacted, and think several moves ahead.

This universe wasn't simply different.

It was *dangerously* different.

Another half hour of wandering the patchwork of rural roads finally brought him to a junction. A weathered wooden sign pointed left.

GENÈVE →

Max exhaled in relief. At last, a direction he recognised.

He tightened the straps on his backpack, squared his shoulders, and set off towards the city.

***

**Saturday, 9th June 2012, 12:38 p.m.**
**Parallel Universe. Diderot farm. Prévessin-Moëns, France.**

Forty minutes after Max disappeared down the road, Renato and Bibiane finished wheeling the last of their painted produce bins into the barn. Bibiane wiped her hands on her dress as her phone rang again. She answered immediately.

Azemar Hennecart's voice was brisk, urgent, all business.

Their conversation lasted less than thirty seconds.

When she hung up, she turned to her husband.

"He wants us to find this stranger," she said. "Keep him talking. Keep him calm. No sudden moves. No confronting him."

Renato frowned. "Tip him off to what?"

She held his gaze.

"They're going to detain him, Renato. That more senior policeman Titbaut Cardone is putting together a team right now."

A cold knot tightened in his stomach.

***

**Saturday, 9th June 2012, 1:10 p.m.**
**Parallel Universe. Geneva outskirts, France.**

"There he is!"

Renato pointed. Max was halfway to Geneva now, walking a quiet suburban stretch of road. Bibiane immediately opened her phone, tapped the five-digit activation code Geneva Security had provided, and set it on the dashboard. From that point on, every word inside the car was transmitted live to Titbaut's team.

Renato muttered, "This time, take it slow. He already thinks we're a bit intense."

They slowed beside Max. He turned, surprised but not alarmed, as Renato lowered the window.

Renato hadn't rehearsed a thing.

He just plunged in.

"Listen... we're sorry about earlier. My wife can get a little... *passionate*."

He grimaced at his own phrasing. Bibiane, stone-faced, didn't rescue him.

"No — *we* are sorry," he corrected, flustered.

Max hesitated. "...Alright."

Renato pressed on. "Look, Bibiane and I... we host gatherings. Sensual gatherings. It's normal here. So when she heard your story about sneaking out of another woman's house—"

Max's face ignited red. His mouth opened, closed, then stalled completely.

Bibiane stepped in with a sudden, measured calm — the kind people use when they realise everyone has skipped the basics.

"Before we make you think we're completely unhinged... we should introduce ourselves," she said. "I'm Bibiane."

The man beside her gave a small, apologetic nod.

"Renato," he added.

Only then did Bibiane gesture toward Max.

"And you? What's your name?"

"Max," he said.

"Max," she said, "I promise that won't happen again. We just wanted to apologise... and offer you a lift. Though it looks like you're already nearly in the city. Do you still want a ride?"

Max considered it. They seemed genuinely contrite. Odd, yes — deeply odd — but sincere. And being in close quarters with locals might give him more cultural detail than wandering alone.

"Sure," he said. "If you could drop me at St Peter's Cathedral? I live near there."

"Of course," Bibiane replied.

Renato unlocked the back door. Max climbed in.

As soon as Bibiane confirmed he'd buckled his seatbelt, she pulled smoothly back into the road.

Renato launched into chatter — jokes, half-confessions, rambling assurances — most of which only made Max fold deeper into the seat. Bibiane spotted it instantly.

She cut in.

"Max," she said gently, "let me be honest. My behaviour earlier... that wasn't really about you. It was about my husband. Renato hasn't been himself."

"Bibiane—" Renato warned, but she ignored him.

"He's been dealing with anxiety," she continued. "Something happened on the farm. Something he can't make sense of."

Max stared out the window, silent.

"He saw a blue sphere appear," she said softly. "Hanging in the air. And a flying machine came out of it."

Max went still.

She saw the micro-reactions instantly — the tightening of his shoulders, the slight lift of his chest as his breath caught, the flicker of alarm in his eyes.

She pushed, gently but deliberately.

"He shot it down," she added. "He's been terrified ever since."

The car fell silent.

Renato twisted around in his seat, raw fear in his face now — the fear of a man who desperately wanted truth, not vengeance.

Max swallowed hard.

"You should pull over," he said quietly. "There's something I need to explain. But it's... complicated."

Renato nearly shouted, "Please! Tell us!"

Bibiane's glare shut him up instantly. She steered toward the curb, easing the car into a parking spot along a busy Geneva street. Pedestrians walked past. Cars drifted by. None of them knew history was folding inward on itself inside a modest little hatchback.

She shifted into park.

Max drew a breath.

And began.

***

**Saturday, 9th June 2012, 1:14 p.m.**
**Parallel Universe. Unmarked security van, Geneva, Switzerland.**

The white van hummed westward along the Geneva–Prévessin motorway, indistinguishable from weekend commuters. Inside, the silence was iron.

Titbaut Cardone drove, eyes fixed ahead.

Behind him sat Azemar Hennecart, jaw locked, pulse hammering visibly in his neck.

Beside Azemar sat Dominic Garner — the Paris specialist recently transferred to the Geneva Security office. He ran a thumb along the chamber of his sidearm, checking it with the slow, methodical calm of someone who'd done this too many times to count.

He looked carved from impact and bad decisions: twice-broken nose, a lip that had never healed straight, two teeth missing, stubble edging toward feral. But his eyes were clean, predatory, precise.

"Weapons check," he said, tone clipped.

Azemar: "Good."

Titbaut: "Ready."

Dominic: "Right."

His phone buzzed once — the relay from Bibiane's car.

He tapped it, then gave a small hand signal to the officer beside him.

Azemar immediately brought up the tablet, swiped across the screen, and opened the vehicle-tracking window. A quick pinch-zoom, a tap, and the map locked onto Bibiane's car.

"That's very close," he said.

A second later, the tablet flicked over automatically and the audio feed from inside Bibiane's car filled the van's cabin.

For the next few minutes the interior sound of the Diderots' vehicle filled the van: faint breath, road noise, and the tense, escalating conversation unfolding between three people.

Max's voice came through, tight but controlled.

"I work for a team of scientists... who accidentally discovered parallel universes exist. We found this place — *this version of Earth.*"

A beat of stunned silence.

Bibiane: "*Version of Earth?*"

Dominic raised a hand. *Listen. Don't talk.*

Max continued: "Your world is like ours, but different. Geneva's different. Cars are different. Some buildings overlap, some don't—"

Renato exploded: "Bullshit! You sent that flying machine to spy on us and to fuck with my sanity!"

Max snapped back, raw panic finally bleeding through his composure: "Yes — and you shot it down, you idiot! And they sent me because of it!"

Azemar muttered, low and urgent, "Is he armed?"

"No indication," Dominic said. "But we treat unknowns as threats. If he bolts or reaches, we incapacitate."

"And if he resists—?"

"*Alive.*" Dominic's tone cut like wire. "Orders are explicit."

The argument in the car surged again.

Bibiane: "Who are 'they'? Why explore here?"

Max: "To understand your people. After the drone, they thought you might be violent—"

"*Fuck you!*" Renato roared — and then the unmistakable bang of a car door slamming open.

Dominic leaned forward instantly. "There. Pull over."

Titbaut braked hard. The van skidded to a stop on the shoulder.

The side doors flew open.

The three men moved as one:

Dominic in front,

Azemar left,

Titbaut right —

weapons raised, lines clean, breathing steady, execution textbook.

Up ahead: chaos.

Renato had Max by the shirt, dragging him bodily out of the back seat. The two men were locked in a clumsy, panicked grapple while Bibiane fought to wedge herself between them.

Dominic didn't shout.

He *detonated* his voice across the road.

"CIVIC CUSTODY — NOW!"

Everything froze.

Renato's grip slackened.

Bibiane stopped mid-movement.

Max went still.

Even passing cars slowed, drivers craning toward the source of the command.

In this universe, those two words carried the force of law — and not the gentle kind. It was the phrase invoked when someone had just been designated an immediate threat to civil order.

Behind Dominic, Azemar and Titbaut kept their weapons level, sights unbroken.

Dominic advanced two measured steps, expression unreadable.

"Hands where I can see them," he said. "Both of you. Now."

For the first time, real dread curled up Max's spine.

Max had botched it. Completely.

He'd walked into this world thinking the assignment was straightforward — explore, observe, ask a few questions, come home twenty-four hours later with notes and a story to tell. It should've been the easiest task he'd ever been given.

Instead, the farmer had lost his temper, everything had spiralled, and now the whole thing was ruined.

What was supposed to be a simple field mission was gone.

And Max was no longer a guest.

He was under arrest — *civic custody*, one of the men with guns had called it, the men who wore no uniform.

***

# Chapter 7

**Saturday, 9th June 2012, 6:30 p.m.**
**Parallel universe. European Security Office, Geneva, Switzerland.**

*Five hours.*

That was how long they had been at it.

Max sat slumped in the metal chair, a half-empty glass of water on the table. Across from him, the four officers — Sauson Bourel, Dominic Garner, Titbaut Cardone, and Azemar Hennecart — had shifted from interrogation into something closer to exhausted bewilderment. They had pressed him on every detail of his story, circled back, pressed again, and reached nothing but the same strange, consistent account.

A knock at the door.

A tray of sandwiches, a jug of coffee, and a bottle of sparkling water appeared on the table. The officers ignored all of it.

Max cleared his throat.

"Can I ask something? I've answered everything I can for hours, but... I still don't understand anything about this world."

Sauson watched him with steady caution. "What do you want to know?"

Max hesitated. "The farmer. When I tried to pay for an apple, he said *money was illegal*. He wasn't joking."

A subtle shift ran around the room. A glance passed between the four officers — not alarm, not secrecy, but calculation. In the hours they'd been questioning him, Max had mentioned money again and again. And banks. And wages. And contracts. To the officers, he sounded like someone discussing ghosts.

Sauson tapped the table lightly.

"We'll take a short break," he said. "Fresh air."

The four men stood, stepped out, and closed the door behind them.

They did not walk far — only far enough to speak without being overheard. The silence of the hallway pressed in around them.

Azemar exhaled sharply. "He genuinely has no idea. He thinks Bugatti builds the best cars in the world." He shook his head, baffled.

Dominic rubbed the fatigue from the bridge of his crooked nose. "If he's telling the truth — and I'm convinced he is — everything here must feel wrong to him. No wonder he's confused."

Sauson crossed his arms. "He's found familiar structures. The geography, the church, the village layout. But the rest? Different enough that his story fits. A world that split from ours at some point... insane, yes. But he believes it."

Titbaut looked between them. "You think he's genuinely from somewhere else?"

Dominic answered before the others could. "I've spent twenty years reading liars. He's not lying. *Not even a little.* He's ignorant of the most basic facts of our society. He asks questions that make no sense. You don't fake that. He's terrified, not deceitful."

Silence settled again.

Sauson finally spoke, voice steady. "I'm detaining him. He stays in custody until we understand the implications. No threats. Full cooperation. But if he's telling the truth, we're looking at the biggest security unknown we've ever faced."

Titbaut nodded slowly. "And the blue shell? The thing that appeared at the Diderot farm?"

Sauson shook his head slowly, as if trying to clear out the nonsense. "Look, I don't buy a word of this. Parallel universe, blue shell, timed return — it all sounds like the sort of thing you hear right before someone pulls a stunt." He glanced at the others, jaw tightening. "But tomorrow at ten I'm going to stand there and watch that supposed portal myself. If something appears — anything — then we deal with it as police, not dreamers."

He pointed at the interview room without aggression, just firm authority. "If the shell shows up, we hold our ground and send a message through. They need to know he's alive, he's in custody, and nothing else comes through until we understand what the hell we're dealing with."

Azemar shifted uneasily. "And Max? He's frightened."

"We tell him a little," Sauson said. "Enough so he understands he is not in danger here — unless he tries to run. After the judge processes him tonight, he'll be moved to a secure room. No handcuffs. Not one of the cells. *But no freedom either.*"

Dominic let out a dry breath. "He's just created a diplomatic crisis with a world that doesn't sound like they believe in diplomacy."

Sauson straightened. "Let's go back in."

***

**Saturday, 9th June 2012, 6:58 p.m.**
**Parallel universe. European Security Office, Geneva, Switzerland.**


The five men sat in the interview room finishing their sandwiches in a silence that felt less like rest and more like a pause between storms. For all its plain décor — a heavy desk, padded chairs, two walls of books — the space carried the stillness of a place where lives drifted off their trajectories.

Azemar finally broke the quiet.

"You know," he said, brushing crumbs from his shirt, "you caused a great deal of anguish for poor old Renato. His wife says he was a wreck for days after that... thing... appeared in his field."

Max lowered his gaze. "I'm sorry. I can imagine how terrifying it must have looked."

Sauson added, "Renato and Bibiane will speak with you again before we take you to the judge."

Max's head snapped up. "Why do I have to see a judge?"

Sauson slowed, choosing his words. "Because you're an unknown, Max. You arrived from nowhere, nobody here knows anything about you, and we have no idea what your intentions are. A judge decides whether you can be released, or whether you need to be held while we learn more."

Max shook his head, frustration breaking through. "And you still haven't explained anything about this world. Why it's different."

A glance passed between Sauson and Dominic — the kind that marked an argument already lost. They had been turning Max's explanation over in their minds ever since he'd given it: that CERN believed the two universes had split at some unknown point, and that he knew nothing more than that.

Sauson exhaled.

"It's because the answer is likely to shock you. Not as much as we've been shocked by what you've told us about the split... but enough."

He stood, crossed to one of the tall bookcases, and slid out a narrow wooden panel disguised as the end of a row of bound volumes. He brought it back and set it on the table in front of Max.

"You asked about money," Sauson said. "In your world it appears to be the centre of everything. Here, we don't have money."

Max blinked. "Yes you've said that but why don't you have money—"

Sauson folded his hands. "For almost a century — since November 1919 — most of our world has lived under a system called the Twelve Rules. It shaped everything about our world today — our laws, our values, the way people deal with one another, and apparently even the different technologies you've noticed. We developed science and engineering along similar lines as it sounds as your world has. What we did not do was build nations driven by profit or conquest."

Max listened, caught between disbelief and a reluctant fascination.

Sauson continued, "I don't know why our histories diverged. Why yours remained, frankly, destructive. But we chose cooperation over competition a long time ago. That doesn't mean misconduct vanished. We still require law, tribunals, social order. Just not your kind of order."

He nudged the wooden panel closer.

"Most nations on this Earth follow the Twelve Rules. They're simple. Everything else — planning, logistics, administration — is just regulation."

Max lifted the panel. The hand-painted lettering echoed the rustic craft of Renato's market displays. He read the title.

THE TWELVE RULES OF SOCIETY

Adopted in the First Year of the New Era — 1919

By the Peoples of Earth in Accord and Peace

Max continued to read.

When he finally lowered it, his face had gone pale. Not frightened — overwhelmed. His thoughts were scattered, struggling to land on anything solid.

The officers watched the shift in him: the quiet internal collapse when a fundamental understanding of life shifts.

Sauson leaned forward.

"This," he said quietly, "is why we hesitated. You told us about your wars, your markets, your money, your hierarchies. To us, your world sounds like an illness history failed to heal."

He sat back.

Max swallowed. He tried to speak, failed, and let the air escape in a thin breath. The revelation wasn't settling — it was overtaking him.

Dominic's gravelled voice cut through gently.

"Take your time, Max. You don't need to understand everything tonight. But understand this: you are safe. And we will treat you fairly."

Max nodded, though the gesture was mechanical, as if he were agreeing to something he had not yet learned to process.

He set the panel back on the table.

And the weight of the profundity of what he'd just read settled across him.

***

**Saturday, 9th June 2012, 8:08 p.m.**
**Parallel universe. European Security Office, Geneva, Switzerland.**

The door clicked shut behind Sauson, and the room seemed to shrink. Renato Diderot entered first — cautiously, almost shyly — a very different man from the panicked farmer who had wrestled Max in the street only hours earlier. His face was lined with exhaustion, but there was a steadiness in his eyes now, the steadiness of someone who had finally come to terms with his fear.

He crossed the room and held out his hand.

"Max... I owe you an apology." His voice was low, honest. "I was terrified. And when a man thinks he is losing his mind, he behaves like a fool. Please forgive me."

Max shook his hand without hesitation. "Of course. Anyone would've reacted the same."

Behind them, Bibiane slipped in and closed the door with her hip. She gave Renato a pointed, affectionate, exasperated look as she took a seat.

"That's because every time he was arrested, he behaved like an oaf," she said.

Renato looked wounded. "Chérie..."

Max couldn't help smiling. They were chaotic, but warm — the kind of couple who argued loudly and cared deeply.

Renato and Bibiane sat in the chairs opposite Max.

Max gestured toward the tray of sandwiches — only an uneaten crust remained. "They've treated me well. Better than I deserve, considering what happened."

Bibiane nodded, her manner softening. "It was a shock for all of us. Imagine standing in your garden and seeing a blue sphere appear out of nothing. Then your flying machine appears from the sky like something out of a folktale." She squeezed her husband's hand. "He thought he was losing his mind."

Renato looked down, ashamed and relieved in equal measure.

"I'm sorry," Max said quietly. "We didn't know anything about your world. We never meant to frighten you."

Renato exhaled. "Thank you."

A quiet settled over the room — the kind of quiet that exists after panic has burned itself out.

Bibiane leaned forward. "The officers told us we're to answer any questions you have. They said you asked about our rules, and that you're going before a judge soon. Is there anything else you want to understand?"

For the next half-hour, they talked. Bibiane explained, carefully and patiently, how the court system worked, how conflicts were handled, why judges existed in a society without money or hierarchy. Renato added small stories — colorful, sometimes inappropriate — that gave the rules texture. Together, they painted a world Max had walked through but still barely grasped.

Gradually, the awkwardness fell away.

Then Max made the mistake of telling Renato how the CERN team reacted to watching him shoot the drone — the shouting, the panic, Gaidon clutching his head, the frantic scramble in the control room.

Renato froze for a heartbeat.

Then he collapsed into helpless, wheezing laughter. Actual tears rolled down his face.

Bibiane covered her eyes. "Renato, please..."

The commotion was loud enough to bring Dominic Garner and Sauson Bourel charging into the room.

"What's going on in here?" Dominic barked.

Renato wiped his face, still half-laughing. "They... they have a nickname for me at their science laboratory."

A breath.

"They call me the 'angry bear.'"

Dominic stared, unimpressed. "That's it?"

Renato thumped the table, laughing all over again.

Sauson shook his head. "It's nearly time. Max, any final questions?"

Max stood. "I think I'm as prepared as I can be."

Bibiane rose and hugged him — warm, steady, lingering.

"Good luck. Truly."

Renato followed, giving him a firm, awkward embrace. "One day, when all this madness is resolved... you must come back. Visit us properly. We host a party on the first Saturday of every month."

Max managed a smile. "I'll keep that in mind."

Then the guards arrived, and the moment was over.

But the warmth stayed with him — unexpected, strange, and profoundly human.

***

**Saturday, 9th June 2012, 9:28 p.m.**
**Parallel universe. Primary Geneva Court, Geneva, Switzerland.**

The courtroom looked exactly like something out of a film — polished timber, a high vaulted ceiling, and the heavy, echoing stillness of a place where decisions carried weight. Only a handful of people were present: Sauson Bourel and the three security officers, Max and his 'defence lawyer', and the judge's empty bench.

Max's lawyer, Lula Renan, leaned towards him. Early forties, sharp-eyed, composed

— the kind of woman who made competence look effortless.

"Remember," she murmured, "this isn't a trial. It's a preliminary enquiry. Answer clearly. And don't panic when he asks strange questions."

Strange questions. That was all Max had been asked since he arrived in this world.

The side door opened. A middle-aged man in simple, dark suit walked to the bench with a quiet assurance built from decades of adjudicating difficult matters.

"Welcome," he said, taking his seat without ceremony. "I am Haylon Oudant. Call me Haylon, Oudant, or Judge — whichever you prefer. This enquiry is in session and is being recorded."

He gestured for introductions.

Sauson stood first and stated his name and position. Dominic, Titbaut, and Azemar followed. Then Lula introduced herself as a legal instructor from the University of Geneva.

Max blinked. A teacher is my lawyer?

Haylon caught the expression and gave a faint, knowing smile.

"You must be Maximilien Rivette. Would you like to introduce yourself?"

Max stood awkwardly. "Ah — yes. I'm Maximilien Rivette. I work as a draftsman at the European Organisation for Nuclear Research. CERN."

Haylon sifted through several pages.

"I've spoken at length with Officer Bourel," he said, "and I must admit — this situation is unprecedented. Two versions of Earth separated by a dimensional barrier. You call it a 'parallel universe'. We are still trying to grasp what that truly means."

He studied Max with unsettling scrutiny, as though trying to see past bone and blood.

"I understand your world remains an economic system based on private wealth and trade. 'Capitalism', you called it."

"Yes."

"That alone is not the concern of this enquiry."

He turned another page.

"What is concerning is your account of widespread wars, nations armed with devastating weapons, and the apparent normalcy of such things."

Max lowered his head. Embarrassment burned hot across his throat.

"You confirm," Haylon continued, "that your world possesses atomic bombs?"

"Yes."

"And that many nations have thousands of them — capable of destroying entire cities?"

"...Yes."

A murmur passed through the officers.

Haylon let the silence linger before continuing.

"Now, we must gather more information about you and your world and whether you represent a risk."

He leaned forward a fraction.

"You told the officers that you work part-time at CERN. What is your full-time occupation?"

"I'm a mechanical designer."

"For which organisation?"

"…Nexter."

"And what does Nexter manufacture?"

Max chose his words with painful care. "Equipment. For the army."

"What kind of equipment?"

"Vehicles. Turrets. Ammunition systems. I design components — structural parts, interfaces, mechanical assemblies."

"'Ammunition systems,'" Haylon repeated softly.

Max nodded.

"And before Nexter?"

Max hesitated. "Various companies."

"I want the one where you spent the most time."

The tightness in Max's stomach returned. "…Dassault."

"You mentioned this earlier — in the interview you said they were… Dassault Aviation."

"Yes."

"And what do they produce?"

"Aircraft."

"Civilian aircraft?"

"Some. But the project I worked on was military."

"The Rafale," Haylon said.

Max looked up sharply. "You know about it?"

"I read very carefully everything you have said today in your interview."

Haylon set the papers down.

"It is a multi-role combat aircraft, is it not?"

"Yes."

Another long pause.

"So," Haylon said quietly, "you have spent more than a decade designing components for machines whose purpose is to deliver explosives, bullets, or missiles."

The heat in Max's face intensified. "I'm not a soldier. I never—"

"I did not ask if you fight," the judge interrupted gently. "I said you help build the tools."

He leaned back, his voice soft but relentless.

"You call yourself a 'draftsman'. But to us, you appear to be a man whose professional life has been dedicated — intentionally or not — to the construction of weapons."

Max stared at the table. "I... I never thought of it that way."

"We abolished war ninety-four years ago," Haylon said. "The very idea that someone could spend a career designing artillery and combat aircraft is grotesque to us. You do not seem cruel. But your work is, in effect, the anatomy of violence."

He paused, letting the words land.

"Do you understand why, from our perspective, you appear to be a very dangerous type of visitor?"

Max's voice cracked. "I'm not a monster."

"No," Haylon said. "Monsters delight in destruction. You simply... built the tools. In our world, that distinction is not as comforting as you might hope."

Dominic and Sauson exchanged grim glances.

Haylon picked up the final sheet.

"Max Rivette. Given the extreme militarisation of your world, the destructive technologies you described, and your professional involvement in their design... I cannot authorise your return at this time."

Max shut his eyes.

"You will remain in the custody of European Security," the judge continued, "and be transferred to Paris for a specialised review. This is not punishment. It is caution."

He gave Max one final, unsettled look.

"This enquiry is closed."

***

# Chapter 8



**Sunday, 10th June 2012, 9:58 a.m.**
**Parallel universe. Diderot farm, Prévessin-Moëns, France.**

The morning light washed across the Diderot farm with a quiet, almost deceptive beauty — the kind of serenity that made the previous day's chaos feel unreal. But everyone present knew exactly what was coming.

Renato and Bibiane had been awake since dawn, helping Sauson Bourel and Dominic Garner set up the tripod, calibrate the camera, and position the three printed signs. Max had given them the timing with absolute certainty: the portal would open at *exactly* 10:00 a.m. The CERN team would be watching. Their job was simple — show the signs, step back, and let the other world absorb the message.

No one felt calm.

The signs leaned against the plant trellises as they finished preparations:

WE HAVE ARRESTED MAXIMILIEN RIVETTE. HE IS SAFE.

DO NOT TAKE ANY HOSTILE ACTION. DO NOT SEND ANYTHING ELSE THROUGH THE PORTAL.

OPEN AGAIN IN EXACTLY FOUR WEEKS FOR FURTHER INFORMATION.

Dominic checked his watch for the tenth time. Sauson ran a hand through his hair, muttering, "This is absurd," not out of disbelief but the weary resignation of a man caught in something far larger than his pay grade.

They had asked Renato yet again to describe what he saw earlier in the week.

"It was big," he said, rubbing his arms as though recalling a blast of cold. "Transparent, but not. Blue, but shifting. Like staring through water and on the bottom, a flat floor with grooves cut into it. And the sound... like the world snapping."

He shuddered.

Bibiane squeezed his arm.

Now, standing ten metres from the circular scar in the soil, they took their positions.

Bibiane held the first sign. Sauson the second along with a small video camera. Dominic the third. Renato stood empty-handed, arms crossed, jaw tight — a man still wrestling with the remains of a trauma he'd once thought was madness.

"Camera on," Sauson said at 9:59. The red light blinked alive.

They stood shoulder to shoulder, facing the empty space.

A single minute stretched into eternity.

Even the birds fell quiet.

Reality tore.

A sharp, flat crack split the air, chased instantly by a rolling boom that thumped through their chests. The blue sphere erupted into existence fully formed — no transition, no fade, just *there* — overwhelming in its scale and presence.

The officers flinched.

Dominic muttered, "Christ..."

The sphere floated ten centimetres above the carved-out soil, shimmering with a cold azure glow. Its surface churned slowly, like tides moving across glass.

Nobody spoke.

The sight crushed language. It was the sort of thing that once would have driven people to prayer.

Renato whispered, "It looks exactly the same."

The fear that had devoured him for weeks was gone now that he wasn't alone. Knowledge had taken the place of terror. He stood straighter.

"Can you see the floor?" he asked.

"Yes," the two officers answered at once — both of them eyeing the metal platform that protruded into the blue volume.

"And can you see the cameras?"

They gave a series of acknowledgements.

Seconds passed.

Nothing moved on the other side. No shift of light, no silhouette.

The sphere just hovered, humming faintly, waiting for an answer that was not coming.

Ten seconds.

Fifteen.

Twenty.

Then—

A soft inward *thump* — as if the air snapped back into place — and the shell collapsed into itself and vanished.

Gone.

The clearing returned to bright morning light and the ordinary sounds of the farm.

Sauson exhaled so hard his shoulders dropped. "Thank God..."

Dominic wiped sweat from his brow. "I think I aged ten years."

Bibiane lowered her sign and blinked away an adrenaline tear.

Renato didn't sigh or shake.

He simply looked at the space where the sphere had been and nodded once.

For the first time since the day he shot down the drone, he looked like himself again — a man who had faced the impossible twice — and finally knew he had not lost his mind.

***

**Sunday, 10th June 2012, 9:58 a.m.**
**Control room, Laboratory 888, CERN, Prévessin-Moëns, France.**

The control room hummed with quiet confidence.

Gaidon and the team had already run through the last diagnostics, verified the countdown, and armed the opening sequence. At exactly 10:00 a.m., the portal would bloom in the other world, and Max would return with whatever knowledge he'd gathered in his twenty-four hours on the far side.

For the first time in days, the mood was relaxed.

Gaidon sat forward in his chair, hands folded, a gentle, anticipatory smile on his face.

He had already begun rehearsing the announcement he would make to CERN leadership — the discovery that would change human history.

Baset glanced at the clock. "What do you think Max actually did for twenty-four hours? That's a long time to stay awake."

Emerancie shrugged. "Probably walked around Geneva all night. He loves the place."

Vincent spun lightly in his chair. "If it were me? I'd have found a nightclub by midnight. Dancing, music, drinks. Whole thing."

Daniel smirked. "I just hope Max hasn't met some strangers at a nightclub and decided to bring them back through the portal."

Gaidon raised a hand. "All right. Ten seconds."

The shift was immediate. Chairs rolled in. Spines straightened. Fingers poised over controls.

The countdown hit zero.

The displays flickered — then filled with the familiar blue-hazed distortion. The automated system extended the remote lenses forward until they gently breached the surface of the shell, giving them a clear view into the parallel clearing.

The team leaned in.

Gasps broke the silence.

Emerancie whispered, "Oh God..."

Daniel said, "What—who are they?"

Gaidon swore. Loudly. Violently.

Four people stood ten metres back from the portal shell. Three held large, painted signs. On the far left stood the angry farmer — arms crossed, expression thunderous. Beside him, a balding middle-aged man. Next to him, a woman holding her sign with both hands. On the right, another man, posture rigid with purpose.

No Max.

Just the signs.

Gaidon read them aloud without even realising he was doing it — the words falling out of him like stones.

"WE HAVE ARRESTED MAXIMILIEN RIVETTE. HE IS SAFE."

His pulse spiked.

The second sign:

"DO NOT TAKE ANY HOSTILE ACTION. DO NOT SEND ANYTHING ELSE THROUGH THE PORTAL."

A cold, electric stillness filled the room.

And then the third:

"OPEN AGAIN IN EXACTLY FOUR WEEKS FOR FURTHER INFORMATION."

Vincent swallowed. "Gaidon... what do you want us to do? Should we shut it down?"

Gaidon didn't answer. He was staring at the screen, his hands shaking, mind blank, lips parted as if trying to form words that wouldn't come.

Emerancie pointed. "They're talking... they're speaking to one another."

Baset leaned forward. "There — off to the side. Another camera. They're recording us."

Daniel turned to Gaidon. "Say something. Do we—"

But Gaidon wasn't hearing them. His face had gone pale, his breath shallow. A long, shuddering exhale escaped him.

Vincent turned fully in his chair.

Gaidon was trembling.

Tears ran silently down his cheeks.

"Gaidon," Vincent said softly, "do you want to shut it down?"

A multi-second pause.

"...Yes."

Vincent hit the shutdown command.

On the monitors, the blue haze imploded in a single breathless collapse —

and the portal sealed shut.

***

**Sunday, 10th June 2012, 10:32 a.m.**
**Gaidon Ballerat's office, Laboratory 888, CERN, Prévessin-Moëns, France.**

The team filed into Gaidon Ballerat's office like a group returning from a funeral. No one spoke at first. The shock of what they'd witnessed through the portal clung to them — heavy, disorienting, impossible to process.

Gaidon sat behind his desk, elbows planted, hands clasped so tightly the knuckles whitened. For minutes after the shutdown, he'd seemed hollowed out — dazed, as if his mind had been punched out of him.

Now the numbness had burned away.

What remained was fury.

He slammed his palm onto the desk with a crack.

"What the fuck went wrong?" His voice cracked with disbelief. "How could someone like Max get arrested? He only had to walk into a suburb, or get a bus to Geneva, take some footage, talk to people, ask for directions!"

The room stayed silent.

Five seconds.

Ten.

Finally, Baset cleared his throat. "I don't think it's about Max. It's about us. We terrified them. If our world discovered a parallel Earth, we'd react with absolute fear. Maybe worse."

Emerancie nodded. "And the farmer was there. The way he stood — arms crossed, glaring. And those other three... who were they?"

Vincent leaned back, replaying the image in his mind. "The woman looked like she was the farmers wife, dressed for... whatever farmers do... and she was the calmest one there."

Daniel added, "The man on the right was definitely police. You could tell by his posture. Confident. Ready. And he looked like someone who's had a few fights in his life."

Baset gestured vaguely. "And the bald man — he looked like he'd stepped straight out of a meeting."

"Enough," Gaidon snapped.

The room froze.

He looked at each of them in turn, eyes sharp with frustration.

"We're not going to solve this by guessing faces on a screen." He took a long breath. "Now... what are we going to do about Max?"

No one answered.

Gaidon pressed on.

"The signs say he's been arrested and is safe. We have no choice but to take them at their word. They knew about the timing. They were waiting. Which means Max told them everything."

His jaw tightened.

"Max is on his own for now. There's nothing we can do." Another breath — strained, irritated, exhausted. "And I don't like them dictating terms about future contact. Four weeks is too long."

He ran a hand through his hair, already thinking three steps ahead.

"I'll talk to Adéhémar. A few days ago he told me he had some hobby heli-drones — decent ones. He said he'd been working on an onboard computer that can fly a pre-programmed route without needing a return signal. If we can send a drone through the portal, and have it fly out, loop around, and come back before the shell closes... maybe we can send some kind of message. They've got to understand we need to know..."

Daniel frowned. "That's risky."

"I don't care," Gaidon said bluntly. "We're out of options. This has been a complete disaster."

The team traded weary looks — unspoken agreement that he was right. There was nothing else to do. No further plans to make.

Just waiting.

Emerancie broke the silence softly.

"What do we tell Max's aunt? She'll panic when he doesn't come home."

Gaidon exhaled, slow and heavy.

"I'll speak to her," he said. "God help me... I'll tell her something."

He pushed back from his desk.

He didn't look enraged anymore.

Just old.

And very, very tired.

***

**Monday, 11th June 2012, 9:00 a.m.**
**Gaidon Ballerat's office, Laboratory 888, CERN, Prévessin-Moëns, France.**

Daniel slipped into the room last, quietly closing the door behind him. The rest of the team were already seated, subdued, waiting. Gaidon didn't waste time.

"Alright," he began, voice frayed. "I've spoken to Adéhémar. He says he'll have his heli-drone ready for later this week. He needs to iron out a few bugs in the autopilot software first. Emerancie, I want you working with him."

"Yeah," she said. "No problem."

Gaidon nodded once and moved on.

"And... I got a call from Fairfax Woods last night."

That name alone drew a few raised eyebrows. Fairfax was high enough in CERN administration that any unexpected interest from him was bad news.

"He noticed our power consumption spikes," Gaidon continued. "Every lab's numbers land on his desk every morning. He worked out we ran the machine multiple times and asked how things were going."

Baset leaned forward. "And what did you tell him?"

"That the system's functioning and we're still ironing out some bugs." Gaidon exhaled sharply. "He wants a full report by the end of the week."

A heavy silence settled.

Emerancie broke it. "Did you speak to Céleste?"

Gaidon's expression tightened. "Yes. And it wasn't easy. I hate lying." He pinched the bridge of his nose. "I told her Max had been called away on another urgent job. But she didn't buy a word of it."

Vincent frowned. "What do you mean she didn't buy it?"

"She already knew," Gaidon said flatly. "Max told her the night before he left. Told her he was going through the portal for twenty-four hours."

The room froze.

Daniel blinked. "He told her?"

"Yes. Everything. So I had to tell her he'd been arrested. I told her what little we know, and I made it absolutely clear she must not tell anyone — *anyone*." He slumped back in his chair. "It took a hell of a lot of convincing, but she agreed."

He rubbed his forehead, exhausted. "This is such a mess. And it gets worse — I still have to deal with Max's boss at Nexter. I don't know how the hell I'm supposed to explain his disappearance."

His voice cracked on the next words.

"Shit. This is a fucking nightmare."

He slammed his fist onto the table. The sharp crack echoed through the room, and for a moment nobody breathed.

***

# Chapter 9



**Monday, 11th June 2012, 11:15 a.m.**
**Parallel universe. Geneva railway station, Geneva, Switzerland.**

European Security wasn't quite a police force and not quite an intelligence service; it was something between the two — a pan-continental organisation that handled the rare cases serious enough to breach the Twelve Rules. In a world without money, without property beyond the personal, and without the machinery of exploitation, most crimes Max knew from his own universe simply didn't exist. Theft, fraud, corruption — they were relics. What remained was the occasional violence, or the truly unusual.

Max, officially "in custody", had never actually felt detained. Because he wasn't violent, wasn't a flight risk, they had kept him in what felt like a small, comfortable hotel suite inside the Security complex: a private bedroom, a small dining area, and a spotless bathroom. He hadn't seen another detainee. Dominic had explained why:

"We rarely need to hold anyone," he'd said. "Most problems are resolved in a day."

And now, after two nights inside that strange, quiet place, Max and Dominic were walking to the nearby railway station. Everything in this universe — the architecture, the cars, the people — felt familiar yet filtered through some gentler logic.

Max kept looking around as they reached the platform. "How come we aren't flying to Paris?"

Dominic shrugged. "Security reasons, I guess. Sauson didn't explain."

"You've spoken to him?" Max asked. "Nobody has told me what happened at the farm yesterday."

"We've been very busy since then," Dominic said. "I only got a few hours of sleep before I had to escort you to Paris."

"Oh."

They sat on a long metal bench. People moved around them without glancing at Max twice. No handcuffs. No guards hovering. Max looked ordinary — just a tired man waiting for a train. But he knew one thing with absolute clarity: he wasn't going anywhere unless Dominic allowed it. The man radiated competence. His build, his posture, the way his eyes tracked the environment — Max suspected he could outrun, outfight, and outthink most people half his age.

"So," Max said quietly, "what actually happened yesterday? At the farm."

Dominic thought for a moment before answering.

"When we were in the courtroom with the judge," he began, "I honestly didn't know what to make of you. The judge clearly thought you were dangerous — someone who might be hiding something. And you have to admit, Max, your story... portals, another Earth... it sounded like a panic-inspired cover story. Something a person might invent when cornered."

Max winced but nodded.

Dominic continued. "But when we went to the farm, and I heard you talk with Renato and Bibiane... that wasn't the voice of a liar. Or a soldier. Or a spy. You just sounded lost. Completely out of place."

He leaned back and exhaled slowly.

"And then, when that thing opened in front of us..." He gave a small shake of the head. "Seeing it with my own eyes — the blue shell, the force of it — that's when I knew. Your story wasn't an act. And whatever danger exists here... it isn't you."

They sat in silence for a while, the railway announcements echoing across the concourse in a soft, melodic chime.

"Nothing really happened in the end," Dominic added. "We just stood there holding the signs. Maybe a minute. Then the sphere vanished."

Max breathed out. "I wonder how Gaidon will take it."

"He's the chief scientist, right?"

"Yes. And he wanted to announce this discovery to the world." Max grimaced. "He's probably going bananas right now."

He sat up suddenly. "Shit — Céleste."

Dominic turned. "Who's Céleste?"

"My aunt," Max said, rubbing his forehead. "In all this — being arrested, the judge — I've barely thought about her. She's going to be furious. The night before I left, we had a fight... and I didn't even get to say goodbye. She'd already gone to work when I left." He groaned. "Bloody hell. I've really messed up."

Dominic didn't answer immediately. He simply watched the trains moving in and out, and then said, with surprising gentleness:

"We'll make sure she knows you're safe."

Max nodded, though the knot in his chest didn't ease.

***

**Monday, 11th June 2012, 1:17 p.m.**
**Parallel universe. Train carriage, France.**

Max was convinced there were at least two more undercover officers on the train. Every so often he caught a glance held a fraction too long — not threatening, just watchful. Enough to confirm they weren't taking chances with him.

Not that he minded. In his world, prisoners didn't cross countries on quiet, comfortable trains or finish generous lunches before being escorted anywhere.

Across from him, Dominic sat with the loose, balanced posture of someone who had spent a career on trains, in interviews, escorting people who were far more dangerous than Max. Between them lay the strange, polite gulf of two men comparing histories that should have matched and absolutely didn't.

"So you really haven't heard of Adolf Hitler?" Max asked.

Dominic shook his head. "No. Should I have?"

"He helped start the Second World War."

Dominic raised an eyebrow. "We didn't have a second world war."

Max blinked. "Right... okay. What about Stalin? Lenin?"

Dominic frowned. "Let me check."

He reached into his bag and pulled out a small, rugged electronic display — thicker than anything from Max's world, built like military equipment rather than a consumer tablet. Dominic tapped through several screens, reading quickly.

"All right," he said after a moment. "Both were part of some political group in the old Russian regions. Arrested early on. Never gained influence. Barely footnotes."

Max stared at him. Stalin and Lenin — two men who shaped half of the twentieth century — reduced here to historical trivia.

"And Hitler?" Max pressed.

Dominic typed again. "Nothing. Doesn't appear to have existed here."

Max leaned back slowly. Their worlds weren't parallel branches — they were divergent realities separated by a century of different choices.

Dominic closed the device and slipped it away. "Our twentieth century looked very different from yours. Not better, not worse — just... a different path."

"What changed it?" Max asked. "What sent everything in another direction?"

Dominic hesitated — not because he didn't know, but because explaining it to someone without the cultural scaffolding was a challenge.

"We call it the evolution," he said finally.

Max looked up. The word landed with an unfamiliar weight.

"Why that word?" he asked.

"Because it didn't start with anger," Dominic replied. "It started with exhaustion. After Armistice Day in 1918, people were done with killing — not abstractly, not philosophically, but viscerally. The carnage was so vast that it shifted humanity's understanding of itself. They didn't just blame governments or generals; they blamed the entire architecture that made war possible."

He gestured at the countryside streaming past the window — green fields, scattered villages, no billboards, no motorways clogged with private cars.

"So instead of rising up, they stepped away. They dismantled the old structures, stripped out the machinery of hierarchy and violence, and built something else. The Twelve Rules came out of that moment — a framework meant to prevent any concentration of power from ever reaching the point where war could happen again. No elites. No permanent authority. Just communities reorganising themselves from the ground up."

He paused, then added, "Once people tasted a life not shaped by fear or obedience, it spread faster than anyone expected. And once it spread, it never reversed."

Max tried to picture it: a civilisation turning away from its own history, not by force or ideology, but by deciding — collectively — to stop repeating the pattern that had nearly destroyed it.

Dominic watched him carefully. "Difficult to imagine, I know."

"It is," Max admitted, "but it... actually makes sense."

Max turned back to the window, watching fields merge into forests, forests into towns.

For the first time since stepping into this universe, fear loosened its grip — replaced by something quieter, steadier, and far more dangerous.

Curiosity.

***

**Monday, 11th June 2012, 6:12 p.m.**
**Parallel universe. Paris, France.**

The train glided into Paris beneath a warm, amber evening sky. Once they stepped onto the platform, Dominic steered Max through the station's wide concourse and out onto the bustling streets. Heat clung to the city hard enough that, after only a few minutes, both men gravitated toward a streetside stall for cold drinks and ice-cream.

Max took the first long, cooling mouthful of his drink and nodded back toward the vendor as they walked away.

"I still don't get it," he said. "If everything's free, why bother running a stand like that? People can just grab the same stuff from a supermarket."

"Correct," Dominic said, wiping a streak of melted ice-cream from his wrist. "Nobody pays for anything. You take what you need. But that young bloke…" He gave a faint laugh. "He's not there out of civic obligation."

"Oh?"

Dominic jerked his chin toward the stall. "He's there to meet girls. Did you see the two he was chatting up?"

Max chuckled. "Yeah. Pretty obvious."

"Exactly. He offers convenience on a hot day, and he gets to socialise. Plus, the food he's serving comes from some of the best small producers in the city. You won't find that sort of quality in a supermarket."

Max considered that — another small window into a society that functioned without money yet somehow remained vibrant and motivated.

Paris itself felt oddly doubled: familiar in its bones — the old stone, the organised chaos of traffic, the murmuring crowds — yet lifted by colour and texture in ways that made his own world feel drab by comparison.

Colour everywhere.

Buildings washed in bright pastels and deep saturated tones. Bus shelters painted with swirling geometric murals. Clothes bursting with pattern and personality. Even people's movements seemed freer, looser, unconcerned with the formal gravity he was used to.

Most wore casual clothes like in his own world, only bolder. And the suits — the very few he saw — were nothing like the corporate armour of home. One man passed in a three-piece ensemble patched together from clashing fabrics in rich jewel tones, striding confidently as though he owned the concept of fashion itself.

Nobody except Max even looked twice.

They rounded the final corner.

Max stopped.

Dominic paused beside him, hands relaxed at his sides, letting him take it in.

European Security Headquarters swept across the block in a graceful arc — concrete, steel, and mirrored glass arranged in broad, flowing lines. The building captured the late sun in sheets of gold and blue that shifted as clouds moved overhead. In the centre of the open plaza stood an enormous abstract sculpture: spirals of colour and brushed metal rising like a captured explosion, dynamic even at rest.

"Wow…" Max murmured. "Your special-police building looks like a museum. Or an art gallery."

Dominic gave a small, matter-of-fact shrug. "We like our public buildings to be worth looking at."

They continued across the plaza. The glass doors slid open silently as they approached, swallowing them into the cool, resonant interior.

***

**Monday, 11th June 2012, 6:33 p.m.**
**Parallel universe. European Security Headquarters, Paris, France.**

The lift carried them smoothly to the upper floors. When the doors opened, Max and Dominic stepped into a wide semi-circular lobby. Curved glass walls followed the arc of the building; a fan of offices radiated from the curve like spokes.

A secretary at a low desk glanced up, recognised Dominic, and made a small gesture toward one of the inner doors without breaking her typing rhythm.

Dominic led Max across the polished stone floor. Max tried to steady his breathing. His palms were damp despite the cool air.

Dominic knocked.

"Come in," a voice called.

They entered a tidy, understated office — dark wood, clean lines, a single abstract painting, and soft early evening light spilling through tall windows.

A man sat with his back to them, speaking quietly into a mobile phone. He turned in his chair as they entered.

Aimes Perrier.

Compact build, broad shoulders, a face marked more by experience than age. Short, grey-streaked hair. Eyes with the steady, measuring quality of someone long accustomed to responsibility. Not threatening, but unmistakably in command.

He finished the call quickly.

"Yes. They're here now. All right. We'll speak later."

He set the phone down and stood, shaking Dominic's hand first.

"No trouble on the train?"

"None," Dominic said. "We travelled without incident."

Aimes turned to Max and offered a firm handshake. "Good to finally meet you."

"Likewise," Max replied.

"Please. Sit."

They took their seats opposite him. Aimes leaned forward slightly, hands folded, gaze direct but calm.

"Well, Max," he began, "I've read the reports from Geneva. I've watched the footage of the device opening. I've gone through everything from the farm, the judge, the officers who brought you in."

He paused, studying Max's face.

"And even knowing all that, it remains... staggering."

He nodded toward the phone he'd just set aside. "That was Félix Koster. One of our senior scientific directors. He's just reviewed the portal recording. Even he's struggling — not with believing what he saw, but with understanding what it means."

Max exhaled slowly. "It shocked us, too. More than I can explain."

Aimes gave a small nod. "I can imagine."

His tone tightened, focus sharpening.

"But we need to talk about *your* world. In detail."

What followed took almost two hours.

Aimes questioned him with steady, methodical precision — never hostile, never hurried, but thorough in a way that left no gaps. He listened closely, only interrupting to clarify a point or to circle back to something Max had mentioned earlier. Dominic occasionally added a question or checked a detail, but mostly he watched.

It was the military and political history that held Aimes the longest.

Conflicts Max assumed everyone knew.

Leaders whose names defined entire eras.

Wars that carved his own century into what it had become — yet here, they had never happened.

Aimes absorbed it all in still, concentrated silence. No notes. No overt reactions beyond the slight tightening of his jaw or a brief narrowing of his eyes as he tried to map Max's account onto a different Earth.

By the time the questions ended, night had settled fully outside the windows. The city lights glowed off the glass.

Aimes leaned back at last, thumb running along the edge of the desk as if grounding himself.

"Your world," he said quietly, "is far more violent than ours. Far more... unstable."

Max swallowed. "Yes."

Aimes nodded once.

"And now," he said, "we have to decide what that means for both of us."

***

**Monday, 11th June 2012, 10:35 p.m.**
**Parallel universe. Paris High Security Jail, Paris, France.**

The night air was warm, carrying the faint sweetness of jasmine from a rooftop garden somewhere above them. Max and Dominic walked the short hundred metres from the European Security Headquarters to the adjoining high-security jail. Paris had settled into its late-night hush; streetlights carved long amber shadows across the pavement.

Max broke the silence first.

"Has any of this... the arrest, the portal... made the news?"

Dominic answered immediately.

"No. Nobody outside the security team and a handful of scientists even knows you exist. And it'll stay that way. This is new, unpredictable. Panic is the last thing anyone wants."

Max nodded, though anxiety still sat like a stone beneath his ribs.

"Right. I get it."

They walked another few steps before Dominic spoke again, his voice quieter, more deliberate.

"One more thing. You must not tell *anyone* where you're from."

Max blinked. "But—"

"Don't," Dominic said gently, cutting him off. "Think about your world. If someone wandered into a police station claiming they were from another universe, what would you call them?"

Max sighed. "Insane."

"Exactly. And here? You'll create problems you can't fix. I've been instructed to warn you: if you talk openly about the portal or your world, the higher-ups will treat it as a threat."

Max swallowed. "So what do I say if someone asks?"

"You won't be answering to anyone except authorised staff," Dominic replied. "The man running this facility has only been told you're a high-sensitivity case. He doesn't know about the portal. He doesn't know about another Earth."

Max rubbed his forehead. "So what does he think I am?"

"He thinks you're to be held under strict protection," Dominic said. He allowed the faintest, humourless smile. "And I made it very clear you're to be handled with kid gloves."

"Why?" Max asked. "Why kid gloves?"

Dominic stopped walking and faced him fully.

"Because, Max... whether or not you want the role, you're an asset. Not a liability."

Max stared at him. "I still don't understand."

Dominic gestured toward the looming structure ahead — a modern, silent fortress of concrete and steel.

"Everyone in here is serving for the worst crimes we still have," he said. "Murder. Assault. A few political extremists. People who can't function safely in society. The guards don't tolerate anything. They run a very tight regime."

A cold ripple passed through Max.

"Then why put me *here*?"

"Because at this hour," Dominic replied, softening, "it's the safest place we have. You won't be anywhere near the others. You'll be placed in a private suite — just like in Geneva. Bedroom, dining area, bathroom. No cells. No block."

Max let out a slow breath — relief, but only partial.

"One more question," he said quietly. "You mentioned extremists. Terrorists. But I thought this world... evolved. No money, no property... I didn't think that kind of violence still existed."

Dominic gave a tired, almost defeated exhale.

"Religion, Max. Fucking religion."

Max didn't ask anything else.

They walked the remaining distance in silence, the entrance looming closer with every step. And for the first time since being taken from the Diderot farm, fear crept back into him — quiet, steady, impossible to ignore.

Tomorrow he would stand before a judge in a world that wasn't his.

***

# Chapter 10

**Tuesday, 12th June 2012, 10:30 a.m.**
**Parallel universe. European Security Court, Paris, France.**

The courtroom was small, quiet, and strangely informal — very much like the one in Geneva. No rows of benches, no spectators, no cameras. Just seven people.

Max recognised four immediately:

Aimes Perrier seated to the judge's left,

Dominic and Sauson beside him,

and Lula positioned closer to the bench, calm and attentive.

The last two men stood near the doors — guards, judging by their posture and the slight bulges beneath their jackets.

The judge entered last. A man in his sixties with silver hair and a contemplative expression, he settled into his raised bench, unfolded a slim computer panel, and surveyed the room.

A moment passed before he spoke.

"Good morning. I am Marcel Rannequin, European Security Affairs Judge. Please call me Marcel." His tone was warm, almost gentle, carrying the same understated authority Max had heard in Geneva.

Introductions followed. Each person stood, spoke, and sat again.

Max's turn came last.

"Ah... I'm Maximilien Rivette, but I prefer Max. I'm a draftsman with the European Organisation for Nuclear Research — CERN."

Marcel nodded. "Thank you, Max."

He turned to Aimes. "Would you begin, please? I've read the full report, though I admit some of the technical details stretch the limits of my ageing brain. Even so, I will do what is right for the people of Europe. And Max — I intend to treat you with complete respect. Your honesty so far has been noted."

He gestured for Aimes to continue.

The Hearing.

The questioning lasted nearly two hours.

It began gently: Max's background, his work at CERN, his role within the project. Then it deepened — slowly but steadily — into the structure of the machine, its purpose, its capabilities, and what Max truly understood.

Max answered everything he could. He emphasised again and again that he was not a physicist. He had designed the chambers, the mechanical frame, the supporting structures, the platform, the rails, the locking systems. But the quantum theory behind it? He had only a surface understanding.

At one point Aimes clarified for the judge:

"Max supervised every mechanical component. In practice, that means he understood how the device behaves physically better than anyone else on the team."

The judge nodded without looking up as he wrote a brief note.

Lunch arrived quietly: sandwiches, savoury pastries, water, juice. The guards brought them in with a surprising level of courtesy.

Before touching anything, Max approached Lula.

"Can I... use the toilet?" he whispered, mortified to even ask.

Lula smiled gently and spoke to the judge. After a short exchange she returned.

"All right. A guard will accompany us."

They walked to a small washroom down the corridor. Lula stood inside the doorway, the guard behind her, both politely averted while Max relieved himself.

As he washed his hands he leaned towards her.

"Does it look... okay? The hearing, I mean?"

Lula placed a hand on his arm.

"It's going well. And Max — you might feel like the one on trial, but you're not. It's your world they're trying to understand."

Max breathed out. "And what do you think will happen?"

She hesitated. "I don't know. But nothing cruel."

He clung to that.

The Decision.

Four hours later the judge called Aimes forward. The two men spoke quietly for almost ten minutes while the room sat in tense silence.

Then Aimes returned to his seat.

Marcel straightened, folded his hands, and looked directly at Max.

"Max," he said softly, "I am ready to give my decision."

Max's heart thudded once, painfully.

"I have found you cooperative and reasonable," Marcel said. "Despite your situation, you have shown restraint, intelligence, and honesty. I believe you recognise why we acted as we did. Our concern was never about you personally — only the unknown you represent."

Max nodded faintly.

"Now," Marcel continued, "I must explain this court's decision. Please allow me to finish before responding."

Max braced himself.

Marcel inhaled.

"To protect the people of Europe, and due to the unpredictable nature of your world, this court orders that you remain here — in this universe — for a period of one year."

Max inhaled sharply. It felt as if the air had been punched out of him.

He folded inward, clutching the edge of the chair. Lula moved instantly, steadying him with an arm around his shoulders.

Marcel pressed on, gentle but unyielding.

"In addition, you will remain in secure custodial accommodation until we determine that neither you nor your world present an ongoing threat."

Max barely heard the words. They swam in and out of focus.

Marcel added, more softly, "We understand you have an aunt in your world — Céleste Guérard. We intend to notify your scientific colleagues of your situation and your one-year stay. We hope they will inform her."

Max stared at the floor. The decision drifted around him like fog.

Marcel stood.

"This hearing is adjourned."

He left quietly.

Aimes placed a steady hand on Max's back. Dominic murmured reassurance. Sauson gave a small nod of sympathy. Lula stayed closest, anchoring him as the room slowly emptied.

But the verdict echoed long after their voices faded.

One year.

In another universe.

And nothing he could do would change it.

***

**Tuesday, 12th June 2012, 8:36 p.m.**
**Parallel universe. Paris High Security Jail, Paris, France.**

Processing Max into the system took fifteen brisk, almost gentle minutes. No shouting. No clanging doors. No aggression. Just a senior guard with a calm voice, reading out regulations like a checklist. Max absorbed barely any of it. His mind was still back in the courtroom, replaying the same line over and over:

A year.

A custodial sentence.

Held until they felt safe.

His stomach twisted.

Dominic stayed close, not hovering, simply present. It didn't help much. Max wasn't angry at him, or at the judge, or even at the guards. He couldn't find the anger yet. It hung around him like fog, drifting between shock, confusion, and a deep, humiliating helplessness.

He stared at a rack of folded green denim uniforms until the shapes blurred together. He lifted one. Put it back. Picked another. Eventually he found the right size, though he couldn't remember actually choosing it.

Dominic saw all of it. He gave the guard a small nod.

"Give us a moment."

The guard stepped out. The door closed with a soft hydraulic hiss.

Dominic waited a second before speaking.

"You look like you've been hit by a train."

Max swallowed. "Dominic... why? Why does your world see mine as such a threat? Why does that justify locking me up? I haven't done anything."

Dominic exhaled slowly, rubbing the back of his neck. "Max... it's not you." His voice tightened. "It's everything your world has done."

Max opened his hands helplessly. "I wouldn't say it's evil."

Dominic turned sharply toward him. There was no hostility — just incredulity.

"Max, think about what you told us today. The Second World War. Tens of millions dead. Death camps. A plan to wipe out an entire people. Industrial killing. And then two atomic bombs dropped on cities." He paused. "You said it like you were reciting a history lesson."

Max felt heat crawl up his neck. He wanted to argue, explain, soften it. He couldn't.

Dominic went on. "And after that horror, instead of stopping, your nations built more weapons. Thousands of them. Weapons capable of burning the world down. Even your France has them."

Max's jaw clenched. He looked away.

"And it didn't end there. Asia. The Middle East. Invasions. Coups. Occupations. Every decade, more violence. Always more."

He let the silence hang.

Max had never felt those facts land like this before — not as trivia, but as indictment.

Dominic continued, quieter now. "You told us your scientists split the atom and immediately turned it into a weapon. Here? When our scientists realised the same thing might be possible, the man who proposed testing it was arrested."

Max blinked. "Just for suggesting it?"

"No," Dominic said sharply. "For pushing it. For trying to convince people to test it. When someone shows that level of recklessness with something that could end civilisation, they don't get a second chance."

Max felt something hollow open inside him. His world had taken every path theirs had sealed off.

Dominic stepped closer, lowering his voice. "Max, your world frightens us because it keeps choosing the same pattern. War after war. Weapon after weapon. And now you've shown us that your people can send whatever they want through that machine. And we have no way to stop it."

Max felt anger rise — defensive, desperate.

"They wouldn't. Gaidon wouldn't allow it. He hates the Americans and their military. He'd never let the machine be used to harm anyone."

Dominic held his gaze for a long, hard moment.

"Let's hope," he said quietly, "that you're right."

***

**Wednesday, 13th June 2012, 10:49 a.m.**
**Parallel universe. Paris High Security Jail, Paris, France.**

Dominic had phoned Aimes the night before, describing Max's state in plain terms: confused, shaken, restless, angry at nothing and everything. Aimes agreed Max needed another visit — not for discipline, but for grounding.

The next morning, Dominic carried a breakfast tray down the silent corridor to the induction wing. Max had spent the night in the "new prisoner cell" — a narrow concrete room with a shelf-bed, a bare toilet, a metal basin, and a camera staring down from the corner. No pillow. No blanket. The overhead light never dimmed.

When Dominic opened the door, Max wasn't sitting or lying down.

He was pacing. Fast. Shoulders locked, breathing sharp.

"How are you holding up?" Dominic asked quietly. "The warden says you've been... vocal."

Max spun around. "Wouldn't you be? The bed has two centimetres of padding, the toilet stinks, the lights never go off, and apparently I'm *lucky* to be here instead of somewhere worse!"

Dominic looked at the cramped cell. He didn't bother disagreeing. "This is standard induction. Everyone starts here until they understand your behaviour."

"I don't care," Max snapped, voice cracking. "Your world keeps going on about peace, dignity, the Twelve Rules... and I'm shoved in a concrete box like a fucking animal!"

Dominic exhaled. "Max... you need to calm down."

"I will *not* calm down! You talk about dignity — doesn't one of those rules guarantee it?"

Dominic's expression hardened. "This isn't about dignity. It's about risk. And right now the warden thinks you're refusing to cooperate. This—" he nodded toward the silver packet of nutri-paste splattered against the wall "—is part of the problem."

Max flushed. "That was a mistake. I was angry."

"The guard said you swore at him."

Max hesitated, shame creeping up his neck. "Yeah. I did."

Dominic closed the door behind him and stepped in properly.

"Max, listen to me. There's something you need to understand before this gets worse. Much worse."

Max froze.

Dominic lowered his voice. "You know Rule Five — the non-violence rule?"

"I know the gist. No physical harm."

"It's more than that," Dominic said. "Rule Five governs response to danger. And there's a line that matters here: 'Where a clear and reasonable danger of harm is foreseen, communities may act to prevent it.'"

Max frowned. "okay...?"

"So," Dominic said, "that clause gives prisons flexibility. A lot of flexibility."

"How much flexibility?"

Dominic swallowed, glanced at the camera, then back.

"Enough that if someone is judged a risk — physical or psychological — they can be placed in RFC."

Max didn't recognise the acronym. "What is RFC?"

Dominic didn't soften it.

"Removal From Contact."

A chill spread across Max's chest. "Meaning what? Solitary confinement?"

Dominic shook his head. "No. Much stricter. Solitary still has voices. Human contact. RFC has none of that."

Max's grip tightened on the edge of the metal basin. "Explain it."

Dominic did.

"RFC is total sensory and social isolation. No voices. No footsteps. No sound. No interaction. Lights on twenty-four hours. No clothing. A slab-bed, a toilet, a basin. Three packets of paste a day through a slot. A camera watching you at all times."

Max's voice thinned. "For how long?"

"Two weeks," Dominic said. "Minimum."

Max just stared at him. "Two weeks of that?"

Dominic nodded.

"And if someone collapses? Loses their mind?"

"They're darted, sedated, treated, and returned. Guards are trained never to speak to inmates in RFC. Silence is part of the protocol."

Max felt nausea rise. "Jesus Christ..."

Dominic continued, tone low and grim.

"RFC breaks people, Max. Some scream for days. Some shut down. Some try to hurt themselves to end it. Most survive it physically, but it changes them. Sometimes permanently." He paused. "And under the Twelve Rules, RFC is legal. It's considered prevention, not punishment."

Max's breathing shortened.

"So what you're telling me is... if I complain again, argue, swear at a guard—"

"Yes," Dominic said flatly. "They'll send you to RFC."

"And you're fine with that?" Max snapped, fear mutating into anger.

Dominic's jaw tightened with frustration and sympathy. "Of course I'm not fine with it. I'm telling you because I don't want it to happen."

Max stared at the floor, sweat gathering on his palms.

Dominic stepped closer. "Max... this version of you — the shouting, the pacing — it's fear talking. You're not violent. You're not dangerous. You're exhausted and rattled. But the guards don't know you like I do."

Max swallowed hard.

"If you centre yourself," Dominic said gently, "and show them you're calm and compliant, they'll move you out of here. Proper bedding. Showers. Real food. Reading material. A routine. All of it changes once they trust you."

A long silence filled the cell.

Max finally whispered, "You're not lying?"

"No," Dominic said. "Not even slightly." He rested a steady hand on Max's shoulder. "But if you keep snapping, they'll send you to RFC. And you won't cope with it. No one does."

Max nodded at last — small, trembling. "okay... okay. I'll behave."

Dominic released a breath he'd been holding. "Good."

Max lowered himself onto the thin bed, eyes hollow.

Dominic lingered a moment, then stepped out.

The door sealed behind him with a quiet click.

Max was alone — shaken, exhausted, and now terrified of a punishment he hadn't known existed.

Removal From Contact.

Two words that weighed heavier than his entire arrest.

For the first time since arriving in this world, Max truly feared what the next day might bring.

***

# Chapter 11

**Wednesday, 13th June 2012, 2:17 p.m.**
**Fairfax Wood's office, Laboratory 888, CERN, Prévessin-Moëns, France.**

Gaidon had barely slept in days. Two consecutive nights manipulating the data with Daniel had shredded his nerves. His hands shook. His heart pounded at irregular, painful beats. For over a year he'd maintained the RACE cover story — a carefully engineered fiction accepted by everyone from junior staff to the Director General. And now he had to lie again. To Fairfax Wood. With a straight face.

He sat in the waiting room clutching the fabricated report so tightly it was beginning to crease. Sweat prickled down the centre of his spine. He tried to breathe evenly, to appear composed, to not collapse into a heap.

The door swung open.

"Gaidon, come in!"

Fairfax leaned out with his usual buoyant smile.

Gaidon stood — and froze.

Constantine Lapôtre, Director General of CERN, was seated inside, legs crossed, casually flipping through a magazine as though this were a routine administration check.

"Bonjour, Gaidon," Constantine said. "How are you?"

Something inside Gaidon snapped like a dry twig.

He walked in like a man being escorted to an execution. Fairfax moved behind his desk. Constantine rose to shake his hand. Gaidon managed to take it, barely, his fingers trembling so violently the Director General's expression changed instantly.

"What's wrong?" Fairfax asked. "You look awful."

Gaidon placed the fake report on the desk with stiff, puppet-like movements. Constantine and Fairfax exchanged a quick, worried glance.

Gaidon tried to speak.

Nothing came.

His throat constricted. His breath hitched. Colour drained from his face until he looked almost grey.

"Gaidon?" Fairfax stepped forward.

And then everything burst.

"We fucked up," he whispered.

Both men leaned in sharply.

"We fucked up!" Gaidon suddenly shouted — voice breaking, tears spilling.

"We manipulated everything. RACE — every file, every test, every report — all of it twisted to show something it wasn't!"

Fairfax froze. Constantine didn't move.

Words tumbled out like a dam collapsing.

"We found a parallel world. Another planet — another civilisation — another us. The greatest discovery in physics and we hid it because we didn't know what else to do. Then that damned farmer shot down the drone. And now—" his voice cracked, collapsing into a hoarse sob, "now we've lost Max. They arrested him. Arrested him!"

He buried his face in his hands and wept, shoulders shaking uncontrollably.

Fairfax and Constantine stared at each other — both stunned, both silently calculating the scale of what they'd just heard.

Then they moved automatically, almost in synchrony, placing steady hands on his shoulders.

"Gaidon... breathe," Constantine said gently, deliberately. "Start again. From the beginning."

It took nearly an hour.

He recounted everything through ragged breath — the first tests, the blue shell, the drone, the farmer, the portal, Max stepping through, the signs, the four-week ultimatum. After ten minutes Fairfax stopped interrupting. After fifteen, Constantine did too. By the half-hour mark, the room was silent except for Gaidon's trembling voice.

When it was over, Gaidon sagged in the chair like a man emptied out.

The silence that followed was long and heavy.

Constantine spoke first.

"Let me be clear," he said softly. "You are not in trouble for this. Not today. Not after what you've managed alone."

Gaidon looked up, hollow-eyed, unsure whether to believe him.

"Next," Constantine continued, his tone sharpening, "we need information — real information. Immediately."

Fairfax nodded. "We can't just sit here while one of our own is imprisoned in this parallel world."

Constantine straightened, shoulders tight with sudden purpose.

"We open the machine again. We send something through — a drone, a probe, anything controllable. And until we understand the full scope of this, not a single person outside this room hears even a whisper."

Fairfax added, "If this leaks before we understand what we're dealing with, governments will descend like wolves."

Gaidon wiped his eyes with the back of his sleeve, voice barely more than a rasp. "Adéhémar's new drone arrives tomorrow. If we modify it... pre-programme a return... we could send it Friday."

Constantine nodded once, decisive.

"Good. That's exactly what we'll do."

Fairfax leaned back in his chair, still visibly stunned but beginning to steady. "Gaidon... this isn't over. We'll get him back."

Gaidon couldn't trust himself to reply.

But he nodded.

For the first time since Max vanished through the shell, something faint and fragile returned to the room.

Not hope.

Not yet.

But a plan.

***

**Wednesday, 13th June 2012, 4:11 p.m.**
**Machine room, Laboratory 888, CERN, Prévessin-Moëns, France.**

The machine room was still — the hum of cooling fans the only sign of life, the tangle of cables resting across the floor like coiled serpents waiting for a signal. The rest of the team was scattered throughout the building, exhausted, shell-shocked, trying to salvage their sanity after hearing about Gaidon's confession.

Vincent checked the corridor twice.

Once more for luck.

Then slipped inside and shut the door.

He took out the phone — the one number he should never have memorised — and dialled before he could talk himself out of it.

Dragonetz answered on the first ring.

"Talk."

Vincent swallowed. "You... you got my message."

"I did," Dragonetz replied, voice smooth and cool. "You said you had something big.

World-changing, if I recall your exact words."

Vincent turned away from the dormant machine, pacing between two tall equipment racks. "Yeah. It is."

"What kind of news?"

Vincent hesitated.

Too long.

"I... can't explain yet."

Dragonetz's tone dropped several degrees. "Can't, or won't?"

Vincent's silence answered for him.

A slow, irritated exhale drifted down the line. "For years you've handed me scraps, Vincent. Lab gossip. Technical crumbs. Nothing of value. Then suddenly you tell me you're sitting on something enormous, and when I ask for detail, you choke?"

"It's different this time," Vincent whispered. "Really different."

Dragonetz said nothing — he didn't have to. The weight of his silence pressed like a hand on Vincent's throat.

Finally: "What can you give me?"

"Telemetry. Data. Enough to prove this is real."

"Proof," Dragonetz repeated. "My boss doesn't move a finger without proof."

"You'll get it," Vincent said, voice shaking. "There's another test on Friday. I'll copy whatever comes off the feed."

Dragonetz paused long enough that Vincent wondered if the line had dropped.

Then the voice returned — colder, flatter.

"We need to meet, tonight."

Vincent's chest tightened. "Meet? I thought— I assumed you just wanted the footage later this week."

"No." Dragonetz's tone left no room for negotiation. "You said you had 'material' already. You're going to hand it to me tonight."

"I don't—" Vincent swallowed. "Where?"

"Prévessin-Moëns cemetery," Dragonetz said. "North gate. Eleven thirty p.m. You'll bring whatever you've collected — notes, photos, any scrap of data. Something that proves this isn't another of your false alarms."

Vincent gripped the phone harder. "The cemetery? Why there?"

"Because nobody goes to cemeteries at night," Dragonetz said. "And because if you're lying to me again, I want space to deal with it."

A heartbeat of silence.

Vincent felt his stomach drop.

Finally he forced himself to speak. "I'll be there."

"You'd better," Dragonetz replied. "If what you have is real, tonight is the last time you'll ever have to worry about money."

The line clicked dead.

Vincent lowered the phone slowly. The machine behind him loomed in the shadows — immense, waiting, unaware that the first betrayal had already been set in motion.

He didn't look back at it.

He only thought of the meeting.

And the money.

***

**Wednesday, 13th June 2012, 11:53 p.m.**
**Cemetery, Prévessin-Moëns, France.**

The cemetery lay still under the warm night air, washed in the dim glow of amber lamps. Every headstone threw a long shadow, stretched thin across the gravel paths like dark, crooked fingers. The hedges whispered with insects, and faint motorway noise drifted in from far beyond the trees.

Vincent sat rigid on a granite bench near the north gate, collar up, hands rammed deep in his coat pockets. His breath came in shallow, uneven pulls. Every time a leaf shifted or a bird rustled, he jerked his head.

He hated the idea of meeting here.

But Dragonetz insisted.

A faint movement between the graves caught his eye.

Dragonetz Coté emerged from the darkness without a single wasted sound — long black coat, gloved hands, posture carved from pure control. His presence alone made the night feel colder.

"You're late," Vincent said, too quickly.

Dragonetz didn't break stride. "You said you had something significant. I assumed that meant you were prepared."

Vincent swallowed and forced himself to stand. "I... am."

Dragonetz stopped before him, eyes flat, unreadable — that unsettling calm of a man who had forced confessions out of people far more dangerous than Vincent.

"The message," Dragonetz said, "you've said you had something big. 'World-changing.' 'Unprecedented.' My boss expects clarity. And I expect competence."

Vincent shook his head, pulse hammering. "Not yet. I can't tell you yet — you'd never believe it without the footage. Gaidon routed all the recordings straight into a secure archive, and I can't get into it. But I've set up a tap on the feed for the next test. It'll still upload to the official locker, but a copy will come to me. Friday, when we run it, I'll have the video and telemetry. Then you'll have proof."

Dragonetz stared at him long enough for Vincent to feel sweat prickling under his shirt.

"And for this proof," Dragonetz said quietly, "you believe you are worth twenty thousand?"

Vincent forced a nod. "Yes. You'll understand when you see the footage."

Dragonetz's expression didn't change. "Do you have anything now?"

Vincent fumbled inside his coat and produced a thick folder — copied logs, sensor fragments, blurred technical sheets. Not enough to expose the truth. Just enough to show the edges of it.

Dragonetz took the folder and flipped through the pages with cold, surgical precision.

"Incomplete," he said.

"It's all I can give before the test," Vincent said. "Once the drone goes through, I'll have the real thing."

Dragonetz had been half-listening, measuring Vincent more than his words — until drone.

The term snapped his attention into focus. Military hardware. Classified projects. Not some crank with a story, but someone brushing against something that mattered.

Silence stretched.

Then Dragonetz reached into his coat and withdrew an envelope — thick, weighty, unmistakable. He didn't hand it over immediately. He held it between two fingers like a warning.

"There is ten thousand euro," he said. "You get the remainder when you deliver the footage."

Vincent reached for it.

Dragonetz didn't let go.

He stepped in close enough that Vincent smelled the faint trace of aftershave and cold leather.

"You dragged me out to a fucking cemetery," Dragonetz murmured, "with scraps. Do not ever call me out half-prepared again."

Then he released the envelope.

Vincent clutched it like a lifeline, nodding too fast. "You'll have the video Friday night. I promise."

Dragonetz turned away first, disappearing between the gravestones with the silent confidence of someone who owned the night.

Vincent watched him vanish before letting himself breathe.

He looked down at the money — heavy in his hand, heavier in his conscience — and felt a surge of sick exhilaration.

A year ago he had slipped the occasional technical detail for a few hundred euro.

Tonight he had just crossed a line he couldn't step back over.

Not for ideology.

Not for justice.

Not to expose wrongdoing.

Just for cash.

***

**Friday, 15th June 2012, 5:53 p.m.**
**Control room, Laboratory 888, CERN, Prévessin-Moëns, France.**

Constantine Lapôtre and Fairfax Wood stood behind Gaidon's team, close enough that the tension passing between them felt physical. The atmosphere in the control room had settled into a strained quiet, the kind that suggested everyone present understood how precarious the situation had become. In the days since Gaidon's breakdown, the two senior CERN leaders had been briefed on everything — the chamber, the recordings, the discovery, and everything they knew about Max's disappearance. The wonder of it had faded quickly, replaced by an unease neither man could shake.

Now the portal was opening again.

Gaidon leaned toward the controls. "okay. Counting down. Seven... six... five..."

The seconds stretched. No one moved.

"Two... one..."

The chamber shells activated and the blue hazed sphere snapped into existence. But the landscape visible through the shell was no longer the quiet patch of forest they expected.

Every voice caught at once.

Two metal frames, each four metres high, stood in the clearing like industrial sentinels. Inside each frame sat a double-barrelled weapon, long black barrels angled outward with an unmistakable, cold purpose. Between them, a computer display blinked awake.

Fairfax let out a startled breath. "Christ..."

The screen began to scroll text.

WE ASKED YOU NOT TO DO THIS.

IT IS FRIDAY, THE FIFTEENTH OF JUNE, 2012.

THE TIME IS 17:53:27.

WELCOME TO THE COMPUTERISED AND AUTOMATED DEFENSE OF

OUR WORLD.

A ripple of swearing moved through the room.

WE ASKED YOU TO WAIT ONE MONTH BEFORE RESUMING COMMUNICATION.

YOU HAVE NOT DONE SO.

HOWEVER, WE UNDERSTAND YOUR CURIOSITY, SO WE PROVIDE MORE INFORMATION.

Gaidon felt himself go cold.

WE RECEIVED COMPLETE COOPERATION FROM YOUR COLLEAGUE, MAXIMILIEN RIVETTE.

WE HAVE LEARNED THAT OUR TWO WORLDS WERE ONCE ONE.

AT SOME POINT AFTER THE GREAT WAR, THEY DIVERGED INTO DISTINCT HISTORIES.

WE DO NOT UNDERSTAND HOW.

Emerancie stared at the screen, her hands unsteady.

WHAT WE HAVE LEARNED OF YOUR WORLD SHOCKS US.

YOUR MILITARY AND ECONOMIC SYSTEMS ARE ABHORRENT TO US.

WE HAVE EVOLVED INTO A STATE OF HUMAN EXISTENCE BUILT UPON COMMUNITY AND LOVE.

OUR WORLDS ARE PARALLEL, BUT IN MANY WAYS POLAR OPPOSITES.

THIS IS THE BASIS OF OUR FEAR.

THIS IS WHY WE DEMAND YOU KEEP OUT OF OUR WORLD.

The room fell still.

Vincent broke first. "What the fuck are we supposed to do? Just sit here?"

Instead of arguing further, he flicked his mouse and quietly logged into the platform control system. One small click — the receiving-chamber platform began to descend.

Then he moved.

In a blur, Vincent lunged at Adéhémar. The first punch caught the slighter man squarely in the jaw, sending him staggering backwards; the second arrived before anyone could even shout, a driving blow that dropped Adéhémar to the floor unconscious.

No one in the room reacted. They just froze.

Vincent stepped over the fallen engineer, grabbed Adéhémar's custom control rig, and hammered a rapid sequence of buttons. The rig chirped to life, confirming the command: the loading robot whirred and began positioning the drone onto the lowered platform.

"Vincent—!" Gaidon reached for him, but the automated sequence had already triggered.

On the monitor, the platform descended. The robotic arms moved into position, and loaded the replacement drone.

Emerancie sprang forward. "Are you insane?" She tried to pull him back from the keyboard.

Vincent shoved her aside with a hard, panicked movement. "Get off me!"

Baset grabbed him from behind, and Vincent swung at him. The room erupted: chairs scraping, a monitor falling, hands grabbing at limbs. The struggle lasted seconds but felt longer, a frantic effort to stop one man from provoking a catastrophe.

They finally brought Vincent down, holding him against the floor as he spat curses at everyone.

Daniel, too slight to help in the fight, kept his eyes fixed on the monitor. The message had resumed.

...THE OUTCOME OF THE TRIAL WAS A DETENTION FOR MAXIMILIEN RIVETTE. HE HAS ACCEPTED THIS AND IS BEING TREATED WELL.

The text shifted to red.

STOP. DO NOT PROCEED WITH THIS COURSE OF ACTION. WE HAVE DETECTED YOUR

The line froze.

The platform finished its ascent.

The drone powered up.

Its rotors spun quickly to full power and it began to ascend.

Both guns in the clearing rotated in perfect synchrony and opened fire. The rounds shredded the drone mid-lift, turning it into a burst of metal fragments. Some of the rounds tore straight through the blue shell and punched into the CERN chamber with terrifying force.

Alarms roared. Red lights strobed across the control room. One of the displays showed the machine room as a portion of the receiving chamber blew outward, sparks cascading across the floor.

Emerancie stepped toward Vincent and kicked him with a fury she had never shown. The crack of bone echoed. Vincent screamed, rolling onto his side, gripping his face.

The control room filled with anger, alarms and raw disbelief — the awful understanding that, for the first time, the two worlds had traded violence.

And they had been the ones to fire the first shot.

****

**Friday, 15th June 2012, 5:58 p.m.**
**Control room, Laboratory 888, CERN, Prévessin-Moëns, France.**

No one in the building had seen a disaster unfold with such speed. When the portal finally powered down—its receiving chamber torn open by gunfire—the control room had dissolved into a stunned, exhausted quiet. Vincent Duke staggered to his feet, gripping his shattered cheek, eyes wild with pain and humiliation. He limped toward the exit without a word.

Just as he reached the doors, Constantine snapped, "You're fired!"

Vincent didn't look back.

A soft groan broke the silence. Adéhémar was stirring on the floor, blinking up at the ceiling as if trying to remember which universe he belonged to.

"Easy—easy," Fairfax murmured, dropping to one knee beside him.

Daniel and Emerancie joined him, helping Adéhémar sit up. His face was grey, his movements unsteady, but he was conscious.

"Can you hear us?" Daniel asked.

Adéhémar managed a small nod, touching the side of his jaw with a wince.

"Jesus, Vincent hit you hard," Emerancie said, voice shaking with disbelief and concern.

They eased him to his feet, each of them supporting an arm. The sight of the team clustered around the smallest man among them seemed to reset everyone's awareness of what had just happened: violence, panic, and a project spiralling out of control.

It took several minutes before anyone trusted their voice. Fairfax looked washed out. Emerancie was trembling. Daniel seemed close to fainting. But the safety checks had to be done, and the system confirmations, and the formal shutdown—each step followed as if by muscle memory rather than conscious thought.

Only then did they descend to the machine room.

It took ninety minutes to remove the argon assembly, another ten to haul it away. Baset climbed down into the chamber with a torch, as he had done on the original RACE device. When he swept the light across the interior, his breath hitched loud enough for everyone to hear.

"What do you see?" Gaidon called down.

Baset swallowed. "Devastation. Total devastation."

He shifted the beam again.

The chamber walls were cratered and warped, a mess of punctures and impact scars. One explosive round had cleanly punched straight through the receiving chamber. Shrapnel trails ran across every exposed surface.

Fairfax muttered, "Jesus Christ…"

Constantine exhaled, long and steady. "This will take months to repair."

He ordered the full shutdown, dismissed the others, then nodded at Gaidon and Fairfax.

"Your office. Now."

When the three reached Gaidon Ballerat's office, Constantine closed the door and didn't bother with restraint.

"A fucking disaster!" His voice struck the walls. "A rogue staff member launches a drone, we provoke a world with automated weapons, and now a fifty-million-euro machine is ruined!"

Gaidon sat heavily behind his desk. He didn't look up; his eyes were fixed on a stack of paperwork he clearly couldn't see. The last few days had hollowed him out.

Fairfax tried for measured concern. "Gaidon… if you'd come to me earlier—"

"Oh, shut the fuck up, Fairfax!" Gaidon snapped, suddenly alive with exhaustion and fury. "You're a pen-pusher. What would you have done? Filed a form? Sent an email? There was only one thing to do once we realised what this machine could do—get more data."

Fairfax's mouth opened, closed again. Gaidon didn't give him a second attempt.

"How was I supposed to know they'd arm themselves? Or that Vincent of all people would lose his mind?"

Constantine stepped closer. "Why would he? Why sabotage everything?"

Gaidon hesitated. Then he answered.

"I think he's been feeding intel to the CIA."

Both men froze.

"What?" Constantine demanded. "Why would you think that?"

"I had Emerancie check his access logs earlier this week," Gaidon said, rubbing his temples. "It appears he may have pulled a ridiculous number of files, we couldn't be certain, and I assume he uploaded them somewhere, all we saw were fragments, clues. Nothing concrete."

Fairfax's face tightened. "What files?"

"A lot of data," Gaidon said. "Again, we couldn't be sure. Vincent knows his way around computer systems. But the one access we were most concerned about was the set of files dealing with potential variations in portal positioning."

Constantine's eyes narrowed. "You told me that was theoretical. Speculative."

"It is. But Daniel and I agree—it might be possible. Not certain. But possible. With the right key, the machine could open a portal in our own world. Specific coordinates. Controlled placement."

Fairfax stared at him, speechless.

Constantine absorbed it first. "So who knew this?"

"I did," Gaidon said. "And Daniel."

The silence that followed was different—heavier, centred around the realisation that the machine was no longer a scientific marvel but something far more dangerous.

Fairfax finally spoke, voice thin. "I don't understand. Why does that matter now?"

Constantine turned to him. "Because if this is true, this machine isn't just a discovery. It's the most powerful weapon on the planet."

The words hung there.

Gaidon's voice was quiet when he finally spoke. "And after what we saw today—after what their message said—can you blame them? They say they evolved into something peaceful. They see us as pure nightmares."

Fairfax ran a hand through his hair, overwhelmed.

No one spoke for almost a full minute.

When Constantine found his voice, it had lost all of its usual certainty. "Gaidon... you realise you can't continue."

Gaidon didn't argue. He only nodded.

"Collect your things," Constantine said quietly.

Gaidon stood slowly. "Fine. But do one thing for me."

He looked up.

"Shut down this project."

Constantine didn't answer.

***

**Saturday, 16th June 2012, 10:44 p.m.**
**Home of Dragonetz Coté, Geneva, Switzerland.**

Dragonetz Coté had phoned his superior half an hour earlier with a tone Nicolas Hightower had never heard from him — urgent, clipped, almost shaken.

"You need to come. Tonight. I have something... unprecedented."

Hightower had excused himself from a dinner with senior Swiss political figures and driven straight across town. The moment he stepped through the door, Dragonetz shut it, turned the key, and checked the latch.

Nicolas raised an eyebrow. "All right. You said 'history-changing'. That's ambitious, even for you. What have you got?"

Dragonetz didn't answer immediately. He crossed to the dining table, opened his laptop a little wider, and drew a steadying breath.

"An hour ago," he began, "I met a man at a cemetery. Vincent Duke. Engineer at CERN. I'd been using him for scraps of information over the last few years."

Nicolas frowned.

"He told me something that sounded completely insane," Dragonetz went on. "Said their team ran an experiment in 2010 — something involving controlled singularities. According to him, it opened a passage to... somewhere else. Not another country. Another universe."

He let that hang for a moment.

"They rebuilt a new machine and just recently sent a drone through first. Then a local farmer shot it out of the sky. Then one of their people — a man named Max Rivette — went through himself and got arrested by whoever lives on the other side."

Nicolas stared at him. "You believe this?"

"I didn't," Dragonetz said. "Not until Duke showed me the video."

He tapped play.

They leaned in.

The footage showed the drone being loaded from one of the laboratory cameras, the chamber platform rising, the shimmering blue portal shell forming around it. Then from a different camera view, through a blue haze, the drone snapped forward into the clearing on the other side.

Two towering gun frames pivoted in unison.

Both sets of barrels opened fire.

The torrent was overwhelming — a disciplined storm of high-calibre rounds that shredded the drone before it climbed a metre. Fragments spun outward. The video stuttered and dissolved into static.

The whole sequence of video cuts lasted less than half a minute.

Neither man spoke. Dragonetz replayed it, slowed the frames, watched muzzle flashes, recoil patterns, barrel cycling, the seamless coordination of the system.

Nicolas finally let out a breath. "That's automated fire. High calibre. Dual-barrel. Caseless, most likely. Thermal acquisition. Full range control. Nothing improvised about it."

Dragonetz nodded. "Exactly. It's real. Whatever that place is — it exists. And they aren't operating with scraps."

"Anything else?" Nicolas asked.

"A written account." Dragonetz slid a printed sheet across the table. "Typed by the engineer — Vincent Duke. He explains the whole day. Says he was fired after the incident."

Nicolas read it quickly. His expression tightened at the references to a parallel world, tightened again at the hints of internal fighting at CERN. When he finished, he placed the page down with deliberate care.

"All right," he said. "Who knows about this? Exactly."

Dragonetz counted.

"Gaidon. His whole team in Laboratory 888. The two senior CERN administrators. And Vincent says the missing guy — Max Rivette — has an aunt who's been told." He checked the sheet. "Céleste Guérard."

Nicolas nodded — not pleased, but satisfied it wasn't worse. "Good. The fewer the better. Containment is still possible."

He closed the laptop softly, as if sealing the evidence.

"I'm notifying Langley tonight. Quiet channel. No written trail. No chatter." He held Dragonetz's gaze. "But we don't wait for them. We make the first move."

Dragonetz remained still.

Nicolas spoke with measured finality. "We shut this down before the Europeans do something irreversibly stupid."

A flicker — fear mixed with anticipation — passed across Dragonetz's expression.

Nicolas continued, his tone quiet but absolute.

"If this technology is real — and that footage leaves no room for doubt — then Europe doesn't get to keep it."

***

# Chapter 12



**Monday, 18th June 2012, 9:30 a.m.**
**Constantine Lapôtre's office, CERN, Prévessin-Moëns, France.**

Constantine knew the moment his secretary mentioned "a science adviser from the US embassy" that the CIA had caught the scent. There was no other reason for an unannounced visit at nine-thirty on a Monday. He told her to send the man in, bracing himself.

Nicolas Hightower entered with a polite smile that looked rehearsed. Constantine stood to shake his hand. The gesture felt obligatory rather than cordial; he knew the type — diplomatic veneer, intelligence core.

"Thank you for seeing me on short notice," Nicolas said. "I'm Nicolas Hightower, senior science adviser with the US embassy in Geneva."

Constantine motioned for him to sit. "What can I help you with, Nicolas?"

"It's come to my attention that CERN has constructed a machine—"

"I know why you're here," Constantine said, cutting him off. "And the answer is no."

Hightower paused. The smile faded. He had expected resistance but not a brick wall in the first thirty seconds. He reassessed Constantine in silence, then adjusted his posture — a shift from diplomatic tone to something colder.

He spoke with deliberate calm. "All right. You're a bold man, and not an idiot. So let's stop pretending. I'm not a science adviser." A slight tilt of his head. "I'm here representing the United States government, and I'm expecting your full cooperation."

Constantine opened his mouth, but Nicolas raised a hand.

"Don't interrupt. I'll be clear." His tone remained even, which made it worse. "We know about the experiments. We know about Gaidon Ballerat. We know about the portal and the so-called parallel world. And, frankly, we know things here have been handled with remarkable incompetence."

Constantine's jaw tightened, but he stayed silent.

Nicolas continued. "Your experiment has exposed this entire planet to an unknown foreign power. A power that has taken one of your people prisoner."

"We control the portal," Constantine said sharply. "They can't threaten us. And as for Max—"

"Can't threaten you?" Nicolas leaned in slightly. "They destroyed your drone in under two seconds with automated heavy weapons. And your machine took hits. Is that accurate?"

A long pause. Too long.

"Yes," Constantine admitted. "But if it wasn't for—"

"Vincent Duke did the only rational thing in the room," Nicolas snapped, losing his composure for the first time. "From everything I've seen, he's the only one who understood the magnitude of what you've stumbled into. And let's talk about that 'government' on the other side — because from my perspective, arresting a man for walking around and asking questions looks hostile."

"They—"

"Stop." Nicolas's voice cut through the room. "I am here to tell you that, as of this moment, the United States is assuming control of the experiment. The machine, the computers, the entire Laboratory triple eight team — all of it now falls under my authority."

Constantine stared at him, stunned.

"You cannot do this," he said quietly. "People will ask questions—"

"Try me."

The words landed like a hammer. Not shouted. Not exaggerated. Just a cold statement of capacity.

Constantine inhaled slowly, his mind spinning for a response that didn't exist. Nicolas watched him like a man observing an equation he already knew the result of.

After a long silence, Nicolas spoke again — measured, almost patient.

"My government wants this resolved immediately. You've failed to recover your missing engineer. You don't understand what you've contacted. And you are in no position to negotiate or experiment further without us."

He stood, adjusting his jacket with an air of finality.

"There's just one more requirement."

Constantine managed, "What?"

"Gaidon Ballerat must be removed."

"I've already done that."

Nicolas nodded once, satisfied. "Good. Then there's only one final instruction."

He stepped closer to Constantine's desk, lowering his voice — not whispering, just stripping away any hint of gentleness.

"You will not speak to anyone about my visit, the footage, the machine, or the portal.

Not a word. If anyone challenges my authority here or interferes with this investigation, the consequences will be immediate. And permanent."

He held Constantine's gaze until the silence became a weight.

Then, calmly:

"I'll need full access. Everything you have. And everything you've kept locked away."

Constantine swallowed, saying nothing. He didn't have to. The signature on the access card would speak for him soon enough.

*** 

**Monday, 18th June 2012, 10:21 a.m.**
**Baset Theron's office, Laboratory 888, CERN, Prévessin-Moëns, France.**

Nicolas Hightower found Baset Theron's office without difficulty and pushed the door open without bothering to knock.

Baset was mid-phone call behind his desk. Daniel Mittermayer sat opposite him — tall, wiry, hair shooting in every direction, and wearing an outfit so violently colorful that Nicolas paused for half a heartbeat. He had walked through warzones and intelligence black sites without blinking, but he had never seen a physicist dressed like a walking optical illusion.

He didn't comment. He simply adjusted his expression and stepped in.

Baset lowered the receiver, scowling. "Who the hell are you?"

Daniel started to speak, but Nicolas lifted one finger — a small, quiet command. Daniel closed his mouth immediately.

"I'm Nicolas Hightower," he said. "United States government. I now have full authority over this experiment."

He held up the access card Constantine had signed off under pressure.

Baset ended his call with a quick promise to ring back and a curt tap of the phone. "Knocking wouldn't kill you."

"I don't need to," Nicolas said, pulling a chair beside him. Daniel eased back a little, the loud colours of his shirt flaring as he moved — impossible to ignore, even in the dim light.

"I know who you are," Nicolas continued. "Baset Theron. Daniel Mittermayer. I've spoken with the Director General. Laboratory triple eight is now under my command."

Daniel blinked. "You're CIA, aren't you?"

Nicolas didn't break eye contact. "Correct."

Baset stiffened; Daniel paled beneath the riot of colour he was wearing.

"This experiment has created a geopolitical crisis," Nicolas said. "A crisis your organisation cannot contain. From now on, secrecy is absolute. Compliance is not optional. If anyone strays from that, the response will be... decisive."

He didn't raise his voice. He didn't need to.

Silence settled across the room.

Nicolas continued, "The machine. The chamber's destroyed, yes?"

Baset nodded. "Seven major components."

"How long to replace them?"

"Six months at least, closer to—"

"Too long." Nicolas's jaw tightened. "I'll push the manufacturers. I can get you priority."

Baset let out a short, dry laugh. "No. You can't."

Nicolas turned his head slightly, a quiet warning. "I can. You underestimate the reach of the —"

"No," Baset interrupted. "You underestimate the engineering."

He leaned forward, elbows on the desk. "You can rush billets, sure. But machining parts this size at our tolerances? There are only a handful of machines in Europe capable of doing it. Every one of them is booked solid."

"Booked with what?" Nicolas asked, already knowing he wouldn't like the answer.

Baset held his gaze. "Your military contracts. Mostly Joint Strike Fighter work. And they're already significantly behind schedule."

Nicolas froze. Daniel shifted again, the colours of his shirt suddenly feeling far too loud in the confined space.

Baset's voice dropped. "You'll get the parts when industrial timetables allow it. Not before then."

For the first time that morning, Nicolas found himself with no immediate response.

***

**Monday, 18th June 2012, 4:32 p.m.**
**Gaidon Ballerat's home, Geneva suburbs, Switzerland.**

When Gaidon opened the door and saw the American standing on his porch — posture rigid, eyes already sliding past him to assess the interior — he didn't bother with small talk.

"What do you want?"

"So Constantine called you," Nicolas said.

"Yeah."

"May I come in?"

"You'd probably shoot me if I said no."

Nicolas didn't react. Gaidon stepped aside.

They moved into the lounge: a lived-in space cluttered with journals, open notebooks, empty cups, and a whiteboard propped against the wall with equations half-erased. It looked like a mind interrupted mid-stride.

They sat opposite each other.

Nicolas began carefully. "I can understand why you're hostile. You make the biggest breakthrough in a century, and then things... unravel."

Gaidon gave a short breath through his nose. "Constantine told me to cooperate and keep quiet. Fine. I'll do that. But I'm done. I want nothing more to do with the machine."

"And nothing you'd like to add?" Nicolas asked.

"No. You've taken over. You have everything you need. Good luck."

The dryness in his voice made Nicolas tilt his head slightly. It wasn't resignation. It was something tighter, something with an edge.

"I visited Baset and Daniel earlier," Nicolas said. "They were polite in a superficial way, but underneath it they were... guarded."

"I'm not surprised."

"That's exactly what concerns me." Nicolas settled back in his chair. "Hostility I can manage. But this feels like more than irritation at a change in command."

Gaidon's jaw tightened.

"So tell me," Nicolas continued. "Is there something I haven't been told? Something about the experiment, or what you found on the other side?"

"No. Why would there be?" The answer was immediate — and too flat.

Nicolas let the room sit in the silence. Years of interrogation work had taught him that people reveal more in pauses than in speeches.

Gaidon looked anywhere but at him.

"You've got the logs, the drone footage, the technical drawings," Gaidon muttered. "There's nothing hidden."

Nicolas didn't argue, didn't raise an eyebrow. But inside, a familiar certainty settled. The man was frightened — not of the CIA, not of political fallout, but of something still sitting in the margin of his mind.

He shifted to a safer topic. "Max is my priority. When the machine is rebuilt, we reopen the portal with something simple. No drones, no provocation. Just a controlled attempt at communication."

Gaidon shook his head. "If Vincent hadn't lost it, none of this would've happened."

Nicolas stood, smoothing his jacket, watching whether the movement unsettled him. "I'll keep you informed. And for what it's worth, I'm sorry it ended like this. My government—"

But Gaidon was already walking into the next room, done with the conversation.

Nicolas watched him go. He didn't call him back.

Before leaving, he let his eyes sweep the lounge again. The whiteboard caught his attention — a smear of hurried handwriting in the lower corner amid the shell diagrams:

displacement vector inside-origin ??? unsafe

He memorised it.

Then he stepped out quietly and closed the door behind him.

One thing was now beyond doubt:

Gaidon Ballerat was lying.

And whatever he was hiding frightened him more than the parallel world ever had.

***

**Tuesday, 19th June 2012, 7:02 p.m.**
**Home of Nicolas Hightower, Geneva, Switzerland.**

The encryption module beside the telephone clicked from amber to green.

Nicolas straightened and lifted the receiver.

"Sir."

David Petraeus came through the line without preamble.

"Hightower, I've read your report three times. Every pass leaves me more alarmed. A parallel universe? Defensive emplacements? A detained civilian? And finally you believe that this Gaidon man is hiding something. This is—" a short exhale "—profoundly destabilising."

"Yes, Director."

"I understand you've taken operational control on-site."

"Yes. The facility is just outside Geneva, on the French side."

"Fine. Geography isn't the concern. Threat assessment is."

There was a brief rustle of paper on the other end.

"Tell me what isn't in the report," Petraeus said. "What you didn't want to commit to paper."

Nicolas let his eyes rest on the dark window across from him. The reflection of the encryption module blinked faintly in the glass.

"Nothing concrete yet. I've begun assembling a team. There's hours of telemetry and drone footage to sift through—"

"I watched all of it," Petraeus cut in. "Every second. An hour of the drone videos, the clearing, the terrain... and then those guns."

His tone hardened.

"I don't care what they claim. A society that mounts twin autocannons at its doorway is not peaceful."

Nicolas did not dispute it. "Their message was full of ideology — 'economic systems abhorrent to them', 'state of community and love'. It sounded almost rehearsed."

"They can recite doctrine all day," Petraeus said. "But a civilian appears and ends up detained, judged in private, handed a one-year sentence. No transparency. No diplomatic overture. Nothing but a verdict."

"I agree. It's hostile behaviour, even if delivered politely."

"Hostile," Petraeus repeated. "And opaque. The two most dangerous combinations we ever deal with."

Nicolas waited.

"So. The machine's down."

"Yes. Their rounds came through the shell. Serious internal damage. Replacement parts will take months."

A low grunt. "I'll have a team at Langley go over everything — physics, weapons analysis, strategic modelling. I want to understand every possible implication before we take a step."

"Yes, Director."

"In the meantime," Petraeus continued, voice settling into the cadence of orders, "contain the story. Anyone asking questions — European officials, CERN staff, journalists — gets nothing unless it comes from you."

"Yes, sir."

"And keep the Europeans calm," Petraeus added. "If they panic, or if word leaks, this becomes uncontrollable."

Nicolas listened closely; he could hear the shift — the slight drop in tone that always accompanied the Director's most pointed instructions.

"We cannot," Petraeus said, "allow the other world to dictate terms. We set the pace. We control the information. And above all—"

The line crackled softly.

"—find out what they're hiding."

The connection cut.

Nicolas lowered the receiver slowly.

Petraeus didn't have to say the rest. It was implicit in every word he'd spoken.

The CIA now regarded the parallel world not as an anomaly —

but as a potential adversary.

And the first quiet step toward escalation had already been taken.

***

**Tuesday, 19th June 2012, 8:14 p.m.**
**Céleste Guérard's apartment, Prévessin-Moëns, France.**

Céleste had been home from the hospital for barely three minutes when a sharp knock jolted the apartment. She wiped her hands on her scrubs and opened the door.

A man stood on the threshold — rigid posture, unreadable expression.

"Céleste Guérard?"

"Yes."

"I'm Dragonetz Coté. Security adviser, U.S. embassy. May I come in?"

The tone was flat and rehearsed. It wasn't a request.

Céleste stepped aside. "This is about Max, isn't it?"

"Yes."

He followed her into the living room. She gestured to the couch. She sat properly; he remained stiff, barely touching the cushions.

"There have been... problems at the laboratory," he began.

"But Gaidon said—"

"He lied," Dragonetz cut in, without the slightest hesitation. "You've been misled from the beginning. That's why we intervened."

A cold pulse went through her.

"What's happened?" she asked.

"There was an accident. Max was exposed to a significant dose of radiation."

Céleste blinked. "But Max told me they'd discovered another universe—"

Dragonetz didn't shift. "I don't know what stories he shared, but there was no such discovery. The experiment involved displacement of gold atoms. Ballerat's negligence put your nephew in danger. The situation escalated. The exposure was severe."

Céleste stared at him.

Max had been anxious, yes — consumed by the work — but truthful. He wasn't capable of spinning fantasies.

And this man was lying with complete ease.

Dragonetz continued, his voice steady, almost monotone. "We moved Max to a secure facility. He's receiving treatment from specialists familiar with radiation trauma. These cases require strict isolation."

There was something unsettling in how quietly he spoke. No aggression, no performance — just a flat, procedural cadence that made her skin tighten. He radiated the kind of stillness she recognised from certain ICU patients: the absence of emotion, not the suppression of it.

"Are you all right, Miss Guérard?" he asked, as if reading from a checklist.

She forced a small nod. "It's... a lot. How long will he be hospitalised?"

"A few months. Possibly longer."

"Where is he being treated?"

"One of our military hospitals. Highly secure."

"Can I see him?"

"No." The answer came instantly. "The contamination level makes visitation impossible. It's for your safety."

"Oh." Céleste looked down at her hands, realising he hadn't even tried to soften the refusal. "I understand."

He stood. "One more thing. Say nothing to anyone. This matter is classified at the highest level."

Céleste nodded again, because there was nothing else she could safely do.

Dragonetz left as silently as he'd arrived.

The moment the door closed, she exhaled slowly, her hands shaking.

Max wasn't in a hospital.

And whatever had happened to him — it wasn't an accident.

****

**Tuesday, 3rd July 2012, 6:32 p.m.**
**Home of Nicolas Hightower, Geneva, Switzerland.**

The encrypted phone module on Nicolas's desk glowed green again. He lifted the receiver.

Petraeus didn't bother with preliminaries.

"Nicolas, good news first. You'll have the replacement parts sooner than expected. I pushed the manufacturing schedule — hard. That engineer... what was his name?"

"Baset. Baset Theron, sir."

"Yes. Him. He wasn't exaggerating about the bottleneck. The favours I had to call in..." Petraeus let the breath run out of him.

Nicolas allowed himself a small sigh of relief. Nothing more.

Petraeus continued, "Our engineers have also altered the original design. Minor adjustments. Won't affect the core behaviour, but the chamber should handle impacts better if those guns open fire again."

Nicolas made a note out of habit, though he already knew the plates wouldn't survive concentrated fire from that close range.

"There's another matter," Petraeus said. "The physics taskforce I pulled together — Oak Ridge, Livermore, MIT — they're confident they understand almost everything."

A pause followed. Nicolas recognised it.

"Except one component," he said.

"The control algorithm," Petraeus confirmed. "The electron-gun sequence that ionises the argon. They can't determine how your people derived it. One of your scientists — Mittermayer — wrote the final version?"

"Yes. I re-interviewed him," Nicolas replied. "He was evasive. Smug. He's concealing something."

"You're probably right." Petraeus didn't sound surprised. "But Oak Ridge found something else in Daniel's notes. Something they decided to test."

Nicolas straightened, pen hovering.

"What did they find?"

"It's simple," Petraeus said. "Almost insultingly simple. Reduce the power to the electron guns and the portal collapses to a much smaller size."

"How small?"

"A fraction of an inch. Almost invisible to the naked eye."

A long quiet settled on the line. Nicolas felt the implications opening one by one — none of them good.

Petraeus continued. His voice was measured, heavy with calculation.

"A portal that small can still pass information. Objects. Devices. Possibly even a material sample. And nobody on the other side would detect it."

Nicolas said nothing.

Then Petraeus's tone shifted — lower, decisive.

"Now here's what I want you to do."

***

# Chapter 13



**Thursday, 12th July 2012, 8:12 a.m.**
**Parallel universe. Paris High Security Jail, Paris, France.**

Dominic walked beside the senior prison guard, their footsteps echoing along the concrete corridor.

"How's he been?" Dominic asked.

The guard gave a loose shrug. "Better. Not perfect — a few sharp edges now and then — but nothing serious. No threats, no shouting. Just... tense."

Dominic nodded. "And the library access?"

"Three days ago," the guard said. "He finally got clearance. Went straight for the history section. Grabbed that massive World History: 1900–2000 volume. Comes back every couple of days for more history. Keeps to himself."

Some of the weight sitting in Dominic's chest eased. "All right."

They reached Max's door. The guard unlocked it and stepped aside.

Dominic entered.

Max sat at the small desk in his upgraded cell — proper bedding now, a blanket folded neatly at the foot of the bed, a few borrowed books stacked on the narrow shelf. The thick history volume lay open in front of him. He pushed it aside when he saw who had come in.

"Dominic?" he said. Wary, but no hostility behind it.

The guard closed the door behind them.

Max looked worn — the kind of tired that comes from weeks of confinement, not a single bad night — but he was no longer the frantic version of himself Dominic had met in the induction cell.

"I didn't think anyone would come," Max said quietly. "It's been... quiet."

"I spoke with the guard on the way in," Dominic replied. "They say you've been keeping it together."

"I'm trying. Some days are harder than others."

Dominic nodded toward the books. "I hear you've made good use of library time."

Max gave a small shrug. "I needed context. History. Your world's so different, and I barely understood any of it."

"It shows you're trying to understand," Dominic said. "Aimes will like that."

Max let out a long breath. "Does it matter enough to change anything?"

"That's why I'm here." Dominic leaned forward slightly. "There's a job offer."

Max blinked. "A job?"

"A placement," Dominic said. "Naval shipyard in Lorient. Drafting and mechanical design. It's still part of your sentence — supervised, structured — but it gets you out of here."

Max stared at him, stunned. "You're serious?"

"Completely. But there's one condition: the warden has to approve it. And he'll only do that if you stay steady. No flare-ups. No arguments. Keep doing what you've been doing."

Max gripped the edge of the desk. "I can do that. I promise."

Dominic allowed himself a faint smile. "Good. That's all that's needed."

He stood. "I'll speak to him today. I'll come back when there's news."

When the door closed behind him, Max stayed seated at the desk, hands resting on the book he'd abandoned. The walls didn't feel any softer, but for the first time in weeks, he could see a way forward — a small path out of the concrete and silence.

And for the first time in a long while, he believed he might actually survive the year.

***

**Thursday, 19th July 2012, 9:04 a.m.**
**Parallel universe. Paris High Security Jail, Paris, France.**

The door slid open with a dull mechanical clunk and Senior Guard Armand Lefèvre stepped inside, a clipboard in one hand and a metal cup of water in the other. Broad-shouldered, silver-haired, built like someone who'd spent his entire life enforcing order — he filled the cell without even trying.

Max was sitting on the edge of the bed, the thick history volume open beside him. He straightened slightly as Armand stepped in.

"You've been stuck into that one these last few days," Armand said, nodding at the book.

Max rubbed the back of his neck. "Trying to understand things."

Armand gave a short, cynical huff.

He made a note on his clipboard, set it on the desk, and — instead of leaving — folded his arms and leaned against the wall.

"So," he said, "what exactly are you trying to find in there?"

Max hesitated. His mouth moved before his brain caught up. "Perspective. On how you see me."

Armand frowned. "How I see you? I barely know anything about you."

Max froze — too late. He'd misjudged the silence of the past month, assumed the guards had been briefed. And worse — he'd forgotten Dominic's warning to say nothing about who he was or where he'd come from.

Armand pushed off the wall, his posture stiffening. "What are you talking about?"

Max swallowed. "You see me as a threat. As someone who... built something dangerous."

Armand's face tightened, but this time with a different emotion: suspicion edging toward alarm. "Why would you say that? Nobody here told me anything about your work."

Max let out a slow breath, trapped by his own mistake. "Because I did something wrong. Very wrong. I helped design the weapons of war."

Armand's voice dropped into something colder, heavier. "Explain."

Max swallowed. "Not weapons directly. Mostly components. Engineering for companies that—"

"What companies?" Armand snapped.

Max froze. "Dassault. Nexter. Places like that." He tried to hide the tremor in his voice. "It wasn't always weapons. Sometimes aviation. Sometimes support equipment —"

Armand pushed off the wall, stepping closer. "Don't dissemble. What did you actually design?"

Max's breath caught. "Artillery housings. Structural assemblies for fighter aircraft. Mounting systems for armoured vehicles. I didn't... I didn't pull triggers. I just worked on the drawings."

Armand stared at him, thrown for a moment.

"You designed weapon systems," he said slowly, as if translating the idea into his own frame of reference. "But for who?"

Max hesitated, searching for a lie that would satisfy and not open more questions. "Different groups. Different... clients. It wasn't one organisation."

Armand's eyes hardened. "So you built machines for terrorists."

Max tensed — but the guard didn't give him a chance to correct it.

"I don't know which group you worked for," Armand said, voice sharpening, "and frankly I don't care. Let me tell you what I do know about war and weapons."

"My grandfather came back from the Great War ruined," Armand said. "Not wounded — ruined. The sort of damage you can't bandage. He'd sit in a chair for hours, rocking back and forth, muttering the names of friends who never came back. And when he slept — if he slept — he screamed like he was on fire."

Max blinked, throat tightening.

"I was seven," Armand went on. "He was an empty man by then. Could barely hold a fork. Couldn't look anyone in the eye. But I remember the sound of him crying. A grown man sobbing like a child. That's what war does. That's what wars machines do. The guns. The shells. The aircraft. The weapons that men like you *design!*"

Max flinched as if struck.

"You think I don't know what those machines look like on the other end?" Armand said, leaning closer. "You think I haven't seen the old footage? Bodies thrown like rag dolls. Trenches where boys drowned in mud so thick they couldn't lift their heads. Entire towns levelled. Millions dead because someone, somewhere, decided that a *bigger* gun was *necessary.*"

"I didn't—" Max began.

"Don't you dare say you didn't know," Armand snapped. "You drew the lines. You made the revisions. You made the work accurate enough so the weapon wouldn't jam when a conscript needed it."

Max's voice cracked. "I never wanted anyone to be hurt."

"Wanting has nothing to do with it," Armand said. "You helped build the system that makes the violence possible."

He stood so close now that Max could see the lines at the corners of his eyes — not cruelty, but the weight of memory and inherited grief.

"We clawed our way out of that nightmare nearly a century ago," Armand said. "We tore out the roots of war. We banned weapons. We rebuilt society from the ground up because we knew what happens when people like you keep designing machines whose only purpose is death."

Max's hands trembled in his lap. "I didn't think—"

"That's the problem," Armand said. "You *didn't* think. You *didn't* question. You just made your drawings and told yourself it wasn't *your* responsibility."

He lowered his voice to a hard, quiet edge.

"But it was. It is. And maybe more than anyone pulling a trigger."

Max's breath shuddered out of him, the truth landing like a weight he hadn't known he was carrying — or hadn't allowed himself to see.

Armand left slamming the door before locking it.

Max sat on the bed, staring at nothing, the history book open at his side.

For the first time, he didn't just understand their fear.

He understood his own role in creating it.

***

**Wednesday, 1st August 2012, 2:42 p.m.**
**Parallel universe. Paris High Security Jail, Paris, France.**

Dominic stepped through the security door as it buzzed open and made his way down the familiar concrete corridor. Senior Guard Armand Lefèvre was waiting for him halfway along, arms folded, posture unmoving.

"You're here about Rivette," Armand said.

"Yes," Dominic replied. "Aimes has approved the placement. Naval shipyard in Lorient. Drafting, modelling. The warden just needs your assessment before the transfer."

Armand considered that for a moment, then gave a single, slow nod.

"He's been fine," the guard said. "No aggression. No swearing. Keeps to himself. Reads constantly. Tense, but that's expected. Never crossed a line." He marked something on his clipboard with the edge of a thumbnail. "A model prisoner, all things considered."

He shifted his weight, expression tightening in a way that wasn't hostile so much as blunt honesty.

"Considering he's a weapons designer," Armand added.

Dominic took the comment without reacting. The guard wasn't seeking clarification and didn't want any.

Armand uncrossed his arms. "If Aimes says he's safe, then fine. No issues from this end."

Dominic nodded. "Then we'll move forward. I'll bring the paperwork tomorrow."

"Good," Armand said. He turned back toward his rounds, already finished with the conversation. "Come back tomorrow afternoon and we'll have him ready to leave."

***

**Thursday, 2nd August 2012, 2:15 p.m.**
**Home of Nicolas Hightower, Geneva, Switzerland.**

Nicolas had just sat down with a glass of indifferent Swiss red when his phone buzzed. Secure line. Washington. He closed his eyes briefly; it was barely dawn there.

He answered anyway. "Hightower."

Petraeus' voice came through clipped, already irritated. "Do you people in Europe ever align your clocks with civilisation? It's eight in the damn morning here and I've got three briefings stacked."

Nicolas didn't bother responding. Petraeus never actually wanted an answer.

"We've got a problem," Petraeus continued. "Your French defence contractor —

Nexter. Their man, what's his name?"

"Johann Richter," Nicolas said. German-born, running a French military subsidiary with the confidence of a man who assumed everyone would return his calls. Nicolas had already rung him in June, spun the story of the radiation incident, emphasised that Max wouldn't be returning to work, would be lucky to survive at all. Richter had swallowed it — but like all bureaucrats, he wanted paperwork.

Nicolas exhaled sharply. "Well, Richter's secretary has been pestering CERN. Apparently she rang one of their administrative staff this morning — demanded documentation so Nexter can process Rivette's final payment and benefits." A pause. "They're rattling cages we don't need rattled."

Nicolas rubbed his temple. "CERN's silenced except for Wood and Lapôtre. The rest know almost nothing."

"Doesn't matter," Petraeus snapped. "Silence creates questions. Questions create audits. Audits uncover lies we don't have the manpower to maintain. We're tying off this loose end. Effective immediately."

Nicolas sat straighter. "You're approving the death notice?"

"Yes," Petraeus said, flat. "Maximilian Rivette dies tomorrow. Choose something plausible — complications, organ failure, whatever your fake medical report says. Deliver it to CERN and Nexter simultaneously. The aunt gets her call after."

Nicolas nodded, though Petraeus couldn't see him. "Understood."

"And for God's sake," Petraeus added, voice hardening, "make sure those people stop asking. I don't want a French HR clerk stumbling into something that collapses the whole operation."

The line clicked dead without a goodbye.

Nicolas lowered the phone, the room suddenly too quiet. Outside, Lake Geneva glinted in the late-afternoon sun — calm, orderly, indifferent. He finished his wine in one swallow, already drafting the wording in his head.

Max Rivette would die tomorrow.

On paper, at least.

And bureaucrats would stop asking questions.

***

**Friday, 3rd August 2012, 9:12 a.m.**
**Parallel universe. Lorient Housing Department, Lorient, France.**

The taxi dropped them outside a modest concrete-and-glass building in the centre of Lorient — nothing grand, nothing ceremonial, just another civic office doing its work without fuss.

Inside, Max and Dominic joined the line of chairs in the small waiting area. Three others were already there.

Max kept his voice low. "So... how does this actually work?"

Dominic answered in the same even tone he used for everything procedural. "Anyone who needs a place to live meets a housing manager. They look at your situation and match you with an available home."

"And who provides the homes?" Max asked.

"The government. Rule Ten — shelter is a guaranteed right."

Max frowned slightly. "But the cost—construction, maintenance—someone has to pay."

Dominic gave him a patient look. "No one pays. Builders work collectively. They build because the community needs housing. You're still thinking in terms of markets and ownership. Let it go, Max. Out here, 'from each according to ability, to each according to need' isn't ideology — it's logistics."

Max nodded. Every assumption he'd grown up with — mortgages, rent, property rights — dissolved under that single explanation. He felt like he was learning how to be a person from scratch.

He glanced around the waiting room.

An elderly man sat with his hands clasped tightly, his shoulders trembling in a way that only meant grief. Quiet, exhausted grief.

"He's lost someone," Max murmured.

"Most likely," Dominic said. "People often move after a partner dies. Too many memories."

Next was a woman in her early twenties, visibly pregnant and alone. She looked calm, already halfway resigned to whatever came next.

Then a boy sat upright near the corner — twelve or thirteen, alert, composed, fingers knotted together.

Max whispered, "Why is a child here alone?"

Dominic lowered his voice. "Rule Four. Freedom of movement. If a young person can't stay with their family — values clashing, escalating conflict — they can leave. Not common, but allowed. Most families reconcile. Some don't."

Max absorbed that quietly. A small change that implied a very different society.

A door opened and a woman with hair dyed in a blazing shade of red stepped out. "Dominic Garner?"

Dominic stood. Max followed.

"Come in," she said with an efficient smile. "I'm Vanessa Jogues."

Her office was tidy, lined with framed photos of completed housing projects. She gestured for them to sit.

Vanessa turned a polite smile toward Max. "Right, Mr Rivette. I was briefed. Single occupant, no dependants, no special needs, no vehicle. Yes?"

"Yes," Max said.

"Good." She slid three folders across the desk. "These are available immediately."

Max opened the first two. Both were sleek apartment complexes with bright interiors and community gardens. Modern, pleasant — but dense. Too many people, too much noise. He imagined footsteps overhead, muffled arguments through walls, the sense of being hemmed in.

Then he opened the third.

A small two-storey building. Only four apartments — two up, two down. A garage. Trees around the property. A modest garden. Fully furnished. Quiet.

Space to breathe.

He set the others aside and tapped the third folder. "This one."

Vanessa nodded. "It's a very good choice."

She gathered a set of keys. "Shall we go take a look?"

Max stood slowly. For the first time since the hearing — maybe since stepping into this world — he felt the faint, steady rise of something he barely recognised.

Hope.

***

**Friday, 3rd August 2012, 10:08 a.m.**
**Parallel universe, Lorient, France.**

Vanessa pulled up beside the small pale-blue apartment building and stepped out, motioning for Max and Dominic to follow. The air smelled faintly of the nearby coast, warm and clean.

Inside, a short hallway led to a staircase. To the left, the lower apartment door sat slightly ajar. A steady pulse of rock music thumped through the frame.

Dominic glanced at Vanessa. "Someone already living down here?"

She checked the file in her hand. "Yes. Victorin Rouille. Mid-twenties. Two years in this building. Recorded as cooperative. No complaints."

Dominic lifted an eyebrow. "What does he actually do?"

Vanessa gave a small shrug. "Unclear. Not much, from the look of things. Doesn't cause trouble, though."

Max wasn't sure whether that was normal here or simply tolerated — another reminder that this world ran on rules he was still learning to read.

They climbed the narrow stairs. Vanessa unlocked the upper door and pushed it open.

The apartment matched the photographs exactly: a compact kitchen, a small lounge opening into a sunlit dining area overlooking the street, and at the back a tidy bedroom and bathroom. Everything smelled freshly cleaned — polished floorboards, new paint, modest furniture chosen more for practicality than style.

Vanessa folded her arms lightly. "Well? What do you think?"

Max walked through the space once, taking in the quiet, the light, the sense of having a door he could close on the world. "I like it. A lot. When can I move in?"

Vanessa pulled a keyring from her pocket and placed it in his hand. "Immediately. I'll register the change of address this afternoon."

She was mid-explanation about maintenance contacts when a voice came from the doorway.

"Ah — I thought I heard footsteps."

They turned.

A tall, thin man leaned against the doorframe, early twenties at most, with dark hair pushed back in a way that suggested he hadn't decided whether he cared about appearances or not. His shirt was loose, patterned in bright, clashing shapes, as if he'd found it in an art studio rather than a wardrobe.

Vanessa gave a faintly resigned smile. "Victorin. Convenient timing."

He stepped inside with an easy nod to Max. "I'm downstairs. Victorin Rouille. If you need anything — sugar, tools, advice on which cafés won't poison you — come by."

Max shook his hand. "Max Rivette."

Victorin studied him for a moment, not suspicious, just curious. "Welcome, then. The building's quiet. I tend to keep odd hours, but I'm not loud. At least not often." He added a quick, self-deprecating flick of a smile. "Anyway... nice to have someone new around."

Vanessa guided them back downstairs a few minutes later. Dominic was about to ask her for a lift into the centre of town when the apartment complex door swung open again.

"Vanessa," Victorin called, pulling on a jacket, "is there any chance you're heading toward the centre of town? My bike chain snapped and I'd rather avoid walking."

Vanessa gestured toward the car. "Fine. Get in."

Victorin joined them without fuss, sliding into the back seat beside Dominic. The faint scent of incense drifted with him, something woody and unfamiliar.

The engine started, the apartment building slipping from view in the rear window.

Max sat quietly, the keys warm in his hand — a small, solid proof that he now had a place in this world, however temporary, and a neighbour who already felt like part of its strange new texture.

***

**Friday, 3rd August 2012, 11:12 a.m.**
**Céleste Guérard's apartment, Prévessin-Moëns, France.**

For the second time in less than two months, someone in a dark suit knocked on Céleste Guérard's door.

This knock was softer than the last — measured, almost apologetic. When she opened the door, the man waiting there carried none of Dragonetz Coté's icy menace. He looked composed, tired behind the eyes, and too careful in his posture to be comfortable.

"Madame Guérard?" he asked.

"Yes."

"I'm Nicolas Hightower. I work with the team overseeing your nephew's case."

His tone was gentle, his French unfaltering. The kind of voice chosen for bad news.

"May I come in?" he added quietly. "What I have to say is difficult."

Her stomach tightened. She stepped aside.

They sat at the kitchen table Max had once cluttered with coffee cups and sketches. Nicolas rested his hands lightly on the surface, as if arranging them softened the weight of what he was about to deliver.

"I'm very sorry," he said. "Max passed away."

The words struck like a blow. Céleste's breath folded in on itself; her fingers trembled against the edge of the table.

"No," she whispered. "He was receiving treatment. Dragonetz told me, he only rang last week—"

"He gave you only what he was permitted," Nicolas said gently. "He wasn't authorised to discuss the details."

Céleste knew the cadence of evasions — two decades in hospital wards had trained her well. This wasn't truth talking. It was containment.

"How?" she asked.

"The radiation exposure Max suffered was severe," Nicolas said. "Cases like this can fluctuate. Patients appear stable, then deteriorate very quickly. That's what happened. When his organs began to fail, the decline was rapid."

The explanation sat neatly inside medical plausibility. Too neatly.

"Where is he?" she asked. "I'd like to see him."

Nicolas shook his head with slow, practised regret. "I'm afraid visitation wasn't possible. The contamination level required immediate incineration in a controlled facility. It was done as a safety measure — for the staff as much as for the public."

Céleste closed her eyes. The reasoning aligned with protocols she knew by heart — and still rang false.

"Was anyone responsible?" she said quietly.

"We're reviewing the conduct of Gaidon Ballerat," Nicolas replied. "There were clear lapses in judgement. If his negligence contributed, steps will be taken."

More polished phrasing. More distance. Nothing concrete.

"Max trusted his colleagues," she said.

Nicolas lowered his eyes, his voice thinning. "Trust is vital in research work. But people make mistakes. This one... was tragic."

Something flicked in his expression then — a tension at the corner of his jaw, the faint tremor of a man reciting a story crafted elsewhere. Whether he believed it or despised it, she couldn't tell.

"I understand this is a terrible loss," he went on. "If you need a liaison for paperwork or support, I can arrange it. But much of the documentation surrounding the accident is classified. Access will be limited."

"Of course," she said, though the softness in her tone had cooled.

Nicolas rose. "Madame Guérard... your nephew was an exceptional man. I'm sorry."

She managed a small nod.

At the door he paused, as if waiting for her to say something he could answer, or forgive. She didn't.

He left quietly. The lock clicked behind him.

Céleste stood motionless for several seconds, then sank into the nearest chair, hands pressed to her mouth as grief broke through in slow, aching waves.

But beneath the grief, another truth settled with absolute clarity.

Max was gone.

But not like this.

Not in the way she'd been told.

Not in the story that man had carried into her home.

Whatever happened at CERN, it was being buried.

She wiped her eyes, steadied her breath, and set her hands on the table.

She would not let it stay buried.

***

**Friday, 3rd August 2012, 11:47 a.m.**
**Parallel universe. Shopping mall, Lorient, France.**

For Max, the outing felt like stepping onto a stage in a play he hadn't rehearsed for. No money. No checkout. No transaction. Just take what you need and leave. His mind kept waiting for the usual cues — prices, receipts, ownership — and every time the expectation collapsed into nothing. Dominic had warned him it would take months before those instincts faded.

They pushed two shopping trolleys down the wide central aisle of the supermarket. Fluorescent lights buzzed overhead; the air smelled of bread and citrus detergent; the floor gleamed like it had been polished an hour ago. Victorin, who had insisted on joining them "because shopping is never a solitary pursuit," drifted ahead, plucking items from shelves and dropping them into the trolley with casual flair.

"So where're you from?" Victorin asked suddenly, spinning back toward them with the unabashed curiosity of someone who never second-guessed a question.

"Max is from Prévessin-Moëns," Dominic said without hesitation. "Not much travel."

Victorin stopped, cereal box dangling from one hand. "Never been to a big city? Why not?"

"Grew up on a farm," Max said. "Didn't feel the need."

Victorin nodded with grave understanding, as if this explained the mysteries of the universe. "Ah. A nature man. That tracks."

The next half hour unfolded in a steady stream of Victorin's commentary. He spoke about nightlife in the industrial district, an art collective that staged performances in abandoned shipyards, a rooftop jazz group that played only improvised sets, and a theatre troupe that performed in complete darkness. He motioned toward the fruit.

"I dated someone who swore she could tell if a melon was ripe just by listening to it roll across a bench. Still not sure if she was serious."

Dominic gave Max a look that conveyed resignation more than annoyance. Max almost laughed.

They worked through the list: clothes, toiletries, kitchen essentials, small appliances. Victorin kept adding "necessities" — novelty socks, a selection of teas, incense, and a tall potted fern that he claimed would "help the space breathe."

Max wasn't sure his space needed to breathe, but the fern stayed.

When the trolleys were full, they simply walked out. No checkout, no scanner, no one watching for theft. People around them did the same — collecting what they needed and leaving without ceremony.

Max kept expecting someone to chase after him shouting, Sir, stop. Dominic noticed the tension in his shoulders.

"You'll adjust," he said quietly.

They reached the taxi rank. Only one vehicle waited. Dominic's patience, worn thin by an hour of Victorin's crazy banter, finally gave way.

"All right. I'm going to the hotel. I'll meet you tomorrow morning for the introduction at the shipyard."

Before Max could answer, Dominic had climbed into the taxi and was already waving as it pulled away.

Max stared after him. "So... what now?"

Victorin blinked at him, as if the question itself were puzzling. "We get a lift."

He pulled out a small phone covered in stickers and tapped the screen.

"A taxi?" Max asked.

"No."

"Then what?"

"A lift," Victorin repeated. "Someone nearby gives us a ride. People do it all the time. Good way to meet new faces."

Max didn't have a reply for that.

Victorin tucked the phone back into his pocket. "Give it a minute. Someone will come."

Max had the quiet, sinking certainty that living above Victorin Rouille would come with surprises he had no way to predict — and no chance of avoiding.

***

**Saturday, 4th August 2012, 9:03 a.m.**
**Parallel universe. Lorient Naval Shipyard, Lorient, France.**

For Max, the shipyard hit him first with its sheer size. Dry docks cut into the coastline in long, geometric trenches, each one large enough to swallow a building whole. Cranes moved overhead with slow, mechanical certainty, their motors humming beneath the clatter of welding and steel plates being manoeuvred into place. Hulls in different stages of construction lined the slips — bare ribs, half-skinned frames, and near-finished vessels — all built with the kind of disciplined engineering that comes from a workforce used to steady, uninterrupted production.

The air smelled of salt, oil, and hot metal. Workers moved with quiet confidence. No rush. No barked orders. Just an environment tuned to cooperation and craft.

As they stepped out of the taxi, Dominic adjusted his jacket and gave Max a moment to take it in.

"Nadine started here at nineteen as an apprentice," he said. "She's now head of engineering. People trust her. She's direct. She expects competence."

"Should I be nervous?" Max asked.

"Yes," Dominic replied simply. "But she'll treat you fairly."

A man in overalls waved them toward a side entrance. "Dominic! Max Rivette? This way."

From the lobby at the entrance of the building they ascended to the tenth floor before following him through a maze of corridors until he stopped at a wide doorway.

Inside was Nadine Verchoux's 'office.'

Calling it an office didn't quite fit. One wall held bookshelves stacked with technical manuals and maritime history. Another housed a large antique drafting table covered in in-progress sketches. A third formed a lounge area — three deep couches around a carved wooden table etched with sea animals.

Nadine looked up from a document. She finished making a note before joining them at the couches.

She was in her mid-forties, lean, sharp-featured, with the alertness of someone who missed nothing.

"Sit," she said.

They did.

Nadine studied Max for a moment — not suspiciously, but as if mapping him. Max shifted despite himself.

"I understand you're a draftsman," she said. "And that your previous work context was... unusual."

Max glanced at Dominic, unsure where the boundaries lay.

Dominic answered calmly. "Nadine is cleared. She was briefed because she'll be supervising you directly."

Nadine folded her hands. "Several weeks ago I was asked to take you on and make sure you can operate here without drawing unnecessary attention. I agreed."

"Attention?" Max echoed.

Dominic leaned forward. "Your technical ability isn't the issue. It's everything else."

Max frowned. "Meaning?"

"Meaning the cultural gaps," Dominic said. "The way you speak, the way you reference things, the assumptions you carry. People will notice quickly that something is... off. Nadine needs a plausible story to explain that before rumours fill the space."

Nadine added, "The simplest cover is one people already understand. In our world, some families isolate themselves — by ideology, by choice, by circumstance. Their children grow up with the usual online network-based education but very little social contact. When they enter the wider community, they're competent but visibly unprepared. We call them 'Shielders.'"

Max absorbed that. "And I would... be one of these?"

"It explains everything people will pick up on," Nadine said. "You struggle with norms. You misread cues. You ask questions no adult here would normally ask. None of that will seem strange if they believe you were raised in isolation."

Max bristled. "So I'm pretending to be some sort of... socially stunted hermit?"

"Not a hermit," Nadine corrected. "Just someone taught by family instead of society. It's a recognised category here. People will accept it immediately."

Dominic said quietly, "Max... it's the safest option. You'll be able to work without suspicion."

The resistance in Max's shoulders eased. He understood the necessity, even if it stung.

"All right," he said. "I'll accept the cover."

Nadine nodded, satisfied. "Good. It will hold as long as you give people as little to wonder about as possible." Then she stood and gestured toward the open blueprints. "Now, let's set identity aside and talk about your actual function here."

She tapped the drawings. "You'll be part of the systems drafting team. Civilian maritime work — cargo vessels, support ships, hull systems, bulkhead design.

Max exhaled slowly — relief mixed with a faint sense of grounding.

Nadine watched him carefully. "You'll do fine," she said. "Just focus on the work. The rest we'll manage."

And for the first time since entering this world, Max felt the faint outline of a life he might actually inhabit.

***

**Saturday, 4th August 2012, 9:24 a.m.**
**Parallel universe. Lorient Naval Shipyard, Lorient, France.**

Nadine Verchoux had every reason to feel pride in the industrial syndic under her stewardship.

From her tenth-floor office, the shipyard didn't just fill the horizon — it swallowed it.

Max stood beside her, stunned, feeling suddenly very small.

The Lorient Naval Shipyard stretched across the junction of the Blavet and Scorff Rivers like a metal city-state. Kilometres of gantries. Buildings the size of stadiums. Dry docks almost big enough to cradle mountain ranges. Long avenues of cranes in slow, deliberate motion. The entire landscape pulsed with the rhythm of a civilisation that had mastered industry rather than drowned in it.

Max had thought CERN was the pinnacle.

He realised now it was a cottage workshop compared to this.

Nadine caught his expression and smiled faintly — the smile of someone who had seen this reaction a thousand times.

"Come," she said. "Seeing it from above is nothing. You need to feel it."

Ten minutes later they entered the sub-assembly complex — a cavernous hall that seemed to swallow sound as much as space. They had been joined by Jean Pacaut, the engineering design manager at the Lorient Naval Shipyard.

Banks of machinery stretched into the distance — not chaotic, not cluttered, but arranged with the deliberate order of a world-class industrial line. The machines themselves were sleek, almost sculptural: articulated arms, gantry-mounted spindles, monolithic milling towers moving with the uncanny grace of ballet dancers.

This was not a factory.

This was a precision ecosystem engineered to the limits of human capability.

An operator noticed Nadine and Jean were taking the two men on a tour, and waved them over to a machining centre the size of a house, so he could extol the features of the machine he was working with. As he talked, Max barely heard him. His eyes were fixed on the machine's movements: smooth, silent, impossibly assured. A leviathan carving steel as easily as a tailor cuts silk.

They passed a fabrication cell where Nadine informed Max they were shaping metals at the atomic scale — shimmering chambers, sealed behind glass, where laser-fed arrays spun glowing patterns across suspended lattices. Max had the unsettling feeling he was watching tomorrow being built in real time.

Everywhere he turned, something defied the limits of his own world.

An hour later in the welding hangar, Max stopped walking altogether.

The space was obscene in scale.

Six hundred metres long.

Three hundred metres wide.

Ninety metres high.

The entire interior glowed with the light of welding arcs — blue, white, electric.

The air trembled with the thunder of machines.

Massive steel plates, each a metre thick and longer than a tennis court, floated through the air held aloft by robotic arms the size of buses. These giants moved with eerie coordination, rotating and aligning slabs of steel with millimetric precision before lowering them into place.

The welding rigs scuttled along the seams like oversized insects, leaving behind rivers of molten metal that cooled to perfect lines.

There were hardly any humans.

Just a handful of technicians perched at control stations, monitoring the ballet of machines that shaped a continent's maritime fleet.

Nadine leaned close so her voice carried over the roar.

"What do you think now, Max?"

He tried to speak. Failed. Tried again.

"It's... breathtaking," he said.

Then, softer, almost afraid: "My world doesn't have anything even half like this."

They watched as a completed segment of hull — the size of an apartment block — was unclamped and lifted by four titanic robotic arms. The motion was impossibly smooth, like giants lifting a sleeping child.

Max felt the awe all the way through his bones.

Outside in the final assembly yard, sunlight washed over a ship so enormous it dominated the river like a floating continent.

Max stared upward.

It was absurd. Impossible. Beautiful.

"That," Nadine said with pride, "is the third hull of the Aurore class."

Max blinked. "How long is it?"

"Just over half a kilometre. Six hundred and forty-five thousand tonnes displacement. Fifty-nine knots cruising speed."

Max couldn't respond.

His mind simply filled with the image of a vessel the size of a city slicing through the ocean at highway speed.

The tour continued — through design halls, prototyping labs, digital theatres — until they reached an office where a small, wiry old man was hunched over a workstation.

Jean Pacaut cleared his throat.

"Max, this is Arguis Ronet — the best drafting instructor we have."

Arguis stood, joints popping, bright-green jeans rustling. He wore an outrageous T-shirt plastered with a heavy-metal band mid-guitar-solo.

He grinned at Max with the warmth of someone who had survived many eras of change and refused to become bitter.

"So," Arguis said, "they tell me you can draw. Let's see if you can think."

Max straightened. "Uh... yes. I—"

"No time for speeches," Arguis cut in cheerfully. "Come along, young man. We have work to do."

He shuffled out with surprising speed.

Dominic, standing beside Jean, gave Max a small wave that translated to good luck — you're on your own.

***

**Saturday, 4th August, 5:07 p.m.**
**Parallel universe. Lorient Naval Shipyard. Lorient, France.**

By the time Arguis finally leaned back in his chair and declared the assessment complete, Max felt as if his brain had been through a full overhaul.

The process had taken the entire afternoon — not because Max was slow, but because the design software here was decades beyond anything he'd used. His entire professional life had been built on systems born in the early 1980s. Thirty years of evolution had made them powerful, yes — but still clunky, patched, layered with compromises.

This world had started earlier.

1964.

That one date alone had knocked the breath out of him.

Nearly half a century of uninterrupted development.

No corporate turf wars. No competing platforms. No licensing restrictions.

Just one continuous, collective push toward better tools.

The result was almost unnerving.

Everything he touched here felt... right.

Intuitive. Elegant. Fast.

As though the software anticipated what he wanted rather than fought against it.

He kept finding himself whispering, "That would have saved us months..."

Or, "God, if we'd had this at CERN..."

But the thing that fascinated him most — the feature he kept circling back to — was the on-demand alloy system. A design interface where materials weren't fixed choices in a catalogue, but dynamic mixtures a designer could conjure like colours on a palette.

Arguis demonstrated by manipulating a five-sided interactive widget floating on the display:

toughness on one axis, elasticity on another, corrosion resistance on a third, conductivity on a fourth, machinability on the fifth.

With each adjustment, the system recalculated composition, cost-in-labour-hours, allowable tolerances, heat-treating paths, and even fatigue simulations.

Max watched it all with the silent awe of someone seeing a machine grant a wish he didn't know he had.

He was still staring when a figure appeared beside the desk.

Arguis glanced up. "Ah. Noah. What's broken now?"

The young engineer looked equal parts annoyed and embarrassed. "The new tool for the DX-45 side panel. Whoever drew it messed up the internal ribs. It clashes with the weldment tolerances. Jean said to find you."

Arguis sighed — long-suffering, theatrical — and rose slowly from his chair like an old actor preparing for the next act. He looked at Max.

"Well? Feel like a walk? I need to stretch these ancient bones."

Max nodded, grateful for the break.

The three of them set off through the factory complex.

As advanced as the place was — as robotic, as automated, as futuristic — one thing hadn't changed in any universe.

Sound.

Smell.

Industry made physical.

Metal being cut, pressed, shaped — a chorus of grinding wheels, deep drills, high-speed spindles. The tang of hot oil in the air, the faint sting of cooling fluid, the warm metallic scent that lived forever in the folds of work clothes.

It hit Max like a time machine.

He was sixteen again. First day as an apprentice toolmaker. Nervous. Excited.

Shouted instructions cut through the machinery's roar, half-heard but unmistakably urgent.

Chips flicked across the concrete in quick metallic bursts, skipping past boots as the cutters bit deeper.

Max paused, taking in the sheer scale of the work around him — a place where problems were solved in steel, and futures were built one weld at a time.

Walking behind Arguis, watching the old man weave through the labyrinth of machinery, Max felt something strange rise in him. Not dread. Not sadness.

Recognition.

A kind of reverse déjà vu — not remembering the past, but foreseeing himself years from now. Older. Greyer. Moving through this same place with the same slow confidence, answering the same questions, shaping younger workers the way Arguis was shaping him.

The thought made his chest tighten.

Not fear. Not quite hope either.

Something in between.

Something like belonging.

***

# Chapter 14



**Saturday, 1st September 2012, 7.49 p.m.**
**Parallel universe. Max's apartment, Lorient, France.**

In the month since Max had moved in, Victorin had become a fixture in his life — not in a needy way, but in the effortless, organic way friendships form when two people simply... click. The age gap barely registered anymore. Victorin brought a kind of easy, chaotic energy into Max's evenings; Max, in turn, provided the older man's calm, a grounded presence the younger man seemed to crave.

Most nights followed a rhythm: Max cooked, Victorin wandered up with some gossip, they watched whatever film looked interesting, and gradually the two apartments developed the comfortable overlap of households that trust each other. Max had once joked, "You spend more time in my place than yours," to which Victorin replied, perfectly sincere, "Obviously. You have better food and better stories."

This world's films fascinated Max. Without money, there was no need for explosions, superheroes, or market-tested sludge. Every film was someone's labour of love — slow, thoughtful, occasionally strange. He and Victorin had spent hours arguing about endings.

Earlier in the week, Victorin had begged him — theatrically, dramatically — to come out for a night on the town. A friend of his, an abstract painter, was opening a new exhibition. Afterwards the entire group planned to hit a nightclub "that plays music too loud for old people but perfect for me," as Victorin had put it.

Max had resisted. Then reconsidered. Then agreed.

Now, at the arranged time, he descended the stairs and knocked on Victorin's door.

It swung open, and Victorin froze.

His eyes widened. His mouth actually fell open.

"Holy shit," he breathed. "No way. Max... you absolute legend."

Max grinned, awkward but pleased. "Too much?"

"Too much? No, you look like you stepped out of a dream painted by someone who hasn't slept in forty-eight hours." He circled Max, snapping his fingers in a little dance of approval. "Women are going to riot. And half the men too."

Max was wearing the suit Dominic had insisted he get, a tailor-made multicoloured suit — a riot of pattern and colour, loud but elegant, tailored to perfection. In his old world it would've looked absurd. Here, it fit him like a declaration: I'm alive. I'm new. I'm allowed to start again.

Victorin clapped him on the shoulder. "Alright, old man. Tonight you party with the youth."

Max laughed, surprising even himself. "Lead the way, troublemaker."

"Gladly."

And together they stepped out into the warm Lorient night — two men from different worlds, literal and figurative, walking side by side as though it had always been this way.

***

**Saturday, 1st September 2012, 9:28 p.m.**
**Parallel universe. Lorient Artist Collective Gallery, Lorient, France.**

The gallery occupied a newly refurbished block in the centre of the city — all clean lines, glass, and white walls glowing under carefully placed track lights. The rooms were crowded but hushed, the kind of reverent murmur that only art spaces manage to command.

Victorin threaded through the crowd with Max in tow, his enthusiasm bouncing off the walls.

"There she is," he whispered, nodding toward a woman greeting visitors beside a massive canvas of swirling violet and green. "Esme."

Max had expected someone loud — some neon-haired creature dripping with paint, the kind of wild soul that fit Victorin's bohemian entourage. Instead, Esme looked like a bank executive moonlighting as a painter. Her charcoal-grey trousers, matching vest, and jacket were immaculate. Her short hair was precisely cut, neat, almost severe.

But her paintings were the opposite: explosions of colour and chaos — sixty works filling the gallery, each a riot of movement.

Victorin performed the introduction. "Esme, this is Max. My new neighbour. He's got taste."

Esme smiled politely.

Max nodded. "Hello, Esme. I love your paintings. They're... fearless."

"Thank you," she said, expression unreadable. "Would you like one? They're disappearing faster than I expected."

Max had already spent time wandering the room, pulled again and again toward the purple-and-green canvas. Up close it was mesmerising; layers of paint collided and overlapped like weather systems on a cosmic map.

"I like this one," he said, gesturing.

Esme slipped her hand lightly around his arm and guided him toward the piece. "Ah. Butterfly Orgy."

The title made him blink. Beside the canvas hung a printed description of the materials and a short imaginative story Esme had written — describing a moment as a child when she became lost in a forest and stumbled upon a swarming, swirling mass of butterflies. The painting suddenly made sense.

"I love it," Max said sincerely. "The way you write about it... it pulls the whole idea into focus."

Esme studied him, really studied him, as though appraising more than his words. "You do love art. I can tell. And that ensemble you're wearing — it's outrageous in the best possible way."

Max glanced down at the tailored, multi-coloured suit Dominic's tailor had created. "Thanks. When I first came here, I saw someone wearing clothes like this and—"

He stopped.

Esme tilted her head, frowning lightly. "When you first came here? Where from?"

Max forced a smile that felt too tight. "A small rural village near Geneva. I barely ever left the farm."

Esme's brows lifted. "Oh. I'm sorry. That sounds like a hard way to grow up. I know someone raised by Shielders."

"Oh." Max didn't trust himself to say more.

But Esme's scrutiny softened. Whatever untruth she detected didn't seem to matter to her. To her, Max was simply a charming older man — stylish, surprising, appreciative of her work.

"Well," she said, brightening, "I'll have the gallery director arrange delivery. No point making you carry Butterfly Orgy home under your arm."

She slipped her hand back through his arm, steering him toward the office to finalise the details — Victorin trailing behind them, already buzzing about the nightclub they would hit next.

***

**Saturday, 1st September 2012, 11:02 p.m.**
**Parallel universe. Wildman nightclub, Lorient, France.**

The Wildman was a sensory overload — a cavernous club pulsing with bodies, colour and noise. Hundreds of young people packed the dancefloor, shifting as one mass under strobes of gold and turquoise. The music was like the electronic dance tracks Max remembered from home, except every few minutes the beat cut dead and some operatic, unhinged vocalist shrieked into the void before the bass dropped again. The crowd loved it.

Max didn't.

He'd retreated to a long, low couch running the length of a mural-covered wall. Like everything else in this world, it had been hand-painted — huge fantasy figures locked in fights, dances, embraces. Erotic, violent, joyful, all at once. It made his head spin.

Across the room, Victorin and his friends were in full flight, dancing like they were trying to summon a god.

Max had just taken a breath when a voice cut through the noise.

"Mind if I sit?"

He turned. A young woman stood before him with a cocktail in hand — luminous skin, neat bob haircut, a light-pink dress that clung to curves in all the right places. Objectively stunning. Max slid over instinctively to make room.

"Sure," he said.

She settled beside him and took a sip of something neon.

"That is a phenomenal pair of threads," she said, nodding at his suit.

"Thanks," Max replied, feeling heat creep into his neck. "I, uh... yeah. It's my... party suit."

She blinked once, slowly. "Right."

Then she smiled politely and turned her attention back to her friends on the dancefloor.

The silence that followed stretched just long enough for Max to feel like an idiot. He glanced at her again — mid to late twenties, confident, poised, absolutely out of his league. But talking was safer than sitting in his own awkwardness.

"Ah — I'm Max," he said.

She looked back, warmth flickering in her eyes. "Clarisse. And now that we're acquainted, tell me something, Max." She shifted a little closer. "What's an older gentleman, in a tailor-made rainbow explosion, doing at the Wildman? You're... not exactly the usual crowd."

Max gave a helpless shrug. "Yes, I know. I'm painfully aware I don't blend in. My neighbour dragged me out tonight. We went to an art exhibition first—"

"Oh! Esme Florin's show?"

Max blinked. "Yes. That one."

Clarisse lit up. "I love her work. Those colours, the movement — she's amazing."

"You know her?"

"Not personally. But anyone who paints like that becomes well-known pretty quickly," she said, watching him with growing interest.

And that was it — the awkwardness evaporated, replaced by a surprising ease. For the next hour, they talked, leaning closer to hear each other over the chaotic shifts between music and screaming vocals. Clarisse asked questions — real questions — and Max found himself answering without overthinking. She found him funny, strangely insightful, and unmistakably different from anyone else in the club.

By the time she placed her hand on his knee, it felt natural.

"Max," she said softly, "would you like to come home with me? It's too loud in here."

He hesitated only a moment, more out of surprise than doubt. "Yes," he said. "I'd like that."

Clarisse stood, took his hand, and led him out into the night. They slipped into the back seat of a taxi, the Wildman's music still thumping faintly through the walls as the cab pulled away.

***

**Sunday, 2nd September 2012, 2:52 a.m.**
**Parallel universe. Clarisse's home, Lorient, France.**

Clarisse Ampère lived in a modest but elegant two-storey home on the outskirts of Lorient — a place with warm lighting, clean lines, and enough quirky décor to make it unmistakably hers. When she and Max arrived, she unlocked the door with the silent caution of someone used to tiptoeing around responsibility.

"My brother's asleep upstairs," she whispered as she hung up her coat. "Fourteen. I look after him."

Max nodded, watching her move — graceful, self-possessed, carrying the weight of a life shaped by loss. Her father had died a few years earlier. Her mother had gone long before that, simply disappearing one day and never returning.

They settled in the lounge — the soft spill of lamplight, two open glasses of wine on the coffee table, and a comfortable silence that didn't feel forced.

Clarisse found Max infinitely refreshing. Men rarely wanted her company; they wanted her body. But Max asked questions, listened, and didn't leer. He was odd — charmingly odd — and more interesting than most people she met in clubs, labs, or anywhere else.

She'd spent part of her twenties working winters in the Alps as a nurse's assistant. She told him about the ski-lift disaster — eight dead, dozens injured, a mechanical failure that had dominated headlines for weeks across Europe.

Max blinked, genuinely shocked.

"I had no idea," he said.

Clarisse frowned at him. "What? Where were you living — under a rock?"

"Like I said... a farm near Prévessin-Moëns."

She held his gaze, unblinking. "Max, you didn't even know about the Première Gardienne. You barely know our history. You don't know events every child learns. What are you hiding?"

He froze — just for a heartbeat — and she caught it. Of course she did.

Her tone sharpened. "Don't insult me. I can tell when someone's lying."

The air between them tightened. Max felt it in his chest, that pull he'd been trying to ignore. He liked her. Liked her enough that deceiving her felt obscene. And she was giving him that look — the one that demanded honesty, not out of anger but out of simple, fierce respect.

He exhaled, a quiet surrender. "All right," he said. "If I tell you, you're not going to believe it. And you can't tell anyone."

It took nearly an hour.

He told her everything — CERN, the portal, the divergence of worlds, the arrest, the jail, the job, the cover story. Clarisse listened, arms folded at first, scepticism plain in every raised eyebrow.

But slowly her posture changed.

She leaned forward.

Her breathing slowed.

Her eyes sharpened.

By the end she wasn't sceptical at all — she was stunned.

"Jesus," she whispered. "No wonder you didn't know who the Première Gardienne is."

Max nodded, exhausted from the telling.

The two of them sat in a quiet that felt heavier than before, but not uncomfortable. The world had just tilted for both of them — differently, but sharply.

Clarisse looked at Max with a new kind of softness.

A decision formed in her mind, sudden and certain: she wanted him in her life. Properly. Not just tonight.

"Would you like some more wine?" she asked gently. "I'll grab another bottle."

Max opened his mouth to reply, but she was already heading to the kitchen.

She rummaged through cupboards, checked under the sink, even looked behind the collection of empty jars kept for recycling — nothing.

"Damn it..." she murmured, then walked back to the lounge.

"We're out of wine," she announced. "But I can offer you—"

She stopped.

Max was slumped in the armchair, head tilted back, fast asleep — deep, unguarded, and gently snoring.

Clarisse stared at him.

"Unbelievable," she muttered.

Then, hands on hips, she sighed with a mixture of irritation and amusement.

"I was going to screw you senseless."

She shook her head, grabbed a blanket from the couch, and draped it over him — her annoyance dissolving into a smile she couldn't quite suppress.

Max slept on, blissfully unaware.

***

**Sunday, 2nd September 2012, 11:35 a.m.**
**Parallel universe. Clarisse's home, Lorient, France.**

Max woke slowly, surfacing from sleep with that strange, weightless moment where he wasn't sure whose ceiling he was looking at. Then the memories from the night before — the club, the conversation, Clarisse — slid back into place. He smiled. He'd met an extraordinary woman, funny, sharp, beautiful... and for hours she'd made him forget every worry he carried.

Max sat up a little straighter in the lounge chair and noticed he wasn't alone. A boy — early teens, mop of dark hair, all elbows and growing limbs — sat cross-legged on the sofa with a bowl of cereal in hand, eyes glued to the television.

The boy glanced over. "Hey. How's it goin'?"

"Ah... good," Max said, clearing his throat. "You must be..."

"Jacques."

"Right. Clarisse did mention she had a younger brother."

Jacques nodded once and turned back to the screen.

Max remembered where the bathroom was and excused himself briefly. When he returned, he settled into the chair again. Jacques didn't mind; he simply nudged the cereal bowl into his lap and continued watching the broadcast — a replay of a major BMX and skateboard event held the previous day.

Max had spent a good part of his life riding a bicycle everywhere, so he could appreciate what these riders were doing — wild, beautiful madness: flips, spins, impossible contortions, all hurled off a ten-metre ramp. Even he couldn't help being impressed.

Jacques, however, was living and breathing every second of it.

"That's Foster," he said without looking away. "Watch, watch — he can spin a seven-twenty easy."

The rider launched, spun twice, and landed so cleanly it made Max's stomach drop.

Max whistled. "Not bad. I liked that other guy... T-something? The one who did that twisty thing."

"TJ. That was a backflip turndown."

"Yeah, that's the one."

Jacques approved of the answer with a tiny nod — the highest honour a fourteen-year-old boy will grant an adult he doesn't yet trust.

Behind them, unseen, Clarisse stood in the doorway watching.

She'd been there for nearly a minute, arms folded loosely, a soft smile blooming across her face. Last night Max had fascinated her — his humility, his strangeness, his heartbreaking honesty about where he'd really come from. And now this: seeing him laughing at BMX stunts, chatting easily with Jacques, fitting into her living room as if he'd always been part of it.

Oh no, she thought. I'm in trouble.

"Good morning, all," she finally said.

"Hey, sis," Jacques replied.

Max turned, startled. "Oh — hello, Clarisse."

Clarisse crossed the room and perched on the arm of his chair, slipping an arm around his shoulders. He looked up at her and she kissed him, a warm, lingering brush of affection that made Jacques oblivious to everything but the screen.

Max stayed for breakfast. When he stood to leave, Clarisse walked him to the door.

"Would you like to spend the rest of the day with me?" she asked. "I have to drive Jacques to his mountain-bike club later. His monthly race meet."

"I'd love to. He's not going to be doing any of those upside-down tricks, is he?"

She laughed. "No. Just racing other kids his age. It's the highlight of his month."

"I can believe it," Max said with a smile.

Clarisse stepped closer. "We've got a few hours before we need to leave."

"Oh? And... what did you have in mind?" Max asked, though her hand sliding into his made the answer clear.

Clarisse leaned in, voice soft, playful, and completely certain.

"Come with me."

She led him toward her bedroom, closing the door gently behind them.

*****

# Chapter 15

**Wednesday, 12th September 2012, 2:35 p.m.**
**Parallel universe. European Advanced Physics Laboratory, Pfronten, Germany.**

The taxi wound through a green valley that looked more like a postcard than a research site. The Pfronten laboratories sat low and wide across the landscape — plain stone buildings, big windows, clean paths. Nothing futuristic. Nothing ominous. Just... competence.

Aimes and Dominic stepped out and took a moment.

"Beautiful place," Dominic murmured.

Aimes nodded. "Hard to look at this and think we're here to build something dangerous."

They headed inside, following signs to the theoretical wing. Felix Köster greeted them at the door of his office with a handshake warm enough to cut through the chill of the mountain air.

"Gentlemen. Come in."

The office was modest: shelves stacked with papers, engineering models scattered on a side table, two whiteboards layered in equations. Through the window the mountains looked impossibly close.

They talked for a few minutes — the usual courtesies — and then Felix leaned forward, turning the conversation to Max and the machine at CERN.

"Max seems convinced they'll try again."

Aimes frowned. "Convinced? After what happened to their drone? Those guns didn't just knock it out of the sky — they shredded it. We know the portal was open at the time, and that blast would've hit the chamber itself."

Aimes sighed. "If the chamber's damaged, then the team at CERN have taken a significant hit to their plans — whatever those plans are."

Felix tapped a finger on the table. "Max agrees. He told me the inner chamber isn't one piece — it's more than a dozen separate segments. Very specialised fabrication.

Difficult to make. But he thinks they'll replace whatever's broken."

Aimes raised an eyebrow. "Replace? That could take months."

"Six, according to Max," Felix said. "Minimum."

Aimes let out a low whistle. "And he's sure they'll do it?"

Felix gave a small, grim smile. "He didn't hesitate. He said they pushed too far to stop now. His exact words were: 'They'll open it again. I know them.'"

Aimes considered that. "So we plan for the portal reopening — but no timeline."

"Exactly," Felix replied. "Could be days. Could be half a year. But it's coming."

"We've been analysing everything Max remembered," Felix said. "Directory structures, CERN's network layout, the quirks in their system he described. And in parallel, we've been decoding the camera your people seized when he was arrested. That part took time."

He reached into the folder he had on the desk and handed Aimes a set of glossy photographs — the camera stripped down on a workbench in Pfronten, every component tagged and numbered.

Aimes flicked through them and gave a small grunt. "It looks ancient."

Felix allowed himself a thin smile. "It is. But digital is digital. Binary's still zero or one, even when the technology's crude. TaloSyn has gone through everything — file signatures, data structures, the behaviour of the recorder chip." He tapped one of the images. "And from that, we're starting to understand how their world handles digital formats."

Aimes closed the last photograph, exhaling through his nose. "All right. That's the camera. Now... what about their computers at this CERN laboratory? Did we learn anything useful there?"

Dominic sat forward. "How much can we expect?"

Felix exhaled — a low sound of disbelief. "More than we thought. According to Max, once you get past the initial login — that absurdly strong password he provided — their entire network is essentially open. No layered permissions. No internal authentication. No meaningful encryption. The system treats every connection as trusted."

Aimes blinked. "None of the usual restrictions?"

"None," Felix said. "Max walked us through the file structure from memory. Project directories, experiment logs, system configs... he described practically everything. If his recollection is accurate, then once we're in, we'll have the run of their system."

Aimes took a moment, letting the implications settle. "So if we manage to get access when the portal opens..."

Felix nodded, a thin smile forming. "Then TaloSyn can extract every file, every document, every scrap of data we'll ever need."

A quiet chime sounded from the small holoprojector on the low table beside Felix's desk — nothing dramatic, just a system coming online. A compact, translucent silhouette lifted from the device, no more than a metre high: an abstract geometric form, rainbow-hued in a muted, shifting way, like light passing through layered glass. It held no face, no limbs — just an artful suggestion of a figure.

TaloSyn's voice emerged evenly, without any hint of presence beyond the projection.

"Aimes. Dominic. Felix. Good afternoon. My friend and colleague Ethan Walker will arrive soon. He has been wanting to meet you two gentlemen."

Dominic exchanged a quick glance with Aimes — not alarmed, just aware they were dealing with something beyond their usual world.

Footsteps sounded in the hallway.

A tall, dark-skinned man in practical work clothes stepped through the doorway — Ethan Walker. Broad-shouldered, self-assured, carrying only a small tablet and the easy professionalism of someone who understood both machinery and people.

He closed the door behind him, nodding to Aimes and Dominic. "TaloSyn's been working hard on analysing Max's information. We can begin whenever you're ready."

The projection pulsed once in acknowledgement — no flourish, just confirmation — then dimmed to a steady, unobtrusive glow.

Ethan turned back to the others, and TaloSyn continued:

"Your colleague Max Rivette provided descriptions of CERN's internal directories that will greatly assist with my plan. When the CERN machine next opens the boundary, their system will broadcast diagnostic traffic. It will be orderly, and it will be enough."

Aimes frowned. "Enough for what?"

The hologram's colours drifted — a quiet swirl, as if thought moved through water.

"Enough for me to follow the noise back to its origin. I do not require passwords. Their machines will not recognise me as foreign."

Dominic looked unsettled. "You're certain?"

"I am prepared," TaloSyn replied.

Not arrogant. Not hesitant. Just factual.

Ethan added. "What TaloSyn means is: yes. It can do it. We simply need a moment of stable contact between the worlds. A few seconds would suffice."

Aimes stared at the holographic figure.

"Once you're in... how fast can you pull their data?"

The figure dimmed to a serene blue.

"Faster than they can detect the loss."

Ethan rested one hand lightly on the desk.

"TaloSyn rarely overstates things."

"Rarely?" Dominic asked.

Ethan grinned. "Never."

Aimes exhaled slowly. "All right," he said. "Tell us what you need from us."

The hologram's colours deepened — like dusk settling across a lake.

"A connection node nearby. And when the portal opens... bandwidth. Enough to hear their machines breathe."

Aimes nodded.

"You'll have it."

***

**Thursday, 25th October 2012, 9:35 a.m.**
**Parallel universe. Aimes Perrier's office, European Security Headquarters, Paris, France.**

Aimes Perrier stood at the window, watching the mix of old stone and new glass across central Paris. The city was changing — shedding decayed relics, replacing them with structures built to last. Some citizens clung to the past with sentimental ferocity, but Aimes had no patience for nostalgia. Progress was the point of civilisation.

Max Rivette, at least, understood that.

He'd read Dominic's latest report that morning. Max had adapted astonishingly well. He worked hard, learned fast, contributed meaningfully, and by all accounts had become valuable both socially and technically. Felix Köster's team had extracted every scrap of information Max could offer and were already making headway.

And then the unexpected footnote: Max had a girlfriend now.

Impossible man, Aimes thought. Falls through a universe, gets arrested, goes to prison, panics, lashes out, ... and within months finds a new life, new career, new romance.

A knock pulled him from his thoughts.

"Come in."

Judge Marcel Rannequin entered first — warm but brisk — and Dominic followed a moment later. They exchanged greetings and took their seats.

Aimes began. "We're here to reassess Max Rivette. I'll be blunt — he's not a problem. In fact, he's become an asset. Productive at work, socially stable, reliable."

Dominic nodded. "His employer loves him. The staff love him. He's settled."

Marcel raised an eyebrow. "Good. And the... situation with his world?"

Aimes leaned back. "Troubling. We deployed the automated gun system and the display, exactly as agreed. We instructed them to cease portal operations."

A pause.

"They ignored it. Tried to send another drone. We destroyed it. And based on the fact we haven't detected any activity since mid-June, we can only assume their machine was seriously damaged."

"Does Max know?"

"Yes," Aimes said. "He's certain Gaidon wouldn't have done anything that reckless on his own, and he thinks someone else — hard-liners, military, whoever opposed his detainment — forced the issue. And if the machine is damaged, he believes they can rebuild the chamber within six months."

Marcel absorbed this quietly, jaw tightening. He had interrogated Max ruthlessly at trial; the violence of Max's world had stayed with him for weeks — the wars, the weapons, the casual cruelty. A damaged world sending another drone wasn't shocking. It was simply who they were.

"So," Marcel said at last. "What's our position?"

Aimes didn't hesitate. "We're preparing. Felix's team continues to refine the theoretical framework. Max has helped immensely. Our models are improving. And we have a small team deployed near the clearing on Renato's farm — round the clock, in case the portal opens unexpectedly. They're equipped to capture any diagnostic traffic and attempt penetration of CERN's networks the moment an aperture forms. In a few months, we expect to understand the physics completely."

"And then?"

"Then we build our own machine."

Marcel nodded once — firm and resolved.

"Good."

***

**Wednesday, 31st October 2012, 1:53 a.m.**
**Control room, Laboratory 888, CERN, Prévessin-Moëns, France.**

The control room sat in near-darkness, lit only by monitor glow and the low hum of cooling systems. Daniel, Baset, and Emerancie had been dragged back to work a week earlier, despite all of them trying to keep their distance. Nicolas Hightower's pressure had been relentless. Even Baset — widowed only days before — hadn't been spared.

They worked through final checks in an uneasy, exhausted silence.

Daniel leaned toward Emerancie, voice barely above a whisper.

"Think this room's bugged?"

She shook her head. "Unlikely. I swept it yesterday. Nothing broadcasting."

"Then why did they go down to the machine room without us?"

Baset didn't answer. He simply pointed at a camera feed.

On-screen, Nicolas, Dragonetz, and Vincent were opening a sealed crate. Inside was a drone — not CERN-built, not even close. Smaller, angular, matte-black. Predatory.

Emerancie whispered, furious, "What the fuck is *that*?"

Baset squinted. "Carbon frame. High-grade. I'd bet it's a third the mass of ours. Look how easily they're carrying it."

Daniel added, "Stealth shaping. Military spec. No question."

They watched helplessly as Nicolas supervised Vincent and Dragonetz strapping the drone to the robot arm that would position it onto the lowered platform from the receiving chamber. No discussion. No explanation. No permission. Just brute authority.

When the Americans finally cleared out, Emerancie let out a shaky breath.

"What are we going to do?"

Neither man answered.

They had no leverage, no protection, and no time.

At length, Baset murmured, "We play it by ear. And if things go wrong... I still have a few tricks."

Before anyone could ask, the control room door snapped open. Nicolas strode in, Dragonetz behind him like a shadow, Vincent close on his heels. The temperature in the room dropped.

Vincent tossed a compact control unit onto the central console — three joysticks, toggles, switches. Purpose-built. American.

Emerancie stiffened. The last time she'd stood this close to Vincent she'd broken his cheekbone. She looked ready to finish the job.

Vincent saw it and smirked.

"What? You gonna hit me again? You craz—"

"Enough," Nicolas said — not loud, but absolute.

Silence. Even Emerancie shut her mouth.

He turned to Baset.

"Status."

Baset kept his voice level. "Machine warmed. Systems stable. Repairs look good."

"When can you open?"

"Whenever you give the order."

"Then open it."

A few keystrokes.

The countdown appeared.

Seven seconds.

Six.

Five.

The room fell utterly still.

Then the shell split open.

The familiar blue haze roared to life — and through it appeared the two massive automatic guns and the towering display screen, both waking like predators sensing motion.

Text scrolled across the display:

DO NOT SEND ANYTHING THROUGH.

FOLLOW COMMUNICATION PROTOCOL.

USE LIGHT MORSE CODE.

WE ANTICIPATE THIS.

The display paused.

Nicolas didn't.

"Shut it down."

Baset obeyed. The haze collapsed and vanished.

Silence reclaimed the room.

The CERN team stared at Nicolas — waiting for the next order, the next threat, the next disaster they'd be forced into.

Vincent broke first.

"So... what now?"

Nicolas didn't bother looking at him.

"We stick to the plan."

He stepped closer to the console, voice low and dangerous.

"Who do they think they are — issuing instructions? Dictating terms?"

A long, heavy pause.

"They've got your draftsman locked in a cell. And we're done playing by their rules."

The message was unmistakable.

The next move would be theirs — not the other world's.

***

**Wednesday, 31st October 2012, 2:12 a.m.**
**Machine Room, Laboratory 888, CERN, Prévessin-Moëns, France.**

The argument had burned itself out. The team were exhausted, furious, cornered.

Nicolas, by contrast, looked like a man discussing tomorrow's weather. He rested one hand on the railing, calm to the point of cruelty.

"Listen carefully," he said. "I have six stealth drones on site. Military-grade. Autonomous. Each with a simple mission profile."

Emerancie snapped, "What sort of profile?"

"To fly, hide, and listen."

Daniel frowned. "Listen?"

"Spy," Nicolas corrected, as if clarifying a stationery order. "They'll bury themselves in the landscape. Their onboard systems will sweep every digital signal they can detect and flag anything of interest. When we open the portal again, they'll transmit everything back in a single encrypted burst."

Emerancie folded her arms, trembling with fury. She didn't trust Nicolas. She trusted Dragonetz even less. But she held her tongue.

Vincent stepped in with a sneer. "It's the only way we'll ever know what's going on over there. Max is gone. We're trying to get him back."

Baset stared at the floor. Powerless.

Daniel looked like he might vomit.

Nicolas continued, unfazed. "One drone is already mounted on the arm. The others are in storage. And yes — I intend to make use of their defence guns."

Daniel opened his mouth, but Nicolas silenced him with a raised hand.

"Let's get back to the control room."

***

"That's enough questions. Baset — start the machine."

Baset typed, each keystroke feeling like betrayal.

The system awoke: timers rolling, relays clacking, fans rising to full speed.

Seven seconds later, the shell unfolded.

The blue window opened.

The other world shimmered into view — crystalline, silent.

The defensive guns stood like the fangs of a metallic predator.

The display screen powered on... then stayed blank. Waiting.

"Baset. Begin the platform sequence."

The repaired hydraulic platform moved faster than it ever had; Vincent had rebuilt and tuned it himself.

The robot arm swung the drone into place. Its electric motors whirred softly, just shy of liftoff.

The platform rose into the haze.

The drone shot forward through the blue membrane—

Gunfire erupted instantly, hundreds of rounds.

The drone climbed eight metres before disintegrating into sparks and carbon shreds.

Emerancie was shaking, white with rage.

Daniel turned away.

Baset watched the telemetry with fists clenched.

Nicolas didn't flinch. Dragonetz didn't blink. Vincent barely registered it.

"Shut it down," Nicolas said. "Next drone in ten minutes."

The portal collapsed. Silence filled the room.

Dragonetz and Vincent left to reload.

Emerancie finally snapped.

"You— You absolute bastard— You'll destroy the machine— You'll kill us all—"

Daniel swore under his breath.

Baset froze. Nicolas stayed silent, unperturbed.

Ten minutes later, Dragonetz and Vincent had returned, the second drone now fixed to the arm.

"Restart the machine," Nicolas ordered.

Baset obeyed.

The shell split open again. The blue haze appeared.

Nicolas leaned in. "Baset — drop the platform."

"Descending," Baset replied.

On the feed, the platform began to sink smoothly out of view as the robot loading system began to ready the drone for loading.

"There!" Vincent pointed. "The farmer."

On the camera feed, the man sprinted through the clearing in his underwear, a rifle in hand. He must have heard the earlier gunfire.

He skidded to a halt about thirty metres out, raised the weapon—

—and his foot slipped sending him to land in the muddy ground. The shot went high, cracking into the trees above the portal.

"Platform loaded," Baset said.

The mechanism reversed.

The platform rose.

The second drone lifted.

A small rocket booster dropped from its belly and fired.

The drone shot upward like a round from a cannon — then, ten metres up, snapped hard left, dropped, and rolled right in a tight, pre-programmed dance.

The defence guns spun and roared — hundreds of rounds in three seconds, a metal chainsaw ripping through the air as they struggled to track the sudden manoeuvres.

They all missed. Not a single strike — and within seconds the guns burned through their ammunition and fell silent.

The drone kept climbing.

Nicolas smiled faintly. His analysts had predicted limited ammunition.

The drone vanished above the treeline.

"All right," Nicolas said. "Begin the second phase of drone operation."

Vincent typed the command.

Instantly, the video feed died.

The portal collapsed to a pin-prick — a glowing mote suspended in the chamber.

Daniel whispered, "Jesus…"

Vincent watched a diagnostic bar crawl across the monitor. "Modules deployed. All four confirmed. They're in quiet mode."

"Good," Nicolas said. "Close it."

Baset shut the machine down.

Nicolas allowed himself a long, satisfied breath.

He had done it.

He had planted eyes in the parallel world.

And no one in the room could stop him.

***

**Wednesday, 31st October 2012, 3:59 a.m.**
**Parallel Universe. Diderot farm, Prévessin-Moëns, France.**

They found it faster than anyone expected.

Barely an hour after the gunfire and the brief shriek of the intruding drone, one of Sauson Bourel's field agents finally spotted the wreck — lodged high in the canopy, tangled like an enormous insect in the forked crown of a beech tree on the edge of Renato's land.

It was the second drone that night. Both times the CERN system had opened the portal, and both times the automated guns had fired without hesitation. Sauson's science team had witnessed everything from the back of their truck, cameras running, flinching at each burst of autocannon fire but sticking to their orders: *observe only, do not approach the clearing unless absolutely necessary.*

During the second deployment, they had even seen Renato himself appear — half-naked, soaked, slipping in the mud as he tried to raise his gun before falling hard out of frame. The team had stayed put, waiting for the firing to stop.

By the time Renato returned — now dressed, mud scrubbed off, still grumbling and furious — more than a dozen operatives had assembled in the partly forested section of his farm, all staring upward at the drone carcass.

Renato marched over, breath hot with anger. "What the hell were you all doing? You heard the guns — twice! Why didn't anyone move? Why didn't you respond?"

Sauson stepped forward. "Because we're under strict orders not to go near the clearing unless we have no choice," he said firmly. "We stay back, we record, and we wait for the right moment." He glanced at Renato's clean shirt and trousers. "Glad to see you came back properly dressed this time."

Renato folded his arms, still simmering but listening now. "Fine," he muttered. "But next time, shout a warning at least."

Harsh portable floodlights had been set up around the area, throwing white columns of light into the branches and catching the drone in a stark, unnatural glow. Shadows from the team stretched long across the grass.

The drone looked nothing like the sleek devices from CERN.

This thing was unsettling — a compact matte-black core with eight spindly limbs, each limb coated in a mesh so fine it resembled the threads of a spider web. The mesh had snared branches as it fell, suspending the machine upside-down in the leaves, the lights glinting off the carbon like wet bone.

Renato spat on the ground. "Fucking bastard thing. Why the hell don't they listen? We tell them again and again — stay out."

Sauson glanced sideways at him, hands in his coat pockets. "You really do hate their toys."

"Hate them? They're vermin. Every time that machine of theirs opens, something goes wrong."

Up the tree, one of the operatives straddled a wide branch like a seasoned climber. He unclipped a handheld unit from his harness — a flat slate with a ring of sensors — and swept it slowly across the drone's body. The floodlights caught the arc of the scanner beam, thin and blue against the machine.

Renato shaded his eyes. "What's he doing now?"

"Multispectrum scan," Sauson said. "Checks for radiological signatures, shaped charges, chemical residues. Anything that might explode or poison half the valley."

"Hmph."

A soft tone sounded from the scanner. The agent looked down and shouted, "No immediate threats. Continuing."

He shuffled along the branch until he was close enough to work on the drone. A small toolkit appeared from his belt.

Renato watched the man loosen a panel no bigger than a hand, unscrewing it one deliberate twist at a time.

"Carefully," Sauson murmured under his breath — more habit than instruction.

Another scan — deeper, longer, confirming the interior was clean.

Then came the delicate part.

The agent threaded a sling under the drone's central body and clipped the line to his harness. A few minutes of work with the knife, and the last strands of webbing gave way. The machine came free, and he lowered it slowly toward the forest floor until two team members stepped forward to take its weight. The lights lit them from below, throwing their faces into sharp planes.

"Got it," one of them said.

"Good," Sauson replied. "Let's move."

They carried the drone out of the trees, past the ruts in the dirt road, and toward the waiting convoy — half a dozen matte-grey technical vans parked in a neat row, rear doors open like receiving mouths. Headlamps from the vehicles added a second tier of illumination, cold and clinical.

Renato walked behind them, shaking his head.

"They'll never stop, will they?"

Sauson didn't answer. The truth was obvious:

***

**Thursday, 1st November 2012. 7:02 p.m.**
**Parallel Universe. Diderot farm, Prévessin-Moëns, France.**

Floodlights washed the roadside on the edge of the farm in cold white light. A ring of high-powered transmission masts surrounded the temporary perimeter, linking the field site directly into TaloSyn's network. Cables snaked across the ground toward a large matte-grey truck whose rear doors had been folded open to form a makeshift laboratory.

Inside, stripped panels of the captured drone were laid out on stainless-steel trays. Its bare chassis sat on a cradle of padded supports, bristling with probes, clamps, and diagnostic taps. A half-dozen engineers worked in tight formation around the exposed circuitry — murmuring, checking, typing.

Sauson Bourel stood at the open doorway of the truck, arms folded. His breath fogged the air. He watched the activity with the same expression he'd worn since the drone was recovered: a mixture of irritation, unease, and a very controlled anger.

Ethan Walker stepped out from behind a rack of monitors, wiping his hands on a cloth. Tall, broad-shouldered, effortlessly athletic even in the unflattering lab overalls, Ethan looked as if he could have been a weightlifter rather than the most respected computer scientist in the syndics.

"Alright," Ethan said, voice deep and unhurried. "You wanted an update."

Sauson gestured at the gutted drone. "How can you be sure of anything this quickly? You've had it for—what?—a day?"

Ethan gave a small shrug. "We've had practice."

"You mean the camera. Max's camera."

"Exactly. That little thing forced us to decode a completely foreign operating environment. File structures, compression formats, the whole computational philosophy behind it. Once you've reverse-engineered one artefact from the other world, the second one goes a lot faster."

He rested a hand on the drone's small central processor node.

"And this," he said, "is built from the same family of logic. Simpler, actually. Less elegant. They've leaned heavily on brute-force processing and hardware redundancy."

Sauson frowned. "Meaning?"

"Meaning their engineering is competent," Ethan said, "but unimaginative. Function over finesse. We've seen enough to map how the subsystems talk to each other."

"And you're certain it's a spying device?"

"Oh yes," Ethan said quietly. "It's purpose-built for reconnaissance. Four onboard microcomputers, each specialising in different kinds of data."

One of the engineers at a nearby terminal turned and held out a stapled printout.

"We anticipated your next question," she said. "This is the phrase-map."

Sauson took the stack. Twelve pages of terms, sorted by priority, printed in crisp black text.

The very first line made his stomach knot:

MAXIMILIEN RIVETTE — PRIORITY 01

Sauson flipped the page.

Lines of related keywords followed:

trial, court, detention, sentence, security, tribunal, arrest, Max, Rivette, prison, release...

Then, on the next page, the tone shifted sharply:

weapons

armour

military capability

munition yield

air power

naval assets

satellite imagery

strike radius

threat response

civil defence

He let the page droop. "So this is what they're desperate to know."

"They're frightened," Ethan replied. "And ignorant. They know almost nothing about us, so they're grasping at shadows."

Sauson tapped the list. "And what does the drone do with the data is receives from our network traffic?"

A young systems engineer answered from behind him. "Most of it gets discarded after parsing. Anything matching the priority clusters is cached."

"And then?"

Ethan leaned against a workbench. "Every four hours — to the second — it sends a burst transmission. Massive data rate. A firehose lasting about two minutes."

"Encrypted, I assume?"

Ethan's mouth twitched into a small, satisfied smile. "Was encrypted."

Sauson raised an eyebrow.

"We cracked it in four hours," Ethan continued. "TaloSyn handled the heavy lifting."

Sauson glanced toward the corner of the truck where a single console sat quiet and dark — except for the faint pattern of shifting colours moving across the glass, like slow breathing.

TaloSyn wasn't active at the moment, but its presence was unmistakable.

Watching. Listening.

Always.

Ethan crossed his arms. "We're now reading every packet the drone tries to send home."

"And the next transmission?"

"Fifty-one minutes," Ethan said, checking his watch. "We'll capture it cleanly."

Sauson let out a slow breath. "And the other thing you hinted at? Gaining access to their network?"

Ethan nodded. "Max's descriptions gave us just enough to build a scaffolding model. Combined with what we pulled from their storage media, we found the weak seams."

"TaloSyn found them," corrected one of the engineers.

Ethan didn't bother denying it. "Yes. With TaloSyn's help, we've infiltrated the peripheral parts of their network. They won't notice unless they start looking very hard."

"Will they look?"

Ethan shook his head. "They don't know we intercepted this drone. And they don't know we're reading its transmissions. They think they've slipped something past us."

He paused, then added in a low voice:

"And to be fair — we are doing exactly what they're doing. Gathering information. Preparing for what we don't yet understand."

Sauson folded the pages, thoughtful. "And the drone's mission? How many keywords relate to weapons?"

"Too many," Ethan said. "They're terrified we might be the threat. And we're terrified they might."

For a moment, both men looked at the silent, spider-limbed machine on the examination cradle.

It had fallen out of the sky less than 24 hours ago.

Now its deployment was a window into the mind of another world.

And that mind was afraid.

***

**Thursday, 1st November 2012, 8:00 p.m.**
**Parallel Universe. Diderot farm, Prévessin-Moëns, France.**

The drone's stripped torso sat on the workbench like a dissected insect, its transmitter module blinking a faint, steady pulse. Sauson stood beside Ethan in the cramped rear of the laboratory truck while the rest of the team clustered in the doorway behind them, watching the final seconds tick down.

"Transmission window opens... now," Ethan murmured.

The blinking sped up.

No dramatic sound.

No flare of light.

Just a tiny diode flickering away as if entirely unaware it was betraying its creators.

Sauson lifted a handheld radio. "Clearing team, status?"

A voice crackled through, baffled.

"No blue shell, sir. Nothing. And no sound from the machine."

Sauson frowned. "What? It must have opened."

"Not that we can see."

Sauson lowered the radio slowly. "So they've figured out how to open it at a microscopic scale." He exhaled. "Of course they have."

Ethan was focused on a diagnostic panel. "It's definitely connected. Protocols exchanged cleanly. They got the whole packet."

The blinking light slowed... then stopped.

"That's the full dump," Ethan said. "Two minutes on the dot. It's also taken instructions from their side."

Sauson turned. "What sort of instructions?"

Ethan raised his right hand — the glove on it lit with faint tracking dots — and made a calm series of gestures. Windows flicked across the monitor at speed.

"Refinement directives," he said. "They want the drone to concentrate less on what it hears in the wild, and more on attempting to access structured networks."

Sauson stiffened. "Government?"

"Oh yes. They want the crown jewels." Ethan continued swiping through data. "Which is... optimistic. And stupid."

"And dangerous," Sauson said.

"No. Not dangerous for us." Ethan angled the monitor so Sauson — and everyone crowding behind him — could see. "This is where TaloSyn steps in."

Sauson gave him a puzzled look. "You're letting TaloSyn handle the counter-espionage?"

"TaloSyn insisted."

"So what's the plan?" Sauson asked.

"A little theatre," Ethan said. "We're letting the drone's logic believe it has a fighting chance. TaloSyn will pretend the encryption on our outer systems gives it trouble — a few milliseconds of artificial 'struggle' — then allow the drone to 'break through' just far enough to think it's found something valuable."

"And what will it actually see?"

Ethan tapped one final command.

The monitor stabilised.

A video feed appeared.

It was Renato's kitchen.

Sauson stared. "What in God's name..."

The video cut again.

Now Bibiane swung through the frame, draped in a feather boa, laughing so hard she nearly fell against the table.

Another cut.

Renato, on his veranda, leading a conga line of locals wearing floral shirts and drinking punch from jars.

Another cut.

A karaoke moment — someone butchering a power ballad in spectacular fashion.

Another.

A slow pan across a barn filled with dancers, strobe lights, beer kegs, and questionable life choices.

Then—

The lights dimmed.

The music swelled.

Renato — unmistakably Renato — burst across the frame wearing nothing but cowboy boots, seen from behind, gyrating like a man possessed.

Gasps filled the truck.

Someone choked.

Someone else wheezed.

One of the engineers actually applauded.

Ethan folded his arms, entirely deadpan.

"TaloSyn thought this constituted 'sufficient cultural disinformation'."

Sauson covered his face with both hands. "They're going to think we run a government composed entirely of... whatever that is."

"Oh no," Ethan said lightly. "TaloSyn made sure the metadata labels it as an official broadcast channel."

The screen froze on a particularly heroic shot of Renato's bare backside mid-dance.

Sauson lowered his hands, stared at it, and groaned.

"My God," he whispered. "We've just introduced the CIA to Community Television: Hedonism Edition."

Behind him, one of the younger techs muttered:

"Imagine them analysing that for military significance."

Ethan didn't miss a beat.

"They'll spend weeks trying to work out whether the naked man is a general."

The entire truck erupted in laughter.

Even Sauson couldn't contain a small, helpless, horrified smile.

***

# Chapter 16



**Monday, November 19th 2012, 8.30 p.m.**
**Nicolas Hightower's office, American embassy, Geneva, Switzerland.**

The phone lit up at exactly 8:30 p.m.

Langley's interim leadership didn't tolerate drift — not after the political firestorm that had detonated around Petraeus. Michael J. Morell had been shoved into the Acting Director's chair the moment the scandal broke, and he'd inherited a mess: a furious President, a shaken Agency, and the revelation — dropped on Obama in a heated argument — that the CIA had been sitting on intelligence about a CERN machine capable of opening a parallel universe.

Morell had made it clear from the first hour: there would be no more surprises.

The encrypted line opened with his clipped, controlled voice.

"Nicolas. Michael Morell."

No preamble. No apology for the chaos back home. Just the man brought in to clean up a secret the President should never have had to drag out of his own intelligence chief.

"I'd like to get straight to it," Morell said.

"Of course."

"I've read your latest intelligence summaries. They're thin. Too thin — especially now that the President has been briefed on your operation. And let me be clear, Nicolas: he found out from us, not from you."

Nicolas said nothing — long enough for Morell to register it.

"I've gone through the reports in full," Morell continued. "I can see your current angle is to dig up anything on this Maximilien Rivette — the guy who kicked the whole thing off in the first place."

"Yes, sir. We still haven't found anything useful. No media references to Maximilien Rivette anywhere in their networks. And the open-access citizen registry showed no match."

"That registry is confirmed? An entire population index visible to anyone?"

"Yes. Like a universal phone book. But he's not there. We checked every variant of his name."

"Not surprising," Morell muttered. "If someone from another universe landed here, we wouldn't parade them in our databases either."

He pushed on.

"Your techs also report that the internal government systems are impenetrable."

"That's correct. Very heavy segmentation. They can't even map the edges of the network."

A brittle pause.

Morell's tolerance for roadblocks was measured in seconds.

"Alright. Let's shift focus. I've just come from a briefing with the scientific review team. Their assessment is blunt: this experiment is the single greatest leap in physics since the discovery of the atom."

Nicolas stayed silent. Morell hated interruption.

"And yet," the Acting Director continued, "there are areas of it they barely understand what they're looking at. They're reverse-engineering a cathedral while standing in the dark with a single match."

After a brief pause Morell continued, "That's the problem. Gaidon Ballerat has had thirty years to build this secret field. And Mittermayer... my people tell me his algorithm — the one governing the ionisation stage — is so specialised several of my experts don't even have vocabulary for it."

"So here's what I need. Apply pressure. Not stupidity. Pressure. Enough to make those two understand we expect full cooperation."

"Understood."

"I want to know exactly what that machine does now, and what it could be adapted to do. I refuse to believe they built a doorway to another universe without exploring other capabilities."

"I'll see to it."

"Good. And Nicolas—"

Morell's voice flattened into steel.

"—never underestimate people who believe they're the moral superior. They will lie with absolute sincerity."

The line went dead.

Nicolas set the handset down slowly.

Another order, another storm coming.

***

**Tuesday, November 20th 2012, 11:07 a.m.**
**Daniel Mittermayer's apartment. Geneva, Switzerland.**

"Daniel, I'm grateful you'd see me. I've got a few more questions."

"OK. But before we start — did the spy drones find Max?"

"No. We've hit a complete dead-end. All we can do is hope they told the truth — that he's safe, and will eventually come back."

"OK. Thanks."

Nicolas studied him.

The reports painted Daniel as a once-in-a-generation mind — the theoretician who'd effectively created a new field — yet he looked like an art student dressed on a dare: violent green corduroy suit, yellow shirt, mismatched shoes.

A savant wrapped in a circus.

Nicolas pressed on.

"I'm here about how the machine is controlled. Specifically, the algorithm that powers the electron guns."

"Sure. What do you want to know?"

"The team says the more they have looked at this machine, the less they understand. The lead scientist called it 'the most esoteric field of physics ever developed.'"

Daniel couldn't help a grin.

"That's what you get when you spend a decade—"

"I get it," Nicolas cut him off. "You're a genius. But that doesn't explain why you won't explain it properly."

Daniel bristled. "I haven't withheld anything."

"Bullshit."

Nicolas leaned in. "My people say you're evasive about how the algorithm was derived and key details as to how it works. They think there might be some possibility to have it work in the manner that you originally designed it for. To open a portal within our world."

There — a tiny twitch at the corner of Daniel's mouth.

Silence.

Daniel looked down.

Got you.

Nicolas lowered his voice.

"There's something you're not saying."

Daniel closed his eyes — a man cornered by truth.

"Yes," he whispered. "There is."

A long, shaky breath escaped him.

"After the original RACE machine failure Gaidon and I spent weeks modelling every aspect of the machine. Changing it. Re-configuring it. Just understanding it — testing every parameter on the CERN supercomputer, in isolation to know what's safe."

Nicolas waited.

"And we found something we didn't want to find," Daniel said. "Two things, actually."

Nicolas straightened.

Daniel continued:

"First: if the coordinate parameters could be altered — and I stress could, because we never attempted it — the maths suggests the machine *might be* able to open a portal between two points in this universe. Any two points."

Nicolas blinked. "As in... anywhere on Earth?"

Daniel nodded reluctantly.

"There are eighteen parameters in total. Six of them — the coordinate set — define position and orientation. Our models imply they could, *in theory*, map to locations inside this universe just as easily as across universes."

"You're telling me we could open a portal inside Vladimir Putin's bedroom?"

Daniel grimaced. "If the machine worked that way — yes, essentially."

Nicolas almost smiled.

Daniel didn't.

"That theoretical possibility terrified Gaidon," he said. "He was convinced that if governments... your government... ever realised it, the machine would become a military system overnight. Instant insertion. Instant extraction. Zero defence. A logistical and strategic weapon beyond anything in history."

Nicolas said nothing.

"But that wasn't the worst of it," Daniel added quietly.

"The military angle is fear number one. The one we could imagine. The one we could predict. The one humans would absolutely exploit."

Nicolas swallowed. "And the second fear?"

Daniel's expression shifted — from anger to something like dread.

"When we modelled that same-universe scenario," he said, "the simulations revealed a catastrophic failure mode. One we never told anyone about."

Nicolas's posture stiffened.

Daniel continued, voice low:

"The white-hole envelope only remains stable because it's paired to a black-hole construct in another universe. The geometry depends on separation — two ends of the same topology held apart by spacetime."

"Meaning?" Nicolas asked.

"Meaning that if the machine ever operates within this universe, the envelope loses its external counterbalance. The stabilising topology collapses. And the white-hole surface can invert."

Nicolas frowned. "Invert how?"

Daniel swallowed.

"Invert into a black-hole surface. Instantly. No warning. One moment you have an expelling envelope... the next, a collapsing one."

The room seemed to tighten around them.

Daniel pressed on.

"In our models, the inversion produces a microscopic singularity — nanometres across, but already consuming the chamber in femtoseconds. It cascades immediately: chamber, lab, valley... whatever mass it touches. There is no containment. No shutdown. Once it begins, it feeds."

Nicolas whispered, "Christ..."

"That's why we buried all the research," Daniel said. "We never published the calculations. We never told the committee. A same-universe operation isn't a weapon or a tool. It's an extinction event waiting for that careless parameter adjustment."

Nicolas finally asked, "How sure are you?"

Daniel didn't blink.

"I can't give you probabilities. But the physics is uncompromising.

We believe if the machine ever operates fully in this universe, the white-hole envelope can invert.

And if that happens..."

He exhaled.

"...it kills everything."

***

**Wednesday, November 21st 2012, 10.30 p.m.**
**Nicolas Hightower's office, American embassy, Geneva, Switzerland.**

"Thanks for taking my call at short notice, sir."

"That's alright, Nicolas. What's going on?"

Michael J. Morell's voice was steady — the voice of a man holding the CIA together after Petraeus's implosion.

"I spoke to the young scientist yesterday — Daniel Mittermayer — and he finally came clean."

"Oh? Good."

Nicolas hesitated.

"Yes and no."

Morell didn't interrupt.

"He confirmed the machine might be capable of opening a portal within this universe — not just into the parallel one. It's theoretical, but the maths supports it."

"I suspected as much," Morell said. "Some of our analysts hinted the physics might allow it."

"Yes, sir. But there's a problem. A serious one."

Nicolas took a breath.

"Daniel says the whole thing hinges on generating a new control 'key' — a prime number so long it needs a supercomputer to validate. If the key's wrong by even a fraction, the simulation either fails... or worse."

"Define 'worse.'"

"He believes — strongly — that an incorrect key could collapse the white-hole envelope. Meaning a microscopic black hole forms in the chamber. Instantaneously. And from there, it swallows the earth into it, then the sun."

A heavy silence.

Morell blinked once, slowly.

"Jesus Christ... you're serious."

He rubbed a hand over his face, trying to regroup.

"So one typo, one wrong key, and poof — planet gone? Not damaged. Not irradiated. Just... gone? Us, the oceans, the dogs, the bloody moon — everything?"

He let out a rough, humourless laugh.

"Shit... that's the sort of thing you shut the whole project down for and pretend it never happened. But we can test this on a computer, right?"

"Yes. I believe so."

He looked back at the speaker, jaw tight.

"Alright. I'll need a full report on this."

"Agreed, sir. And he wasn't manipulating me. He was terrified. A physicist terrified of his own equations."

Nicolas pushed on.

"I also put him on the phone with Gaidon Ballerat. They've agreed to produce a full disclosure report — every risk, every failure mode, all of it. It'll be ready by Friday."

"Good. We'll review it as soon as it lands."

Morell exhaled sharply — the sound of a man dealing with problems at geological scale.

"On another matter: I spoke with the President this morning. He wants any future drone flights stopped."

"Understood," Nicolas said. "No more provoking the defence guns."

"It's not just that," Morell continued. "He's seen the intercepted video footage your team forwarded — there was a lot of some community TV station from this town Prévessin-Moëns."

Nicolas winced.

Morell went on, dry as concrete:

"The President's exact words were: 'All we know for sure is that the farmer likes to dance around butt naked.' Then he told me to shut down the spy programme altogether. We've learned nothing, so it ends."

Nicolas pinched the bridge of his nose. "Yes, sir."

"The President wants a different approach. Open the portal, use lights, send Morse. Ask for proof of life. Anything. A message, a photograph — whatever they'll give us. We need to know this Rivette kid is alive before we proceed with anything else."

"Yes, sir. I'll pull the new CERN team together. Give me a few days."

"Make it happen, Nicolas."

The line clicked dead.

***

# Chapter 17



**Friday, 7th December 2012, 9:35 a.m.**
**Parallel universe. Aimes Perrier's office, European Security Headquarters, Paris, France.**

The position of Première Gardienne had never been created for power.

In a society governed by the Twelve Rules, the role existed simply because people occasionally needed someone calm, steady, and persuasive enough to coordinate between regions. Maxine Jacquet had resisted the appointment for years — which, of course, made her the obvious choice.

Her only privilege was clothing: a small collective of designers insisted she dress impeccably for the rare moments she faced a camera. Today she wore a pale-blue tailored suit over a soft rose blouse, the kind of look that implied effortless authority — classic, sculpted, sophisticated — the unmistakable aura of a woman who could still a room with a single raised eyebrow.

She sat opposite Aimes Perrier, drumming her fingers once, lightly, the only sign she was displeased.

"Let me understand this clearly," Maxine said, voice smooth but edged. "They were warned — explicitly — not to send anything through the portal."

"Yes," Aimes replied. "The computer displays made that point unmistakable."

"And yet they sent two more flying machines."

"A spying device, Première Gardienne," Aimes confirmed. "We recovered the second intact. Ethan Walker's team — along with TaloSyn — opened it and uncovered everything. It analysed our signals, our speech, our networks... the usual arrogance."

Maxine's eyes narrowed — thoughtful, not angry. Even her irritation had a surgeon's precision.

"What have we learned about the operators on their side?"

"From Max's testimony, the original CERN scientists were curious, not hostile," Aimes said. "The behaviour now? Entirely different. Our analysts believe someone else has taken control — military, or intelligence."

"That is consistent," Maxine murmured. "Curiosity sent Max here. Militarism sent those drones."

A moment of silence.

Maxine looked out toward the winter skyline — old stone meeting new glass, evolution instead of erasure. It was a view she considered a responsibility.

"And if they escalate again?" she asked quietly.

Aimes hesitated. He knew that beneath Maxine's calm sat an unwavering line: the safety of the people.

"We don't have many options," he admitted. "We can warn them. Or we can shut them out."

"You mean destroy the portal on their side," Maxine said.

"Yes."

She considered the idea with chilling clarity — not as a threat, but as engineering.

"Place an explosive charge in the shell the moment it opens," she said. "It would end this permanently."

Aimes nodded.

"And they could rebuild it eventually."

"Yes," she said. "But the message would be unequivocal."

A knock on the door.

"That will be Max," Aimes said.

Max entered with Dominic beside him. He froze for a heartbeat when he realised who was present.

Maxine stood — gracious, warm, unmistakably commanding.

"Hello, Max. I'm pleased to finally meet you."

"Hello, Miss Première Gardienne— ah, Maxine," he stammered.

She smiled. "Please take a seat gentlemen."

They sat. Aimes began without ceremony.

"Max, it has been nearly six months. Your sentence was precautionary. We now consider you no threat at all."

He slid a thick folder across the desk.

Max barely looked at it. The moment was too heavy for paper.

Maxine leaned forward. "Your world's behaviour has shifted. The drones they sent were gathering military information. That is not curiosity — that is fear. Fear becomes danger."

Max's face fell. "This isn't CERN. Gaidon would never do that. Someone else must be in charge. Someone military. And... my non-return probably triggered it."

Maxine absorbed this, then asked gently but firmly:

"Do you wish to return to that world, Max? Truly?"

Max's answer came slowly. "I love the life I've found here. I've learned more in six months than in twenty years back home. I've met someone... I'm finally happy. But yes. I need to go back. Not to stay — to explain. To tell Céleste what happened. And to show them this place works. They won't believe any of it without something real."

Dominic seized the moment.

"We were thinking the same. Let Max take a message. A video. Examples of how our system of Twelve rules works here. TaloSyn has tested his old camera — we can expand the storage and match the encoding."

Aimes nodded. "Exactly. A clear demonstration of life here. No threats, no demands — just truth."

Maxine's expression softened. "Would you help us create that message, Max? You understand both worlds better than any of us."

Max nodded. "Of course."

Maxine smiled. "Good. And please remember — you return alone. No one else crosses that threshold."

"Understood."

Aimes added, "There's one more thing. Over the past few nights, CERN has been sending us Morse messages every two hours — always at set times, always in darkness so the lights show clearly. They've asked repeatedly for 'proof of life.' They want to see you."

Max's breath caught — relief, worry, hope all tangled.

Aimes continued. "If you're willing, we can arrange to meet them at the farm tomorrow night. We'll signal the time at the next two-hour window."

Max nodded, more certain now. "Yes. I'd like that. And I'd like to see Renato and Bibiane again."

Maxine rose and took his hand, steady and warm.

"Then let's begin. If your world can be changed, Max... you may be the one to start it."

For the next hours, they worked together — drafting, planning, imagining the audacity of peace.

***

**Saturday, 8th December 2012, 8:35 p.m.**
**Parallel universe. Diderot farm, Prévessin-Moëns, France.**

The helicopter skimmed low over the winter-bare fields, its downdraft scattering dry leaves across the frost-hardened soil. It settled behind Renato and Bibiane's barn, rotors slicing the cold night air. Max stepped out and braced against the bitter wind — the kind that cut straight through clothing and into bone.

Bibiane got to him first, wrapping him in a fierce, maternal hug that crushed the cold out of him for a moment. Renato followed with a heavy slap on the back. Dominic received polite, cautious handshakes.

They walked toward the forest. Their breaths billowed in white plumes. The mud beneath the thin crust of frost clung to their boots, sticking and releasing with wet sucking sounds as they crossed the dark fields. Sparse moonlight spilled over the late-season crops, turning them silver.

Max spoke about his work in Lorient, about Clarisse, about the strange exhilaration of living in a world governed by the Twelve Rules. Renato and Bibiane updated him on the farm, the failing tractor, the weather turning sharply colder.

By the time they reached the treeline, they'd fallen into an easy rhythm of talk, the familiar voices softening the cold.

Dominic raised a hand.

"Alright, Max — the gateway's scheduled to open at nine. Ten minutes. Last chance: are you still willing?"

"Yes."

Dominic nodded. "Good. Since last time, we've installed cameras, hardened comms relays, and"—he gestured vaguely—"all the hardware the engineers insisted on."

Renato snorted.

"Oh yes. 'Hardware.' Two bloody war cannons."

Dominic suppressed a grin. "Defensive measures only. And I am going to turn them off. For now."

Bibiane pulled her coat tighter, breath trembling in the cold.

"And what stops Max from simply... walking home?"

Dominic surprised them all with his plain answer.

"Nothing. He's free to go if he chooses."

Max felt their eyes on him — three silhouettes in the dim glow of their portable lamps, watching him breathe clouds of white into the night.

The pull of the old world flickered — familiar streets, familiar voices — but it was a ghost now, not a home.

"I'm staying," he said. "At least until my year is over. And after that, I only want to return long enough to explain, to show them what exists here. Then I come back. I've found a life worth living — and someone worth loving."

Renato smiled. Bibiane squeezed his hand. Dominic gave a small, approving nod.

"Alright." Dominic checked his phone, disabling the automated weapon stations. "Safe to proceed."

They stepped into the clearing.

The night was harsh and still — the kind of air that burned the lungs. Portable floodlights had been placed at the perimeter, throwing pale cones upward into the bare branches. Beyond them, the forest was pitch black.

The ground still bore the faint circular scallop where the gateway touched soil, but the clearing now resembled an austere forward outpost. Two communication signs stood like pale sentinels. Two matte-grey weapon stations loomed at the corners of the clearings, tall cylinders with twin barrels jutting from their centres. Their metal caught the cold light and gleamed under the strong sharp lighting. It reminded Max of the artillery weapons Max had designed for Nexter.

Dominic checked his watch.

"One minute."

Max asked, "Do we know who they're sending?"

"No."

Dominic drew a compact pistol — unadorned, practical, completely controlled in his hand.

In the stark floodlight, Max saw the truth of him clearly: a man who had been too close to violence too many times.

The gateway opened with a violent, instantaneous concussion — a shockwave that slapped the air and made the farmers flinch. A four and a half metre diameter sphere of blue transparency erupted into existence, crackling faintly along its edges like frozen lightning. The steel platform inside descended, humming from somewhere below ground.

Then it rose again.

A figure stepped through the shimmering curvature.

A tall, bearded man in his sixties — lean, composed, wearing a light grey suit, eyes that measured everything. He moved with the clipped assurance of someone accustomed to command.

"Hello, Max," he said. "I'm Nicolas Hightower. I'm now in charge of the experiment at CERN."

Max stepped forward but kept distance. Something predatory lived beneath the politeness.

"What happened to Gaidon? I expected him."

"He's still with the team. Just not in charge."

A glance at Dominic, then at Renato and Bibiane — a quick threat assessment. "After your... disappearance, I was assigned to bring you home."

"Are you alright, Max? Treated well?"

"Yes."

"I understand you were charged as a spy. Detained for a year. That true?"

"Yes."

"But you're a draftsman. That's absurd."

"I was sent here to gather information," Max said carefully. "They have legitimate security concerns."

Half the truth. The other half — his world's instinctive militarism — Nicolas didn't deserve to hear.

"We don't like not knowing what's on the other side," Nicolas said.

Max almost laughed.

"You control the gateway. You send machines through. You ignore warnings. What exactly do you fear from them?"

That hit its mark. Nicolas stiffened.

"You have nothing to fear," Max continued. "This world is peaceful. They only want you to stop sending drones."

"And you?"

"I finish my year. Then I return. If you'll open the gateway."

"Of course. People back home are worried sick. Your aunt Céleste—"

"Tell her I'm fine," Max said. "Tell them all."

Nicolas took a step closer.

"You sure you don't want to come back now? We've reinforced the machine. Added defensive systems. Armed teams. You'd be safe."

Max recognised the lie instantly.

"No. I'm staying until the year is done."

Nicolas assessed him — no hesitation, no fear.

"Very well. I'll report that you're alive and unharmed."

He backed into the shimmering sphere. The platform dropped. The gateway vanished with a sudden implosion of light and a muffled *whump*.

The clearing fell silent — the only sound was the winter wind.

Max turned to the others.

"He's CIA. Not a scientist. And he lied about the weapon system in their machine."

Dominic holstered the pistol.

"Thought as much. Let's head back. Aimes will want this report immediately."

Renato clapped Max on the shoulder, breath fogging in the cold.

"Good performance, Max. Very diplomatic."

Max exhaled — relief, resolve, and the first real warmth of hope cutting through the winter night.

He wasn't just surviving here anymore.

He was shaping the future of both worlds.

And for the first time since stepping through the gateway six months earlier, Max knew exactly where he belonged.

***

**Saturday, 8th December 2012, 10:26 p.m.**
**Parallel Universe. Diderot farm, Prévessin-Moëns, France.**

Max stayed on after Dominic's helicopter lifted away toward Paris, its lights dwindling over the dark fields. Aimes had been relieved — genuinely relieved — to hear that Max was committed to the plan and had handled the meeting with the American calmly. With that done, the tension of the night slowly dissolved into something far kinder.

Renato and Bibiane insisted he stay the night. "No arguments," Bibiane had declared, wagging a spoon. "You've had a day. You're not going anywhere."

By late evening, the farmhouse felt like the heart of the world.

The long dining table — already enormous — had sprouted extra chairs dragged in from sheds, the porch, even the tractor garage. It still wasn't enough. People lined the walls, perched on armrests, sat cross-legged on the floor with plates balanced on their knees. Three dozen neighbours had wandered in as they always did whenever Renato announced one of his "celebrations of life."

It wasn't a party so much as a ritual: good food, laughter, arguments about vegetables, too much wine, music turned up just a little too loud.

A warm human tide.

Max found himself seated midway down the table, caught between conversations. The room smelled of baked apples, herbs, woodsmoke and spilt red wine. It was chaotic and friendly — the sort of night his old world had somehow forgotten how to make.

Bibiane settled opposite him, smiling with that same mix of mischief and maternal warmth she'd shown the morning he first arrived in their universe.

"So," she said, nudging a bowl of roasted chestnuts toward him, "your new girlfriend — Clarisse, oui? You must tell me everything."

Max felt himself blush, which Bibiane found delightful.

"She's twenty-seven," he began. "She works as an industrial chemist. Very clever. And... she's just..."

He trailed off, trying to find the right word.

Bibiane supplied it for him.

"Good for you."

He laughed. "Yes. Exactly that."

Bibiane's outfit — a short red skirt and a pink shirt patterned with swirling colours — was pure Bibiane: loud, joyful, unapologetically alive. She leaned in conspiratorially.

"And does she adore you as much as you clearly adore her?"

Max tried not to grin too hard. Failed.

"I think so."

Bibiane clapped her hands once, delighted. "Then that is that. You are staying for breakfast tomorrow so I can hear the rest."

Across the room, Renato popped open another bottle of wine and shouted, "To Max! The only man we know who can cross universes and still remembers to visit!"

Everyone cheered. Someone banged a ladle on a pot.

Max, laughing despite himself, raised his glass.

For the first time since he'd crossed into this world, he felt something simple and pure settle in his chest.

He belonged here.

At least for a while longer.

And tonight — surrounded by warmth, by chaos, by people who treated him like family — that was enough.

***

# Chapter 18



The school didn't look like a school.

Max had expected classrooms — rows of desks, glossy walls, that vaguely chemical smell of floor polish. Instead he stepped into a huge open hall carved into the southern edge of the shipyard itself. Sunlight cascaded through towering windows that overlooked cranes, dry docks, and half-finished hulls. Inside, the air hummed with purposeful noise — teenagers building, arguing, laughing, focused in that effortless way young people are when they're doing something that actually matters to them.

He paused by a brass plaque:

*Centre d'Essais Techniques pour Jeunes Curieux*

Technical Exploration Centre for Curious Youth.

Finally, a name that said exactly what it meant.

A woman in her forties approached with grease and oil smudged hands and a tired knot of hair. Practical overalls, a pin labelled *Mireille* — Coordinatrice.

"Welcome," she said. "Arguis mentioned you'd be filming around the shipyard. He said you were curious about how the students work."

"That's right," Max said. "Just gathering footage. Nothing formal."

"Good. They'll ignore you after the first minute," she said. "Let's go for a walk."

One section of the hall was glass-walled to contain the noise — a compact machining workshop, small in footprint but equipped with full-scale, professional tools. Racks of scrap alloy, and an array of tooling, workbenches arranged like small engineering bays.

A cluster of students were gathered around a milling machine, mid-argument.

"It'll chatter in the final pass," a girl in a yellow hoodie said flatly.

"It won't," the boy opposite insisted. "Your feeds are too conservative."

Mireille leaned toward Max. "They're building a gearbox for a pedal cart."

"To race?" Max asked.

She shook her head. "To help an elderly neighbour haul firewood in winter."

The girl noticed Max's camera and gave a brief nod of acknowledgement — nothing more.

"If you want a test cut, we're about to run one," she said, already turning back to the machine.

They clamped a small block of alloy into place. One student loaded a toolpath. The machine spun up, smooth and confident.

Max leaned in instinctively, watching the cutter skim through metal with a flawless finish.

"This equipment is better than what we had at CERN," he muttered.

The boy shrugged, amused. "Factories upgrade. We get the older models. Still great machines."

Max swallowed the tightness in his chest and kept filming.

Up on a mezzanine, the atmosphere softened. Low couches, coffee tables, sketch tablets, proof models, and several teens sprawled in comfortable chaos. Every screen ran UniGraphNext — the same drafting suite Max had learned at the Lorient shipyard.

A boy of about fourteen waved a distracted greeting as they approached, but didn't stop working.

"I'm redesigning a folding kayak," he said, eyes fixed on his tablet. "Arguis says I'm overcomplicating it again."

Max leaned down. Across the screen: a cascade of iterations — early blocky forms, refined hinge studies, then elegant solutions emerging step by step.

"You designed all this?" Max asked.

"Yeah. I take the kayak out every weekend. Carrying it on the tram sucks. So I'm fixing the problem."

Mireille nodded. "Their interests shift, their projects shift. We just make sure they have the tools."

Max filmed quietly as the boy adjusted a hinge angle with the casual fluency of someone who had never been taught to doubt himself.

Further in, the smell shifted to solder and warming electronics. Dozens of teens worked on circuits, microcontrollers, and code. Max spotted a stripped-down harbour rescue drone — just like the ones he'd seen over Lorient.

A girl with braided hair noticed they were passing and gestured briefly.

"We're rewriting the controller firmware for the rescue system."

Max frowned. "That's real hardware."

"Not this unit," she said. "Training model. But the code ports fine."

Her screen showed crisp, disciplined logic — cleaner than some professional code Max had reviewed at CERN.

A boy nearby added, still typing, "Working on new failsafes. Storm visibility's a nightmare."

The girl nodded. "We want it to recognise when the operator's lost orientation and stabilise automatically."

They weren't performing for him. They were simply explaining the task they were already doing.

Max filmed without interrupting.

After an hour, Mireille brought Max to a balcony overlooking the full hall. Below, dozens of teenagers shifted between work and laughter, concentration and improvisation — a living engine of curiosity.

"Everything they need is here," Mireille said. "Tools, mentors, community, purpose."

Max let the camera run as he spoke softly, more to himself than to her.

"This... this is exactly what my world needs to see."

Mireille tilted her head. "Part of your film?"

"Part of the truth," Max said.

Emotion rose sharp and unexpected. He looked away.

Mireille noticed, but didn't comment. She simply offered a small, knowing smile.

He kept filming until the battery died.

*****

**Saturday, 22nd December 2012, 10:20 a.m.**
**Parallel universe. Max's apartment, Lorient, France.**

Max had just finished setting up the small tripod on his kitchen table when the screen of his laptop computer lit up. Felix's face appeared — tired, unshaven, surrounded by the muted chaos of a lab in full swing.

"Morning, Max," Felix said. "Quick update."

"Yeah, go ahead," Max replied.

Felix pushed his glasses up, then leaned closer to the camera. "We're past the halfway point on the machine simulation runs."

Max nodded. "And the physics simulations?"

"Promising," Felix said. "Terrifying, but promising."

He hesitated — a rare thing for Felix — then continued.

"We're close to reproducing the exact stability curves of your world's machine. TaloSyn scraped the data logs from CERN to cross match against our computer modelling."

Max leaned back in his chair. "How long until you begin to build the machine?"

Felix exhaled. Long. Slow. Honest.

"Six months, maybe more. We've got every file, folder and drawing from CERN but this is still an enormous challenge. But we're getting closer every day."

A softer look passed over Felix's face — unusual, almost out of character.

"You doing alright, Max?"

"I'm good," Max said. "Busy. Filming. Asking questions. Learning things I never imagined existed."

Felix nodded. "Keep doing that. Whatever you bring back to your world... it might matter more than you realise."

Max swallowed, feeling the weight of that truth settle into him.

"I will," he said.

The call ended. The room went quiet again.

Max sat there for a moment, staring at the blank screen, realising that for the first time since arriving in this world... he wasn't confused anymore.

He had a purpose.

*** 

**Tuesday, 25th December 2012, 11:32 a.m.**
**Parallel universe. Max's apartment, Lorient, France.**

Max opened the door just as Clarisse raised her hand to knock.

She laughed, surprised.

Behind her, Jacques — all elbows, enthusiasm, and teenage curiosity — gave Max an eager wave.

"Joyeux Noël," Clarisse said, stepping in and kissing him lightly on the cheek.

The apartment smelled of roasted vegetables, fresh bread, and the citrusy steam from the pot on the stove. Max had spent the entire morning cooking. Not because it was expected — no one in this world cared about gifts or spectacle — but because today felt worth the effort.

Jacques wandered immediately to the balcony.

"Whoa. Look at the harbour from up here."

Max smiled. "It's even better at sunset."

They settled around the small dining table. Three plates. Simple decorations: a sprig of holly from the communal garden downstairs and a beeswax candle Clarisse had made herself.

They ate. They talked. They teased Jacques gently about his chaotic haircut.

At one point, Clarisse rested her hand on Max's wrist and whispered, "This is perfect."

For a moment, he couldn't reply.

Six months ago, he'd spent time alone in a concrete cell — six weeks of isolation, fear, and confusion.

Now he sat here, sunlight warming the table, surrounded by people who wanted him, not out of duty but out of affection.

He realised — quietly, suddenly — that he belonged.

Clarisse noticed the look on his face.

"You're thinking something serious."

"Just... grateful," Max said. "I didn't grow up with family Christmases. My parents died when I was tiny. My aunt raised me, but—"

He shrugged. "This feels different."

Jacques grinned. "Because we're more fun?"

Clarisse flicked him on the ear. "Because he's loved, idiot."

A soft knock sounded at the door.

Max opened it to find Victorin, scarf crooked, hair wind-tousled from cycling.

"Only stopping by," Victorin said, handing over a loaf of still-warm brioche. "Didn't want to interrupt. Just wanted to wish you a peaceful day."

"You're part of the family now," Clarisse called from the table. "You can interrupt whenever you like."

Victorin chuckled, eyes kind. "Then I'll come for dessert later."

He left as gently as he'd arrived.

Max closed the door and looked back at the table — Clarisse smiling, Jacques stealing another roasted carrot, the candle flickering warmly between them.

He exhaled, slow and steady.

For the first time in his life, he understood what a home actually felt like.

***

# Chapter 19

**Wednesday, 2nd January 2013, 9.12 a.m.**
**Machine Room, Laboratory 888, CERN, Prévessin-Moëns, France.**

The machine room thundered as always — a constant, bone-deep roar of pumps, coolant lines, and high-frequency inverters. Conversation here didn't travel; it dissolved into vibration. It was perfect camouflage.

Daniel stood by the diagnostic console, pretending to scrutinise a thermal graph. Constantine slipped through the access door, ducked under a thick cable bundle, and joined him.

"You picked the right place," Constantine said, pitching his voice just enough to cut through the noise. "We could be reading poetry at each other and nobody would know."

Daniel gave a thin smile. "That's the idea."

Constantine leaned a little closer, the industrial hum swallowing the movement.

"I spoke with Nicolas Hightower. They've given up on the parallel world. Completely. They've stopped chasing the drone data."

A flicker of relief warmed Daniel's chest — brief, fragile.

Then he saw Constantine's expression.

"And now?" Daniel asked.

Constantine let out a frustrated breath.

"Now they want something worse. Nicolas is pushing hard. They're demanding we shift resources — heavy resources. They want master-key testing simulations."

Daniel went still.

Constantine pressed on, voice tight.

"They want to brute-force the master key. New combinations. Massive sweeps. They told me to allocate double the supercomputer time. Possibly triple."

Daniel's fingers tightened around the railing.

"How many keys?" he asked.

"As many as we can generate," Constantine said. "Tens of thousands. Hundreds of thousands if the cluster holds. Nicolas called it a 'strategic evaluation'.

Daniel looked back at the lattice towers humming behind them. The machine he had helped build. The machine he feared in ways no one else at CERN truly understood.

"They won't find it," Daniel said quietly.

Constantine frowned. "You sound certain."

"I am."

Daniel turned slightly, letting the noise swallow everything but the shape of his words.

"There is one key, Constantine. One topology that stabilises the white-hole envelope across universes. Derived from constraints so narrow they might as well be cosmic coincidence. The more I think about it, the more I believe it was... engineered. "

"And any other?"

"Fails," Daniel said. "Every single one. They can test a million keys. Ten million. A trillion. None will work. The portal will never open inside this universe. The physics won't allow it."

Constantine blew out a breath — frustration mixed with relief.

"They'll be furious when nothing works."

"They'll blame us first," Daniel said. "Then the mathematics. Then reality itself."

He took another breath. "But this is the safest path. If Nicolas insists on testing, we let him test. Because nothing they try can succeed."

Constantine rubbed his forehead.

"I hate wasting this much compute time. Half our winter run schedule will be stalled."

"I know." Daniel's voice softened. "But if we push back, they'll assume we're hiding something. Cooperation is safer. And it costs us nothing — because the outcome is already fixed."

Constantine's shoulders lowered, tension easing.

"So you'll work with him?"

Daniel nodded.

"I'll cooperate. Exactly as they want. Run the simulations. Validate the keys. Document the failures. Then present the results."

A thin, weary smile. "Physics will do the rest."

A deep rumble shuddered through the floor as one of the coolant pumps switched cycles.

***

**Saturday, 19th January 2013, 10:42 a.m.**
**Parallel universe. Flowers hotel, Paris, France.**

Max followed Félix Charlier — the Lorient shipyard's contacts manager — through the revolving doors of the Flowers Hotel, a grand old building whose marble floors had survived three centuries and many architectural revolutions.

Inside, the largest conference room had been cleared of the usual arrangement of furniture. No stage, no podium, no seating plan. Just a series of long modular tables arranged in a loose circle, already crowded with folders, tablets, cups of coffee, metal samples, and three half-finished pastries someone had abandoned during an argument.

Max breathed in the atmosphere — bright, chaotic, alive.

This was planning day.

And anyone could attend.

Félix gave Max a conspiratorial smile.

"Welcome to the great annual metals circus."

Max blinked. "There are... fifteen delegates?"

"Sixteen," Félix corrected. "The Australians sent two this year — one for bauxite, one for finished aluminium. And before you ask: yes, they fight. Every time."

As they approached, Max saw the group in full force.

Two German steel syndics were arguing with a Swiss machinist over rolling tolerances. The Swedish stainless representative kept loudly insisting that chromium shipments had been delayed because the Norwegians were "hoarding cranes again." The Australian bauxite pair were animatedly describing the state of their coastal fleet to anyone who would listen, including a horrified Belgian.

In the middle of it all, the rare-earths group — three people in faded mining jackets — waited patiently, sipping tea.

Félix stepped forward and clapped once, sharply.

The room settled. Mostly.

He introduced Max, and then the meeting began — not with a chairperson, but with whoever felt like speaking first.

Today that was the Swedish stainless delegate.

"We can meet Lorient's stainless quota," she said, "but only if we get the new heavy rolling machines your yard promised last year. The old ones are chewing through bearings like they're made of cheese."

Félix nodded. "We've nearly finished the prototype. Thirty percent stronger, safer to maintain. But to manufacture it at scale, we need a guaranteed supply of ultra-fine titanium powders."

All eyes turned to the rare-earths group.

Their spokesperson shrugged cheerfully.

"We can do that. But our separation rigs are dying. We need replacement actuators. Strong ones."

One of the Germans leaned forward.

"You get us a detailed spec, we'll build them. But we want something too. We'll provide mild steel slabs for Lorient — the full annual tonnage — but only if we receive the specialised lift-arms for the mining vehicles we're upgrading."

The Australians laughed. "Good luck getting the lift-arms. We need those same components for the new dry-dock cranes."

"Then propose a swap," someone muttered.

"We just did!"

"No you bloody didn't!"

Voices climbed over one another while tools scraped, chairs shifted, and a stack of diagrams skidded dangerously close to the edge of the bench.

Max braced for a meltdown — the kind that, in his old world, ended with slammed doors and stonewalling.

Instead, the rare-earths miner, an older woman with dust in her hair and the calm of mountains in her eyes, raised her hand.

"Friends," she said simply.

The room fell quiet.

"We all know the rule," she continued. "Everyone leaves with enough. No one leaves with everything."

Félix exhaled in relief.

"Exactly. Let's break it down."

He moved around the circle, drawing out needs, constraints, and offers.

It took hours.

Whiteboards filled. Coffee vanished. Two people shared a sandwich by quietly tearing it in half. Someone's toddler wandered in at one point and was immediately given crayons and a dedicated corner of the table.

Max filmed everything.

He was stunned by one thing above all:

No one in the room was protecting a profit margin.

They were protecting function. Community needs. Safety. Efficiency. Reliability.

By late afternoon, the final jigsaw piece clicked.

The Germans would supply mild steel in exchange for specialised lift-arms and maintenance systems.

The Swedish stainless syndicate would receive the new rolling machines in exchange for doubling the chromium share for Lorient's hullwork division.

The Australians would secure fifteen new coastal-class ships built at Lorient — in return for prioritising refined aluminium and bauxite allocations for the shipyard for the next five years.

The rare-earths group would get their actuators, and in return provide the exotic powders the atomic-scale printers needed.

Everyone signed the allocation report.

No one looked disappointed.

Max leaned over to Félix.

"Does it always end this well?"

Félix gave a proud, almost paternal smile.

"It always ends fairly. That's the point."

Max looked around the room — stained coffee cups, tired faces, warm handshakes, laughter growing again now that the work was done.

It felt... sane.

Human.

Hopeful.

And he knew the camera footage he'd captured today would be gold — not for propaganda, but for truth.

A glimpse of a world where coordination wasn't imposed from above.

A world where cooperation wasn't a fantasy.

A world that worked because everyone in it wanted it to.

*****

# Chapter 20



**Wednesday, 30th January 2012, 9:35 p.m.**
**Parallel universe. Lorient General Hospital, Lorient, France.**

Max followed the night-shift coordinator through the double doors and into the emergency ward.

For a moment he simply stood there, taking in the noise, the movement, the strangely familiar rhythm of a hospital doing its best to outrun chaos.

Clarisse had warned him.

Not about the blood — he expected that.

Not about the pace — he'd seen that in films.

But about people.

The sheer weight of their private tragedies.

"Just shadow tonight," the coordinator said. "Observe. Ask questions. Hand things to people when they ask. And don't faint."

Max gave a nervous smile.

He wasn't entirely sure that last one was guaranteed.

The first hour was easy.

A woman in her fifties with a persistent cough who left with antibiotics.

A teenager who'd fallen off a BMX bike and was more embarrassed than injured.

A man needing stitches who apologised for wasting everyone's time.

A cheerful nurse fitting a temporary dental mould for an elderly man who had wandered in at 11 p.m. saying, "My teeth don't fit anymore and I can't sleep."

Max almost laughed — not out of mockery but out of the absurd wholesomeness of it.

A hospital that also did dental work at night.

And nobody paying.

Just people helping.

Then the mood changed.

A young woman was brought into a quiet room, breathing fast, arms wrapped around herself as though holding her ribs together.

Max and a psychiatrist sat with her.

She spoke in broken sentences — about feeling "wrong", about "failing", about lying awake every night convinced her life didn't matter.

Max expected trauma. Abuse. Something catastrophic.

But as the questions continued, it became clear:

She was just desperately, chronically lonely.

When she stepped out to use the toilet, the psychiatrist let out a long breath and murmured:

"She doesn't need medication.

She needs someone to eat dinner with."

Max felt it like a punch.

This world — organised, fair, non-hierarchical — still had the same aching emptiness that money and politics couldn't explain or fix.

He nodded, quiet.

The psychiatrist clapped him gently on the shoulder.

"We'll connect her with a local circle. They're good people. No one here gets left alone for long."

Before Max could reply, the radio crackled.

A voice, tense.

Traffic accident.

Two patients inbound.

Serious.

Everything shifted — voices sharpened, bodies moved with a speed that wasn't panic but precision.

Max followed the trauma team into the resus bay.

Two stretchers burst through the doors.

A young man, conscious but sobbing uncontrollably.

A young woman, unconscious, blood pooling beneath the stretcher, skin too pale.

Max stepped aside as the professionals took over.

They cut clothing, called vitals, adjusted tubes, pushed drugs.

He heard fragments:

"Blood pressure dropping—"

"Right pupil blown—"

"Where's the crash data—?"

"Breath sounds absent left side—chest tube now—"

The man on the other stretcher was screaming her name.

"Élodie! Élodie wake up—please—please—"

A nurse held him in place, speaking softly, firmly, grounding him with her hands.

A doctor leaned close to Max and whispered:

"He admits to drinking. His friend disabled the safety monitor in the car. The car refused to start — so they hacked it. Clever idiots."

Max felt his stomach turn.

So even here — in a world without corporations, without advertising, without the cult of consumption — human stupidity still found a way.

The trauma surgeon arrived — a tall, thin black woman with the kind of presence that made everyone step back half a metre without thinking.

She examined Élodie, her face set into the unreadable calm of someone who has done this too many times.

She issued orders without raising her voice.

Needles moved.

Machines hummed.

Blood transfused.

For twenty minutes they fought.

Then her hand froze on the girl's sternum.

The monitors told the rest of the story.

The surgeon looked at the girl, then at the team, and gave the tiniest shake of her head.

Everything stopped.

No alarms.

No chaos.

Just silence that stretched across the room like a scream with no sound.

The young man realised before anyone spoke.

He collapsed forward, a howl tearing out of him — not words, not language, just primal grief.

The nurse caught him as he folded onto the floor.

Max felt tears building before he could stop them.

The surgeon stepped away from the table, pulled off her gloves slowly, almost delicately.

She walked into the small anteroom beside the resus bay.

Max watched her through the glass.

At first she stood perfectly still.

Then her shoulders began to shake.

She pressed both hands to her face.

A soft, broken sob escaped her, then another, and then she slid down the wall until she was sitting on the floor, elbows on her knees, forehead resting on her palms.

No one interrupted.

No one pretended not to hear.

This was part of the job here — not a crack in professionalism, but an acknowledgement of humanity.

Max turned away, unable to watch without falling apart himself.

He had seen harshness in his capitalist world — violence, poverty, cruelty — but this hit differently.

Here, even in a world designed to spare people unnecessary suffering, the worst suffering still found its way through.

Human frailty.

Human error.

Human heartbreak.

Clarisse had been right.

He was confronted.

Not by brutality — but by its inevitability.

By the realisation that even in a better world, tragedy would always, always happen.

But the care...

The solidarity...

The compassion that pulsed through the hospital like a second circulatory system...

That was different.

That was worth bringing back.

Max wiped his eyes.

He understood now.

His home-world didn't need perfection.

It needed this.

People doing the right thing because it was the right thing.

Not for money.

Not for prestige.

Just because the person in front of them needed help.

***

**Wednesday, 6th February 2013, 2:17 a.m.**
**Data Centre, CERN, Prévessin-Moëns, France.**

The room felt hollow at this hour.

Rows of monitors glowed with simulation windows. A dozen plots pulsed in angry reds and blues. The hum of the supercomputer filled the silence like heavy weather.

Daniel leaned forward in his chair, elbows on his knees, eyes locked on the screen.

He looked exhausted.

But alert.

Almost afraid.

Nicolas stood behind the circle of scientists, arms crossed. He had been pacing minutes earlier. Now he had settled into a simmering impatience.

"Run it again," Daniel said quietly.

The physicist at the console — Dr. Lebrun — nodded and tapped a few keys.

The simulation restarted.

A new master key.

A new attempt to configure the machine to open a portal within this universe.

The same disastrous outcome unfolded.

The containment chamber appeared on screen — its virtual geometry rendered with perfect precision.

The portal shell formed.

The electron-gun lattice stabilised.

And then—

The white-hole envelope inverted.

Instantaneously.

What should have been an expelling surface became a collapsing one.

A black singularity bloomed — microscopic, maybe a nanometre across — yet already devouring the chamber in femtoseconds. The simulation stuttered as the numbers skyrocketed.

The mass-accretion plot went vertical.

Earth gone in 4.2 seconds.

The Sun swallowed 37 seconds after that.

The solar system erased before the minute mark.

The model froze on the final frame: a small, stable black hole drifting alone where the Sun had once been.

Lebrun exhaled shakily.

"Same as the last fifteen runs."

Daniel rubbed his face with both hands. "Because we still don't understand the relationship between the key and the shell geometry. And they want us to guess."

Nicolas stepped forward.

"Enough. You're telling me every configuration except the one you used — the one that got Rivette lost — ends in total annihilation?"

Daniel turned in his chair.

"Yes," he said bluntly. "Because the original key worked for reasons we still don't understand. It wasn't luck. It wasn't brute force. Someone — somehow — found a perfect fit for the underlying physics. And until we know why, using a new key is like firing a gun at our own heads and hoping for a misfire."

Nicolas scoffed.

"You're exaggerating. The computer is a model. Models fail."

Daniel almost laughed.

"Not at these scales."

Gaidon's absence pressed like a weight on the room; his suspension left Daniel carrying all the dread alone.

Lebrun brought up a new graph — a simple line chart that climbed from sanity into cosmic terror.

"Look," Lebrun said, voice low. "A black hole with a radius of one nanometre has a mass of about a billion tonnes. It forms, and then the argon shell collapses . Once it exists, there is nothing to stop it."

Another physicist — Dr. Keller — added, "And because the event horizon forms instantly, there is no meaningful window for intervention. Light can't escape. Certainly no human action can."

Nicolas glared at the monitor.

"You're telling me this machine could destroy the Earth in less time than it takes to tie a shoe?"

Daniel replied with cold precision.

"In less time than it takes to blink."

Silence.

Nicolas's jaw clenched.

"This... has to be wrong. We need progress. Not more doomsday charts."

Daniel rose from his chair — slowly — as if tired of protecting the man from the truth.

"*Listen* to me," he said, voice firm but not raised.

"If we run the wrong key on the actual machine, the first sign of failure will be the machine casing collapsing inward at a significant fraction of the speed of light. Then we die. Then the planet dies. Then the Sun."

Keller added softly, "You cannot threaten a singularity, Mr. Hightower. You cannot bargain with it. It is pure geometry."

***

# Chapter 21

**Friday, 8th February 2013, 6:06 p.m.**
**Parallel universe. Max's apartment, Lorient, France.**

Max opened the door.

Ethan Walker stood in the hallway — tall, dark-skinned, athletic, carrying that steady, grounding presence Max had heard so much about.

"Max," Ethan said warmly. "Good to finally meet. Félix Köster speaks very highly of you."

They sat at Max's kitchen table, half-covered in cameras, memory cards, cables, coffee cups, and a forest of scribbled notes. Ethan unfolded a compact workstation and tapped the edge of the screen.

"I stitched together the four strongest clips from your police rotation," he said. "Rough edit only. But it's good. Really good."

Max nodded. Suddenly nervous.

"Alright. Let's watch."

Ethan dimmed the lights.

The screen lit the room.

***

Clip One — "Synthetic Hammer"

A shaky, streetlamp-lit frame.

Valentin Marin crouched beside a teenager sprawled on the curb, screaming between ragged bouts of retching. His hands shook so hard his whole body trembled; sweat poured off him in sheets.

Two terrified friends hovered uselessly.

Valentin checked the boy's pulse with clinical calm.

"Heart rate's high, but not danger-high," he murmured. "He's on Synthetic Hammer. Cut-rate chemistry. Too many uni kids playing mad scientist."

The boy screamed again — a long, hysterical wail.

Valentin didn't flinch.

"You're safe, Louis. It's going to pass. Keep breathing."

A paramedic jogged into view.

Valentin stood.

"Take him to the clinic. His family doesn't need to see him like this; it'll shame him. Let him come down first."

The stretcher lifted the boy away.

Ethan paused the footage. "You caught that perfectly. Raw, but dignified."

Max swallowed. "It shook me."

"Good," Ethan said quietly. "It should."

***

Clip Two — The Cinema Brawl

Night. Neon lights flashing OFFRE SPÉCIALE across the pavement.

Two men hammered at each other while a stunned crowd watched.

Valentin shoved through bystanders, breathless but focused.

"Stop!" he barked.

One man turned on him — bloodied lip, furious eyes.

"He stole her from me! She's mine!"

Valentin stepped in so close their noses nearly touched.

"No," he said calmly. "She is not anyone's. And if you love her, mon ami... you will stop behaving like a child."

Confusion killed half the man's anger.

Maëlle Dupré — towering, muscular, carved-stone expression — hauled the second man forward by his collar.

"Both of you," she said. "Mediation office. Tomorrow. Ten sharp. Wear clean shirts."

A ripple of uneasy laughter passed through the crowd.

***

Clip Three — Domestic Violence Call

A cramped apartment.

Anna stood at the doorway, mascara smeared, clutching a half-empty glass like it was a prop she'd forgotten how to use. Her mood swung every few seconds — angry, tearful, defensive, back to angry again.

Marc sprawled on the couch, heavy-limbed and glassy-eyed. His knuckles were raw. He reeked of alcohol and stale sweat.

Anna waved her arm vaguely toward him.

"I didn't— I wasn't even— he just... he starts, and then I— you know what he's like, it's not—"

Her voice snapped upward suddenly.

"Marc! Look at this— look at *you*! You're *useless*!"

Marc mumbled something into his chest, then lurched upright, swearing under his breath — half-formed syllables, more noise than words.

Valentin stepped in quickly, hands raised but calm.

"Marc. Sit down. Not like this."

Marc blinked at him as if trying to remember who he was.

"Don' tell me... don'— she's the one... she—" His arm jerked toward Anna. "She's always— always yap... yappin'—"

"Sit," Valentin said again.

Marc wavered — then lunged, sudden and stupid, aiming himself more at the general direction of his wife than at any real target.

Maëlle moved before Anna even realised he'd shifted.

A sharp step, a hooked leg, a twist of her hips — Marc hit the floor face-first with a grunt, limbs sprawling like dropped laundry.

He tried to push up, but Maëlle already had a knee in place and his arm trapped cleanly behind him.

"Stay down," she said, not unkind, just done.

Anna staggered back against a wall, pointing at everything but the problem.

"This is so— so stupid! We were fine! We were— he was fine till you— you people turn up and stick your— your *rules* everywhere—"

Valentin took Marc's wrists as Maëlle cuffed him. Marc slurred a messy protest:

"Didn't... didn' do... nuffin', she... she started— she always— always—"

Valentin hauled him up with steady hands.

"Alright, mate. Enough. We're finishing this outside."

Anna kept muttering, spinning in circles of blame — at Marc, at the police, at the walls.

Neither officer reacted. This was normal for them. Friday-night normal.

Only when Marc was secured and Anna was no longer in reach did Maëlle look over at Max, who had stayed a few steps back, camera steady, completely unobtrusive.

Her voice was low, weary, matter-of-fact — the voice of someone who handles a dozen of these before dawn.

"Make sure your film shows the truth," she said. "This is what real policework looks like."

***

Clip Four — At the Station

Filmed discreetly from a corner:

Valentin and Maëlle in the break room, hands around steaming mugs.

Maëlle stared at the wall. "Some nights I want to throw my badge in the river."

Valentin nodded. "Pain doesn't disappear in a good society. We just try to stop it becoming permanent."

Maëlle snorted. "Speaking of permanent pain — whoever invented Synthetic Hammer? I'd like a word."

"With your fists?" Valentin asked.

"Yes," she said honestly. "But I know it won't fix anything. So... no."

They laughed — exhausted, hollow. The kind of laugh that only comes from surviving humanity at its worst.

Valentin's voice softened.

"Most people are fine. The damaged ones... they learn to tuck it away until it leaks out."

***

Silence.

The screen went black.

Ethan leaned back. Max realised he'd been holding his breath.

Ethan spoke first.

"You didn't shoot propaganda. You shot the truth. Your world needs to see exactly this. Not perfection. Compassion."

Max's voice caught.

"It surprised me. Seeing the same old problems. The same human failures."

"Yes," Ethan said. "The same pain. Except your world punishes pain."

He touched Max's shoulder gently. "This world treats it."

His eyes stayed on the blank screen — seeing far beyond it.

Ethan's voice was quiet but certain.

"Let's build the rest of your documentary with that clarity. Not: 'look how perfect we are.'

But: *'look what becomes possible when no one is allowed to give up on anyone.'*"

Max nodded slowly.

This wasn't just video footage.

It was a message.

A challenge.

A mirror pointed at the world he came from.

***

**Friday, 15th February 2013, 9:15 a.m.**
**Parallel universe. Lorient Naval Shipyard, Lorient, France.**

Max arrived early, as always — coat dusted with salt-wind, coffee still steaming in hand.

The engineering office was already humming softly, screens alive with wireframes and part trees, the usual murmur of early-morning concentration.

For the last week he'd been working shoulder-to-shoulder with two other drafters on the redesign of the componentry inside the rear access doors of the H-47 maritime rescue drone-carrier — dozens of small articulating brackets, micro-servos, safety interlocks. Small details. Big consequences.

He was in the middle of explaining a geometry constraint when the conversation died mid-sentence.

Footsteps approached.

Max looked up.

Nadine Verchoux and Jean Pacaut were walking toward the cluster of engineers, both smiling in that unmistakable "we're here on purpose" way.

Nadine folded her arms lightly.

"Hello Max. How are you this morning?"

"I'm well," Max said, trying not to sound nervous.

"It's come to my attention," she continued, "that you've completed your last test for the entrance exam."

"Yes. Yesterday."

He exhaled. "It wasn't easy."

Nadine's smile widened.

"Well... you did extraordinarily well. You scored ninety-seven out of one hundred. That puts you in the top bracket — and the computer analysis flagged your adaptive constraint work as..." She glanced at Jean. "...exceptional."

Before Max could reply, a ripple of laughter spread through the office.

Arguis was approaching.

Slow, determined steps.

Jeans.

A pale yellow T-shirt that shouted I AM THE PARTY above an image of a jubilant semi-naked man being hoisted aloft in a nightclub.

Under his arm, something framed.

Nadine chuckled as he reached them.

"Perfect timing, Arguis."

The old man nodded, eyes warm, face creased with pride.

He stepped forward and held out the frame.

"Max," he said, voice gravelly with age and sincerity, "I am proud to have been your teacher. You have worked with focus, humility, and genuine joy. Your dedication to the craft is obvious."

Max took the frame with both hands.

It was a certificate — hand-lettered, calligraphic, precise, beautiful.

For a draftsman, it meant more than any printed award ever could.

A wave of applause rolled outward through the engineering office.

Chairs scraped back.

People emerged from cubicles and workstations, smiling, clapping.

Within seconds there were nearly a dozen people around him — each shaking his hand, patting his back, congratulating him.

Jean raised his camera above the crowd.

"Alright — picture time! Everyone squeeze in!"

They gathered around Max as if he'd been part of the team for years. Arguis stood proudly at his side. Nadine placed a supportive hand on his shoulder.

"Perfect," Jean said, firing off several shots. "Got it!"

Max stood there for a moment, framed by colleagues, laughter, morning light.

He felt something unfamiliarly strong flood his chest.

Belonging.

Recognition.

A kind of pride he had never earned in his old world — thirty years of service, and not once had anyone stopped to tell him he had done well.

Here, in a world he had stumbled into by accident, people saw him.

And celebrated him.

Max swallowed hard.

He wasn't sure whether to laugh or cry.

It didn't matter.

Everyone around him understood.

***

**Sunday, 17th February 2013, 8:47 p.m.**
**Daniel Mittermayer's apartment, Geneva, Switzerland.**

The knock came long after dark.

Daniel glanced up from the kitchen table — papers everywhere, two emptied mugs, laptop closed. He knew who it was before he reached the door.

Nicolas Hightower stepped in without waiting for permission. Calm on the surface, but with a brittle, clipped edge in his movements — a man holding too much frustration under too much discipline.

"Daniel," he said. "Tell me about the core structure of the algorithm."

Daniel closed the door.

"What about it?"

Hightower paced once through the living room, stopped, and fixed his stare on him.

"You told us the master key — the prime — never changed between the original RACE experiment and the breakthrough. Only the peripheral parameters changed."

"That's correct."

"Then explain why that key fits so perfectly. Why it works. Why it's the *only* one that works."

Daniel hesitated.

"It's complicated."

"I'm not leaving," Nicolas said. "Start talking."

Daniel exhaled and gestured toward the cluttered kitchen table, his half eaten meal sitting on its plate.

Nicolas declined.

"Fine. Stand there if you like. Just listen."

Nicolas folded his arms.

Daniel began.

"When Gaidon and I first attacked the problem, the biggest barrier was time. The compression phase of the ionised argon occurs in less than ten trillionths of a second. There is no chance for real-time correction. No feedback. Nothing. Everything must be pre-programmed."

Hightower nodded curtly.

"OK. You have explained this part before. I know this."

"No," Daniel said quietly. "You know the summary. Not the reality."

He dragged a notepad toward himself.

"We tried symmetrical compression. The shell destabilised — the collapse always started at the equator. So we tried patterned compression. That also failed. Differently. Useful failure. It told us where the collapse *began*."

"And?" Nicolas pressed.

"So I wrote an algorithm."

"A solver?"

"Sort of."

Daniel gave a tired half-smile. "A blindfolded solver."

He continued.

"It generated thousands of random compression patterns per second. Tested each in simulation. Passed the results to a learning agent I built. The agent didn't search for answers — only for direction. Failure vectors. Points of stability."

"And then?"

"And then it found something neither of us anticipated."

Daniel tapped the pencil.

"A very specific set of integer intervals resisted collapse."

Nicolas narrowed his eyes.

"What kind of intervals?"

"Prime-derived sequences."

Nicolas rubbed his forehead. "All right, remind me—why is it always a prime number with this damn machine?"

"No," Daniel replied. "I'm telling you that when we structured pulse timings using certain prime relationships, the shell stopped folding. It started to shrink. And I mean shrink very rapidly. The key fixes the problem, the problem being not to dissimilar to squeezing a balloon unevenly, so it reshapes smaller instead of popping."

Hightower absorbed that.

"Once we had found that specific master key the supercomputer found the rest of the parameters in the algorithm in minutes."

A thin silence stretched across the room.

Nicolas's jaw tightened.

"You need to explain *why* nothing works. We've spent a week in the data centre watching every candidate key produce white-hole inversion."

Daniel shook his head, helpless. "I can't. We don't know why that prime behaves differently from the rest. We only know that it does."

"And you'll watch a thousand more do the same."

Nicolas's patience snapped.

"Then show me the damn key. I need to see it."

Daniel held his gaze — no fear, just exhaustion.

"Fine."

They moved to the kitchen table. Daniel opened the laptop and typed the password when Nicolas asked.

The system unlocked.

"Where is it?" Nicolas demanded.

Daniel guided him through a directory labelled RACE_Archive_Internal.

Inside were two items: a text document and an audio file.

Nicolas squinted.

"What's the MP3?"

Daniel leaned back against the wall, suddenly weary.

"The algorithm. Slowed down. Expressed as notes. Sixty seconds long."

"You're joking."

"I wish I were."

Nicolas clicked it.

A strange, metallic chiming filled the room — jagged, shifting, eerily structured.

"You named it *Song of Argon Containment*?"

Daniel shrugged. "We were tired."

"Physicists," Nicolas muttered. "Unbelievable."

He stopped the playback.

"The master-key. Show me."

Daniel gave him a brief, almost puzzled look. "You've talked about it for months, Nicolas, but you've never actually asked to see the number."

Daniel opened the text file.

One line filled the screen:

1,111,111,919

Nicolas read it aloud, each cluster slower than the last.

"One... one-one-one... one-one-one... nine-one-nine."

He turned to Daniel.

"What am I supposed to *do* with this?"

Daniel's restraint cracked.

"You've *seen* the simulations," he said, voice tight. "You've watched every *wrong key* collapse the shell. You've sat in the room while the supercomputer showed us universes dying in femtoseconds."

His voice rose — not angry, but desperate.

"That number — that stupid, absurd number — is the only configuration that holds. Every other key collapses. Every other attempt ends with white-hole inversion. Ten digits stand between stability and annihilation."

Nicolas didn't speak.

For the first time since arriving in Europe, the armour slipped — not fear, not awe, but a sober recognition of the scale of what lay in front of him.

He closed the laptop gently.

Pocketed nothing. Took nothing.

Just stood there, breathing slowly.

Finally he said, "We're not done. But... at least now I understand more."

He turned and walked to the door.

Daniel didn't move until the latch clicked shut.

Only then did he sink into the chair, staring at the prime he wished he had never uncovered — the number that separated the two parallel universes.

***

# Chapter 22

**Wednesday, 27th March 2013, 10:30 a.m.**
**Parallel universe. Lorient Shipyard, Lorient, France.**

Max walked out into the courtyard exactly when he said he would. He'd already taken Clarisse's call ten minutes earlier — she was on her way in her little blue hatchback, annoyed-but-laughing about the spare key fiasco — and she'd told him Victorin had answered the door when she stopped by the apartment.

He spotted them immediately — Clarisse with a small moving box tucked under one arm, Victorin trotting beside her like an overeager retriever trying to be useful.

Max smiled as they approached.

"You two made good time."

Clarisse lifted the box.

"I tried to pick up a spare key from Vanessa Jogues, but she wasn't at her desk. The other woman in the office didn't know anything. So I went to your apartment... and found him."

Victorin pressed a hand over his heart in theatrical offence.

"I tried to help! But then we hit the tiny complication where—"

Max cut him off.

"—where you lost your key privileges because you stole a turkey out of my fridge."

Victorin held up a finger.

"Temporarily borrowed. And I remain forever wounded by your lack of forgiveness."

Clarisse snorted, trying not to laugh.

"Anyway," she continued, "since neither of us could get in, we drove straight here. And now..." she tapped the box with her knuckles "...I'm officially moving in."

The words hit Max with a quiet, steady warmth.

He leaned in, and she kissed him — gentle, decisive, belonging.

Victorin whipped out his phone.

"Photo!"

"Victorin, don't—"

Click.

Too late.

He turned the screen so Max and Clarisse could see a perfectly candid shot: both of them mid-laugh, sunlight turning the edges of Clarisse's hair gold.

Victorin's grin softened into something sincere.

"Truly... I'm happy for you both."

Clarisse reached for Max's hand.

"Come on," she murmured.

"Let's take the box home."

Max intertwined his fingers with hers and squeezed.

***

**Thursday, 4th April 2013, 7:41 p.m.**
**Parallel universe. Max's apartment, Lorient, France.**

Max had just finished cleaning the kitchen when his phone buzzed.

He wiped his hands on a towel and answered.

"Hey, Max — it's Ethan."

Max smiled; he always sounded halfway between amused and exhausted.

"How'd it go?"

"It's done," Ethan said. "Your camera is now officially a bottomless pit. Forty-five hours of high-resolution storage. Non-volatile, shock-protected, waterproof. Probably over-engineered, but that's how we do things."

Max let out a low whistle. "That's incredible. I'll need it. I've got... a lot."

"I've seen a number of the files you sent," Ethan replied. "Shopping for groceries, the police work, hospital nights, the shipyard, your classes at the Mid-Technical School — and your personal clips with Clarisse, hanging out with Victorin. That's about four hours. Good range. Honest. Human."

Max leaned against the counter, feeling a small, unexpected flush of pride.

Ethan went on, "TaloSyn's added another four or so — a historical sequence. Early struggles, the Twelve Rules, first-decade footage, social transitions. But the rest isn't just filler. TaloSyn's realised the Twelve Rules look simple and they're not. So it's pulled in material that shows how they actually work in practice."

"That'll help people understand."

"Oh, there's more," Ethan said. "Civic instruction pieces, local assemblies, training videos, problem-solving sessions from all over the world. Anywhere a civil society sat down and tried to explain its own rules to ordinary people. TaloSyn's mined it all. It's using those countless hours as a scaffold — to show how this framework turns into real decisions, real behaviour, day after day. Your world won't change overnight. But it'll have a mirror it's never had before."

Max exhaled slowly, letting the weight and hope of that settle.

"So... anything else I should do?" he asked.

"Just keep filming," Ethan said. "Real life is the strongest argument we have."

They exchanged a few lighter words — weekend plans, Clarisse's work schedule, a joke about Victorin's chaos-field — before Ethan signed off.

"Night, Max. And... good work. Really."

"Night, Ethan," Max replied, warm and steady.

He set the phone down, looked at the small camera on his desk, and felt a rising certainty that what he was making might actually matter.

A lot.

***

**Thursday, 2nd May 2013, 10:43 p.m.**
**Home of Nicolas Hightower, Geneva, Switzerland.**

Nicolas opened the door before the second knock — John Brennan didn't visit socially, and certainly not unannounced.

The newly appointed CIA Director stepped inside with that tightly contained force he was known for, the kind that suggested the room itself should brace.

"You have something for me," Brennan said, not bothering to sit.

Nicolas shut the door.

"I don't."

Brennan's expression didn't change, but the temperature in the room seemed to drop a degree.

"You're telling me," Brennan said, "that after weeks of work, after being given priority access to more computational power than any civilian program in American history — you have nothing."

"We've thrown every simulation we can find at the computers," Nicolas said. "Every variation, every master-key, prime numbers, big ones, small ones — every pattern the analysts could dream up. It all collapses."

Brennan's jaw tightened. "Then your team is failing."

"My team includes Daniel Mittermayer," Nicolas said, "and every top quantum specialist Washington could scrape together on short notice. They all agree."

Brennan finally moved — a slow turn, a colder stare.

"And what exactly do they 'agree' on?"

"The key is unique," Nicolas said. "Not one of a set. Not a variation. Just a strange, solitary number that works when nothing else does."

Brennan exhaled through his nose, long and sharp.

Nicolas continued, unflinching.

"We used sixty percent of the U.S. supercomputing network. That's more total compute than the climate center, the nuclear stewardship program, and cryptanalysis combined. And the outcome is always the same."

Brennan's voice was flat.

"Black holes."

"Every time," Nicolas said. "Instant collapse. Chamber, facility, planet — seconds. Not survivable."

He gestured to a folder on the coffee table.

"That's the past two hundred and forty-eight hours of simulation logs. Read it if you want to lose sleep."

Brennan didn't touch it.

A long, heavy silence settled — frustration, humiliation, and physics refusing to obey American power.

Finally Brennan lowered himself into a chair, the fatigue visible.

"So I have to walk into the Oval Office," he said, "and tell the President that our strategic window — our chance to outrun every rival on Earth — is closed."

"Yes," Nicolas said.

Brennan rubbed a hand across his face, the edge draining out of him.

"For God's sake."

For a moment neither spoke.

Then Brennan straightened slightly.

"What about the Frenchman? The draftsman. Max." Brennan sighed before continuing. "I've been briefed on what Petraeus ordered you to do in regard to tying up a loose bureaucratic end, The death certificate. The fake accident. Christ." He shook his head. "We can't kill him, and we sure as hell can't let that paperwork stand. When Max walks back through that machine, every lie Petraeus signed is going to blow straight back into our faces."

Nicolas said nothing.

Brennan continued, voice low and tight.

"We'll have to do what this Agency always does when a bad decision ages badly: lie better, cover harder, and pray the mess doesn't rot through the floor." He exhaled sharply. "We'll find a way to patch it. But the day he steps out of that chamber, we're cleaning up a bureaucratic corpse none of us created."

He rubbed at his temple, as though steadying the weight of it.

"Yes. And..." Nicolas hesitated. "We've been communicating. Not directly. Via light signalling. Morse. Their people insisted on it when they shut us out in December. We keep to a strict schedule."

Brennan frowned. "And they're still answering?"

"In their way," Nicolas said. "Mostly status updates. But three days ago they asked, plainly: 'Are you prepared for Max to return on 9 June?'"

"And we said?"

"That we are. Because we have to be."

Brennan rose slowly, shoulders heavy, the night finally catching up with him.

"So that's it. No weapon. No breakthrough. And we just... take him back."

Nicolas nodded.

Brennan lingered at the door long enough to mutter, half-resigned:

"A draftsman caused all these problems and brings the United States to a standstill. Remarkable."

He left without another word.

Nicolas stood alone in the quiet flat, feeling — for the first time — something like acceptance.

The universe had drawn a hard line.

And even America couldn't cross it.

***

# Chapter 23

**Monday, 3rd June 2013, 12:04 p.m.**
**Parallel universe. Lorient Shipyard, Lorient, France.**

The rooftop wind carried the smell of salt and steel — cranes groaned, welding torches spat sparks that glittered in the sunlight, and somewhere below a siren whooped twice in a cheerful docking signal only shipyard workers seemed to understand.

Max and Aimes stood by the waist-high safety barrier, ten storeys above the yard, watching a half-finished cargo ship shimmer under the afternoon sun.

Aimes rested both hands on the railing.

"Max," he said quietly, "we need to talk about the danger you are facing."

Max kept his gaze on the ship — on the clean, purposeful geometry of a world that had finally made sense to him.

"I don't see it as much of a risk," he said. "I'm one person. What threat could I be?"

Aimes exhaled — not impatient, just worried.

"You're not a threat. It's what you bring with you. A new way. A better world. All that power in your world isn't just going to bend over and change. They will see you as a threat."

Max finally turned toward him.

Aimes continued, "I've seen the final cut of your documentary. So has the Première Gardienne."

Max raised an eyebrow. "Oh?"

Aimes nodded once. "She said, very simply: 'They won't like it. They will hate it. They will see it as a direct threat and shoot the messenger.'"

Max gave a small, uncertain smile. "That's the risk I will have to take."

"She actually means it literally," Aimes said.

He stepped a little closer, lowering his voice even though they were alone.

"Max, you've spent nearly a year in a society built on trust, cooperation, and dignity. You've lived inside a system designed to lift people, not crush them. Your old world isn't like that. You told us yourself."

Max didn't look away.

"Yes. I did. But…" Max paused, lost for words.

"So you know there's a small chance they might not believe you," Aimes said. "Or worse — they may believe you and fear what you represent."

The wind tugged gently at Max's shirt as he faced the yard again — the clang of steel, the laughter of workers, the absence of tension. A world not perfect, but profoundly sane.

"Aimes," Max said quietly, "Gaidon sent me here to walk around for twenty-four hours, get some real human intel, return to the portal, wait, and go home. That was it. One day in another universe. Nothing more."

He drew a slow breath.

"The only thing that's changed is the time frame. It's a year instead of a day. But the mission is still the mission — I'm going back to report what I've learnt about this world."

Max paused, then shook his head.

"But that's not the whole truth. The part that won't go in any report is what I've learnt about myself."

His voice lowered again, not confessional, just honest.

"I spent my life designing weapons for people I'd never meet. Tools for conflicts I didn't understand. And I never questioned it. Not once. I never stopped to think how I was just a cog in a machine that existed to kill."

He swallowed, eyes fixed on the yard below.

"Maybe my going back is my way of trying to atone for that."

The wind shifted. A shipyard crane gave a deep metallic groan.

Aimes spoke softly. "I'm afraid for you, Max. Truly. They could silence you. Discredit you. Use you. Even punish you."

Max nodded. He'd already thought it through a hundred times.

"I know. But something has to be done. Billions of people are living under the yoke of a corrupt, immoral, and inefficient system, and very few of them live meaningful lives. I owe it to them to show there is another way."

Aimes searched his face — hoping for doubt, finding none.

Max inhaled once, steady.

"When I was in the cell," he said, "I read those early history books — the ones about the year after Armistice Day 1918, when people were fighting for the Twelve Rules against the elites who wanted to stop them. They had a phrase they used to steel themselves when everything looked impossible."

Aimes tilted his head. "What phrase?"

Max's voice dropped to something resolute, almost solemn.

"History remembers the brave."

He looked Aimes squarely in the eyes.

"And right now... that has to be me."

Aimes closed his eyes for a moment — not defeated, but accepting the weight of it.

When he opened them, he extended his hand.

"Then I'll walk with you as far as I'm allowed."

Max took the hand firmly.

Below them, the shipyard kept moving — cranes swinging, welders sparking, voices rising — a living reminder of the world he would soon have to leave behind.

***

**Friday, 7th June 2013, 4:00 p.m.**
**Parallel universe. Lorient Shipyard, Lorient, France.**

The shift whistle blew, echoing across the shipyard like a farewell trumpet, and Max shut down his workstation for the last time.

The engineering office was already filling with people drifting toward him — casual, smiling, oblivious to the truth beneath the surface.

Jean Pacaut clapped him on the shoulder.

"So, monsieur bicycle-designer... ready for mountain air and tiny Swiss cafés?"

Max forced a grin.

"Ready as I'll ever be."

A ripple of laughter rolled through the office.

Someone opened an enormous bottle of sparkling cider; someone else produced a tray of pastries; someone cranked up a little speaker playing jaunty Breton pop.

The crowd tightened around him — colleagues from drafting, metallurgy, simulation, fabrication; people he'd known for just ten months but felt he'd known for years.

They toasted to "Max's new adventure."

He toasted back to "the best workplace I've ever had."

His phone buzzed in his pocket.

He slipped away toward the far window and answered quietly.

"Felix?"

Felix spoke over the faint hum of machinery in the background.

"We're nearly there, Max. The team in Pfronten has just signed off on the final drawings of our Parallel Universe Machine. We  expect to have everything ready for final assembly in October. The computer simulations say it'll work."

Max closed his eyes, absorbing it.

"Good luck tomorrow, Max. Truly."

He hung up and turned back toward his friends — toward the life he was leaving.

And then Arguis Ronet materialised through the crowd like a mythic creature.

Today he wore neon-orange trousers covered in hand-painted spirals, a purple T-shirt emblazoned with a leather-clad man leaning casually against an oversized bulldozer, and one electric-green sneaker and one cobalt-blue sneaker.

He held a piece of paper — no, a parchment — because of course he did.

"Silence!" he declared, though nobody had asked for it.

The room quieted instantly; Arguis always got silence.

He cleared his throat with theatrical weight.

"My dear colleagues," he began, "and Max — our lost son of another... arrondissement."

Laughter.

Arguis continued, flourishing his parchment.

"This man arrived among us wearing clothes so plain I feared he was a ghost. And then — mon dieu — he began to learn.

He learned fast.

He learned well.

He learned beautifully.

And he reminded an old fool like me why teaching is worth it."

Max felt warmth bloom in his chest.

Arguis stepped closer, lowering his voice but not his flair.

"You brought us joy, Max.

You brought curiosity.

You brought humility — which is rare in engineers and extinct in designers."

More laughter.

"And now," Arguis said, lifting his glass, "you go off to make bicycles or lovers or both — I don't judge — and we will miss you terribly."

Thirty glasses lifted.

"To Max!"

Max lifted his own glass, throat tight.

"To all of you," he said. "I couldn't have asked for a better place to learn."

The toast crashed joyfully through the room.

Max smiled — deeply, genuinely — even as the ache behind it grew sharp.

His world would end tomorrow.

Or begin.

***

**Saturday, 8th June 2013, 5:08 p.m.**
**Parallel universe. Max's apartment, Lorient, France.**

The suitcase sat by the door like a verdict.

Max zipped his jacket slowly, deliberately, as if dragging out the last seconds might change their meaning.

Clarisse stood in the middle of the small living room, arms wrapped around herself, eyes fixed on him with a desperation neither of them pretended to hide.

"You don't have to do this," she said quietly.

Her voice wasn't angry — just broken around the edges.

Max stepped forward and touched her cheek with the back of his hand.

"I do."

She shook her head.

"No. Max... you're doing what you believe is right. And I understand that.

But don't ask me to pretend it doesn't break my heart."

He tried to hold her gaze but she overwhelmed him — Clarisse Ampère, brilliant and fierce and fragile in the places she tried hardest to hide.

She stepped closer, hands on his chest.

"I love you," she said, the words trembling out of her.

"I love you, Max. Stay. Stay with me."

The room went impossibly quiet.

Max swallowed, feeling the ache swell up through him like pressure from deep water.

"I love you too," he said, finally saying it without hesitation.

"But I have to do this."

She pressed her forehead against his sternum, her breath catching.

"Why? Why must you be the one who fixes their world? Why must you go back there alone?"

He held her tightly, closing his eyes.

"Because someone has to.

Because somebody has to show them there's another way.

Because if I don't try, then nothing changes — and everything stays broken."

Clarisse's hands curled into his shirt.

"You don't owe them anything."

"I know," he whispered.

"But I owe myself the truth of who I want to be."

She exhaled a shuddering breath — half anguish, half surrender.

Then she lifted her face to him and kissed him with the kind of intensity that comes from knowing the moment is finite.

It lasted too long, and not long enough.

When she finally stepped back, tears had won the fight she was trying not to have.

"You come back," she said.

"You come back to me, Max Rivette. Promise me."

Max nodded, voice cracking.

"I will. I promise."

He picked up the suitcase.

Opened the door.

Paused on the threshold.

Clarisse stood in the doorway's shadow, shoulders trembling, chin lifted in that proud, stubborn way he loved so much.

"Go," she whispered.

"Before I drag you back inside."

Max managed a thin, aching smile.

He stepped into the hallway.

The door closed behind him like the end of a chapter.

***

# Chapter 24

**Saturday, 8th June 2013, 10:48 p.m.**
**Parallel universe. Diderot farm, Prévessin-Moëns, France.**

Max stepped out of the taxi and into the familiar gravel of Renato and Bibiane's driveway.

Music thumped faintly from the barn — deep bass pulses, sporadic cheering, the unmistakable soundtrack of one of the Diderots' infamous "celebrations of life."

Light spilled out in flickers as bodies moved past the open door: dancing silhouettes, bursts of laughter, someone waving a bottle of something glowing neon blue.

Renato was already waiting on the porch, arms crossed, a grin carved across his weathered face.

"You look like a man who's walked a thousand kilometres in one afternoon," the farmer said.

Max exhaled, tired in a way that came from inside the ribs.

"It's been a long day."

Bibiane swept out behind her husband, wearing an outrageous sequined shawl that shimmered in the porch light.

Without hesitation, she wrapped Max in a fierce hug.

"My poor boy," she said into his shoulder.

"You have chosen the worst night to try and sleep here. Half the region's libertines have shown up."

Renato snorted.

"It's not a party until someone gets naked on the hay bales. And I think Jean-Pierre beat his own record — only took him an hour and a half this time."

Max almost laughed — almost — the exhaustion blunting his usual amusement.

Bibiane saw it immediately.

She guided him toward two chairs set away from the chaos, under the old apple tree.

They sat.

The music thumped.

Someone outside the barn shrieked with joyous abandon.

Renato cracked open a bottle of home-made cider and handed it to Max.

"Drink. It won't fix anything, but it makes listening easier."

Max took a sip.

The cold sweetness hit him like a memory of childhood — tree sap, sun-warm fruit, the taste of summer with no consequences.

Bibiane rested a gentle hand on his arm.

"Clarisse?"

Max nodded.

"Yeah."

Renato leaned back, letting the chair creak.

"She asked you to stay, didn't she?"

"Yes," Max said softly.

"She loves me. I love her. And I'm still leaving."

Bibiane inhaled slowly, sympathetically.

"You're doing something impossibly brave. That doesn't make it less cruel."

Max stared at his hands, knuckles white around the bottle.

"It feels like I'm tearing myself in half."

Renato studied him for a long moment.

Then he spoke the way older men do when life has carved wisdom into them by force.

"To make two worlds understand each other," Renato said, "someone has to go first, and that person ends up alone for a while. It's frightening. But without that step, nothing changes."

Max swallowed hard.

From the barn came the unmistakable sound of someone trying — and failing — to belt out an old rock anthem.

Bibiane rolled her eyes.

"That's Jacques Legrand. He thinks he can sing when he's drunk."

There was a pause at the three listened to an atrocious singing voice shrieked out.

"He cannot."

Renato shrugged.

"Better than last month. He only got two songs out before he vomited."

Max finally cracked a real smile — small, but real.

Renato stood and clapped Max on the shoulder.

"Come on let's get you up to the house. You have a big day ahead of you."

***

**Sunday, 9th June 2013, 9:58 a.m.**
**Parallel universe. Diderot farm, Prévessin-Moëns, France.**

The morning light was thin — a washed early-summer grey that softened the edges of everything.

Max stood in the clearing's damp grass with Bibiane, Renato and Dominic gathered loosely around him, each giving him space without stepping away.

He touched the strap of his small backpack, the same one he'd carried through on day one, camera buried inside.

No one seemed willing to speak first.

Birds called tentatively in the trees, as if even they understood the wrongness of the moment.

Renato broke the silence only long enough to mutter, "Two minutes," checking his old brass watch.

Bibiane wiped her cheeks, though she wasn't crying — not yet — just bracing.

Dominic stood a step behind Max, hands clasped behind his back, face carved into its usual hard angles.

Only his eyes betrayed him: softer, resigned.

Max exhaled slowly, looking at each of them in turn.

Nothing needed to be said — everything had already been said last night, and the night before, and in the weeks leading up to this morning.

Renato checked the watch again.

"One minute."

Bibiane reached out and took Max's hand.

Her grip was warm, steady, maternal in the deepest sense.

"You come back," she whispered.

It wasn't a command, or a plea.

It was a truth she needed the world to hear.

Max squeezed her hand and let go.

The clearing held its breath.

The gateway opened with its signature sharp, load-crack — a violent, air-splitting jolt that punched through the clearing — and a four and a half metre sphere of blue transparency snapped into existence.

Max stepped forward.

Renato straightened but said nothing.

Bibiane covered her mouth.

Dominic nodded once.

Max paused at the threshold — one heartbeat, two — then stepped through the shimmering blue sphere, which crackled softly as it parted around him. He crossed onto the steel platform and stood there for barely a second before it began to descend, taking him out of sight.

A few seconds after he vanished, the sphere contracted inwards instantly — shrinking to a point — and collapsed with a soft whump that rippled across the clearing.

And the clearing fell silent again, as if he had never stood there at all.

***

**Sunday, 9th June 2013, 10:00 a.m.**
**Machine room. Laboratory 888, CERN, Prévessin-Moëns, France.**

Max stepped out onto the narrow steel platform, the settling of the machinery behind him sounding like the last breath of a fading dream.

The room felt colder than he remembered — fluorescent, metallic, impersonal — a world that seemed to have shrunk in his absence.

Nicolas Hightower was waiting for him. And he wasn't alone.

Four men in civilian clothes stood in a loose formation behind him. No uniforms — just the unmistakable discipline of people trained to move fast and without hesitation.

Nicolas stepped forward with a smile that never reached his eyes.

"Welcome back, Max."

Max didn't respond.

Nicolas continued as if they were picking up a normal briefing.

"You'll notice the original team aren't here to greet you. Daniel, Gaidon... they're off-site today."

The line sounded rehearsed. Nicolas didn't give Max space to question it.

"We've made some adjustments," he went on.

"New procedures. New safety requirements."

He signalled one of the men, who wheeled forward a sealed medical case — clinical, heavy, unmistakably serious.

Max stiffened.

"What is this?"

"A precaution," Nicolas said, smooth as glass.

"You've been away for a full year. No one knows what you might have been exposed to."

"I feel fine."

"I know." Nicolas nodded sympathetically — or at least performed the sympathy.

"But this is protocol now. Before you meet anyone, we need a full medical screen. Bloodwork, scans. Routine."

Max didn't move.

"It's temporary," Nicolas added softly. "A few days. Not a real quarantine — just a controlled assessment."

Everything about the phrasing was too neat. Too prepared.

Max stepped back half a pace.

"I want to see the old team."

"You will," Nicolas said immediately.

"After the checks. It's safer this way. For everyone."

Max's eyes moved to the four silent men. Not one blinked.

"How long?" he asked.

"Forty-eight hours at most. Maybe less if everything looks good."

There was no real choice.

Max gave a short nod.

Nicolas exhaled as though something important had just been secured.

"Good. Thank you."

He turned to lead Max toward the exit corridor — and that's when one of the security men extended a hand, palm up, a simple, wordless signal.

Max looked at him, then realised he wanted the small backpack slung over his shoulder — the same one he'd carried into this universe, his camera still inside.

Reluctantly, he handed it over.

The man accepted it without comment and stepped back into position.

They continued down the corridor, the four men falling in around him — not touching, but close enough to steer him without giving him a choice.

They reached the lift, its doors already open, and crowded in together.

The ascent was silent.

When the doors slid back at ground level, the cool air hit him first. A black van idled a few metres away, windows opaque, engine humming with a low mechanical growl.

The men tightened their formation, guiding him toward the van.

Max glanced back at the building. His bicycle was still there, leaning against the wall — exactly where he'd left it one year ago to the day.

Nicolas opened the van door.

"Once the tests are done," he said softly, "we'll sit down and talk about what you've brought back."

Max stepped inside.

The door shut.

The lock clicked.

And the ride to Geneva began.

***

**Sunday, 9th June 2013, 10:45 a.m.**
**Private clinic commandeered by CIA, Geneva, Switzerland.**

Forty-five minutes after leaving CERN, the van glided down a concrete ramp into an underground car park. Max felt the pressure shift — deeper, quieter — the way basements swallow sound.

The door slid open.

No sunlight.

Just strip lights reflected off polished concrete.

"Out," one of the men said.

Max stepped onto the cold floor. Nicolas was already waiting, posture immaculate, expression unreadable.

"This way."

A fire door opened onto a corridor that could have been part of any private Swiss clinic — white walls, soft lighting, a faint whiff of antiseptic — except it was silent. Too silent. No footsteps, no wheelchairs, no murmur of nurses. Just the hum of perfectly maintained ventilation.

A doctor entered the first exam room almost immediately. Middle-aged, neutral accent, no introduction.

"Shirt off. Arms forward."

ECG pads. Blood drawn. Pupils checked. Reflex tests.

The man wrote nothing down — as if his memory was the clipboard.

He left without a word.

Two minutes later a different doctor entered. A woman this time. Dark hair pulled tight, evaluating eyes.

"Stand. Look ahead."

Neurological sweep. Balance test. Light sensitivity.

Again, total silence.

Then she vanished.

The third doctor brought Max to imaging.

A small MRI suite — modern, clean, empty except for the humming machine.

"Lie still."

Full-body scan. Brain scan. Lung capacity.

The man watched the monitors like a hawk but said nothing.

The absence of sound pressed in on Max.

A hospital with no staff noise wasn't a hospital.

It was a set — a stage built for one patient.

Two hours after arriving, Nicolas reappeared.

"That's all for now," he said with a courteous nod.

"Thank you for cooperating."

He guided Max back to the van waiting in the silent car park.

The door shut.

Darkness again.

No clues where he was, or where he was going next.

***

**Sunday, 9th June 2013, 5:12 p.m.**
**Secret CIA prison, Geneva, Switzerland.**

The recorder clicked off forty-five minutes in.

Max had spoken without a break — calm, detailed, almost unnervingly coherent — walking them through every facet of the parallel world: its towns, its work culture, the police, the hospitals, the schools... and finally, the Twelve Rules.

When he finished, Nicolas and Dr Conrad Hale exchanged a glance that said everything; then they rose, muttered something about "consulting for a moment," and stepped out. The door sealed behind them with a soft hydraulic sigh.

Max sat alone for several minutes, listening to nothing but the steady hum of the ventilation and, faintly, the edge of incredulous voices drifting down the hall. Their disbelief wasn't surprising, but the intensity of it was. He imagined the two men arguing about whether he was delusional — or whether the delusion was theirs.

When the door finally opened, Nicolas and Hale looked subtly altered: less sceptical than before, more unsettled, as if the break had only deepened their confusion. Nicolas returned to his chair, leaned in, and flicked the recorder back on with a precise, almost ceremonial click.

"All right," he said, voice tight. "Let's go through this again."

Max exhaled quietly. He recognised that tone — disbelief wrapped in procedural courtesy, the kind used when the listener refuses to concede ground.

Nicolas leaned back, steepling his fingers.

"So now that we've heard your summary... let's address the obvious."

He paused, studying Max with a mixture of suspicion and professional curiosity.

"You claim—"

"I told you what happened," Max said.

"Fine," Nicolas replied. "You told us. But we need to know if any of it is remotely credible."

Hale leaned forward, adopting a gentle tone Max instinctively mistrusted.

"Max, we want to understand. Truly. But we need clarity. So let's start here:"

He consulted his notes.

"You're telling us that an entire civilisation operates under... what did you call them?"

"Twelve Rules," Max said.

"Twelve rules," Hale echoed. "Twelve."

"Yes."

"And these rules," Nicolas said slowly, "govern their entire societal structure?"

"Yes."

Nicolas looked down at his notepad, then back up.

"So now we understand your claim. But the part we cannot believe — the part any rational person would struggle with — is that Rule Twelve is... what again?"

Max met his stare without blinking.

"Money is illegal."

Silence fell so abruptly the room seemed to tighten around it.

Hale blinked, trying to recalibrate.

"No currency. No credit. No tokens. No trade instruments. Nothing?"

"Nothing."

Nicolas scoffed under his breath.

"That's not a society. That's a fairy tale."

Max leaned forward slightly.

"It works."

"For them," Nicolas said. "Not for humans."

"They are humans."

"Humans don't function like that."

Max held his gaze, unflinching.

"I lived there. They do."

Nicolas tapped the table once — a sharp, irritated crack.

"Look at what you're asking us to swallow. A world without hierarchy, without coercion, without financial incentive, without secrecy, without corruption — all balanced by twelve rules written a century ago by... who, exactly?"

"I don't know. They were reached by consensus," Max said. "But they're real. They follow them."

"And they somehow avoid collapse," Nicolas said. "Avoid exploitation. Avoid war."

"They have no elites."

"And that," Hale said, "is precisely what makes your story unbelievable."

Max gestured toward the door.

"You took my camera. The footage is real. Just watch it."

"We will," Nicolas said. "But right now what we see is the probability of delusion. Or conditioning. Or manipulation."

"It's not," Max said sharply. "I worked there. I contributed. I had a home. I had a partner. They treated me with respect even when I was a prisoner. Ask me anything about their society. Anything."

"We are," Nicolas said. "And your answers defy everything we know about human behaviour."

Max leaned forward, voice low and steady — the kind of steadiness that makes a man listen even when he doesn't want to.

"That's because you don't know what humans are like when they're not forced into competition."

Nicolas's expression hardened.

"Enough."

Hale closed his notebook, the motion final.

"I think that's all for the day."

Two guards entered, silent and precise.

Nicolas rose.

"Max, we're placing you back in your room for now."

Max stood slowly, a knot tightening in his chest.

"What room?"

There was no answer.

The guards escorted him down the corridor — identical doors, identical silence — until one opened.

A cell.

Concrete walls.

No window.

A hard cot.

A stainless steel toilet and sink.

The air carried the sterile smell of metal, disinfectant, and institutional neglect.

The door slammed shut, a clang that vibrated through the floor and straight up Max's spine.

He stood in the dim, cold light, breathing carefully.

He closed his eyes and thought to himself, "History remembers the brave."

***

**Monday, 10th June 2013, 3:02 p.m.**
**Secret CIA prison, Geneva, Switzerland.**

The secure room was colder than the rest of the floor — a deliberate few degrees down. Nicolas felt it the instant the outer door sealed behind him with a padded, deadened thump.

Five people were inside. No badges. No insignia. Just the pallor of people who had been staring at screens too long and had not slept enough to hide it.

Equipment racks lined the walls, all running off isolated power: forensic-grade monitors, diagnostic hardware, sealed analysers. No cables led out. No signals could leak.

A man stepped forward  mid-forties, suit slightly creased, the posture of an academic shoved into government work.

"Professor Dalton Carver. Technical assessment."

He didn't shake hands. "You need to see this."

Carver gestured to Max's camera — disassembled on a bench. "The camera's a standard Sony Handycam, but…" He hesitated. "It isn't standard anymore."

Nicolas raised an eyebrow.

"Someone — on the other side — modified the internals. Seamlessly. Expanded memory far beyond anything commercially available. Enough to store the full forty-five hours of 4K footage he brought back. No mismatched solder. No tool marks. No power-draw anomalies. It's… elegant. Like it grew that way."

Nicolas didn't like that.

Carver turned to the monitors.

"We've reviewed thirty-four hours so far."

"And?" Nicolas asked.

Carver's jaw flexed once. "Not only do we not understand what we are seeing, but it's not fake."

Nicolas scoffed. "Everything is fakeable."

"Not this," Carver replied. "Not at this scale."

He gestured to the central screen. A hospital scene rolled. Not glossy. Not staged. Just real — with all the uneven lighting, stray noises, and unselfconscious movement real life refuses to tidy up.

"Look at it," Carver said quietly. "The human behaviour. The timing. The overlapping conversations. The background actions no director would bother to choreograph. This isn't performance. This is life happening around a camera that barely matters to the people in frame."

He switched clips.

A street. Max walking with two people. Someone bumps into him and apologises in a hurry. A child cuts across chasing a dog. A cyclist yells something indistinct from the edge of frame.

"This isn't a set," Carver said. "You'd need a whole city as extras — thousands of people who aren't acting."

Nicolas opened his mouth, but Carver continued before he could speak.

"And the industrial sequences..."

He clicked again.

The shipyard appeared — vast, sunlit, impossibly detailed. Workers moved through labyrinths of cranes, gantries, scaffolds and hull plating. Everything about it felt... lived in. Functional. Not built for a camera.

"If this is a fabrication," Carver said, "someone constructed an entire working port, shipyard, housing district, transport network, and hospital system just to trick us — and populated it with millions of people behaving like actual human beings."

He turned to Nicolas.

"Hollywood best CGI couldn't fake a five-minute scene like this. Not with unlimited budget. Not with the best visual effects teams alive. Because you can't choreograph this many small, unintentional, natural things at once."

Nicolas stared at the screen, at a welder pausing to stretch his back, at a crane operator adjusting his seat, at a pair of workers laughing at something off-camera.

Carver's voice softened.

"You asked us to find the trick. We haven't found one. Not a seam. Not an inconsistency. The camera is real. The footage is real. And whatever world this came from..."

He gestured to the endless shipyard on the monitor.

"...is more advanced than ours. Technically. Socially. Organisationally. In every measurable way."

Silence filled the room.

Nicolas swallowed, the truth landing like a weight he didn't want but could no longer deny.

"If it's real," he said quietly, "then everything we're doing here... is wrong."

No one answered.

Only the hum of the sealed room — and the distant clang of hammers from a world they had never imagined existed.

***

# Chapter 25

**Monday, 10th June 2013, 5:04 p.m.**
**Secret CIA prison, Geneva, Switzerland.**

The secure line blinked green twice before connecting. Nicolas stood alone in the operations office, the shipyard footage still echoing in his skull like a migraine made of steel.

"Hightower. After reading your initial report on the return of Maximilien Rivette, I didn't know what to make of it. You said you didn't believe a word of it. That he'd had some sort of psychotic break. You also mentioned he'd repeatedly referred to some kind of video evidence, and that you were looking into it. What's the latest from the review team you put together?"

The voice was unmistakable — clipped, hard-edged, impatient.

John Brennan, Director of the CIA.

"Sir," Nicolas said. "We've completed the initial assessment. Professor Dalton Carver and his team have—"

"Spare me the preamble," Brennan cut in. "Begin with your conclusion."

Nicolas swallowed. He had practised this sentence twice. It still felt unreal.

"Maximilien Rivette is... telling the truth, sir."

Silence. Not static — real, heavy silence, as if Brennan had briefly stopped breathing.

Nicolas pushed on. "Carver's team has gone line by line through the footage. Forty-five hours. Hospital sequences, street scenes, domestic interiors, infrastructure. And—"

"You believe it," Brennan said flatly.

Nicolas exhaled. "Yes, sir. I didn't at first. I questioned Rivette, challenged him, pressed him. He held his story. But the footage..." He hesitated, remembering the scenes at the vast shipyard. "There's no mechanism by which Rivette could fabricate it. There's no mechanism we could use to fabricate it. Carver is certain. His entire team is certain."

Another long pause. When Brennan spoke again, the softness in his voice made the words worse.

"Rivette must never see the light of day."

Nicolas closed his eyes. He had known it was coming. Hearing it spoken by the Director still hit like a physical blow.

"Yes, sir."

"The footage is to be secured immediately," Brennan continued. "I want a maximally encrypted copy prepared under Carver's supervision. Physical transport only. No digital transmission, no network exposure. You will hand-deliver it to a courier team. That copy goes straight to Washington."

"Yes, sir."

"And I will take it personally to the President," Brennan added. "Obama needs to see what we're dealing with."

Nicolas felt his pulse spike. If Brennan was willing to walk this into the Oval Office, the implications were far larger than he'd imagined.

"You will maintain compartmentalisation," Brennan went on. "Rivette is to remain isolated. No further interviews. No contact with anyone except authorised medical checks."

Nicolas hesitated. "Sir... what is the long-term plan for him?"

"Containment," Brennan said. "Permanent."

Nicolas stared at the wall, jaw tight. "Understood."

"And the techs?" Brennan asked.

"They're loyal," Nicolas said. "Shaken, but loyal."

"They've seen something we don't want anybody to see," Brennan replied. "They will have to be made aware of the need for utmost secrecy."

Nicolas felt cold. "What are your orders regarding them?"

"They'll be compensated," Brennan said. "Handsomely. Six figures each. New contracts, new NDAs, whatever legal wallpaper keeps them calm."

"And after that?"

Brennan's tone turned to solid ice.

"After that, they will be monitored for the rest of their natural lives. And if so much as a whisper escapes one of them — even in a bar, even to a spouse — they will be removed. Quietly. Immediately."

Nicolas felt his throat tighten. "I will convey the expectations, sir."

"No," Brennan said. "You will not. I will call Carver myself after we hang up. It'll be taken more seriously if it comes from me."

Brennan continued:

"Your job is to keep Rivette locked down. I want his guards keeping only the absolute minimum of contact with him. No engagement beyond what's operationally required." He paused. "Whatever he stepped into... we do not let that idea spread."

"Yes, sir."

Brennan exhaled once, hard. "I'll be wheels-up in four hours. Prepare the package and secure the prisoner."

The line went dead.

Nicolas lowered the handset slowly. His reflection stared back from the dark screen: pale, strained, older than he had looked that morning.

Outside the office, down two corridors and behind three locked doors, Max Rivette was sitting alone in a concrete cell, unaware that five minutes of razor-sharp shipyard footage had just sentenced him to life in a place without windows.

And somewhere deep inside Nicolas, a quiet, unwelcome thought took hold:

Brennan is wrong. We are doing the wrong thing.

He sat with that thought for only a second.

Then he buried it.

And walked out to obey his orders.

***

**Wednesday, 12th June 2013, 10:03 a.m.**
**The Presidents office, Washington DC, United States of America.**

The room felt cavernous without the usual constellation of aides, advisors, note-takers, and Secret Service shadows. President Barack Obama stood near the Resolute Desk, arms folded, gaze fixed on the small, matte-black laptop that a technician had just finished scanning and isolating. Once they left, the door sealed, and only two men remained:

John Brennan.

And the President of the United States.

Brennan sat stiffly, the laptop angled between them on a small side table normally reserved for briefing folders and coffee. Obama lowered himself into the chair opposite, elbows on his knees, expression already tense.

"All right, John," Obama said quietly. "Let's see what couldn't wait."

Brennan typed in a long string of characters, the kind no human memorises unless the stakes are extraordinary. The screen flickered. Then the first frame appeared.

A hospital ward in another universe.

They watched for several minutes without speaking. Obama absorbed every detail —

the medical charts openly accessible at the foot of each bed, the calm interactions, the efficiency unmarred by bureaucracy or fear. His eyes were analytical, but something else crept into them: a faint, reluctant admiration.

Brennan fast-forwarded. Streets. Homes. Workplaces. Conversations. Then the documentary portion — clean edits, coherent commentary, social structures that made no sense to an American capitalist frame of reference, and yet worked. The footage felt like a mirror held up to everything broken in their own world.

And then the shipyard.

Obama leaned forward, hands clasped. The sheer scale, the seamless cooperation, the absence of coercion or hierarchy — it struck him harder than any speech, any briefing, any think-tank report. Tens of thousands of people working without visible authority, without money changing hands, without ownership. And it worked. It worked better than anything America could produce.

Brennan finally closed the lid but didn't move the laptop.

For a long moment, Obama stared at the empty screen, jaw set, mind racing.

When he finally spoke, his voice was low and controlled. "Well," he said, "now I understand why you brought this directly to me."

Brennan didn't answer.

Obama rubbed his forehead with both hands. "John... if that system is real, it is a political—no, a civilisational—detonation. Nothing in our structure survives learning that a moneyless society with bottom-up governance outperforms us on every metric that matters."

"It would destabilise global power centres," Brennan agreed. "Instantly."

Obama nodded grimly. "And the people who put me in this office? Wall Street, defence contractors, big donors... they'd see this as an existential threat. They'd burn half the world to the ground rather than let a 'Twelve Rules' system get traction." He sighed heavily. "And the public? They would riot. Half in hope, half in fury."

Brennan didn't blink. "We can suppress it."

A long silence stretched between them.

Obama finally looked up. "Shut down the CERN experiment."

Brennan accepted the order with a small nod.

"No more inter-universe travel," Obama continued. "No more portals. Weld it shut, burn the files, pull the funding — I don't care. Make it disappear."

"Understood."

"What about the CERN scientists?" Brennan asked. "They'll fight it. They'll demand answers."

"Tell them to keep their mouths shut," Obama said coldly. "Or else."

Brennan waited for elaboration. None came.

Obama straightened, his face now carved from granite.

"We give them a national security directive. They defy it, they lose their careers, their visas, their pensions — whatever pressure you need. And if anyone tries to leak this—" He hesitated only a heartbeat. "—we treat it as espionage. Full stop."

Brennan absorbed this with the stillness of a man who had seen bad orders and worse necessities.

He drew a slow breath. "There's a problem, though. Gaidon and his team will ask about the missing man. Max Rivette."

Obama's head snapped toward him. "Explain."

Brennan hesitated — only a fraction.

"Sir... officially, Rivette is already dead."

Obama frowned. "Since when?"

"Petraeus authorised a death certificate last year, in August. Bureaucratic pressure from CERN — they needed documentation for final pay and benefits, and Petraeus didn't want them digging. It was meant as a temporary stopgap." Brennan exhaled through his nose. "But Rivette himself is alive. We're holding him in a secure facility."

Obama stared at him, incredulous. "So on paper he's dead, but in reality he's in our custody."

"Yes, sir."

Obama let that hang in the air for several seconds.

Then Brennan continued carefully, "Sir... we can use this. Tell Gaidon and his team a similar story to what Petraeus filed — that Rivette died soon after he first travelled through the portal. A radiation accident, catastrophic contamination, a collapse on the far side. They know that we searched extensively for information on Max and we turned up nothing. We tell them our surveillance eventually picked up the true story; we demanded the body be sent back. His return was handled quietly. We put all the blame on Max's death on the other side. They lied to us for a year, we use that to tie everything together and it solves several problems at once."

Brennan paused before adding, "And if they ever mention this, we can use this to make they're life hell. They will have a different version of events, of just *who* killed Max, and *when* Max died,  and that will make them look bad. They'll look like *they're* the ones lying, in order to cover up Max's death."

Obama considered this, jaw tightening. "Who actually knows about the death certificate?"

"A handful of CERN bureaucrats," Brennan said. "And Rivette's employer. That's it."

"Good," Obama said. "Then we'll have a strong talk with those people. The line holds: Rivette died. Tragic, scientific, irreversible."

He gestured sharply.

Brennan nodded once. "Understood."

Obama leaned back, exhaling slowly. "John... I hate this. You know that. But that world? If even ten percent of what we saw gets out, we won't control the narrative. We won't even control our own country." He looked tired in a way Brennan had never seen. "Sometimes the right thing and the stable thing aren't the same. And in this job, stability wins."

Brennan stood, closing the laptop and sealing it inside the hardened case. "I'll proceed immediately."

Obama didn't rise. "Make sure no one else sees that footage. And no one ever sees Max Rivette again."

Brennan gave a single, sharp nod, left the office, and disappeared into the machinery of the state.

Obama remained seated for a long time, staring at the place where the laptop had been.

After a while he whispered to the empty room:

"This world deserves better than us."

***

**Wednesday, 12th June 2013, 2:05 a.m.**
**Gaidon Ballerat's home, Prévessin-Moëns, France.**

Gaidon Ballerat awoke to a tapping sound.

He lay still for a moment, listening, half-convinced it was a dream. Then came a second tap, sharper, unmistakably intentional.

He groaned into his pillow. "If that is a bird, I swear I will relocate the entire species."

The tapping paused.

Then came a whisper, too close for comfort. "Gaidon!"

He bolted upright. That wasn't a bird. That was trouble.

He shuffled to the window, pulled the curtain back, and nearly swore out loud.

Daniel was crouched outside, face pressed sideways against the glass like an overgrown child.

"Open up!" Daniel hissed.

"What are you doing?" Gaidon whispered furiously. "It is two in the morning!"

"Open the window, let me in!"

Gaidon sighed, lifted the latch, and stepped back as Daniel clambered inside in a chaotic heap. He fell onto the floor with a graceless thump.

"You could have used the door," Gaidon muttered.

"I'm trying not to get killed," Daniel whispered back.

"What. Why?"

Daniel sat up, hair wild, face flushed with adrenaline. "I have something. Something big."

"Oh wonderful," Gaidon said. "Let me fetch my heart medication."

"Gaidon, listen," Daniel insisted. "This started Sunday morning. I was at CERN, doing ATLAS calibrations, when my phone pinged."

"Your what?"

"My power monitor from laboratory triple eight," Daniel said. "One of the automated alerts from the RACE days. I never disabled it."

Gaidon stared at him.

"You left a live monitor on the machine after shutdown?"

Daniel winced. "Yes. Not my proudest oversight. But it saved us. The alert was real-time — the machine drew power."

Gaidon's expression flattened. "Power? How much?"

"Significant," Daniel said. "A full operational spike. Then it vanished almost instantly under a security lockout."

"And you tried to access it," Gaidon said.

"Briefly," Daniel admitted. "Then I realised who controls that machine now. The CIA doesn't issue warnings. They issue consequences. So I backed off."

Gaidon nodded once. "That is the first sensible decision you've made in years."

Daniel let the comment pass. "But the next day I couldn't shake it. The timing, the pattern of the spike — it was too familiar. So I tried again."

"And?"

"Nothing. The network was sealed. CERN on the surface... but something far heavier underneath. I couldn't get anywhere near it alone."

"So what did you do?"

Daniel looked sheepish. "I called Emerancie Favre."

Gaidon blinked. "Emerancie? She left CERN."

"That's why I called her," Daniel said. "She's furious about how she was pushed out. You know her—give her a conspiracy and she'll sharpen her knives before you finish the sentence. I told her what I'd seen. She didn't hesitate."

"And she helped you break in," Gaidon said slowly.

"She taught me how," Daniel corrected. "Kali Linux, custom scripts, a bypass toolkit on a USB. I watched her work for two hours. She made it look like knitting."

Gaidon sighed. "God help us."

"Yesterday afternoon," Daniel continued, "I sat at my desk in ATLAS, opened a dummy project window to look respectable, plugged in her drive, and started digging."

"And you weren't caught?"

"They weren't looking for someone like me," Daniel said. "They think the old team is broken up and terrified."

Gaidon's face tightened.

"They made sure of it. After Nicolas sent those spying drones in October, Baset, Emerancie, Daniel — even Vincent — were removed from the group. Transferred, reassigned, scattered. In their place the Americans ran things: button-pushing, basic operations, nothing requiring understanding. They dismantled our team so no one would question anything."

Daniel swallowed. "Exactly. They weren't watching for anyone who still cared."

Daniel leaned forward. "I broke through. Not far, but far enough. I found the power logs. Sunday morning. Exactly the same pattern as the activation last year. The machine ran for fifty-two seconds. Identical curve."

Gaidon felt his pulse shift. "Fifty-two seconds, that's enough time for someone to..."

"Use the machine to transfer," Daniel said quietly. "Either in or out."

"What about video?"

"Scrubbed," Daniel said. "Everything wiped clean. No camera feeds, no sensor telemetry. Just shadows where there should be data. But there were traces — timestamped blank files, overwritten directories. Someone erased things after the fact. And they did it fast."

"And you're sure the machine ran?"

"I'm sure," Daniel said. "And the timing isn't a coincidence."

Gaidon sat on the edge of the bed, staring at nothing.

"One year," he murmured. "They told him a year."

Daniel nodded. "To the minute."

The room went silent.

Gaidon whispered, "They sent him back."

Daniel swallowed hard. "That's what I came to tell you. Max returned on Sunday morning."

Gaidon closed his eyes. "And they hid it."

"Yes."

"They'll never tell us what they did with him."

"No," Daniel said softly. "But we know he's here. Somewhere. And they're lying to everyone."

Gaidon rubbed his face. "Why did you come through my window?"

"Because if I used your door," Daniel whispered, "and the CIA has your house flagged, I'd be dead before sunrise."

Gaidon blew out a breath. "You are an idiot."

Daniel smiled weakly. "Maybe. But an idiot who found something."

Gaidon met his gaze. "So what now?"

Daniel swallowed. "Now we find Max."

***

# Chapter 26



Max Rivette had stopped trying to count the days. The cell gave him nothing to measure them with — the lights never dimmed, the air never changed, and no sound leaked in from the corridor. Time flattened into a featureless slab.

Meals arrived without warning: a metal tray sliding through a narrow slot at the base of the door, three times a day by his best guess. No voices. No footsteps. Just the scrape of steel on steel and the retreating click of a mechanism.

Every few days — he thought — the door would unlock and two silent guards would escort him to a shower. No conversation, no eye contact. Ten minutes, then back inside.

Since that first interview with Nicolas, no one had spoken a word to him. No doctor. No questions. Not even a token welfare check. Eventually the truth settled over him with a slow, icy finality:

He wasn't being assessed.

He wasn't being monitored.

He had been put away.

Locked out of sight. Locked out of mind.

And left there.

The realisation echoed against older memories he thought he'd left behind. He had spent six weeks in the holding centre in the parallel world, unsure of his fate, unsure of the rules, unsure of everything except that he had been removed from ordinary life. That experience had frightened him at the time, but it had also shown him something important—that he could survive confinement without losing himself. The walls had closed in then too, but he'd come out intact.

Now, in this featureless concrete room, those memories offered a strange form of ballast. He knew he had endured worse uncertainties than this; he knew he had the resilience to face isolation without disappearing into it.

He sat up on the narrow bed and let his thoughts drift toward Clarisse Ampère. Whenever he felt the edges of panic rising, he imagined her standing in the doorway of her apartment, arms folded, giving him that patient, slightly amused look she always used when she thought he was overthinking something. The memory softened the harshness of the cell. He remembered her laugh, the way she would place a hand briefly on his shoulder to steady him, and the promise he had whispered to her before leaving —the promise to return. It had felt sincere and certain at the time. It still did.

He wasn't sure how he was going to keep that promise from inside the CIA's walls, but the promise itself mattered. It reminded him that life existed beyond this concrete slab, that a world he cared about was still waiting for him.

Just as important was the reason he had returned at all. He had spent a year living in a society that operated on principles entirely foreign to this one. Their cooperation wasn't theoretical. Their stability wasn't propaganda. He had seen what life looked like when people weren't organised around fear, competition, and hierarchy. The memory of that world, its confidence and cohesion, felt like something he carried inside him now, something no prison could fully suppress. Even here, stripped of freedom and contact, the knowledge remained intact.

Max let his feet rest on the cold floor and steadied his breathing. There was no way to know how long the CIA intended to keep him here. The answer might well be "indefinitely." But he had no intention of letting this place hollow him out. He had survived a year in another world, survived losing everything familiar, survived learning how to live completely differently. This cell wasn't going to undo that.

There would be moments later—small windows, brief opportunities, gaps in attention. He didn't fool himself into thinking escape would be simple, but he also knew systems built on secrecy had weak points. If he kept his mind clear and refused to let fear drive him, he'd notice things. People slipped. Procedures faltered. Nothing remained airtight forever.

He leaned back against the wall and let his thoughts settle. Clarisse was part of his anchor. The twelve-rule world was another. Between the two, he felt something steady return to him. Not optimism—something quieter, more durable.

Whatever came next, he intended to face it with his eyes open.

***

**Friday, 28th June 2013, 11:37 a.m**
**Céleste Guérard's apartment, Prévessin-Moëns, France.**

Her phone lit up: APPEL ANONYME.
A public line, or someone masking their number. Never a good sign.

Still, she answered.

"Bonjour?"

"Madame Guérard? This is Gaidon Ballerat."

Her grip tightened around the cup. She hadn't heard that name — or that voice — in a year. Not since the morning Max vanished into the other world. That call had begun the spiral that ended with the visit from the American official.

"Yes, I remember you," she said carefully. "Why are you calling?"

A pause. "I need to speak with you about Max."

The breath left her chest in one sharp, involuntary shock.

"There's nothing to speak about," she said, voice tightening. "Max is *dead*."

Gaidon's tone sharpened instantly. "Dead? Who told you that?"

She let the bitterness rise — bitterness she'd buried out of necessity, not acceptance.

"That American man..."

"Nicolas Hightower," Gaidon said immediately. "CIA. Dangerous."

She didn't argue. "He told me Max was contaminated. That the body had to be destroyed."

She swallowed. "And before him, another man from the embassy said Max had been exposed to a massive dose of radiation. They blamed you." Her voice cracked. "*I blamed you.*"

Silence wavered across the line.

"So unless you have something real," she said, regaining her composure, "don't call me with *lies*."

"I'm not calling with lies," Gaidon said. "The machine activated again. Sunday morning. To the exact minute Max left our world. I saw the power logs myself. I helped build the machine — I know its signature. Someone ran it, and someone scrubbed the records immediately afterward. When the CIA seals something that fast, they're not protecting people. They're protecting a narrative."

Céleste braced herself against the counter.

"You're telling me he's alive."

"I'm telling you he was sent back," Gaidon said. "And the moment he returned, someone took him. I don't know who has him now — but the CIA is involved. That much is certain."

She said nothing at first. Her mind couldn't compute the collision of grief, anger, disbelief, and the faint, dangerous tremor of hope.

"They told me he was dead," she whispered. "Both of them. And you're saying it was all... invented."

"Yes," Gaidon said. "Whatever Hightower told you, it served *their* needs, not yours."

Her pulse quickened, panic rising. "Why lie to me? Why bother lying to *me*?"

"Because you're a loose end," Gaidon said. "Because controlling you helps control the story. Because if you knew the truth, you'd start asking questions they don't want asked."

She closed her eyes. "If he's alive... I don't know what to feel."

"I wish I had certainty," Gaidon said. "But I swear to you — I'm going to find out what happened to him. I'm not stepping away. Not after everything."

Céleste steadied herself, voice firmer now. "Then be careful. These men fabricate stories the way other people breathe."

"I know what they are," Gaidon said. "And I'm not letting them decide the ending."

Something in his voice — the resolve, the anger — cut through her numbness more clearly than any evidence could.

"If you learn anything," she said, "you call me immediately."

"I will," he promised. "I'm sorry they lied to you."

She didn't respond. The call ended a moment later, leaving her alone in the quiet kitchen — the tap still running, the cup cooling in her hand.

Her grief didn't vanish. But it shifted, cracked, reconfigured itself. Underneath it was something she had forgotten how to feel.

Not quite hope.

But the shape of possibility.

For the first time since the Americans came to her door, the story was moving beneath her feet.

***

**Friday, 28th June 2013, 12:04 p.m.**
**Munich Airport, Germany.**

Nicolas Hightower sat in a busy departure lounge, surrounded by restless travellers and the metallic echo of airport announcements. He was reviewing a report on a secure tablet when his CIA-issued mobile gave a sharp two-tone buzz — the alert reserved for surveillance flags.

He answered immediately.

"Hightower."

A technician from the Geneva facility spoke quickly. "We intercepted a call that matches your parameters. Sending audio now."

There was a click, followed by the recorded conversation: Céleste Guérard's voice rising in distress, Gaidon Ballerat contradicting her, claiming Max had been returned and was being held by the CIA, promising to "get to the bottom of it." The call was short — under three minutes — but every second was dangerous.

When the audio ended, the technician returned. "Pulled from her passive buffer. No secondary access."

"Good," Nicolas said. "Send me the transcript. Secure the original."

He ended the call and stood, moving to a quieter alcove near a row of darkened shops. His expression had flattened into operational neutrality.

He dialled another number. After several rings, a French voice answered.

"Commissaire Verdan."

"Leon, it's Nicolas Hightower. I need your immediate assistance."

Verdan sounded cautious, searching his memory. "Hightower... CIA liaison, yes? What's happened?"

"We have an urgent situation involving one of your citizens," Nicolas said. "A CERN staff member—Gaidon Ballerat."

There was a faint pause while Verdan sorted through vague recollections. "I may remember the name. It was connected to that particle project, wasn't it?"

"Yes," Nicolas said, "and that project involved technology sensitive enough to be classified at the highest level. Ballerat has now made unauthorised contact with a protected civilian — a woman he has no legal or ethical right to approach."

Verdan's tone sharpened. "What kind of contact?"

"Pressure," Nicolas said. "He confronted her with fabricated claims about the former experiment, made insinuations about government actions, and attempted to steer her toward a false narrative. We have the entire call recorded."

"And you're certain it was pressure?"

"It was deliberate," Nicolas said. "We've just identified a credible terrorist plan seeking access to information from the project. Ballerat's behaviour aligns with someone attempting to obstruct or warn others. Whether willingly or under influence is unknown, but the impact is the same."

Verdan absorbed this quickly, but with visible unease. "If he's interfering in an active investigation, that changes things."

"It does," Nicolas replied. "And we can provide documentation to justify immediate action. There are irregularities in his conduct, security breaches tied to his credentials, and inconsistencies in project logs under his supervision. Enough for a warrant, enough for detention, and enough to keep him isolated until we determine what role he's playing."

Verdan hesitated. "You're requesting an arrest."

"I'm requesting you move now," Nicolas said. "We cannot allow him another conversation. If he reaches anyone else, he could compromise an operation that involves both our governments."

The commissaire exhaled slowly. "Understood. Send the evidence you have. I'll initiate the process and have officers dispatched."

"You'll have the files within the hour."

Nicolas ended the call and looked out across the airport tarmac, where ground crew moved like small figures between aircraft tails. The normalcy of the scene contrasted sharply with what he had just set in motion.

He returned to his bench, opened a secure form, and entered the necessary details. The paperwork was precise, clinical, built from a mixture of truth, omission, and expertly assembled fiction.

When he typed the final line — "Subject: immediate containment recommended" — he sent the form through the encrypted channel.

Across the border in France, machinery began to move.

Phones would ring.

Uniforms would gather.

A door would soon be knocked upon.

And Gaidon Ballerat, unaware of the storm turning in his direction, had already run out of time.

***

# Chapter 27

**Mid-September 2013.**
**Secret CIA prison, Geneva, Switzerland.**

Max Rivette had reached the point where the days no longer distinguished themselves. Everything blended together: the dull tray of food slid inside three times a day, the identical concrete walls, the fluorescent light that never changed, and the silence enforced by guards who treated him as if he barely existed. Early on he tried asking questions, but after receiving the same blank indifference each time, he stopped trying.

The routine was simple.

Eat.

Wait.

Shower twice a week under supervision.

Return to the cell.

Repeat.

There were no explanations, no updates, no sign of Nicolas Hightower. In the first month, Max had still expected Hightower to appear with some bureaucratic nonsense, a new interview, a review, anything. By mid-September, that hope had worn down to nothing.

It reminded him, uncomfortably and sharply, of what Dominic had told him in the parallel world: the description of RFC — Removal From Contact. Hearing those details had terrified him at the time: the sensory deprivation, the silence, the fluorescent lights that never dimmed, the guards who did not speak, the bland food packets shoved through a slot. He remembered the chill that went through him when Dominic explained the rules in that cramped induction cell in Paris, remembered standing there while learning just how far that society would go in the name of preventing harm. He had never experienced RFC, but the idea alone had been enough to keep him cautious and cooperative.

Now, here, he understood something Dominic's explanation hadn't captured. RFC in the parallel world had been cold, bureaucratic, and arguably excessive — but it still had structure, oversight, and a rationale rooted in a system that at least pretended to be humane. Here, in this CIA-run black site, isolation was simply cruelty without justification. No context. No review. No path out.

The guards didn't look him in the eye anymore. They didn't acknowledge his presence except to move him from one room to another. He wasn't being assessed. He wasn't being evaluated. He was being erased.

On this particular morning, Max was sitting on the edge of the bed, elbows on his knees, staring at the floor. The numbness in his chest had been building for weeks, and today it felt close to breaking open. When he finally spoke, his voice was hoarse.

"Why am I here?"

No one responded. The question fell flat against the concrete.

He stood and approached the door. "Guard. I need to speak to Hightower."

Silence.

He tried again, harder. "Get me Hightower!"

The sound of a boot shifting outside the door was the only acknowledgment he received. It wasn't enough.

Frustration rose quickly — too quickly. The lack of human contact had reshaped his thoughts, pushed them into corners he'd never imagined. In RFC, Dominic had said, the silence could unravel people. Here, the silence felt designed to achieve exactly that result.

Max pressed his forehead against the door and tried to breathe, but the tension kept climbing. He told himself to centre, to remember Clarisse, to hold onto the image of her at the kitchen table, the smell of morning coffee, the promise he made to return. But the cell didn't allow clarity. It swallowed everything.

When a guard finally appeared — a large man with a blank expression — Max felt something inside him snap. He stepped toward the door before he had fully decided to. "I asked for Hightower," he said. "You heard me."

The guard didn't respond. He simply opened the slot and pushed a meal tray inside.

Max kicked the tray across the floor.

The lock clacked.

The door swung open.

Only then did Max see the guard — and the reaction was immediate: a slight tightening of the jaw, the first flicker of emotion Max had witnessed in months. A second guard stood behind him in the corridor, both moving with the same efficient, practised coordination.

They stepped inside.

"I want answers," Max said, though he already sensed what was coming.

Something inside Max broke.

He didn't think. Didn't plan. He just launched himself at the first shape in the doorway — a ragged, explosive burst of movement from a man who had been silent too long.

His shoulder slammed into the guard's chest. Max clawed for the man's throat, for his face, for anything he could hurt.

The guard reacted instantly.

A forearm snapped up under Max's chin, driving his head back. A brutal torque twisted his arm behind him, and Max was slammed sideways into the wall so hard the breath tore out of him. The second guard was already on him, sweeping his legs, pinning him down with a knee across the back of his thighs.

Max thrashed anyway — wild, directionless, animal. He didn't care what they did to him. He just needed the world to feel him again.

The guards didn't strike him.

They didn't shout.

They just held him — inexorable, immovable, trained strength pressing him into the concrete until the fight drained out of his muscles one trembling inch at a time.

The message was unmistakable:

You can rage.

You cannot win.

And for the first time since he entered that cell, Max felt the full collapse of his own sanity closing in around him.

Max stopped resisting almost as quickly as he had started. The fight drained out of him in seconds. When they released him, they left without a word, closing the door and locking it as if closing the lid on a box.

His breathing shook. The cell felt smaller than it had that morning, smaller than it had the week before. He didn't know how much longer he could maintain the line between himself and the crushing isolation that surrounded him.

For the first time since returning to his own world, he whispered something he didn't want to believe.

"I don't know how much more of this I can take."

The silence that followed was complete, and it pressed against him from every side.

***

**Thursday, 3rd October 2013, 9:00 a.m.**
**Special Assize Court, Paris, France.**

Three months earlier, they had taken Gaidon Ballerat from his home at dawn. No explanation, no warrant he could read, no familiar faces — just armed gendarmes and a sealed order. He had spent the time since in a maximum-security facility outside Lyon, in the block reserved for high-risk inmates: terrorists, organised-crime leaders, people the state no longer trusted to breathe unmonitored air.

He was not allowed contact with anyone from his former team. No Daniel, no Baset, no Emerancie, not even a note or second-hand message. His only human contact had been a court-appointed lawyer who visited once every two weeks and always looked apologetic before he even sat down.

"It concerns the experiments at Laboratory 888," the lawyer had told him during the first meeting, hands folded as if preparing Gaidon for a death sentence.

"Experiments in what sense?" Gaidon asked.

"I'm not permitted details," the lawyer replied. "The classification level is... unusually high. The magistrates consider the matter extremely serious."

Every visit after that had been the same: Gaidon pressing for answers, the lawyer shrugging helplessly.

"I'm not being given anything more," the man repeated. "Not even the full indictment."

Three months.

Three months in isolation, fed only fragments of implication and dread.

And now this.

Gaidon Ballerat was led into the courtroom in handcuffs, escorted by two gendarmes who avoided eye contact. The room was built for secrecy rather than justice: reinforced walls, sealed windows, and an atmosphere thick with the sense that the verdict had been written long before he arrived.

The judge didn't bother with ceremony. He signalled to the clerk, who began reading the charges in an even, almost bored voice.

"Gaidon Ballerat, you stand accused of aggravated homicide resulting in the death of Maximilien Rivette, conspiracy to commit acts endangering state security, and soliciting and receiving payment from a known terrorist group."

Gaidon's stomach dropped.

"Death?" he whispered. "They— they're saying I killed him?"

One of the guards tightened his grip on Gaidon's arm, urging him to stay still.

The clerk continued, tone unchanged. "The state contends that Mr Ballerat intentionally exposed Maximilien Rivette to lethal radiation during the Prévessin-Moëns experiment, in order to prevent Rivette from revealing Mr Ballerat's alleged cooperation with a terrorist organisation seeking access to classified CERN technology."

Gaidon nearly rose from his chair, barely held down by the guards.

"That's insane," he said. "None of that happened. Max was—"

The judge struck his gavel once. "You will remain silent unless asked to speak."

Gaidon glared at him. "You're accusing me of murder. You expect me to sit here quietly?"

His assigned defence lawyer — a bland, clean-cut man with the mannerisms of an accountant — laid a hand on his forearm. "We will respond at the appropriate time," he murmured.

Gaidon looked at him and saw exactly what he was dealing with.

A plant.

Handled by the CIA.

Hopeless by design.

The judge continued flatly.

"Certain evidence in this case has been designated secret défense under counter-terrorism statutes. The material will be reviewed in restricted session. Defence counsel will have limited access, subject to clearance."

Gaidon blinked. "Limited access? So I don't even get to see what I'm accused of?"

His lawyer adjusted his glasses, avoiding eye contact. "I'll be permitted to examine a summary, strictly on-site. I cannot reproduce it or discuss its contents in detail."

The prosecutor stepped in smoothly.

"The classified evidence includes operational logs, internal communications, and irregularities in the functioning of Laboratory 888. These items raise serious concerns about the defendant's conduct and intent in the days preceding Rivette's planned *accident* which eventually resulted in his death."

Gaidon barked out a humourless laugh. "Intent? You've invented an entire fantasy world. Max wasn't killed by radiation. He came back—"

Another gavel strike. Sharper this time.

"You will control yourself," the judge said. "This court will not tolerate disruption."

The prosecutor continued as if nothing had happened. "Additionally, the state asserts that the defendant attempted to intimidate Maximilien Rivette's aunt, Céleste Guérard, in order to obstruct her cooperation with federal investigators."

Gaidon felt the blood drain from his face. "I didn't intimidate her. I called to tell her the truth!"

"Mr Ballerat," the judge said sharply, "this is not a forum for theatrics. Your counsel will address the allegations when permitted."

Gaidon looked to his lawyer again. The man calmly rearranged his notes, showing no intention of challenging anything that had just been said.

This wasn't a defence.

This was pageantry.

The judge shuffled his papers. "Given the classified nature of the case, the court will recess until tomorrow morning, when the state will present its evidence in closed session."

Closed session.

Unattended.

Unquestioned.

They weren't even pretending he had a chance.

As the guards came to escort him away, Gaidon looked around the empty courtroom —no journalists, no observers, no hint of sunlight—and felt the full weight of what had been arranged for him.

This wasn't a trial.

It was disposal.

And tomorrow, they would bury him completely.

***

**Monday, 4th October 2013, 9:00 a.m.**
**Special Assize Court, Paris, France.**

The courtroom felt even smaller than it had the day before. The air was dry, the lighting unforgiving, and the emptiness behind the gallery rail gave everything a hollow, staged quality. Gaidon Ballerat had barely slept in the holding cell beneath the courthouse; the exhaustion showed in the way he carried himself as the gendarmes escorted him to the stand.

His defence lawyer offered no reassuring glance, no whispered reminder of strategy. He simply nodded in Gaidon's direction as though acknowledging a colleague at a bus stop. The meaning was clear: you're on your own.

The judge addressed him in a formal monotone. "Mr Ballerat, you will answer questions clearly and concisely. Any deviation from the subject matter will be treated as obstruction. Do you understand?"

"I understand," Gaidon said, though his voice cracked slightly from lack of sleep.

The prosecutor rose with a stack of papers he had no intention of using. He didn't need evidence; he had narrative. This was theatre, and he was already the one holding the script.

"Mr Ballerat," the prosecutor began, "you claim you had no involvement in the events leading to Maximilien Rivette's death. Is that correct?"

"Yes," Gaidon said. "Because he isn't dead. I—"

The prosecutor cut him off. "We are not here to indulge fantasy."

Gaidon's hands clenched at the edge of the witness stand. "It's not fantasy. Max was returned. The machine—"

"Returned from where?" the prosecutor asked, tone sharpened to a blade. "From a parallel universe?"

A faint, mocking ripple passed through the courtroom—no laughter, just a shift in posture, the quiet discrediting of a man who no longer had the right to dignity.

"Yes," Gaidon said. "I know how it sounds, but it's the truth. The machine activated again on the anniversary of his disappearance. I saw the logs myself. The CIA wiped the data. The CIA took him—"

The prosecutor leaned forward. "So your defence is that the CIA abducted a man who, according to every official document, died from radiation exposure?"

"They lied," Gaidon said. "They lied to his aunt. They lied to the team. They lied to you. They—"

Again the prosecutor cut him off. "Mr Ballerat, are you aware that your story exactly mirrors the behaviour of individuals who have previously fabricated conspiratorial narratives to evade responsibility?"

"My story?" Gaidon snapped. "This isn't a story. This is what happened."

The prosecutor flipped an empty page for effect. "Let us clarify. You claim that a classified scientific experiment opened a gateway to a parallel world. That Mr Rivette travelled through it. That he lived there for a year. And that he was returned by this same magic gateway, intercepted by intelligence personnel, and concealed from the public. Is this your testimony?"

Gaidon opened his mouth, stopped, then tried again. "Yes. Because it's the truth."

"So the CIA," the prosecutor said smoothly, "orchestrated a multinational cover-up of an event that defies all known physical laws, simply to frame you for a murder that—according to you—never occurred?"

"Yes," Gaidon said, frustration pushing past caution. "Because Max knew something. Because they didn't want the world to know what he saw."

The prosecutor gave a slight, satisfied nod, as though he had been waiting for that line.

The judge intervened. "Mr Ballerat, be advised that the court will not entertain unsubstantiated scientific fiction. You are required to answer the charges, not invent new ones."

Gaidon's breath quickened. "I'm not inventing anything. Look at the machine's power logs from June. Look at the CIA's movements that week. Look at the—"

The prosecutor interrupted again, voice raised just enough to appear decisive. "Mr Ballerat, the court does not have to 'look at' anything. The evidence has already been reviewed by the appropriate authorities."

"Evidence I'm not allowed to see!" Gaidon shouted, finally losing control. "Evidence you created! You're burying me because you're hiding something far bigger than me!"

Two gendarmes stepped closer.

The judge banged his gavel twice. "Order. This behaviour confirms the court's concerns regarding your emotional instability."

"I'm not unstable!" Gaidon said, trying to steady his breathing. "I'm telling you the truth. Max came back. They took him. I can prove—"

"You can prove nothing," the prosecutor said coolly. "What you have demonstrated today is an elaborate attempt to deflect from your own responsibility in a man's death."

Gaidon stared at him, fury tightening every muscle in his body. He knew the moment he'd lost control that this was exactly what they wanted. They hadn't needed evidence. They needed a performance, and he had just delivered it.

The judge gathered his papers. "This session is adjourned until tomorrow morning. "

The gendarmes moved in and took Gaidon by the arms. As they led him out, he looked back at the empty gallery where no one would ever hear the truth he had tried to tell.

***

**Tuesday, 12th November 2013, 9:00 a.m.**
**Special Assize Court, Paris, France.**

The verdict day arrived with the same chill that had filled every hearing before it. No journalists waited outside the building. No cameras followed the gendarmes escorting Gaidon Ballerat into the courtroom. The hall was nearly as empty as it had been on the first day — a few officials, a clerk, the defence lawyer who might as well have been a cardboard cutout, and the judge whose indifference had never once shifted.

Gaidon took his seat without looking at anyone. Six weeks of this process had drained him of the energy to resist. The second day of testimony had broken him; every attempt to tell the truth had been twisted into evidence of instability. By the end of that session, he had stopped trying. Nothing he said had mattered. Nothing was meant to.

The judge adjusted his spectacles and began reading the court's decision with the flat cadence of someone delivering an administrative ruling, not a life sentence.

"This court, having evaluated both the classified evidence presented by the state and the testimony provided, issues the following findings in the matter of Gaidon Ballerat versus the State."

Gaidon lifted his eyes only once — a brief, instinctive movement — but the judge never met his gaze.

"The defendant is found guilty of aggravated homicide, conspiracy to commit acts endangering national security, and deliberate collaboration with extremist elements."

A silence settled across the chamber, heavy and stale.

"The court finds that Mr Ballerat, having led the research programme known as the RACE experiment, pursued unauthorised lines of inquiry that posed a direct threat to public safety. Although the experiment initially showed scientific promise, evidence provided to the court demonstrates that the defendant knowingly exceeded operational parameters, falsified progress reports, and concealed emerging dangers."

A bitter sadness rose in Gaidon's chest. He had spent ten years of his life on RACE — long nights, failed prototypes, and worked countless hours, documenting everything. He had never falsified anything. He had been almost painfully honest about its limitations. But the court treated their fiction as fact, their story as scripture.

"The court further finds," the judge continued, "that following a series of professional setbacks and the realisation that the RACE project would not achieve its stated objectives, Mr Ballerat initiated contact with an anarchist terrorist organisation operating within Europe."

Gaidon closed his eyes. A nameless group — impossible to disprove, impossible to fight.

"It has been established that Mr Ballerat offered access to components of the RACE technology in exchange for financial compensation, in the amount of seven hundred and fifty thousand euros."

He barely heard the rest. The number didn't matter. They could have said five euros or five million; the fabrication stood either way.

The judge turned a page without pausing.

"The state has submitted documents, encrypted exchanges, and financial records indicating that the defendant intended to provide the RACE system as a foundation for weapons development."

His defence lawyer did not react. He didn't take notes. He didn't move. He had not objected once throughout the entire process.

The judge continued.

"The most serious matter before the court concerns the death of Mr Maximilien

Rivette, an employee under the defendant's supervision and the sole individual to discover the defendant's illicit activities."

Gaidon's jaw tightened. There it was — the centrepiece of the lie.

"The court finds that Mr Ballerat acted with clear intent when he orchestrated Mr Rivette's exposure to a lethal dose of radiation on the 9th of June 2012, thereby ensuring Mr Rivette could not reveal the defendant's collaboration with said extremist organisation."

A few lines on a page, delivered without emotion, had rewritten Max's fate and Gaidon's life in a single stroke.

"Mr Rivette succumbed to his injuries six weeks later at a secure private medical facility. The defendant made no attempt to assist him, nor to notify authorities of the cause."

Gaidon stared at the wooden edge of the dock, unable to speak. Any protest would be recorded as further proof of instability. He had learned that the hard way.

The judge reached the final page.

"Given the severity of the offences and the risk posed to national and international security, the court sentences Gaidon Ballerat to indefinite detention in a designated high-security facility. He shall be housed under conditions appropriate to individuals deemed a continuing threat to public safety. The terms include extended solitary confinement as determined by security assessments."

There was no dramatic finale.

No gavel strike.

No declaration of adjournment.

The judge simply closed the folder, handed it to the clerk, and rose. The gendarmes moved in without prompting.

Gaidon didn't resist. He didn't speak. He let them take his arms and guide him toward the door. The hallway outside smelled faintly of cleaning solution, and as the security door clanged shut behind him, he realised this had been the last room he would ever see as a free man.

The world had decided what he was.

And there was no one left to contradict it.

***

**Tuesday, 12th November 2013, 2:12 p.m.**
**Special Assize Court, Paris, France.**

The press briefing took place not in the main courtroom but in a narrow, echoing corridor designed for controlled messaging — two podiums, a line of uniformed officers, and a handful of pre-screened journalists who already understood they weren't going to learn anything unexpected.

A government spokesperson — polished, calm, expressionless — stepped up to the microphone, a prepared statement gripped firmly in both hands.

"Ladies and gentlemen," she began, "the Special Assize Court has concluded its deliberations in the matter of *State versus Gaidon Ballerat*. We are authorised to release the following summary."

She did not glance at the cameras.

She simply read.

"Mr Ballerat, formerly a senior researcher at CERN, has been found guilty of aggravated homicide resulting in the death of Maximilien Rivette, conspiracy to commit acts endangering state security, and soliciting and receiving payment from a known terrorist organisation."

Several heads in the crowd lifted — homicide always drew attention — but the spokesperson pressed on before anyone could interrupt.

"The court determined that Mr Ballerat engaged in unauthorised correspondence with a terrorist organisation, providing its members with sensitive information derived from experiments conducted at CERN. This information was intended to enable the development of advanced weapons for use against the civilian population. Furthermore, the court found that Mr Ballerat deliberately exposed a CERN employee, Mr Maximilien Rivette, to a fatal dose of radiation in an effort to conceal his activities."

She paused for effect. A few cameras clicked.

Not many.

Interest was present, but thin.

"In light of these findings, the court has issued a sentence of indefinite detention in a high-security facility. Given the classified nature of the evidence, no further details will be released."

A journalist toward the back raised a hand. "Is there any comment from CERN on these allegations?"

"The organisation has cooperated fully," the spokesperson said, offering the most neutral smile imaginable. "They support the court's conclusion that Mr Ballerat acted independently and without the institution's knowledge."

Another hand shot up. "And what about Mr Rivette's family?"

"A representative of the government has met with them privately," she answered. "We ask that the public respect their privacy."

It was a line designed to shut down any follow-up. It worked.

Within ten minutes, the briefing was over.

Twenty minutes later, the first short articles appeared online:

CERN Scientist Jailed for Terror-Linked Homicide

French Court Finds Researcher Responsible for Fatal Radiation Exposure

Security Breach in Particle Research Facility Leads to International Investigation

Headlines like these travelled quickly, but without the fuel of politics, celebrity, or spectacle, they burned out just as fast. A few commentators speculated about what 'classified evidence' might mean. Others recycled the press statement almost word for word. By the next morning, the story was already sliding down the news rankings. By the end of the week, it was overshadowed entirely by a government budget dispute and a celebrity scandal.

Within days it became one of those strange, half-remembered stories that most people heard once and didn't think about again — a footnote in the jittery catalogue of post-9/11 security cases.

And for the few who knew what had actually happened, the silence that followed was exactly the point.

***

# Chapter 28

**November 2013.**
**Secret CIA prison, Geneva, Switzerland.**

The days had blurred into something shapeless. Maximilien Rivette had stopped keeping track of how long he'd been in the cell because every attempt to count ended in the same quiet collapse: nothing changed, nothing improved, and nothing reached him from the outside world. Whatever thin thread of purpose he'd walked in with had frayed under the constant isolation.

He tried to anchor himself by remembering the parallel world — Clarisse's steady presence, the calm certainty with which people handled conflict, the feeling of being surrounded by something functional and sane. But the more he reached for those memories, the further away they slipped. He began to doubt himself. Doubt his choices. Doubt the mission he'd once believed in so fiercely.

Some nights, lying awake under the fluorescent lights that never dimmed, he replayed the moment he stepped back into his own universe. *Was it worth it?*

He had told himself it was. He had told himself the truth mattered. But as the days crushed inward, even that conviction felt flimsy.

He was yelling again tonight.

Not because it helped, but because silence had become unbearable. When the guards ignored him, he shouted louder. When they acknowledged him, even with irritation, it was something — a sign the world still existed beyond the concrete.

A guard appeared at the door with the evening tray. Max hurled the previous tray toward the slot before the man could slide the new one in.

"Talk to me!" Max shouted, voice hoarse. "Tell me why I'm here! Tell me what the hell you want from me! I'm not done! I'm not dead! I'm not—"

The guard snapped.

"Shut the fuck up."

The words hit harder than the guards ever had. Max froze mid-breath.

The guard leaned closer to the door, scowling. "You think anyone cares? You think you matter? Now that Gaidon is locked up for killing you in that radiation accident, you're even more disposable than before."

Max went still. Utterly still.

He didn't respond. Didn't blink. Didn't breathe for a long moment.

The guard shoved the tray through the slot, muttered something under his breath, and began to walk away. By the time the footsteps faded, Max was still rooted to the same spot, staring at the door as if something written on the metal might explain what he'd just heard.

*Radiation accident.*

*Gaidon locked up.*

*Killed you.*

He replayed it in his mind, word by word. The guard hadn't been careful; it had slipped out in anger. Not a rehearsed line. Not an official message.

It was information.

Real information.

The first he'd heard in months.

Max sat slowly on the edge of the bed, letting the shock settle. If the guard believed he was supposed to be dead, then someone had created a story — a lie big enough to justify whatever had been done to him. And if Gaidon had been arrested, then something outside was moving. There was a chain of events unfolding beyond these walls, and he wasn't as forgotten as the silence had made him believe.

His mind, dulled by the monotony of confinement, began to work again. Painfully at first, then faster. The guard had no reason to invent that detail. It was too specific, too casual, too bitterly delivered to be a fabrication.

Someone had told the world he was dead.

And if they needed him dead, then he was more valuable alive than he had realised.

For the first time in weeks, a faint current of energy stirred in him. Not comfort — nothing close to that — but clarity. The world was still turning. People were still acting. Lies were being told, and lies always pointed to something important beneath them.

Max set the tray aside and leaned back against the cold wall, not to rest but to think.

He wasn't done.

He wasn't finished.

And now, finally, he wasn't in the dark.

He had a thread — thin, fragile, dangerous — but a thread nonetheless.

And he wasn't letting go.

***

**Saturday, 23rd November 2013, 1:11 p.m.**
**Prévessin-Moëns public library, France.**

The news of Gaidon Ballerat's conviction had washed through the region in the usual way — a few headlines, a cluster of startled conversations in cafés, then the inevitable fade as newer stories pushed it down the page. For most people, it was just another security trial. For Céleste Guérard, it explained the silence.

The phone call she'd received from Gaidon months earlier had left a mark she tried not to revisit. The urgency in his voice, the insistence that Maximilien had been returned, the warning not to trust the Americans — it had all seemed like grief or guilt twisting a man who'd lost control of his own work. But now, with the news repeating the state's narrative of radiation and terrorism, she found no comfort in the explanation. The official story didn't sit right. It was too convenient. Too clean.

Gaidon had vanished.

Maximilien was declared dead.

And no one would speak to her plainly.

So she decided to look on her own.

The public library in Prévessin-Moëns was quiet on Saturday afternoons. A few students, a couple of retirees, a librarian shelving biographies — nothing out of place. Céleste signed in on one of the communal computers, sat down, and stared at the blank search bar for a long moment.

She typed the only phrase she had:

RACE experiment CERN

The results were thin. Most were outdated references from academic conferences years earlier. A handful were speculative blog posts. None were useful.

She tried again.

"CERN RACE team"

"RACE experiment staff"

"RACE project researchers"

More of the same: disappointing, vague, sterilised.

Then a single line caught her eye — a cached index page from a CERN archive. It wasn't detailed, but it listed a handful of contributors from the early development years. Most were administrative. One name stood out. Max had told her about this physicist — the one whose outrageous, colorful outfits utterly belied his genius.

Daniel Mittermayer — computer modelling and simulation lead.

She recognised none of the others. She didn't need to. Daniel was enough.

It took her five minutes to pull up an old academic profile with a contact number and a personal website. He had left CERN by then — the page noted work in Geneva's tech sector. That alone made him safer to approach than anyone still bound by security contracts.

Céleste closed the browser history, wiped her fingerprints from the mouse, and left the library with a sense of purpose she hadn't allowed herself to feel since June. She didn't know where this path led, but she knew it was the first real step she'd taken toward understanding what had happened to her nephew.

What she didn't know — couldn't know — was that every keystroke she'd entered had already been recorded.

Nicolas Hightower's digital surveillance net had been in place from the moment the Gaidon operation began. He had ordered an automated sweep over global search traffic for any unusual intersections: queries linking any CERN RACE personnel with either Maximilien Rivette or Gaidon Ballerat. On their own, Rivette and Ballerat triggered too much noise — half the curious citizens of Europe had searched those names during the trial week. But the other names? The ones never mentioned publicly?

Those were the tripwires.

Baset Theron.

Emerancie Favre.

Vincent Duke.

Adéhémar Baille.

Daniel Mittermayer.

Names scrubbed from official messaging, fully absent from the sham trial.

Anyone researching two of them together — especially with either Rivette or Ballerat — moved to the top of the threat board. Another filter narrowed the field further: geographic proximity. Searches originating within forty kilometres of Geneva were reviewed manually.

In the first two weeks, the system had flagged four individuals — all former CERN employees who, out of personal curiosity, had looked up old colleagues after hearing about the trial. Dragonetz Coté visited each one. His approach was quiet but effective: a polite reminder of ongoing classified investigations, a warning wrapped in diplomacy, and a cold smile that told them a second visit wouldn't be pleasant. All four stopped searching immediately.

The system returned to silence.

Until 1:27 p.m. on Saturday.

The alert pulsed bright red on the monitoring console.

ALERT: MATCHED QUERY PATTERN

Origin: Prévessin-Moëns

Search terms: "RACE experiment CERN" → "CERN RACE team" → "Daniel Mittermayer RACE CERN" → "Daniel Mittermayer contact"

User location: public library terminal 3

Name attached to login: Céleste Guérard

A soft chime sounded.

Then a second one — the proximity filter adjusting the threat index.

The automation pushed her to the top of the list.

A technician escalated it to Nicolas's personal channel.

FLAG: POSSIBLE FAMILY MEMBER OF DECEASED SUBJECT 'RIVETTE'. FURTHER ACTION ADVISED.

He read it once.

Then again.

Months earlier, he had told Dragonetz that if Céleste resurfaced, they were to move immediately.

She had just resurfaced — and she had done so by entering exactly the combination of searches that suggested she already suspected the official story was a lie.

Nicolas closed the report, reached for his phone, and issued the order with the same steadiness he used for every necessary operation.

"Locate Coté. Tell him he's needed in Prévessin-Moëns. Immediately."

***

**Sunday, 24th November 2013, 2:03 a.m.**
**Céleste Guérard's apartment, Prévessin-Moëns, France.**

Dragonetz Coté had arrived before sunset. He parked two streets away, walked the rest of the distance, and took up a position where he could see the entrance without drawing attention. He watched for hours, motionless. The apartment lights shifted occasionally — kitchen, hallway, bathroom — nothing unusual. She came home shortly after six, carrying her handbag and a thin folder. She never left again.

Nothing suggested she intended to contact anyone. No activity on her devices. No movement outside. She kept to the apartment for the rest of the night, silent and withdrawn.

By midnight the street was empty, the temperature dropping. At one a.m., lights in the other apartments went out. Dragonetz waited another hour, just to be sure. He approached the building without hesitation, stepping around the spots where the entry cameras couldn't catch him. The back stairwell door had a cheap lock; he opened it in less than eight seconds.

Inside the hallway, he moved with quiet efficiency. No sound carried. No movement disturbed the stillness. He reached her door and used a thin, flexible tool to slip past the lock. It gave quietly. No alarm. No one else inside.

Céleste was awake.

He found her seated at the kitchen table, shoulders shaking, hands pressed to her face. A cold cup of tea sat untouched beside her. She didn't hear him enter. She was too far gone in her grief to sense anyone near her.

Dragonetz paused only long enough to confirm she was alone.

Then he moved.

One step behind her.

A hand on the back of her neck to steady her.

The other pressing a small autoinjector against her skin beneath the hairline.

The device contained a dose of succinylcholine chloride — a paralytic that acted in seconds, left the heart unprotected, and metabolised so completely that most coroners mistook the end result for a natural cardiac event.

She gasped, startled more by the sudden human touch than the pain. She turned slightly, eyes widening when she realised someone was standing over her. She opened her mouth — not to scream, but to speak — and then the drug hit her bloodstream.

Her muscles loosened instantly.

Her breath faltered.

Her body slumped against the kitchen table.

He held her upright long enough to ensure the dose took full effect, then eased her gently to the floor so she wouldn't make noise. She was gone before she touched the tiles. No struggle. No words. Just a soft exhale as the life left her.

Dragonetz checked her pulse out of habit.

Nothing.

He wiped the small mark on her skin with a cloth, retrieved the injector, and let the apartment fall back into the stillness he had found it in.

Satisfied, he left the way he had entered, closing the door behind him with the quiet care of a man placing the final tile in a pattern.

By the time he reached his car, the street was silent again.

Another job completed.

Another loose end removed.

No trace that would trouble anyone who mattered.

And the only person in the world who still carried the truth about Maximilien Rivette was dead.

***

**Tuesday, 3rd December 2013, 12:34 p.m.**
**Parallel universe. European Advanced Physics Laboratory, Pfronten, Germany.**

Light snow drifted in diagonal sheets across the roofs and courtyards of the Pfronten facility. The place looked exactly as it had in summer — low, wide buildings of pale stone, long windows catching the weak light, pathways kept clear with quiet diligence. Nothing dramatic, nothing high-tech bristling at the sky. Just the same calm, orderly competence the site had always projected, now wearing a thin winter coat.

Aimes Perrier cleared security, logged his arrival, and followed Félix Köster down a corridor lined with pinned diagrams and diagnostic readouts.

"The instability is fixed," Félix said, scanning a column of figures as they walked. "Three full-duration cycles. All stable."

"So the long activation is safe?"

"Yes. Everything is ready."

Aimes nodded; Félix's judgment meant more to him than the numbers.

They reached Félix's office — a modest room with a desk on one side and a small seating area near the window. On the low table, the holoprojector flickered faintly with TaloSyn's colorful abstract waveform.

They sat.

Aimes began without delay. "Félix, we need to address the broader picture. We've heard nothing from Max for six months. Nothing."

Aimes gathered his thoughts.

"He mentioned an intelligence group from his world... the—"

The holoprojector brightened.

"The CIA," TaloSyn said. "That is the organisation he described."

Aimes nodded once. "Yes. That."

He exhaled. "We've had no movement on their side. No emergency signal. No atmospheric disturbance. And based on what Max told us... there's a chance—"

TaloSyn's colours sharpened slightly, becoming darker.

"More than a chance. An extremely high probability," it said. "But not a certainty."

TaloSyn continued. "Max described institutions shaped by secrecy, centralised authority, and force. Those traits increase the likelihood that he has been detained. But we cannot determine his status with the information we have."

There was a quiet silence for several seconds before Felix spoke up. "So we proceed on the assumption he may be alive, and possibly held. Nothing more."

"That assumption is appropriate," TaloSyn said.

Félix leaned forward. "Then the machine's readiness matters even more."

"It does," TaloSyn replied. "And it is ready."

Aimes paused, then frowned. "One thing I still don't fully understand — why place the receiving chamber a kilometre up the mountain? I know distance was part of it, but not the full reasoning."

Félix nodded. "The choice was straightforward. A mountaintop minimises risk — far less likely to have roads, buildings, or people located at the portal opening. When the portal reopens, we want somewhere safe to conduct our operation, not a house or a highway."

He continued, "After the feasibility run in October, the risk committee formalised the decision. TaloSyn designed the chamber to be semi-portable — difficult to move, but possible with planning. It can also raise itself six metres for alignment, the same principle CERN used."

Aimes gestured for him to continue.

"When we opened the first micro-shell," Félix said, holding his fingers a few centimetres apart, "TaloSyn kept the aperture tiny. Just enough for cameras. What we saw was untouched forest — winter-dark, no structures, no human presence. Much safer than opening inside a populated area."

"And the specific ridge?"

"TaloSyn triangulated it as the safest coordinate: low foot traffic, no tourist routes, stable terrain. We confirmed it twice. After the micro-shell closed, we pulled through a few severed branches — harmless, but a reminder that if we'd opened elsewhere, we might have dragged something far worse."

Aimes nodded. "So the ridge wasn't guesswork."

"Not at all. And after that, we relocated the entire receiving chamber — including the underground infrastructure — about fifteen metres so that the opening aligns with the edge of their ski slope in their world. Statistically the least dangerous point of contact."

Aimes let that settle. "Good. Then we move forward."

TaloSyn's external display changed to a slightly larger, more colorful, slowly shifting abstract display that reflected its optimism.

"The long-duration activation will succeed. All remaining variables are accounted for."

Aimes rose. "Then today becomes the turning point."

Félix stood with him. "We run the activation. Once confirmed, we start planning."

"TaloSyn shrank slightly, its colours becoming more muted.

"All variables are controlled. When the chamber opens, we proceed."

Outside, snow drifted through the valley — quiet, steady, indifferent.

A kilometre up the ridge, the receiving chamber waited beneath the pines, poised on the boundary between two worlds.

The parallel world had run out of patience.

***

**Tuesday, 3rd December 2013, 2:54 p.m.**
**Parallel Universe. European Advanced Physics Laboratory, Pfronten, Germany.**

The control room in the Pfronten valley lab looked exactly like the rest of the facility: functional, disciplined, built by people who valued results over theatre. A long technical console dominated one wall, its surface crowded with high-resolution monitors, input panels, and live data feeds from APEX-3's subsystems. Felix Köster sat at the central station, three technicians spaced along the console beside him. Aimes Perrier stood a little back from them, hands clasped behind his back as he studied the screens.

One monitor displayed a pair of coordinates.

47°32'57.6"N — 10°33'04.8"E

Aimes pointed at the display.

"What's that location?"

"Oh—just the lat-long," Felix replied, adjusting a power curve. "It's where the portal manifests in both universes. The mountain ridge."

Aimes absorbed this without comment.

Felix brought up the activation interface. At the bottom of the screen sat the machine's designation:

APEX-3 — Anisotropic Portal Exchange System

Aimes raised an eyebrow. "APEX-3?"

Felix shook his head. "Not mine."

The holoprojector on a nearby low table flickered alive. A thin, rainbow-toned figure resolved above it: TaloSyn.

"I named it," the projection said. "Your staff were referring to it simply as the machine. That was imprecise. APEX-3 accurately describes its function and developmental iteration."

Felix didn't argue. He checked the final diagnostic.

"We're set for a ten-second shell. Full diameter. No traversal."

The technicians confirmed their parts in turn.

"Argon system ready."

"Compression chamber stable."

"Harmonics green."

Felix placed his hand over the activation key.

"Beginning countdown."

A hush settled over the room. The console lights dimmed. Cooling systems deepened to a heavier hum. TaloSyn's projection sharpened, its internal patterns accelerating as it tracked dozens of sensor streams.

"Seven seconds."

The receiving-chamber monitors showed what they always did at rest: the interior of the chamber — curved steel walls, frost halos on the seams, a standard reference grid. Four cameras sat just inside where the shell surface would form, spaced around the equator, their feeds stitched into a composite view.

"Five seconds."

Aimes kept his eyes on the feed. This would be the first full-scale shell they'd attempted.

"Three."

APEX-3's background hum sank into a deeper register.

"Two."

Settings locked. Power steady.

"One."

Felix activated the system.

In the sender chamber beneath their feet, the event announced itself with a muffled load-crack as the pulse ignited, followed by a soft pressure-shift and a spreading blue haze. No flames, no theatrics — just the controlled precision of a machine doing something nature had never intended.

On the monitors, the receiving chamber feed appeared as the shell formed.

The steel walls vanished, replaced instantly by the transparent blue shell.

The cameras quickly moved through the shell to sit a few millimetres inside the boundary, looking out.

The screens showed a snow-covered ski slope in the capitalist world — Breitenberg's upper run, wind sweeping thin veils of powder across the ridge. A distant alpine skyline cut against a washed-out winter sky. No skiers crossed the frame. No lifts. Just empty snow, trees, and the faint suggestion of piste markers far off to one side.

A heartbeat later the audio feed kicked fully in — a hard, concussive crack rolling across the valley on the other side, the sonic shock of the shell's instant appearance reverberating off rock and snow. The microphones clipped for a fraction of a second, then stabilised into the thin hiss of cold wind over the ridge.

Snowflakes floated into the blue curvature and slipped through untouched, crossing from one world into the other without even a shimmer of resistance.

TaloSyn brightened.

"Shell is stable. Harmonically clean."

Felix watched the timer.

"Five seconds."

The composite view held: the same slope, the same empty ridge, the same steady fall of snow beyond the invisible curvature of the shell.

"Eight seconds."

"Shutting down."

In the chamber on the mountain, the shell collapsed. On the monitors, the ski slope vanished, replaced once more by the internal walls of the receiving chamber, frost outlines and grid markings snapping back into place as if nothing had interrupted them at all.

The air in the control room relaxed as the technicians exhaled. Felix leaned back, relief mixing with the guarded posture of an engineer who trusted results only after repetition.

"Successful," he said. "Full-diameter shell held without drift."

TaloSyn dimmed to a resting glow.

"APEX-3 is now capable of traversal. All parameters fall within safe margins."

Aimes didn't respond immediately. His gaze stayed on the main monitor—on the hard steel walls of the receiving chamber now restored where the snowy slope had been moments earlier.

Someone from their world could walk through that.

Not yet. Not today. But soon.

Felix watched him, reading the direction of his thoughts.

"So... what next?" he asked quietly. "Are we going to send someone through? We've developed the surveillance drones. They're ready. All we need is the order."

Aimes didn't answer.

He didn't need to.

The next step was already taking shape in his mind.

***

# Chapter 29

**Wednesday, 25th December 2013, 10:31 a.m.**
**Parallel Universe. European Advanced Physics Laboratory, Pfronten, Germany.**

Two weeks of preparation had reshaped the entire mood of the Pfronten lab. Once APEX-3 proved stable, the team moved immediately into reconnaissance. They kept the receiving shell small — never larger than seventy centimetres across, just enough for one of the 30-centimetre quad-rotor drones to pass through cleanly. The moment the drone entered the capitalist world, Felix shrank the shell to a narrow two-centimetre aperture to maintain a faint, low-power tether while keeping the opening almost invisible to anyone on the other side.

The drones flew low and fast across the snow-covered slope above Pfronten, mapping what they could before their limited batteries forced them to signal for return. When that signal came, APEX-3 reopened the portal to seventy centimetres, for the drone to settle on the hydraulic platform before closing the link again. It was enough for them to build a rough map of roads, buildings, and communication nodes in the capitalist world.

They learned quickly that this world was harsh. A drone nearly lost itself in a downdraft. Another clipped a cable and spiralled before regaining stability. Ice froze a propeller once, forcing an emergency recall. And while the little onboard processor couldn't penetrate networks, it could sniff enough digital noise to let their analysts piece together where major systems were clustered.

By Christmas morning, it was obvious the drones could only do so much. If they wanted answers — real answers — someone had to go.

Ethan Walker stood below and to the right of the receiving chamber, close enough to step onto the platform the moment it dropped, far enough that the hydraulics wouldn't catch his coat. He wore the expedition pack built for him—ruggedised laptop, stripped-down hardware, and the weight of two kilograms of gold coins. In a capitalist world, gold still spoke the clearest language.

Ethan checked his harness once, then faced the chamber. Above him, the receiving chamber was silent—no shell yet, no distortion, just the normal mechanical hum of fans and coolant lines.

Felix's voice came over the intercom from the control room.

"Stand by. Portal engagement in ten seconds."

A dull, muffled thump rolled through the chamber, followed by a green indicator light snapping on — confirmation of a successful link. It was strange, really: metres above Ethan's head a white-hole surface had just taken shape and attached itself to a black-hole construct a kilometre away, yet the moment felt routine.

A second later, the hydraulic platform began its descent with controlled precision. As it dropped into view, the air around it shifted—the gentle, unmistakable crackling whisper of the blue shell forming across the aperture. A shimmering lens of pale cobalt filled the laboratory, rippling faintly like film over water.

The platform lowered fully and locked in place.

Ethan stepped onto it without hesitation.

Up in the control room, the cameras showed every angle—the shell, the platform, Ethan centred in the safety lines.

Felix spoke again.

"Platform rising."

The hydraulics reversed, lifting Ethan toward the glowing curvature. The platform ascended steadily, the blue surface waiting above him like a held breath.

Then the platform carried him up through the portal—

and he was gone.

On the monitors, the receiving- chamber feed flicked once. A 4.5-metre blue sphere appeared on the snowy mountain in the capitalist world, framing Ethan, static crawling gently along its surface. Snow drifted into it and continued unchanged.

"Shell stable," Felix reported.

Ethan stepped toward the platform edge. He paused, only once, gathering his breath. The weight of the backpack shifted against his shoulders — laptop, instruments, and dense gold pulling him slightly off-balance.

Aimes watched without speaking.

Ethan reached the edge and jumped cleanly through the sphere. On the monitors, the cameras from the receiving chamber captured him emerging in a controlled landing, boots sinking into fresh powder. He staggered for half a second under the pull of the load before steadying himself. The wind lifted his coat and spun snow around his legs.

He adjusted the straps, turned, and began descending toward the valley — slow at first, then more confidently as he found footing through the uneven white crust. The pack dragged him backward on steep sections, forcing him to brace himself in a half-crouch with every few steps.

APEX-3 held the shell until he had cleared the immediate landing zone, then closed it.

The sphere vanished.

And with it, Ethan Walker — the first man since Max — stepped into another parallel universe, but this was different, he was here to discover what had happened to his friend.

***

**Wednesday, 25th December 2013, 11:49 a.m.**
**Pfronten Hotel, Germany.**

The small lobby smelled faintly of pine, the kind of scent that clung to every Alpine hotel in winter. Ethan stepped inside, stamped the snow from his boots, and took a moment to steady the weight of the backpack against his shoulders. The walk down the mountain had left him aching from the cold and the strain of balancing the load, but he kept his composure as he approached the desk.

A young receptionist looked up from her computer. She couldn't have been more than twenty. "Guten Tag. Zimmer?"

Ethan switched to flawless German, warm and polite. "Yes, please. How much for a room?"

She quoted a price. Ethan nodded, then hesitated with just enough tension to sell uncertainty.

"There's something I should explain," he said quietly. "I am in a difficult position. I don't have any European currency with me."

Her eyes flickered with confusion. Before she could respond, Ethan reached into his coat and placed several small gold coins on the counter. The receptionist's eyebrows shot up. She stared at the coins, then at him, uncertain what to do.

"Could you call your manager?" Ethan asked.

She didn't need telling twice. She disappeared into the back office and returned moments later with a middle-aged man in a charcoal vest and tie. He carried himself like someone who had dealt with both grifters and genuine aristocrats over the years and was still learning to tell the two apart.

The receptionist whispered an explanation. The manager picked up one of the coins, turning it between his fingers. He examined the unusual crest stamped on it, then weighed it in his hand.

"What country is this from?" the manager asked, looking directly at Ethan.

Ethan held his expression steady. "A small place in West Africa. Not widely known.

My family had these minted decades ago. I... left home recently, and this is all I have available to trade."

He kept the delivery calm, measured—just enough vulnerability to make the story believable, not enough to invite pity. Combined with the expensive-looking winter coat, the perfect German, and his posture, the effect landed exactly as intended.

The manager studied him again, assessing the inconsistencies and trying to reconcile them with what he saw: a man who appeared educated, composed, and unruffled despite clearly being out of place.

"Do you mind," the manager asked, "if I test the coin?"

"Of course not," Ethan said.

The manager disappeared for a moment and returned with a small ceramic plate. He set it on the counter, found a corner where the glaze had chipped, and drew the edge of the coin firmly against the rough surface. A bright gold streak marked the plate.

He nodded once. "It's real."

The receptionist looked impressed; the manager looked thoughtful.

Ethan waited, neither apologising nor pressing his advantage. Patience was part of the persona.

Finally the manager set the coin back on the counter. "How long would you like to stay for, Herr...?"

"Walker," Ethan supplied smoothly. "Ethan Walker. And I'm not sure yet. A few days, perhaps longer, depending on what arrangements I can make."

The manager considered him for another moment, then nodded. "We can accommodate that."

He gestured to the receptionist to begin the paperwork, still glancing occasionally at the gold coin as though it might change its nature if he looked away too long.

Ethan kept his hands folded loosely on the counter, his expression polite but neutral. He had made it off the mountain, slipped into the first shelter he could find, and bought himself time. Everything from here would depend on how well he could navigate a world built on suspicion, money, and systems designed to swallow strangers whole.

But for now, he had a room.

A door he could lock.

A place to go to work.

And that was enough.

***

**Friday, 27th December 2013, 4:38 p.m.**
**Pfronten Hotel, Germany.**

For two days Ethan Walker lived in quiet anonymity inside the Pfronten Hotel, moving only between his room, the lobby, and the breakfast hall. The heavy laptop and the compact cluster of tech gear he'd carried across the portal were now spread across the small desk by the window—an improvised workstation built from a mixture of his parallel worlds hardware and capitalist infrastructure.

He'd solved the connectivity problem on the first afternoon. The laptop had faced several network handshake protocols, flagged others as insecure, and briefly confused the hotel router before Ethan coaxed them into agreement. It took him three hours to write a patch that allowed the device to speak the archaic dialects of capitalist internet infrastructure. Once it stabilised, the connection worked flawlessly.

What he found online, however, made less sense.

On the technical side, the capitalist internet was crude but legible—layers of outdated architecture patched together with commercial hacks, advertising-driven service layers, privacy holes large enough to drive trucks through. He mapped it out in notes: routing standards, DNS structures, ISP hierarchies, the absurd complexity of licence agreements, the fragmentation of legal jurisdictions. All usable. All predictable.

The content was another matter.

News websites drowned themselves in gossip. Forums were riddled with feuds, conspiracy theories, and people shouting at each other for no purpose at all. Entire sections of the internet appeared dedicated to pictures of cats with malformed spelling. Another vast section revolved around sexual content so aggressive and so omnipresent that Ethan had to recalibrate his browser filters twice just to stop it appearing in the margins of pages.

He sat back at several points simply trying to understand the logic. It wasn't the presence of entertainment that confused him—it was the scale, the obsession, the sheer amount of time people appeared to spend producing things that served no collective purpose whatsoever.

It took him a day and a half before he felt confident enough to begin searching for Max.

He kept the searches simple:

Maximilien Rivette

CERN Rivette case

Prévessin-Moëns incident

Laboratory 888 Rivette

What appeared made his stomach tighten.

The trial of Gaidon Ballerat dominated the search results. Articles from November 2013 repeated the same narrative with slight variations: Gaidon had caused a radiation accident at CERN that killed Maximilien Rivette. Some reports embellished, others trimmed the details, but all delivered the same conclusion—Max had died six weeks later and Gaidon had been jailed.

Ethan sat in silence for a long moment, hands hovering above the keyboard. The dates were wrong. The explanation was wrong. Everything about the reporting was fabricated so cleanly, so thoroughly, that he knew he was looking not at journalism but at a political operation. The only reasonable conclusion was that Max had been hidden, not killed. And if they were lying about the death, then the truth was something the capitalist state considered even more dangerous.

He stopped searching.

He closed every trace of his internet presence by deleting the temporary logs he'd created. There was no sense in leaving a pattern behind. He had learned what he needed to know: Max was alive, and someone had gone to considerable trouble to bury the fact.

The rest of his time he spent exploring the systems themselves. Peer-to-peer protocols amused him—primitive, brittle, but clever in their own way. The decentralisation principle felt almost familiar. He set up a Pirate Bay account under a disposable alias, more as an experiment than out of any need to download the content itself. It helped him understand the faultlines in this world's information networks, gave him a picture of how data moved outside official channels.

By late afternoon of the third day he packed the laptop, rewired a few connectors, and repacked the gold coins deeper into the lining of the pack.

The walk back up the mountain took him nearly two hours. The pack dragged at his shoulders, the gold shifting just enough to upset his balance on icy inclines. More than once he paused to steady himself against a tree trunk or a jut of rock. The cold bit deeper with each step, the wind dragging at his coat, but he kept moving.

Eventually he reached the top of the mountain where he knew the portal was waiting in stealth mode.

He touched the small device in his glove—the trigger they'd agreed upon.

A point of air shimmered.

Two centimetres widened to seventy.

Then, with a soft, silent swell, the portal expanded to its full four and a half metres.

They had learned to control shell size gradually, starting from the earliest 2-centimetre tests. Now the transition came without drama — no shockwave, no concussive crack. That only accompanied an initial formation.

What appeared instead was the sudden, precise arrival of the blue sphere, its surface humming faintly with internal static.

The steel platform rose smoothly from the receiving chamber floor on the other side, hydraulic arms lifting it into perfect alignment with the snowy ground.

Ethan stepped onto it.

A moment later, the sphere snapped out of existence.

The mountain was dark and empty once more.

Now the Pfronten lab would learn what he had seen—and what he suspected had happened to Max.

***

**Saturday, 28th December 2013, 6:24 p.m.**
**Secret CIA prison, Geneva, Switzerland.**

Max had no sense of how many days had passed. The lights never changed, the meals arrived on no pattern he could track, and the guards refused to speak unless shouting a command. Time dissolved into a blur of pacing, muttering, half-sleep, and stretches of disorientation where he couldn't tell if he was lying down or drifting somewhere outside himself.

That evening, while sliding Max's tray through the slot, one of the guards muttered to another, "If I see another box of bloody Christmas leftovers I'm gonna lose it."

The words cut through Max like a blade.

Christmas.

He hadn't known. There had been no marker, no hint, nothing to distinguish the day from any other. The realisation hollowed him out, leaving a sharp ache behind his ribs.

He tried to hold himself together, but the isolation was grinding him down faster now. The silence seemed to press in from all directions, smothering thought, stealing any anchor he might cling to. His mind kept circling back to the warning Dominic had given him in the parallel world—the description of Removal From Contact. It returned in a jumble of remembered phrases, distorted by exhaustion: lights that never dimmed, food packets pushed through a slot, guards who never spoke, weeks of sensory starvation.

"RFC!" he shouted at the wall. "You think you can break me? You won't break me, you bastards! I know what this is!"

His voice came out raw, cracked. He slammed his fist against the steel door until his hand shook. The guards ignored him at first; then he heard a scuff of boots and the snap of a baton being unclipped. Before he could brace himself, the door burst open and the nearest guard drove a blow into his ribs that sent him sprawling. A second strike caught him across the shoulder. Max curled instinctively, trying to protect his head from the flurry of baton strikes.

"Shut up," one of them barked. "Just shut your fucking mouth."

They stepped back only when he lay still, breath coming in thin, painful pulls. The door clanged shut again, sealing him back inside the unchanging light.

He stayed on the floor for a long time, waiting for the pain to clear enough that he could get air into his lungs. When he finally managed to push himself upright, the truth settled with a clarity he could no longer deny. Whatever this place was meant to be, it wasn't medical, and it wasn't temporary. It served a purpose—one designed not to interrogate or extract information, but to erase the person held inside it. No voice, no outside world, no recognition that he existed. Just a routine built to wear him down until he stopped expecting anything at all.

The silence wasn't an accident.

It was the mechanism.

Max eased himself onto the cot, back against the cold wall, feeling every bruise. The danger here wasn't only the guards or the beatings; it was the possibility that this isolation might eventually start to feel normal. He closed his eyes and focused on the faint hum of the ventilation system—the only sign of life beyond these walls—and forced himself to hold onto it as proof that the world hadn't disappeared completely, even if everything inside him felt like it was slipping.

He whispered to himself, barely audible.

"Stay awake. Stay yourself."

It wasn't courage.

It was survival.

***

# Chapter 30



**Friday, 27th December 2013, 9:17 p.m.**
**Parallel Universe. European Advanced Physics Laboratory, Pfronten, Germany.**

Felix Köster was halfway through Ethan's preliminary report when his handset vibrated.

The caller ID — Aimes Perrier — left no decision to make.

He answered at once.

"Aimes, he's back. Ethan returned about an hour ago."

"How bad?" Aimes asked. No greeting, no small talk.

Felix glanced at the open report on his screen. "Bad. And clumsy."

"Go on."

"They've built an official story," Felix said. "Full public narrative. According to their news channels, Gaidon Ballerat was tried as a terrorist and traitor. Sealed evidence, state-security language, all very theatrical. And Max…" He paused. "Max supposedly died six weeks after a radiation accident at CERN in June 2012."

There was a short, flat silence on the line.

"June 2012," Aimes repeated. "The month he walked into our universe."

"Exactly," Felix said. "They're telling their world he died while he was living here, around the time whe started working at the Lorient shipyard."

Aimes let out a slow breath, more contempt than surprise. "So they've managed to cover this all up, sell something to their public that has a veneer of truth."

"They don't need truth," Felix replied. "They need something simple enough to repeat. Ethan says the same script runs everywhere — national broadcasts, regional outlets, archived summaries. Same phrases. Same date. Same images. It's coordinated propaganda, not the reality."

"And Gaidon?" Aimes asked.

"They've buried him under it," Felix said. "Official villain. Secret contacts, invented conspiracies, all tied to this fabricated 'accident'. He's their explanation for everything they can't admit about the machine, and by extension our world."

Aimes moved to the window, watching Paris traffic slide past far below, the city lit in comfortable ignorance.

"So they've told their population Max is dead," he said. "While knowing perfectly well he spent a year in our world."

"Yes," Felix said. "They know the dates don't fit. They know the reality doesn't fit. They just don't care. The point isn't truth — it's sealing the story."

"And TaloSyn's view?" Aimes asked, though he already knew the answer.

"It doesn't hedge," Felix said. "Calls it what it is: a cover operation. They needed Max erased and Gaidon discredited, and they needed it fast. The trial, the accident, the radiation story — all tools."

Aimes was quiet for a moment.

"Then the only useful thing in their lies," he said at last, "is what they're afraid of."

Felix nodded to himself. "Max."

"And what he knows," Aimes said. "Which means, one way or another, they didn't let him walk away." Aimes's jaw tightened.

"All right. What else?"

Felix scrolled through Ethan's technical notes.

"He mapped their global network. It's crude by our standards, but enormous. One layer is peer-to-peer — open, decentralised, virtually impossible to purge once something spreads."

"You're saying they have an uncontrolled information network," Aimes said.

"Yes. Mostly used for films and music, but the mechanism doesn't care. Ethan believes he can adapt our tools to push data into it."

"Which data?"

Felix didn't hesitate.

"The forty-five hours Max recorded — the full archive. Shipyard, hospital, police rotation, council sessions, Clarisse, the documentary footage. All of it. He thinks he can release it in a way their government can't completely suppress."

Aimes rested a hand on the cold pane, watching headlights blur along the wet Paris streets.

"If we do this, there's no taking it back. Once it's out, their authorities will never contain it."

"That's the point," Felix said quietly.

Another silence — short, decisive.

When Aimes spoke again, the softness was gone.

"Ethan returns," he said. "He takes the full archive. No edits. No filters. What Max lived is what their world will see."

"You're certain?"

"Max returned wanting to help them," Aimes said quietly. "He believed their world could change. I told him their system would crush him before it listened — and it did. We may not be able to save him now, but we can still carry his truth to the people he tried to speak for."

Felix nodded to himself.

"I'll brief Ethan. He'll be ready to go as soon as possible."

"Good. Then send him," Aimes said. "If their world insists on living inside lies, we give it one unkillable truth and let it spread."

The line went dead.

Felix set the handset down, glanced again at Ethan's notes on the capitalist network topology, and rose.

They had waited long enough.

It was time to let the truth loose.

***

**Sunday, 29th December 2013, 10:04 a.m.**
**Pfronten Hotel, Germany.**

Ethan stepped into the lobby with the same composed stride he had used the day he first arrived.

The manager looked up from the counter, eyebrows lifting slightly.

"Herr Walker. Welcome back. You were gone for a couple of days — I hope everything is in order?"

Ethan adjusted the single backpack on his shoulder.

"Yes. My father is in Monaco for the holidays. He asked to see me. I met him there briefly and returned as quickly as I could."

The manager nodded, reassured.

The receptionist emerged from a back corridor, saw Ethan, and lit up with a delighted smile.

"You've returned! We wondered when you'd come back."

"Good morning," Ethan said politely.

She stepped closer.

"Do you need any help with your bag, sir?"

"No, but thank you for asking," he replied, "but I can manage."

The manager moved back behind the counter.

"And shall you be paying with...?"

Ethan reached into his coat and placed two small gold coins on the polished surface.

"You liked these so much before."

The receptionist let out a soft gasp.

"Oh, you are so generous!"

The manager picked up one coin, felt the weight, nodded with quiet satisfaction.

"This is perfectly acceptable. Your room remains ready for you."

"Excellent," Ethan said. "Thank you."

He shifted the backpack more securely over one shoulder and headed up the stairs.

The receptionist gave him an eager wave; the manager returned to his paperwork, clearly pleased to have such a profitable guest check in again.

Upstairs, Ethan unlocked his room and stepped inside.

The quiet was immediate, steady, familiar.

He placed the backpack on the desk and began unpacking with practised efficiency.

The laptop.

The small transmitter modules.

The secure drive containing forty-five hours of Max Rivette's world.

Everything was intact.

He checked the Wi-Fi signal, confirmed the network speed, and powered up the laptop.

In a few minutes he'd begin the work that would change a world.

For now, he unpacked the final items and glanced toward the window, listening to the muted sounds of the hotel hallway beyond the door.

He was back in place.

And the next phase was ready to begin.

Ethan closed the door to his room, set the heavier bag on the desk, and powered up the laptop. The screen came alive almost instantly. The encryption modules recognised his identity and the scattered nodes he'd prepared the day before. Each dormant link pulsed green, waiting for activation.

He logged in to his Pirate Bay account. The simple interface appeared — crude, inelegant, but decentralised in a way the parallel world understood instinctively. It didn't need to be beautiful. It only needed to work.

He created a new torrent.

Maximilien Rivette_Documentary_FullArchive_45h_1080p

Size: ~200 GB

Trackers: Multiple, redundant, globally distributed.

He clicked Create & Seed.

The hashing bar crawled across the screen, pulling together hours of footage: Max's year in the parallel world, the shipyard, the hospital, the courtroom, the streets of Paris, Clarisse, the police, the documentary elements he had TaloSyn add. Every detail, every conversation, every visual cue. All of it prepared to slip into a world built to suppress exactly this kind of truth.

A few minutes later, the torrent went live. Ethan watched the seeding window stabilise — the initial upload was slow, as expected, drawing only on the hotel's single uplink. It didn't matter. This was just the ignition point.

He unzipped the pack and removed the first of the twenty palm-sized transmitter-computers. Each was no larger than a compact power bank, encased in matte black — deliberately anonymous. Inside each one: a high-density battery good for two weeks, a wide-spectrum adaptive Wi-Fi module, onboard storage holding exactly one-twentieth of Max's archive, and code written to monopolise roughly eighty percent of whatever downstream connection it could find.

But none of them would touch the hotel's network.

Not yet.

Ethan placed all twenty devices on the desk in a neat grid and opened his laptop. The torrent file—forty-five hours of footage, cleanly indexed and cryptographically signed—was already prepared in the client window. His machine would be the initial seed; and once deployed the modules contribute their part in the seeding process.

He powered up the first unit. Its indicator glowed faint blue as it linked directly to the laptop over the secured local handshake channel. Ethan assigned it Segment 01, confirmed its integrity, then pushed the configuration. The light shifted to steady white —ready.

He repeated the process with the second, the third, then the next five.

Each one connected only to the laptop.

Each one received its precise role: which twentieth of the archive to carry, which hash tree to verify against, which part of the eventual swarm it would pretend to be the origin for.

Soon the desk shimmered with a quiet constellation of indicators, each blinking through configuration states in its own rhythm: authentication, sync, assignment, lock-in.

No external networks.

No broadcasts.

Just preparation.

Ten minutes later, the last device pulsed white.

He initiated the swarm.

The torrent client spun up, seeding all segments simultaneously. The modules absorbed their assigned blocks at high speed through the local secure link, each confirming its piece of the total before disconnecting into standby mode.

Only when all twenty had been successfully provisioned did Ethan power down the laptop's wireless adapters entirely.

Now the modules would wait until physically deployed, each seeking whatever Wi-Fi signal it encountered—home routers, café hotspots, municipal repeaters—and injecting its fragment of the archive into the global swarm. The full file would never pass through any single network. It would spread the way spores do: everywhere, quietly, relentlessly.

He gathered the modules into a plain grey cloth shoulder bag, slung it over one shoulder, and stepped out into the cold evening air.

The town lay ahead—modest shops, quiet residential streets, the invisible glow of routers behind shuttered windows.

Perfect terrain.

Ethan began walking, scanning for the strongest signals as he moved.

The distribution phase had begun.

A bakery on the corner had a surprisingly powerful router — he left one unit beneath a low hedge beside the entrance. Another node went behind a row of bike racks near the train station. One slipped under the edge of a wooden bench outside a ski rental shop. Two went behind a municipal sign near the community centre, where the public Wi-Fi reached out generously across the square.

Each placement took a minute at most. Ethan moved naturally among locals and tourists, invisible in plain sight. His clothes were tidy, his posture confident, and his expression politely unreadable — the sort of man people remembered only vaguely, if at all.

By early afternoon he had placed twelve units. By mid afternoon, all twenty were in position: under bushes, behind flower boxes, beneath park benches, tucked behind drainpipes, concealed between stacked crates behind a restaurant. Every unit found a network. Every unit began its relentless, quiet work.

As he made his final sweep through the town, Ethan paused at a small bridge overlooking a frozen stream. The rooftops of Pfronten were dusted with new snow, and the glow of multiple access points shimmered across the screen of his scanning device.

The swarm was alive.

Twenty tiny machines, each drawing breath from a different corner of the town.

Twenty hidden engines, pushing the truth into a world that had buried Max Rivette.

Ethan closed the scanner window, slipped the device into his coat, and turned back toward the hotel.

The seeds were sown.

Now they only needed time to grow.

***

**Sunday, 29th December 2013, 9:45 p.m.**
**Kenneth Rice's apartment, Seattle, United States of America**

Earlier that day Kenneth Rice sat hunched over his desk in a dimly lit apartment that smelled of stale fast food and the sweet smell of hashish. His second monitor flickered with an endless scroll of torrents — mostly films, mostly trash — until one title stood out simply because it made no sense.

Maximilien_Rivette_Documentary_FullArchive_45h_1080p

He squinted, rubbed his eyes, and leaned closer.

"That name... where have I heard that?"

The drug haze made the memory slippery, but he eventually shook it loose: a news article months ago about a French lab worker who died in some sort of radiation accident. It had barely registered at the time — a blip in the global news storm — but the name was the same. And the file size? Obscene. No amateur hoaxer uploaded a forty-five-hour documentary in 1080p.

Curiosity cut through the fog, sharper than anything he'd taken that evening.

He clicked Download.

Then ticked the box for sequential downloading — he wanted the first chunk immediately, not in six days.

By the time the clock edged toward three in the morning, the first of twenty segments had finished. The second was creeping along at seventy-eight percent. The rest crawled behind like a reluctant parade.

Kenneth opened the first file.

A black screen faded into a calm, beautifully lit shot of a clean workshop. A voice — deep, steady, almost impossibly clear — began narrating.

Then images:

A shipyard.

Rows of vessels under construction.

A man — mid-forties, maybe — smiling awkwardly at the camera as he worked at a computer.

Cut to a hospital with open-air wards and soft daylight.

Cut to a community meeting where people actually listened to one another.

Kenneth blinked hard.

The camera quality was flawless, the colour grading professional, the structure deliberate. No shaky cuts, no cheap filters, no digital artefacts. Whoever filmed this had time, resources, and skill — far beyond what internet hoaxers normally bothered with.

Then the narration mentioned The Twelve Rules.

Kenneth paused, dragged the video slider back twenty seconds, and listened again.

Twelve rules for governance.

No hierarchy.

Shared ownership.

No monetary system.

He frowned, paused the video, and opened his browser.

Maximilien Rivette death radiation CERN accident

Multiple hits.

All consistent.

He was dead.

So what the hell was this?

He stared at the paused frame — Max walking through a shipyard, greeting workers who seemed utterly at ease with themselves and with him. Nothing about it looked staged. Nothing about it smelled like fiction.

Kenneth closed his eyes for a moment, trying to clear the fog in his head.

It didn't work. But something else did: a faint spark of fear.

Or awe.

He couldn't tell which.

He pushed the drugs aside — literally shoved the bowl of hash laced tobacco off the desk. It hit the floor and stayed there. His attention locked onto the torrent instead. The data bar showed 14% availability, meaning only a portion of the archive was currently reachable. New peers were popping up rapidly though — one in Germany, two in Eastern Europe, another in Canada, all in the last ten minutes. The swarm was small but active.

He clicked over to the torrent's comment page.

Someone had already posted:

"This isn't fake. Whoever made this has money — serious money."

Another user responded:

"Gov psyop? Why 45 hours?"

A third:

"Downloading. First vid is insane. Where did this footage come from?"

Kenneth hesitated, then added his own comment:

"I'm 30 min in. This is documentary-level production. Looks legit. If this guy is supposed to be dead, something is off."

He refreshed the page and watched the peer count grow.

His heart thumped a little harder.

The drugs weren't doing that — this was something else entirely.

He turned back to the screen, unpaused the video, and kept watching.

Whatever this was, he had stumbled onto it early.

Very early.

And he couldn't shake the feeling that before the day was over, thousands more would be watching exactly what he was watching now.

*The ripple had begun.*

***

**Thursday, 2nd January 2014, 11:15 p.m.**
**The Presidents office, Washington DC, United States of America.**

The West Wing had settled into its late-night quiet — a hush broken only by distant footsteps and the soft hum of ventilation. John Brennan walked the final stretch toward the Oval Office, escorted by a single Secret Service agent who knocked once, waited, and opened the door.

President Barack Obama sat behind the Resolute desk, sleeves rolled to his forearms, papers pushed aside. The fireplace behind him crackled softly, the only warmth in the room.

"Sit," Obama said, eyes fixed on nothing in particular.

Brennan took the chair opposite.

The door clicked shut.

Obama leaned forward, hands clasped. "All right, John. Why am I here at eleven at night?"

Brennan didn't ease into it. "Sir... something surfaced. And we didn't detect it. We found it by accident."

Obama's eyes narrowed. "Explain."

"A servicemember at Joint Base Lewis–McChord was torrenting a commercial film — a 2013 blockbuster. During the download he noticed a massive file being shared by others. It kept reappearing. He ignored it until he recognised the name."

Obama's voice went flat. "He was pirating movies."

"Yes," Brennan said. "And he was reluctant to admit it. But he informed his superior. The officer recognised the significance and escalated immediately. That's the only reason this reached us."

Obama gestured impatiently. "Show me."

Brennan opened the slim government laptop he carried, tapped a few keys, and spun it to face the President.

On screen: a torrent index.

A single name dominating the page:

Maximilien_Rivette_Documentary_FullArchive_45h_1080p

Below it:

Seeders: 312

Peers: 1,949

Obama stared at it for several seconds, then looked up sharply. "Tell me this is some kind of deepfake."

Brennan shook his head. "It's Rivette's archive. All forty-five hours. The footage he recorded in the other world."

A taut silence followed.

Obama's jaw clenched. "I thought you destroyed every copy."

"We did." Brennan said. "Every drive. Every digital instance. The camera hardware. The laptop. We pulverised the components. Nothing survived."

"Then how," Obama said slowly, "is a forty-five-hour documentary from another universe being traded by goddamn teenagers online?"

"We don't know," Brennan admitted. "But the upload is deliberate, clean, and absolutely not from our side."

Obama leaned back, staring at the ceiling as the fire popped behind him. "A fully functional, non-capitalist society. On video. With testimony."

"People are already discussing it," Brennan said. "Forums, tech circles, darknet boards. They're debating its authenticity. The production quality makes it hard to dismiss."

"How far will this spread?" Obama asked.

"Unstoppable," Brennan said. "Even if every seeder shut off tonight, the swarm would persist for weeks."

Obama stood abruptly and paced behind the desk, gripping its edge. "The one thing that could ignite political upheaval — living proof that a non-capitalist system not only works but outperforms ours — and it's circulating like leaked porn."

Brennan stood but didn't speak.

Obama pulled in a slow breath and snapped into command mode.

"First: do whatever it is that you do to stop this."

"Understood," Brennan said.

"Second: total information lockdown. No press comments. No back-channel confirmations. Nothing that legitimises this."

Brennan nodded. "And the source?"

Obama shook his head sharply. "I assume we'll never find it. Whoever released this knows exactly what they're doing."

He leaned forward, voice steady but laced with fury.

"Focus on containment. Not origin. I'm not frightened of a file. I'm frightened of what people do with the idea of a better world — especially if they can see it."

Brennan straightened. "We'll move immediately."

Obama didn't thank him. He just stared down at the laptop glowing on his desk, the torrent statistics ticking upward in real time.

Then something in him snapped.

He picked up the laptop with both hands, turned toward the fireplace, and hurled it into the flames. The screen cracked with a sharp pop, plastic warping as the fire swallowed it.

"God damn it!" Obama shouted.

Brennan said nothing.

Obama watched the laptop burn, chest rising and falling, the fire reflecting off his eyes.

"The lie held for six months," he said quietly. "Now the truth is loose."

He turned back toward Brennan.

"And it's going to land somewhere we can't reach."

***

# Chapter 31



**Friday, 3rd January 2014, 9:45 p.m.**
**Secret CIA prison, Geneva, Switzerland.**


Nicolas Hightower didn't enjoy being summoned. Especially not at nine in the evening, and especially not by a message from John Brennan that consisted of only three words:

Check on Rivette.

He knew what that meant. Brennan had seen the internal reports: Rivette shouting through the door, Rivette refusing meals, Rivette pacing until his feet bled, Rivette lunging at a guard and needing to be restrained. The staff were used to difficult prisoners, but this one had begun to unravel in ways even they found unsettling.

Nicolas arrived at the facility with his usual controlled stride, signed through the layers of security, and made his way into the detention wing. The hallway smelled faintly of disinfectant and metal — the same sterile tang that clung to every CIA black site he'd ever worked in.

A guard briefed him quietly. "He's been volatile. Barely sleeps. Shouts half the day. Tries to talk to the cameras. Keeps repeating things about isolation."

Nicolas nodded once. "Unlock it."

The guard hesitated, then keyed the door.

Max was sitting on the floor with his knees pulled up, elbows resting on them. He looked thinner, older. His hair had grown out unevenly and his jaw was dark with rough stubble. When he looked up and saw Nicolas, his expression didn't flicker with surprise — only a hard, exhausted hostility.

Nicolas stepped inside and the door closed behind him. "Maximilien."

Max barked a laugh that had no humour in it. "Look who finally grew a conscience."

"I'm here for an update," Nicolas said evenly. "That's all."

"An update," Max repeated, mocking the word. "You people took me, locked me in here, cut me off from everything, and now you want an update?"

Nicolas ignored the provocation. "Tell me how you've been."

"How I've been?" Max pushed himself to his feet, unsteady but burning with anger. "What do you think? You dumped me in a hole and left me to rot. I don't even know what month it is. I don't know if it's day or night. I don't know if anyone even remembers I exist."

He took a step closer. "What about my aunt? Céleste Guérard. She'd go to the police, you know that. She'd be asking where I am."

Nicolas kept his expression neutral. "Your aunt won't be asking anyone anything."

The words landed like a stone dropped in still water.

Max froze.

"What does that mean?" he asked quietly.

Nicolas realised too late what he had said. He saw the shift in Max's eyes — the way confusion snapped into focus, pulling a thread tight.

"Say it again," Max whispered.

Nicolas tried to backtrack. "You're not in a position to demand—"

"You killed her." Max's voice didn't rise. It didn't crack. It simply solidified. "You killed Céleste."

"That's enough—"

Max moved.

There was no hesitation, no warning. One moment he was standing in front of Nicolas; the next he launched himself forward with a force that caught Nicolas off-guard. His fist slammed into Nicolas's jaw, and before Nicolas could regain balance, Max drove a knee into his ribs. The impact forced air out of him, sharp and involuntary.

Nicolas stumbled but stayed upright. Max came at him again — wild, exhausted, furious — and that was enough to break Nicolas's restraint.

He caught Max by the collar, twisted hard, and forced him down. Max hit the floor but kept struggling, hands clawing at Nicolas's jacket, trying to pull him off balance. Nicolas pinned his forearm against Max's chest, trying to hold him still, but the man fought like someone who had nothing left to lose.

"Stop," Nicolas snapped.

Max didn't.

Nicolas's patience broke.

He drew back his fist and struck Max square across the temple. The resistance in Max's body faltered, stiffened, then gave out. His head hit the floor with a dull thud and his hands slackened. The fight collapsed out of him in an instant.

Max lay motionless.

Nicolas stood over him, breathing hard, jaw aching where the punch had landed. He straightened his shirt, adjusted his jacket, and glared down at the unconscious man.

He hadn't intended to say anything about the aunt.

He hadn't intended for any of this.

He reached for the intercom. "Medical to cell one," he said, voice steady again. "Now."

The line clicked.

He looked once more at the man on the floor.

Then he walked out.

The door locked behind him with a metallic snap.

***

**Sunday, 5th January. 2014.**
**4chan forums, Internet, Market places, Homes, Businesses.**

The American government's sudden "piracy crackdown" lasted exactly forty-eight hours before people realised what had actually triggered it. The timing was too neat, the press releases too vague, the list of banned domains too wide and too clumsy. PirateBay vanished. KickassTorrents went dark. A dozen mirrors disappeared in the same hour.

But the torrent had already spread.

By Sunday morning, more than two thousand people across the world held the full forty-five-hour archive locally, tucked onto hard drives, NAS boxes, USB sticks, and encrypted folders. Once it existed everywhere, shutting down the public trackers only removed the signposts — not the road.

Word travelled fast. Someone on 4chan posted screenshots of the the enormous shipyard. Someone else uploaded a few seconds of video of Max with Clarisse. A group on an Italian message board posted Italian subtitles they'd made overnight.

Across the world, small local news outlets began chasing the story in their own ways.

One clip from Melbourne, Australia started circulating almost immediately — partly because it was absurd, partly because it was unmistakably real.

Channel 9 News had sent a junior reporter to Collingwood Town Hall after receiving word that a man was openly distributing burned CDs labelled "MAXIMILIEN RIVETTE – FULL ARCHIVE".

The fifty-second broadcast became an underground classic.

The camera panned across the Sunday computer-swap crowd.

Then it settled on a man standing beside two folding tables stacked with freshly burned discs and a battered laptop.

A lower-third caption slid onto the screen:

LUKE RUSSELL — LOCAL VENDOR

Luke barely glanced at the camera, still arranging a stack of discs while two uniformed officers chatted with him in the most casual way imaginable.

The reporter stepped forward.

"Sir, are you aware this material is being linked online to a major global cyber investigation?"

Luke shrugged, completely unfazed. "Mate, people sell worse on these stalls every weekend. It's not Hollywood. It's not *copyrighted*. It's just *information*."

Cut to one of the officers.

"We've checked it," he said. "Doesn't fall under state offences. Looks like some kind of documentary. If it's illegal, that's Federal Police territory."

The second officer nodded, holding three of Luke's discs loosely in one hand.

"We watched a bit on his laptop. Strange stuff. Not our jurisdiction."

The reporter — confused, slightly rattled — wrapped up quickly.

"So the material continues to spread despite international warnings... and apparently with no local enforcement."

The segment ended with the two officers wandering off, discs still in hand, while Luke went right back to his stall and resumed handing out more.

A small clip.

Barely a minute long.

But it proved to everyone watching:

The torrent wasn't just surviving.

It was thriving — in broad daylight.

The torrent kept moving, quietly and without a centre.

Burned discs passed hands in cafés, markets, libraries, school carparks.

Blu-rays changed pockets in bars and university corridors.

Entire copies were smuggled between strangers on trains with only a whispered instruction: "Watch this. Don't delete it."

The government warnings — "terrorist training material", "fabricated propaganda", "dangerous foreign disinformation" — landed flat. The clips spoke for themselves. Max's voice did. The footage did. The faces of the people in the other world did. Nothing about it had the cadence of fabrication, and the more the authorities insisted otherwise, the more obvious their panic became.

Discussion flared across the internet's underbelly — encrypted IRC rooms on Rizon, EFNet, and Freenode; invite-only torrent boards that sprang up after Demonoid went dark; buried threads on Something Awful and 4chan's /x/, /g/, and /pol/ boards; Reddit subcultures in r/conspiracy and r/technology; and onion-routed message boards that had grown out of the pre–Silk Road darknet crowd. The places where rumours usually went to die were suddenly the places where this one caught fire. The tone changed day by day. At first it was curiosity. Then disbelief. Then the gradual, stunned realisation that the twelve rules weren't a fantasy at all. They weren't ideology. They weren't theory.

They were lived reality.

People began posting questions that no government wanted them asking.

Why is their world healthier? Why is their system stable? Why do they have no homelessness? Why is their justice humane and ours cruel? Why are their leaders elected bottom-up while we vote for people who don't know us?

In ninety per cent of countries, the news slipped past firewalls within hours. The videos spread faster than takedown notices could be drafted. Even in places with heavy censorship, copies were traded by hand faster than censors could identify new distributions.

It didn't feel like rebellion yet.

Just a shift — quiet, patient, and unmistakably growing.

People weren't talking about revolution.

They were talking about possibility.

And in living rooms and break rooms and back alleys across the world, someone always said the same thing after watching the introduction:

"If this is real... everything we were taught about power was a lie."

The seed had taken root.

***

# Chapter 32



**Tuesday, 7th January. 2014, 11:07 a.m.**
**The Presidents office, Washington DC, United States of America.**

The moment the door closed, Obama understood the mood. No greetings, no small talk — just grim faces, folders clutched too tightly, and that particular silence that meant the intelligence community had run out of excuses.

"Alright," Obama said, taking his seat. "What have we got?"

The Homeland Security adviser cleared his throat. "Mr President... the video is still spreading. Our best estimate is that several million people have already seen at least part of it. The number is rising too quickly for us to chart."

Obama's jaw tensed. "Define 'several million.'"

"At least four million by last night," the adviser said. "We've been shutting down trackers and pirate sites as fast as we can, but every time one disappears, three more pop up. It's whack-a-mole on a global scale. And that's no longer the biggest problem."

Obama looked up sharply. "Go on."

"People have started sending chunks of the footage directly by email. Personal mail. Work accounts. University servers. Encrypted attachments. They're breaking the archive into pieces and passing it around like contraband. Encryption use has exploded in the last forty-eight hours. We can't inspect half of what's moving now."

"And downloads?" Obama asked.

"Impossible to measure," the adviser replied. "Tens of millions have at least fragments of the footage. Full copies... we know there are still thousands out there, maybe more. Once it left the torrent network, it became a grassroots relay system. There's no central choke point anymore."

He leaned back, absorbing it. "So what I'm hearing is: you can't put this back in the box."

"We're trying," the adviser replied, but the words sounded pathetic even to him.

Another aide stepped forward, anxious to show progress where none existed. "We've begun preliminary lists of individuals to detain on material-support grounds. Anyone who has knowingly downloaded, seeded, or redistributed—"

Obama stopped him with a hand. "How many?"

"Sir?"

"You're proposing mass arrests. Give me a number."

The aide hesitated. "Potentially millions."

"Millions." Obama repeated it flatly, not as disbelief, but as confirmation of just how absurd the suggestion was.

Silence settled again. The machinery of the American national-security state — satellites, wiretaps, interception programs, data-harvesting systems that spanned continents — still couldn't put a dent in a 200-gigabyte video file that seemingly half the world now had on a hard drive.

"Next question," Obama said, his tone sharpening. "How did this get out? Tell me what we know about the leak."

"We don't know," the CIA deputy admitted. "There's no sign of internal compromise. The copy we seized was destroyed in Geneva. The camera was destroyed. The laptop was destroyed. No off-site duplication. No backups. No forensic residue."

"Meaning what? That it materialised out of thin air?"

"We're examining cyberattack vectors, foreign actors, domestic infiltrators—"

Obama cut him off. "You're telling me the origin of the most destabilising piece of footage in modern history is unknown."

"Yes, sir."

He let the weight of that settle. There was no anger — anger would have implied he believed someone in the room still had control.

A final aide came forward with a tablet. "The counter-narrative is almost ready. A reconstruction of the CERN accident. We have a special-effects team drafting the visuals. With two more days we can release a plausible fatal-radiation scenario and a timeline consistent with the public record."

Obama looked at the man for a long moment.

"And you think people will believe it," he said softly.

The aide swallowed. "We... hope enough will."

The President turned his gaze to the window, watching the grey winter light settle over Washington. For the first time since the video surfaced, he didn't speak.

He simply understood — the government of the United States was no longer steering events. It was being dragged behind them.

***

**Tuesday, 7th January 2014, 7:11 p.m.**
**The Presidents office, Washington DC, United States of America.**

The day had begun with confusion and irritation.

It ended with something closer to panic.

Every hour dumped a new crisis report on the President's desk.

China announcing emergency cyber-controls.

France detaining "suspected digital saboteurs."

Brazil, India, and South Korea reporting unprecedented traffic spikes as millions searched for mirrors of the documentary.

The European Union issuing a continent-wide advisory warning citizens not to download "potentially weaponised digital material."

By noon, P2P packets were being throttled across half the planet.

By mid-afternoon, they were being blocked outright.

By early evening, governments were issuing statements that sounded increasingly desperate.

Inside the Oval Office, the wall of monitors had become a mosaic of red alerts: international outages, blackouts in data centres, anonymous leaks, mass arrests, and a new problem category analysts had invented only hours earlier — recall actions.

Obama stood before the screens, arms folded, watching in grim silence as the torrent continued its runaway spread. Analysts had stopped trying to estimate the number of copies in circulation; the swarm was too large, too fractured, too global.

The NSA director had quietly admitted that morning:

"There may no longer be a ceiling, sir."

The national security adviser stepped forward with a tablet covered in updates.

"Every government is asking us what the hell is happening. Germany reports over two hundred arrests tied to protests. India wants a joint taskforce. Australia claims they're detaining 'cyber extremists'—your guess is as good as ours."

"And none of them," Obama said, "can stop a forty-five-hour video."

"No, sir."

He flipped to the next page. "And there's something else. People are turning up at government buildings—state, local, federal—demanding officials step down. They're calling it the recall movement."

Obama frowned. "Recall?"

"Yes, sir. They're quoting that line from the documentary. Rule Two.

Delegates shall be recalled at once if they act against their charge."

Obama pinched the bridge of his nose. "And they're applying it to... who, exactly?"

"Everyone," on of the many advisers in the room added. "Members of Congress. City councils. Mayors. School boards. They're showing up with printouts of Rule Two like it's constitutional scripture. And they're organised. Peaceful so far, but coordinated."

"In Sacramento this morning, four thousand people marched into the plaza chanting 'Recall now! Recall now!' Toronto, Berlin, Sydney, Johannesburg — same thing. They're walking in with printouts of Rule 2 treating it like constitutional scripture."

Obama rubbed his temple. "Jesus."

"They're calling it delegated governance, the corrective principle. They're saying: 'If it works in that world, why not ours?'"

Obama stared at him.

"A legitimacy crisis," he said quietly.

Another adviser added, "Mr President, millions have watched at least part of this documentary now. Tens of millions have seen excerpts, breakdowns, or commentary. P2P takedowns aren't slowing it. When we shut down a tracker, three more appear. When we pressure a hosting company, mirrors pop up on 4chan, Demonoid clones, and private warez boards. Users are emailing chunks of the video to one another. USB sticks. Sneakernet. And encryption adoption has gone vertical in the last twenty-four hours."

Obama closed his eyes. "This is bad. Really, really bad."

The communications director entered with a sheet of talking points that had clearly been rewritten all afternoon.

"We need a televised address tonight," she said. "Something steady. Reassuring. We frame this as a coordinated cyber-extremist action."

Obama scanned the page. It was the usual crisis boilerplate:

vague threats, cyber-terrorism, extremism, foreign actors.

Language that sounded authoritative while saying nearly nothing.

An hour later, Obama stepped before the cameras.

He spoke with the calm precision that had carried him through wars and recessions. He warned Americans that "a decentralised cyber-extremist movement, likely tied to anarchist elements," was circulating dangerous digital material designed to destabilise nations. He spoke of plots to cripple infrastructure, to confuse the public, to undermine the constitutional order. He promised decisive action and international coordination.

It sounded presidential.

It sounded controlled.

And it sounded like someone trying to dam a river with his bare hands.

When the cameras blinked off, the room felt hollow.

The advisers dispersed quietly. The national security team huddled near the doorway. No one said it aloud, but every face reflected the same understanding:

Nothing they did was slowing it.

Outside the White House walls, millions kept downloading.

Millions kept sharing.

Millions kept arguing, debating, organising, demanding.

And across the world, people with printed copies of Rule Two were standing in front of government buildings, asking their leaders to step aside.

The torrent wasn't just spreading.

It was becoming belief.

And belief was something no government on Earth had ever been able to stop.

***

**Wednesday, 8th January 2014, 8:06 a.m.**
**Secret CIA prison, Geneva, Switzerland.**

Max had given up trying to mark the passage of mornings, but the moment the guards took him without explanation and led him down the corridor, he knew something was different. They were taking him back to the interview room — the one he'd first sat in the day he was brought here.

They sat him in the metal chair, tightened the cuffs, and hooked the short chain to the ring welded into the tabletop. One of them checked the restraint twice, as if expecting trouble. Then they stepped out and closed the door.

A minute later, Nicolas Hightower walked in.

He wore the same neat suit, the same neutral tie, the same carefully composed face — but there was something off in the way he held himself, like a man who hadn't slept properly in several days. He closed the door with more force than necessary and sat down opposite Max.

Neither spoke at first.

Eventually Nicolas broke the silence. "We're going back over your recordings."

Max watched him carefully. "You already have everything I told you. Every location. Every date. Every face I could name."

"That's not enough anymore," Nicolas said. "I need more detail. How much raw footage there was. How it was made. Who made it."

Max frowned. "Why does that matter now?"

"Because it does," Nicolas snapped, a fraction too quickly.

Max had spent days replaying their last conversation in his head, trying to use it to stay sane. Now he replayed this single answer in real time.

"You've lost control of it," he said quietly. "Haven't you?"

Nicolas's gaze hardened, but he didn't deny it.

Max continued, more certain as he spoke. "You took my camera. You took the tapes. You took the laptop. You locked me in a box and made sure I couldn't speak to anyone. And yet here you are, asking how the video was made. That only happens if something slipped through your fingers."

"Careful," Nicolas said.

"So it's out there," Max said. "Somewhere. Someone found it. Someone copied it."

Nicolas's jaw tightened. It was a small tell, but on him it might as well have been a shout.

"We're trying to understand where this has come from," he said. "That's all. Who else knew the scope of what you filmed? Who might have had access? Names. That's what you're going to give me."

"There is nobody on this side," Max said. "I stepped through that portal with one camera and a backpack. Whatever's happened since... you did that, not me."

"That's not how this works," Nicolas replied. "You don't get to hand us a bomb and then pretend you had nothing to do with the explosion."

Max let that sink in. A bomb. So the footage wasn't just loose; it was causing damage.

He met Nicolas's eyes. "You can blame me all you like. I filmed a year of my life. I didn't tell anyone here about it, because I've been thrown in a cell and *removed from contact*."

Nicolas's patience frayed. "You returned with forty-five hours of footage showing a society that makes ours look broken. That video is tearing through the world, undermining governments, fuelling riots, and collapsing trust in institutions. Don't sit there and pretend you don't understand the impact of that."

"And what did you expect?" Max shot back. "That you could bury it and everything would stay neat?"

For a second, the mask dropped. Nicolas leaned forward, voice low and dangerous.

"You are buried," he said. "That was the point. No name. No records. No visits. No questions. You don't exist."

Max surged forward, yanking his arms as far as the chain allowed. The bolts in the table groaned.

Nicolas stood abruptly, came around the side of the table, and forced Max back into the chair with his forearm. When Max resisted, Nicolas planted a hand on the back of his head and drove it down against the metal table.

The impact rattled through Max's skull. White light flashed at the edges of his vision. He tried to twist away, but the cuffs restricted him. Nicolas held him there, palm hard against his scalp, pressing just short of causing real damage but far beyond anything that could be called restraint.

Nicolas moved in close. "You're only alive because I convinced the people above me not to dispose of you. That argument won't hold forever. Don't pretend this is mercy."

Max's breath came in sharp bursts against the tabletop. Pain radiated behind his eyes, but beneath it something had changed. The fog that had been smothering him for months had burned off.

Nicolas held him there a few seconds longer, then released his grip and stepped back. Max stayed where he was, forehead resting on the cold metal, because lifting his head felt like too much effort.

Without another word, Nicolas walked to the door, opened it, and left.

The lock clunked home.

Max stayed hunched over the table, vision slowly clearing, mind clearer than it had been since the day he walked into the portal.

For the first time in months, the thought that formed wasn't despair.

It was simple, and sharp, and certain:

They're losing control.

***

**Wednesday, 8th January 2014, 10:30 a.m.**
**CNN Newsroom, Atlanta, United States of America.**

The mid-morning bulletin cut in abruptly, replacing a segment on midwest weather with a stern disclaimer graphic:

NATIONAL SECURITY ANNOUNCEMENT

The anchor, a polished professional with the steady cadence of someone used to high-stakes scripts, looked directly into the camera.

"We begin with breaking developments out of Washington. The White House has confirmed that the recent global internet restrictions are linked to the death of French citizen Maximilien Rivette — a case now at the centre of what officials describe as a coordinated attempt to spread fabricated material online."

Behind her, the screen shifted to a generic image of the CERN complex.

"Over the past several days, anonymous groups have released what intelligence officials say is a series of highly sophisticated fake videos. These recordings claim that Rivette was involved in experimental research and travelled to what the creators describe as a 'utopian parallel society.' Analysts say the footage is a mixture of digital manipulation, staged content, and advanced video compositing."

She paused, then continued with a note of practised gravity. "The government maintains that Maximilien Rivette was murdered during an alleged containment breach at CERN. Officials have released what they describe as 'contextual evidence' to support that claim."

A short clip played — blurred, de-colourised, deliberately degraded. It showed two men in protective suits lifting a body from a metallic structure. The lower third caption read:

OFFICIAL FOOTAGE – CERN INCIDENT, JUNE 2012

"This is the government-verified footage," the anchor continued. "According to officials, it shows Rivette following a radiation incident during a particle-displacement experiment. They maintain he died six weeks later from the resulting exposure."

The video cut again — this time to a heavily edited courtroom clip of Gaidon Ballerat. The audio had been flattened and cleaned to the point of sounding synthetic.

"In a statement released moments ago, the Department of Justice provided this footage from the trial of Gaidon Ballerat, Rivette's former supervisor. In it, Ballerat appears to admit to negligence and concealment. Authorities say this contradicts claims circulating in online forums that the experiment was part of a larger conspiracy."

The clip ended abruptly.

The anchor shifted her papers and lowered her voice slightly, signalling the gravity of the next part.

"The Department of Homeland Security has also issued a legal advisory. Beginning today, possession, distribution, or viewing of the fake Rivette videos falls under new counterterrorism regulations adopted in coordination with our European partners. Officials warn that these videos are being used to recruit, mislead, and destabilise critical infrastructure."

A new graphic appeared:

CYBER TERRORISM ADVISORY – LEVEL 3 RESPONSE

"Federal agencies report that individuals hosting or sharing these files may be engaged in what they describe as 'material support for extremist terrorist activity.' Several arrests overseas have already been confirmed. Domestic enforcement guidelines are expected later today."

She paused, letting the message settle.

"We will continue to follow this developing situation as governments worldwide attempt to combat what they describe as a large-scale disinformation effort. Viewers are strongly advised not to download or share unverified material relating to the Rivette incident."

The anchor transitioned to the next segment with professional ease, but the tension in the room was visible in the background — producers rushing between desks, phones ringing, editors rewriting headlines in real time.

Out in the world, the torrent continued spreading.

Inside the newsroom, the official narrative had just begun.

***

# Chapter 33



**Wednesday, 15th January 2014, 10:30 a.m.**
**CNN Newsroom, Atlanta, United States of America.**

The newsroom looked composed, but only at the surface. Behind the anchor's desk, producers moved with the stiff, clipped motions of people who were following orders they didn't believe in. The anchor sat perfectly framed in the centre of the screen, posture immaculate, expression neutral. Only her eyes gave anything away — tired, and quietly appalled.

A red banner slid across the bottom of the broadcast:

NATIONAL CYBER EMERGENCY – LEVEL 5

"Good morning," she began. Her voice maintained the usual steady cadence, though there was a faint tightness under it. "We have a major update from Washington. The White House has announced what officials describe as an 'extraordinary, temporary measure' in response to ongoing cyber disruptions."

She paused — not for effect, but as if she needed that half-second to accept the next line herself.

"Beginning tonight at midnight Eastern Time, civilian access to the global internet will be suspended."

She continued reading with perfect professionalism, but her tone slipped, just slightly, on certain words — almost like she was choosing which parts of the script deserved credibility and which did not.

"Government representatives say this *restriction* is necessary to counter the continued spread of what they call malicious digital *fabrications* connected to the death of French citizen Maximilien Rivette."

A flicker of hesitation.

"According to federal agencies, the material remains 'highly destabilising.'"

On the studio monitors behind her, a graphic displayed blocks marked Federal Gateways, Secure Endpoints, and Restricted Regions. It looked authoritative. It also looked pointless.

"Essential infrastructure networks — hospitals, aviation, emergency services — will remain online under federal management. All private services will operate in a limited mode through approved channels."

Her eyes flicked briefly to the camera, a microsecond of unspoken commentary. Then she returned to the script.

"International partners are implementing parallel measures. The European Union has announced staged reductions in data access. Australia and Japan issued coordinated advisories this morning, and other nations are reviewing identical restrictions."

She moved to the next sheet, but the momentary sigh she gave before reading was barely masked by the microphone. It wasn't fatigue. It was disbelief.

"These actions, according to officials, are intended to remain in place until the Rivette footage is 'fully contained and *neutralised*.'"

Her jaw tightened ever so slightly at the phrase. She didn't correct it. She didn't editorialise. She just read it... with a tone that suggested she didn't buy a word.

"This is the first time in U.S. history that a nationwide internet suspension has been enacted."

Another pause. Longer this time. She looked directly at the camera — not with confidence, but with a look that quietly said I know you're not fooled.

"We'll update this story as soon as additional guidance is provided by federal authorities."

A small breath.

Her professional smile returned, but it didn't reach her eyes.

"Stay with CNN for continuing coverage."

As the camera pulled back for the transition bumper, she held her expression steady — but her fingers tightened around the papers in front of her, the only visible sign of what she was really thinking:

They're losing control, and they want me to pretend this is normal.

***

**Friday, 17th January 2014, 10.32 p.m.**
**The Presidents office, Washington DC, United States of America.**

The room felt crowded even though there were only six people inside. Aides, advisers, intelligence chiefs — each carrying a folder or tablet like it might bite them. Obama stood behind his desk, jacket off, sleeves rolled. He'd been reading reports for hours and none of them got any less bleak.

The National Security Adviser started first. "Sir, we've restored civilian access. With filters. And mandatory monitoring protocols. It's the only configuration that didn't collapse critical infrastructure outright."

Obama nodded. "How bad were the disruptions?"

"Worse than expected," she admitted. "Transport grids mis-synced, hospital networks lost authentication keys, supermarkets couldn't process deliveries, banks stalled payment pathways. Half a million small businesses completely unable to function."

Another adviser jumped in. "Public reaction is mixed. Most are relieved it's back. Many are furious. Several nations imposed night-time curfews to limit unrest."

Obama dropped into his chair. "And the video?"

Director of National Intelligence cleared his throat. "Penetration is higher than early estimates suggested. Our current models show approximately fifty percent of the first-world population has seen at least part of the footage."

"Belief level?" Obama asked.

"Split. Roughly half accept the possibility. The other half think it's a hoax. The shutdown actually strengthened the conspiracy angle."

Obama leaned back, rubbing the corner of his eye. "So we made it worse."

The Director hesitated. "Somewhat."

The Communications Director stepped forward. "Sir, conservative commentators are pushing the line that it's Anonymous propaganda built with advanced CGI. They've flooded talk shows, blogs, radio segments. It's gaining traction."

"And the countermeasures?" Obama asked.

"Minimal impact," she said. "People don't trust the official CERN footage. Too many inconsistencies. Too clean. Too staged."

Obama almost smiled. Of course they don't. They were inconsistencies because the real footage — the footage he'd watched in this room — had redrawn the lines of reality.

The Homeland Security deputy chimed in. "There's more. Curfews in France, Spain, and South Korea went into effect tonight. Germany's government is split. Australia is threatening to block all foreign internet traffic until they get assurances about containment."

"So everybody's panicking," Obama said.

"Correct, sir."

He tapped his desk lightly with one finger. "And nobody, not one of you, can tell me how the file got out?"

The room froze.

"No, sir," the DNI said quietly. "No sir, the person that originally seeded the file was sophisticated enough to cover their tracks"

Obama nodded slowly, exhaling through his nose. If he closed his eyes he could still see the shipyard, the hospital, the faces in the parallel world — the world Max had described and lived in for a year. A world that worked. A world that now existed on millions of hard drives around the globe.

He opened his eyes again.

"All right," he said. "Give me the last item."

The national security adviser swallowed. "Projection models say we cannot suppress discussion of the video. Even with filtering. The curiosity threshold has been exceeded."

"So in plain English," Obama said, "people won't shut up about it."

A few heads nodded.

"And we can't arrest millions?" one adviser added helplessly.

"No. That crosses a line we don't cross — not even now."

Silence.

Obama leaned back in his chair, finally letting some of the exhaustion show. "Well... I suppose this is what happens when you try to put toothpaste back in the tube."

A few people blinked, unsure if that was the joke.

Obama added dryly, "Except in this case, the toothpaste is sentient, angry, and apparently has a better social system than we do."

He lifted his hands. "So. Let's figure out how to manage that."

***

**Saturday, 18th January 2014, 11:47 a.m.**
**New York City, New York, United states of America.**

The cold air off the Hudson carried a restless charge. New York had felt uneasy for days, ever since the internet flickered back to life in its filtered, throttled form. People were moving differently now — quicker, impatient, half-watchful. Every conversation on the street seemed to circle the same questions.

A crowd gathered in Union Square, not as part of any official demonstration but because no one wanted to sit at home anymore. Students, office workers, retirees, artists, night-shift delivery drivers who hadn't slept yet — all talking over one another in a way that felt raw rather than chaotic.

Someone had brought portable speakers. Someone else held a cardboard sign with the words WHERE IS MAX? written in thick marker. Others carried printed images from the documentary, already grainy from being copied a thousand times.

A young woman in a puffer jacket stood on a bench and spoke as if she'd been pushed forward by the mood around her.

"We can't wait for politicians," she said. "Half of them are already facing recall crowds at their offices, and the rest are too busy trying to smother this to listen. We've seen only a fraction of what Max saw — what he lived — and we don't need their permission."

A man near the front called out, "Yeah, but what happened to him? They shut everything down after the video dropped."

Someone else added, "I heard he was arrested."

"No, disappeared."

"No, the CIA grabbed him — that's what people are saying."

The contradictions didn't matter. What mattered was the fear in their voices.

The woman lifted her hands to steady the crowd. "Look, we don't know. None of us. And that's the point. He risked everything to show us that world. He didn't just film it — he lived it. And now he's vanished, and nobody in power is giving a straight answer."

A hush moved through the square. People shifted closer, drawn by the weight of the truth spoken aloud.

A young man near the speakers said quietly, "If what he showed us is real... then he's the most important witness on the planet. And witnesses disappear when governments panic."

No one contradicted him.

Off to the side, a group of university kids were debating the Twelve Rules with the intense seriousness of people who had stumbled onto purpose for the first time in their lives. Two were planning a gathering for that night — an improvised forum. Another was building a mailing list. All of them moved with the energy of people who sensed history speeding up.

Across the river in Jersey City, protests had already tipped into clashes after police tried to disperse a crowd outside a transit hub. Photographs of tear gas drifting through the streets were spreading across the remaining social channels. In London, tens of thousands had overtaken Trafalgar Square. In São Paulo, a march had turned into a street battle. In Seoul, riot police were forming lines in front of the National Assembly.

Every city seemed to be reaching the same conclusion without speaking to the others: if governments were panicking, the video must be true. And if it was true, the world they lived in was smaller, pettier, and more brutal than the one Max had shown them.

Someone in Union Square shouted, "They can't stop all of us!"

Another voice answered, "They're hiding him!"

A third: "He deserves protection, not a prison!"

People cheered. A kind of fever moved through the crowd — not violent, not yet, but sharp-edged with frustration and possibility.

Sirens wailed several blocks away. The crowd didn't disperse. It pressed closer together, as if sharing warmth against the cold and against the government's tightening grip.

Somewhere in the middle of it, a man repeated the question that had become the movement's heartbeat:

"Where is Max?"

No one had an answer. But the question travelled through the crowd like a spark looking for tinder, and by midday it was already racing across a dozen cities the same way.

***

**Sunday, 26th January 2014, 3:48 a.m.**
**Secret CIA prison, Geneva, Switzerland.**

The night staff at the black-site facility were used to surprises, but not this one.

Nicolas Hightower arrived without warning, flashed his credentials, and demanded access to Maximilien Rivette's cell. His voice carried a hard edge, the kind that made men move first and think later.

The jailer on duty — a thick-set Swiss man named Keller — hesitated when Nicolas told him to shut off the cameras.

Keller hesitated, shifting his weight. "Mr Hightower... this isn't a good idea."

Nicolas stepped in close. "You will disable the cameras and hand me the keys. Now."

Keller swallowed. Something was wrong; the polished calm he'd seen on earlier visits was gone. Nicolas looked frayed, brittle, like a man who'd been holding a door shut against a storm and just lost his grip.

"Sir, if this goes on record—"

"It won't," Nicolas growled. "Unless you'd like to spend the rest of your life answering for obstructing a national security operation. Turn them off."

Keller's nerve cracked. He reached for the console, flicked the feeds to black, and unlocked the ring of keys before handing them over.

Inside his cell, Max had been half-asleep on the thin mattress when the lock turned. He sat up sharply, blinking into the harsh fluorescent glare.

Nicolas stepped inside. Alone.

Max's stomach dropped. Nicolas never came without guards, who would wait outside the door. Never at this hour. And never looking like this — a brittle fury stretched over something hollow and exhausted.

"What do you want?" Max asked, trying to keep his voice steady.

Nicolas shut the door behind him with careful, unnatural control. The kind a man uses when the alternative is breaking something.

"I'm here," he said quietly, "to deal with the last loose thread in this catastrophe."

Max stared. "So they fired you."

A short, humourless exhale escaped him — not quite a laugh, not quite a breath.

"No. Worse. I came from a briefing where Brennan hinted — in that sly little Washington way of his — that all of this... this implosion... traces back to me. Not formally. Not in writing. They're cowards. But the implication was carved into the room."

His voice tightened, shaking with anger that barely had a shape.

"They're terrified, Max. All of them. The whole machinery of power — presidents, generals, billionaires, institutions built over a century — and now they're acting like cornered animals because of a forty-five-hour video."

He took a step forward, eyes bright with something unhinged.

"Do you have any idea what you've done? I spent my life defending this world. Its order. Its hierarchies. The idea that civilisation must be protected by strong hands, decisive hands. We built systems — flawed, yes, but necessary — to keep chaos from swallowing everything."

His jaw worked, a tic forming along his cheek.

"And now you stroll back from your... your twelve rules utopia, holding a mirror up to our world, and suddenly half the planet is questioning everything. As if decades of structure and sacrifice can be waved away by some commune with sunshine and cooperation."

Nicolas's breath hitched — a dangerous, fragile sound.

"You don't understand what's happening out there. Countries teetering. Markets convulsing. People refusing orders. Soldiers hesitating. Entire governments paralysed because they've seen your anarchist little paradise where everyone holds hands under the Twelve Rules."

He shook his head, fury warping into disbelief.

"And they like it. They want it. They're abandoning everything we built because a man like you lived there for a year."

Max raised his hands slightly. "Nicolas... they aren't abandoning anything. They're imagining alternatives. That's not an attack. It's not a threat. It's just—"

"Don't patronise me." Nicolas's voice cracked, the first sign of something breaking beneath the anger. "You think I don't see what's happening? Order is dissolving. Authority is evaporating. And people — people are cheering."

He jabbed a trembling finger at Max.

"You don't grasp what this means for men like me. I was a protector. A guardian. I spent my entire career shielding the weak from monsters — real monsters — fanatics, warlords, extremists who thrive in the cracks of civilisation. Sometimes violence is the only language those men understand. Sometimes force is all that stands between stability and ruin."

His tone turned almost sermon-like, but fractured, as though he was quoting a doctrine he no longer fully believed.

"We were the wall, Max. The last, necessary wall. And now the world looks at your idyllic commune and starts whispering that maybe the wall wasn't needed. That maybe we were the problem. That maybe the enemy was the system itself."

He blinked hard, swallowing something bitter.

"They're wrong. They're children dazzled by a mirage. And you—"

His voice wavered.

"—you are the messenger carrying that poison."

Max felt the temperature in the room shift, the air compressing around Nicolas's unravelled certainty.

"You kill me," Max said quietly, sensing the direction Nicolas was spiralling, "and nothing changes. The truth is out. People have seen it. You can't force them to unlearn hope."

Nicolas stepped closer, his expression tight and feverish.

"Oh, don't lecture me about hope. Hope is a weapon. You brought back a version of it wrapped in communist scripture and called it salvation. But all I see is the end of the world I swore to defend."

His hand moved, slow, deliberate, revealing the gun.

Max held his breath.

Nicolas's voice dropped to a trembling whisper, equal parts rage and heartbreak.

"You're the spark that lit this. And sparks..."

His eyes locked onto Max with a terrible clarity.

"...can be stamped out."

Down the corridor, Keller sat at the console, sweat beading at his temple. Something about Hightower's voice echoed in his head — the frantic edge, the break in discipline. Against every instinct for self-preservation, Keller reached out and tapped the camera feed back on.

The screen came to life.

The audio came with it.

He froze.

Hightower: "I should have done this the night you returned."

Max: "You're not thinking clearly."

Hightower: "I am thinking more clearly than I ever have."

Keller stood so fast his chair toppled. He grabbed the master keys and ran.

Inside the cell, Nicolas stepped closer, raising the pistol.

Max braced. "Don't do this."

"It's already done," Nicolas whispered.

He lifted the gun toward Max's head.

Footsteps. Close. Nicolas glanced toward the door.

Max attacked.

He lunged low. Nicolas reacted late — not used to someone charging bare-handed. Max drove a shoulder into his ribs, shoved him back, and grabbed at the arm holding the gun.

The weapon flew from Nicolas's grasp and hit the floor with a metallic clatter.

Max grabbed it first and came up fast, chest heaving, the barrel aimed squarely at Nicolas.

Keller reached the doorway at that exact second, eyes wide.

"Max—don't shoot!"

Max didn't look away from Nicolas. "I don't want to," he said, voice raw. "But I will if I have to."

Nicolas's expression twisted — not fear, but rage, total and blinding. He lunged, hands out, trying to tackle Max to the ground.

Max didn't give him the chance.

He fired once.

The bullet tore cleanly through Nicolas's temple. The body crumpled to the floor, the impact echoing sharply against concrete.

Silence swallowed the cell.

Keller stared at Nicolas's body, helpless as the blood streamed from the man's temple, his own shock pinning him to the doorway. Max kept the pistol pointed down, then looked at the jailer.

"Where the hell am I?"

"Geneva," Keller whispered.

Max nodded once. "Give me the keys. I won't shoot if you don't force me."

Hands shaking, Keller passed them over.

Max backed into the corridor, eyes never leaving the jailer.

Then he turned, sprinted down the hallway, unlocking the doors as he went, and out into the freezing Geneva night.

He didn't know where to run.

Only that he needed to keep running.

And he did.

***

# Chapter 34



**Sunday, 26th January 2014, 4:05 a.m.**
**Geneva, Switzerland.**

Max tore through the back streets without any sense of direction, lungs burning in the cold air. His clothes were soaked with sweat despite the winter freeze, and his hands shook as he clutched the pistol. Every few steps he expected a spotlight, a siren, a shout — anything to signal that the world had snapped shut around him again.

Instead, the city was coming apart.

He heard it before he saw it: a deep, rolling chaos, the sound of a crowd on the edge of breaking. Police sirens cut across the night. Fire engines echoed from somewhere closer. Shouts bounced off the old stone facades.

When he reached the first major street, he saw why.

A thousand people filled the broad intersection — young and old, students, factory workers, office staff still in business coats, pensioners gripping banners, teenagers carrying makeshift shields. Riot police formed a tight line, shields raised, helmets lit by the glow of burning rubbish bins.

The two groups were colliding in waves. Firecrackers burst between them. Tear gas drifted in pale ribbons. Someone with a megaphone shouted about the shutdown, about censorship, about "the video" and the "lying bastards in Washington." Someone else hammered a saucepan with a wooden spoon. Someone farther back sobbed quietly into a friend's shoulder.

Max realised the rage wasn't focused — it was everywhere, spilling out of every corner of the street like a boiling pot with no lid.

He shoved the pistol into his trouser pocket. It didn't sit properly; the grip jutted out, obvious to anyone who bothered to look. He crossed the road as casually as he could manage, head down, acting like a man simply trying to get home before the situation worsened.

Halfway across the road, a young man at the edge of the crowd turned his head sharply. His eyes widened.

"Hey—" he whispered to the woman beside him. "Hey, look. Look."

She followed his gaze. Her expression changed instantly.

"That's him," she breathed. "That's Max."

Max froze. His heart slammed against his ribs. For a moment he considered running again, but something inside him gave way — a sudden, disorienting wave of emotion he had held back for months. Tears spilled before he could stop them.

He didn't try to wipe them away.

The young man approached slowly, palms open, as if afraid a sudden move might break whatever delicate state Max was in.

"Are you... are you really him?" the man asked. "Maximilien Rivette?"

Max's throat locked up. He forced a nod.

"Yes," he whispered. "I'm Max."

The woman stepped closer. Her eyes swept over him — the bruises, the torn shirt, the blood on his collar, the gun angled awkwardly from his trouser pocket. She looked horrified and protective at the same time.

"Okay," she said, steadying her voice. "You can't stay out here. Not with police about to push through the back lanes."

Behind her, the riot line surged forward another metre. The crowd pushed back. The sound was like a living thing.

Two more people joined them — a man in a wool coat and a woman carrying a bike helmet. Both recognised him within seconds.

"He's hurt," the man said. "And if he stays here, he'll be crushed in the charge."

The woman with the helmet stepped to Max's side and put a hand on his arm.

"We're getting you off the street," she said. "Now."

Max didn't argue. He let them guide him away from the edge of the riot, through the shadows, down a narrow passage between shuttered shops.

For the first time since he'd fled the prison, he felt something other than fear.

He felt seen.

And for the first time in months — he wasn't alone.

***

**Sunday, 26th January 2014, 6:35 a.m.**
**Geneva apartment. Geneva, Switzerland.**

Max sat at a small kitchen table, hunched forward like someone still half-expecting a door to crash open. The apartment was warm, dim, lived-in — mismatched mugs on the counter, a drying rack of plates, a radio unplugged and pushed aside. Dawn light crept through the blinds and painted thin stripes across the floor.

Across from him sat the couple who'd taken him in: a woman in her late forties with tired eyes, and her partner, a broad-shouldered man with greying hair pulled back into a short tail. Neither had introduced themselves properly; everything had happened too fast. The woman was making tea, grounding herself in the small ritual as she spoke.

"Start from the beginning," she said gently. "Not the whole year in the other universe. The whole world knows that part. Just... what happened to you here."

Max tried. His voice faltered on the first attempt. He swallowed, tried again.

"I was taken the moment I came back. No charges, no explanation. They kept me in a cell. No news. No daylight. No idea what month it was. I thought I was going to die in there."

The couple exchanged a look — not disbelief, but grief.

The man asked quietly, "The man you killed — was he CIA?"

Max nodded. "He told me the world was collapsing and he blamed me. He'd come to kill me."

The woman set a mug in front of him. Her hands trembled when she let go.

"And now you're out," she said. "But not safe. Not with surveillance like this. They'll be hunting you."

Max pushed his hair back with a shaking hand. "I need to see someone. My colleague. Gaidon Ballerat. If any of the team survived, he'll know what—"

The man cut him off with a slow shake of the head.

"Max... Gaidon's gone. Not dead — but locked up. Life sentence. They had him tried for killing..."

He stopped, searching Max's face as if the word itself didn't sit right.

"...you."

Max stared, hollowed out. "What did they say he did?"

The woman answered. "They claimed he killed you. Exposed you to radiation. Said he was working with terrorists. It was absurd, but they pushed it everywhere."

A tight, sick silence filled the kitchen.

Max exhaled shakily. "So they buried me twice. In prison... and in the news."

"They had to," the man said. "The video was tearing everything open. People trust what they've seen of your world more than what they hear from ours."

Max rubbed his hands over his face. "I need a way to show the world I'm alive — and that everything they're saying about me is a lie."

The couple didn't disagree — but neither of them rushed to agree, either.

The woman sat down beside him. "Max, there's no way to upload anything, the internet's barely alive. It's filtered, throttled, watched. Every connection is monitored. They're arresting people for searching the wrong terms."

"And if we tried to broadcast something from here," the man added, "they'd be through our door within the hour. You more than anyone need to stay out of sight."

Max set the mug aside, untouched. His pulse thudded in his throat.

"So what do we do?" he asked finally.

"For now," the woman said, "we wait."

The word tasted bitter, but he knew she was right. Nothing outside was predictable — not the riots, not the crackdowns, not the sudden declarations from Washington or Brussels or Beijing. Every government was improvising. Every street was shifting.

"We watch the world for a few days," the man continued. "We see which way things move. The truth is already spreading. If we act too soon, they'll crush you. If we wait, there might be a moment — a real moment — where speaking out actually matters."

Max leaned back in the chair. His body wanted to collapse, but something in him refused. He nodded.

"All right," he murmured. "We wait."

The couple exchanged another glance — the kind two people share when they both know that waiting might be the hardest thing they will ever do.

Outside, distant sirens rose and faded.

***

**Sunday, 26th January 2014, 7:10 a.m.**
**Secret CIA prison, Geneva, Switzerland.**

Dragonetz Coté stood in the prison's operations room with the fluorescent lights buzzing faintly overhead. The place smelled of disinfectant — the residue of a facility built for silence, not chaos. Keller, the night jailer, was still locked in a holding cell down the hall, trembling so hard his keys had rattled in his hand when Dragonetz arrived.

The emergency line connected on the third ring.

Brennan answered on the second ring, irritation already bleeding through.

"Dragonetz, this had better be worth interrupting my sleep."

"It is, sir." Dragonetz didn't bother with preamble. "We've got a situation."

"It's about Nicolas Hightower," Dragonetz said. "He's dead. Rivette shot him."

A beat of silence.

"How?" Brennan asked, the annoyance cooling into something harder.

"Single shot. Execution-style," Dragonetz said. "The guard called it in straight away. When I got here he was barely holding it together — shaking, rambling, trying to explain what he'd seen."

Brennan's voice flattened. "Which was?"

Dragonetz swallowed once.

"Hightower tried to execute Max. But Max took the gun off him... and killed him."

"What about Rivette?"

"He's gone," Dragonetz said. "Escaped less than a minute after the shooting. Jailer was forced to handover the keys at gunpoint. Security cameras show Max unlocking the three security doors before running into the street."

Brennan swore softly. "You're telling me a prisoner we declared dead months ago is now loose in the centre of Geneva."

"Yes, sir."

"And Hightower walked into a black-site alone and got himself killed." Brennan exhaled into the receiver. "Of all the idiotic—"

He cut himself off.

Dragonetz waited. He knew better than to fill silence when a Director was weighing consequences.

Finally Brennan spoke again, quieter, with that low, dangerous clarity reserved for moments when the stakes were beyond salvage.

"We can't involve local law enforcement. Not even covertly."

"I'm aware," Dragonetz said. "We can't request support without explaining who we're looking for. And the moment anyone hears the name Rivette in the police network, our entire narrative collapses."

"We need Rivette found," Brennan said. "Alive, preferably. But if that's not possible—"

Dragonetz understood the rest without hearing it.

"Yes, sir."

"I'll try to assemble a team I can trust," Brennan said. "People without paper trails. Contractors, former field operatives... maybe two or three from the paramilitary side who know how to move without leaving prints."

"How long?"

"Twenty-four hours," Brennan answered. "Maybe slightly less if I pull rank."

Another pause. "Until they arrive, you stay put. Keep the site secure. Contain the fallout. And for God's sake — no noise. No outreach. No unilateral moves. Eyes only."

"Understood."

"Good. I'll be in touch."

The line went dead.

Dragonetz looked around the grim hallway. Hightower's body was still being processed in the cell; technicians were documenting the scene in silence.

The prison felt different now — nothing like a place of control. It felt exposed. Vulnerable. A secret with its lid blown off.

Dragonetz straightened his collar and exhaled once, quietly.

Max Rivette was somewhere in Geneva.

And Dragonetz Coté had twenty-four hours before the Director's handpicked hunters arrived.

He turned toward the corridor, his heels clicking sharply on the concrete.

There was no room for mistakes now.

***

**Sunday, 26th January 2014, 2:35 a.m.**
**The Presidents office, Washington DC, United States of America.**

The West Wing was half-asleep at this hour, running on skeleton staff and dimmed lights meant to lull the building into a soft hum. Barack Obama pushed through the doorway of the Oval Office in a dark robe and slippers, two aides following him with hurried, apologetic expressions.

John Brennan stood waiting in a suit that looked like it had been thrown on in a hallway. Beside him was a senior national security adviser who looked equally grim. Both men turned as Obama entered.

"All right," Obama said, voice thick with fatigue but already sharpening. "Someone start talking."

Brennan stepped forward. "Mr President... we have a situation in Geneva."

Obama rubbed his temple. "Of course we do. Go on."

Brennan took a breath. "Nicolas Hightower, our man on the ground in Geneva, is dead."

Obama's eyes opened fully. "What?"

"Killed inside the secure facility. Shot at close range."

"By who?"

"By Rivette."

Obama stared at him for a long, incredulous second.

"Sir... Rivette escaped the facility. He killed Hightower and forced a guard to release him. He's somewhere in Geneva right now."

One of the aides leaned against a chair as though his knees softened.

Obama paced once, robe swaying, then turned back sharply.

"Let me get this straight. The man we've spent a year pretending died in a radiation accident just killed one of our own and is now loose in a major European city in the middle of a global crisis?"

"Yes, sir."

Obama threw his hands up. "We are *fucked*."

No one corrected him.

Brennan pressed forward. "I'm assembling a small retrieval team. People we can trust. No official trace. They'll be in Geneva within the day."

Obama lifted his hands, then let them fall. "This is spiralling. The internet collapses, half the world is rioting, and now the one living person who knows the entire truth is out there giving us the finger."

He pressed his palms into the Resolute Desk and leaned forward.

"Find him before someone else does. Before a camera does. Before he speaks to anyone. You understand me?"

"We do," Brennan said.

"And John?"

"Yes, sir?"

Obama leaned in until Brennan could feel his breath. His voice dropped to something cold and lethal.

"John, if you walk through that door with one more surprise, I swear to God I will put you in the ground myself. Not SEAL Team Six. Me. Do you understand me?"

Silence flattened the room. No humour. No bravado. Just the exhaustion of a man who had been pushed past every reasonable limit.

Brennan swallowed. "Understood."

Obama straightened slowly, as if forcing himself back inside the shell of a president.

"Go," he said, voice tight. "And don't let this get any worse."

The men left quickly, the door closing with a soft, guilty click.

Obama remained where he was, staring at the dark window, the lukewarm coffee untouched beside him. A dead operative overseas. A fugitive who wasn't supposed to exist. A lie collapsing faster than any government could catch it.

*****

# Chapter 35

**Monday, 27th January 2014, 4.10 p.m.**
**Parallel universe. Aimes Perrier's office, European Security Headquarters, Paris, France.**

Aimes's office overlooked the winter-grey sprawl of Paris — the wide avenues, the quiet plazas, the calm that unfavorably compared to the chaos unfolding in the capitalist world. Ethan Walker and Dominic Garner were already seated when Maxine Jacquet stepped inside. All three had been called urgently, and Aimes's expression confirmed it wasn't routine.

He didn't offer coffee. He didn't sit.

He simply said, "We've received the latest drone pull."

The surveillance drones — slim, silent flyers pushed through a portal barely large enough for their wings — had been crossing into the capitalist universe every night at 2 a.m., slipping down the ridge above Pfronten and vanishing into their networks. Each mission returned with fragments, but the fragments were becoming darker by the hour.

Aimes tapped the console on his desk.

The wall-screen came alive with news thumbnails, shaky protest videos, police cordons, crowds forcing their way into municipal buildings.

Maxine frowned. "It's getting worse."

Aimes nodded grimly. "Much worse. Their governments are losing control. Millions in the streets. Demands for resignations everywhere — from village mayors to federal ministers. They're calling it a recall movement. Inspired, they say, by Rule 2."

A second tap brought more footage:

Tear gas. Barricades. Office windows smashed as crowds shouted for politicians to step down.

"All this from a video," Maxine murmured.

"No," Aimes corrected softly. "All this from the truth finally finding oxygen."

"And the absence of any genuine trace of him," Aimes continued, "no leaks, no chatter, no sightings... suggests he's either been killed, or permanently removed from public view."

The room held its breath.

Ethan leaned forward, voice steady. "Their censorship algorithms are tightening every hour. They're wiping out entire subnetworks. But when they push that hard, counter-currents form. People switch to encrypted clusters."

Dominic nodded. "Anything we can track?"

"Not from here," Ethan said. "From this universe we only see surface traffic — what's loud, what's public. For the deep patterns, someone has to work inside their world. On their machines. With their routing."

Dominic stepped in. "Which is why we need direct access. Not to manipulate — to observe. If Max is alive, the signs won't be on broadcast channels. They'll be buried in private nodes and encrypted clusters. Ethan needs a machine in their system."

Aimes nodded. "The drones can only skim their world. They're scouts, not surgeons."

Ethan added quietly, "Get me in front of their hardware, and I can follow the threads they're trying to bury."

Maxine folded her hands. "You're asking to operate inside an unstable system across a dimensional boundary. Without certainty. Without knowing whether Max is still breathing."

Dominic didn't blink. "Yes."

Ethan matched him. "If Max is alive, he deserves to be found. If he's gone... then his truth deserves not to die with him."

Maxine looked at each of them — Dominic, Ethan, Aimes.

Then she nodded.

"You may act. All of you. Whatever tools you need, you'll have. Whatever access TaloSyn can provide — it is yours. Short of taking a life, you are authorised to do whatever is required to find Max, or to support those in their world who are trying to reclaim their society."

The words settled heavily across the room.

Dominic inclined his head. Ethan did the same.

Aimes straightened. "We begin tonight. We get Ethan and Dominic into their world."

Maxine turned back to the glowing screen — protests, smoke, shattered windows, signs demanding recall.

"If Max is alive," she said, "bring him home.

If he is not... then make sure his truth doesn't drown beneath their lies."

Dominic and Aimes exchanged a sharp, concentrated look.

Ethan closed his laptop with a soft, decisive click.

The next move belonged to them.

****

**Tuesday, 28th January 2014, 4.23 p.m.**
**Pfronten Hotel, Germany.**

Ethan had cleared the small desk beside the bed and unfolded his equipment with the neat, practised movements of someone who never wasted motion. The hotel curtains were drawn just enough to hide him from the street, and the soft hum of his suitcase-sized processing unit filled the room with a low, steady vibration.

Dominic stood near the foot of the bed, hands in his pockets, watching the rapid blur of Ethan's typing on his laptop.

"What now?" Dominic asked. "There's no internet. Or is there?"

Ethan didn't look up. "When I first came here, I had to work out how their networks actually function — protocols, file structures, routing conventions. The architecture isn't ours, but the principles are close enough." His fingers kept moving, deliberate and fast. "Their security's good by their standards, but not by ours. The infrastructure is intact. It's only the civilian access that's been cut."

Dominic leaned closer, keeping his voice low. "The receptionist said the government shut the entire internet down."

"They did," Ethan replied calmly. "But only at the access layer. They didn't destroy the backbone. They can't — half their essential infrastructure depends on it. Hospitals, transport grids, law enforcement, emergency networks."

Dominic nodded. "And you can get into that?"

Ethan tapped a key, and a cluster of diagnostic windows flickered to life on his screen. "Their cryptography is twentieth-century logic dressed up in twenty-first-century hardware. This unit"—he rested a hand on the compact, powerful processor beside him —"is generations beyond anything they can conceive of. Once it threads through their packet verification layers, it'll masquerade as one of their own systems."

"How long?"

Ethan glanced at a column of numbers racing down a window. "Half an hour, maybe less."

Dominic allowed himself a thin smile. "You're telling me you're about to walk through the front door of a locked-down world?"

"I'm telling you," Ethan said, "that their governments turned off the lights for the public, but left all the doors to the control rooms wide open. And I have the keys."

Dominic breathed out, the tension in his shoulders easing for the first time that day. "Good. We need eyes. We need truth. And we need to know what Max walked back into."

Ethan nodded, still typing. "We will."

For a moment neither man spoke.

In the quiet hum of the hotel room, separated from a collapsing world by nothing more than plaster walls and snow outside, they shared a rare smile — not of triumph, but of purpose.

The system on Ethan's screen chirped once, a muted, confident tone.

"First lock's open," Ethan said.

Dominic pulled up a chair. "Then let's see their world."

***

**Tuesday, 28th January 2014, 9.10 p.m.**
**Geneva apartment, Geneva, Switzerland.**

Évelyne Jacquard set a mug of warm tea on the table beside Max, her movements gentle, almost maternal. The apartment was quiet except for the soft murmur of a late-night radio bulletin drifting in from the kitchen — low enough not to intrude, loud enough to feel like another human presence in the flat.

Max hadn't touched the tea. He sat hunched slightly forward, elbows on his knees, staring at nothing. His eyes were open, but he wasn't present.

Évelyne watched him for a moment before speaking. "Max... are you alright?"

He blinked once, as if surfacing. "Sorry. I drift off sometimes." His voice carried the gravel of exhaustion — not the simple kind, but the sort that clung to a person after too many months in a place designed to erase them.

"It's understandable," she said softly. "What you've been through... nobody walks away from that unchanged."

Max exhaled, long and unsteady. "It's not just that."

She waited.

He swallowed, throat tight. "My aunt. Céleste Guérard." The name alone pulled something sharp across his expression. "They killed her. Because she looked for me."

Évelyne's face fell. "Max... I'm so sorry."

"She was my only family," Max murmured. "And I never even got to say goodbye."

He rubbed a hand over his face, the weight of everything pressing down in silent increments. "I don't even know where she's buried. Or if they gave her anything more than a number in some cold room."

Évelyne stepped closer and touched his shoulder — a simple gesture, steady and human. "I'll find out."

He lifted his head slowly. "You don't have to—"

"I want to," she said. "She deserves that much. And so do you."

Max's eyes glistened, but he held himself together. "Thank you."

Évelyne squeezed his shoulder once, firm and certain. "Rest tonight. I'll start making calls in the morning. Whatever they tried to hide... we'll shed light on it."

Max nodded, not trusting his voice. For the first time since escaping, he felt a thread of something close to hope — thin, almost fragile, but real.

***

**Wednesday, 29th January 2014, 11.03 a.m.**
**Pfronten Hotel, Germany.**

Ethan crooked a finger at Dominic. "Come here. You need to see this."

Dominic stepped behind him, leaning over the back of the chair. The laptop's display showed a block of text, crisp and clinical, stamped with a CIA header.

Dominic read aloud under his breath. "'Rivette is still at large. There is little possibility of finding him with the limited human resources available to my team.'"

He straightened. "Where the hell did you find that?"

"I searched for Max's name inside their internal network," Ethan replied, fingers still dancing across the keys. "This one is from about two hours ago. There are dozens more. All of them exchanges between someone called Dragonetz Coté and the top CIA official — a John Brennan."

Dominic blinked. "You broke into the CIA's network? That has to be one of the most secure systems on this planet."

"Oh, it is," Ethan said, matter-of-fact. "But it was open in two hours."

Dominic stared at him. "Two hours."

Ethan tapped the small, hard-edged device sitting beside the laptop — the portable processing unit they'd brought back from their world. "Do you remember that little machine we buried in the snow near the portal site?"

"Yeah."

"It's micro-bursting packets every thirty seconds through the 2-centimetre return link," Ethan explained. "Each burst routes straight into the receiving chamber, then hands off to TaloSyn."

He tapped the screen, watching the data rate flicker.

"TaloSyn barely notices the load. I'm using less than a hundredth of one percent of its file-cleaning subsystem — the part it uses to tidy corrupted archives and purge redundant storage. That's all I need."

Dominic blinked. "That little?"

"It's absurd," Ethan said with a tight smile. "If TaloSyn could reach this universe without the portal bottleneck, it would break their encryption in real time. As it is... the only thing slowing us down is the bandwidth. Not the computation."

He nodded at the trickling data stream.

"TaloSyn is dismantling their ciphers like they're made of damp paper. We're just feeding it the scraps as fast as the link allows."

Dominic let out a low whistle — a sound of genuine admiration. "You weren't kidding."

"The funny part is the shape of their security," Ethan went on. "The first barrier took two and a half hours. The second layer, where they keep departmental access, took six more. But the last lock — the individual password layer — that was the comedy."

Dominic raised an eyebrow. "Go on."

Ethan flipped to another window. "I started at the top. John Brennan, Director. You'd expect something meaningful. A phrase, a cipher, a credential token."

"And?"

"And his password was *password123*." Ethan looked up, deadpan. "Three s's. Took three milliseconds."

Dominic barked out a laugh. "This world really is held together with string and arrogance."

"Exactly." Ethan switched back to the message logs. "Now we sift. Coté's updates are detailed. We find the last point where Max was mentioned, the last recorded location, the radius of the manhunt — everything we need."

Dominic rested a hand on the back of the chair, expression tightening with purpose. "Good. If Max is alive out there, we're going to find him."

Ethan nodded, scrolling through the flood of secret communications now laid bare. "Now we just read. And follow the trail."

***

**Wednesday, 29th January 2014, 4:20 p.m. GMT**
**Multi party video conference.**

The screens flickered into place one by one — London, Washington, Berlin, Tokyo, Moscow, Ottawa, Paris, Canberra, Brasília, New Delhi, Pretoria, — faces drawn, voices already tight even before the first agenda item was raised. No one bothered with greetings. No one pretended this was a routine summit.

The British Prime Minister opened bluntly:

"We are facing the largest civil disturbance in recorded human history."

No one disagreed. Every leader on the call had the numbers in front of them — daily updates that felt like dispatches from a collapsing world.

Global fatalities: somewhere between 32,000 and 40,000.

United States: 802 dead yesterday, thousands injured.

EU riots: seventy-four cities in active unrest.

India: mass strikes and street blockades.

South America: government buildings torched.

Australia & NZ: unprecedented protests.

Africa & Middle East: large-scale demonstrations erupting despite shutdown attempts.

No one tried to soften it. The States were burning, and the pressure could no longer be contained with polite diplomatic language.

The Americans went on the defensive first.

The US Secretary of Homeland Security leaned toward his camera, jaw tight.

"We want to be absolutely clear — the so-called documentary is an Anonymous fabrication. A digital forgery. Nothing more. The man in question is deceased. His death was caused by Gaidon Ballerat. Anything else is disinformation."

Germany's Interior Minister snapped back immediately:

"If it's fake, explain the consistency across the forty five hours of video. We've had our analysts look at it. They're not convinced its fake."

Washington shut that down flat.

"Your analysts are wrong."

The French delegate leaned forward, face drawn, voice sharp.

"We have riots in Paris that make 1968 look like a picnic. People believe this Rivette man is alive. They believe your government has either murdered him or has him buried in a black site never to the light of day. Why should anyone here trust your denials?"

The American answered coldly:

"Because we're telling you the truth."

It didn't land.

The debate spiralled toward the only topic that mattered: the internet.

Japan raised what many were thinking.

"Should we isolate ourselves? Cut national networks off entirely?"

"Impossible," said the Canadians.

"Too late," said the Australians.

"Commercially suicidal," said the British.

"And strategically catastrophic," warned the French.

The US pushed hard:

"Shut down your P2P infrastructure. Block remaining nodes. Anyone distributing the video must be treated as a national security threat."

The German representative shook his head.

"Half our population has already seen it."

"Forty percent here." — UK.

"Over sixty in ours." — Denmark.

"We can't arrest our way out of this." — South Africa.

The Americans dug in.

"You must. We have. And we will continue to."

The temperature in the room climbed until diplomacy collapsed.

A Brazilian minister slammed a hand on the desk.

"People are dying because of your secrecy. Because of this video. If this Rivette man was killed by your agencies—"

The US delegate cut her off sharply:

"He wasn't. And this line of questioning ends now."

The French delegate muttered — not quietly enough —

"Your country has lied before. *It's your national sport!*"

Washington exploded.

Raised voices overlapped. Several ministers shouted over translations. Two cameras shook as aides tried to calm their leaders. The Australians cursed. The Americans doubled down. The British demanded order. The Russians laughed openly. The Germans threatened to disconnect.

And then the moment of rupture:

The American delegation stood up and walked off camera.

One by one, their screens went dark.

The remaining governments sat there in stunned silence, the static hum of twenty open microphones filling the void.

The British PM finally exhaled and muttered:

"Well. That's that."

The call ended without resolution, without unity, and without hope that Washington would cooperate.

The world was burning, and the governments supposed to contain the fire had just torn up the map.

***

**Wednesday, 29th January 2014, 9:02 p.m.**
**Pfronten Hotel, Germany.**

Dominic had been hunched over the laptop for hours, sifting through the torrent of intercepted intelligence with the precision of a forensic analyst dissecting a crime scene. CIA routing chatter. Handler lists. Movement logs. Sanitised briefs. Misleading decoys. And then something uglier tucked between the lines — a report noting that Max had been accidentally told about the murder of his aunt by the CIA. And then the parts that mattered — glancing references to Geneva, to a secret CIA prison, and the clipped, shaken admission from Dragonetz Coté that Maximilien Rivette had slipped through their control.

By the time he leaned back, the hotel notepad was a dense lattice of names, dates, arrows, and cross-links. For the first time since crossing over, the fog was lifting. They finally had direction.

The door opened.

Ethan stepped in, shoulders dusted with snow, wearing the exhausted satisfaction of a man who had managed three miracles on the way upstairs. Dominic closed the notepad.

"Did you get it?"

Ethan held up a small envelope. "Yes. I gave the receptionist the last of the coins." He tapped the envelope on the table. "Twelve hundred euro in cash."

Then he dangled a pair of battered car keys. "And these. She's lending us her Renault. Twenty-five years old, one headlight out, and held together by optimism. The gold helped her discover a deep, previously unknown commitment to hospitality."

Dominic allowed himself the smallest grin. "Amazing what a handful of metal will do in this world."

"Indeed," Ethan said, pocketing the keys.

They worked quickly, packing their notes and equipment into their backpacks, wiping down anything that might leave a trace. Within minutes the room looked untouched — just another anonymous guest room in a sleepy Bavarian hotel.

Dominic shouldered his pack, met Ethan's eyes, and nodded once.

"Geneva," he said.

"Geneva," Ethan echoed.

And they stepped out into the cold.

***

**Thursday, 30th January 2014, 5:15 p.m.
Secret CIA prison, Geneva, Switzerland.**

From the street, the building still looked like the Admiral Hotel — the same glass, the same awnings, the same quietly anonymous frontage. Only someone who knew what it had become would sense the sealed edges, the reinforced hinge lines, the blinds that never moved.

Dominic pressed the intercom beside the main door.

"Dominic Garner and Ethan Walker," he said, voice flat and practised. "We have an appointment with Dragonetz Coté."

They already knew Coté wasn't inside. Ethan had seen to that — a fabricated sighting of Maximilien Rivette in a district three kilometres south had dragged the CIA man out of the building at speed. The ease of puppeteering a hostile intelligence service using its own email and phone systems had amused both men more than they would admit aloud.

A moment of silence hung on the line.

"He is unavailable," the voice finally replied.

"When will he be available?"

"Not right now."

Dominic took his finger off the button and looked at Ethan. "Officious little shit. Watch this."

He pressed the buzzer again.

"That isn't going to work," he said, tone shifting into the register of a man used to issuing instructions. "Mr Coté will want to know why you turned us away when we have a scheduled appointment. We've already been briefed. This visit is a formality — a handover and a key collection. If we lose time because you blocked us, he will take that personally."

Another silence, this one edged with nerves.

"...All right. The door is open. Second floor."

The lock clicked. Dominic pushed the door, and they stepped inside.

The interior was nothing like a hotel — stripped walls, reinforced frames, cameras disguised as smoke detectors. As they climbed the stairs, another door on the landing unlocked automatically. Dominic noted the mechanism. Powered locks. Layered control. They had poured money into this place to keep one man contained.

They entered a small reception area. Two CIA men were waiting — one at a laptop, typing with the flat expression of someone doing triage, and another standing to greet them.

The standing man stepped forward with an apologetic half-smile and extended his hand.

"James Marshall. Sorry about the delay. We found the communications eventually. I understand you're from the European Security Directorate and have intelligence regarding the POI."

Dominic handed over his identification. Marshall glanced at it long enough to look credible before returning it.

"Yes," Dominic said. "We believe Rivette has a psychological attachment to a particular location. If he's lying low, he'll drift there sooner or later."

Marshall nodded. "Most of the team rushed out. Strong chance they've got a lead." He turned to the analyst beside him. "Anything?"

The man shook his head. "Still searching."

Ethan stepped forward. "We'll find him. Did you secure the vehicle we requested?"

Marshall opened a drawer and produced a set of keys. "Black Mercedes van. Marked for Geneva Fire Security Services. Should blend in. It's parked fifty metres down the street."

Dominic turned the keys in his hand. "Appropriate for what we're walking into."

Marshall gave a tight smile. "Use the secure email system for updates."

"We will," Ethan said. "You'll have the POI soon."

They left the room with the keys and a quiet satisfaction — the CIA, frantic and hollowed-out, had handed them the tools they needed without ever realising who they had just let through the door.

***

**Thursday, 30th January 2014, 9:15 p.m.**
**Cemetery, Prévessin-Moëns, France.**

The cemetery lights hummed faintly against the cold night air, each lamp rising from the gravel paths like a thin metal spine. Dominic tightened the last mounting bracket and stepped down the ladder, which Ethan steadied with one gloved hand.

"That's the last module," Dominic said, lowering the small boxed camera into place and securing the weather cover. The CIA's equipment was crude by their standards, but it did its job — each unit wired into the lamp's power feed and streaming high-resolution video back to the monitors in the van.

"Let's hope he hasn't already been here," Ethan murmured. "I'd hate to think we missed our chance."

He adjusted the freshly mounted camera and kept talking, low and matter-of-fact.

"The CIA never had anyone watching this place properly. Too many angles. Too many approaches. I've also got monitors on every colleague Max has worked with in the last decade — all online, all easy enough to scrape. If he tries to reach out to anyone, we'll see it."

He straightened, eyes scanning the street.

"But this is still our best shot at catching him."

Dominic scanned the neat rows of lit paths, each lamp now carrying one of their hidden eyes.

They gathered the tools quietly, boots whispering through the thin frost on the gravel. The van waited at the edge of the grounds, lights off, a black shape under the bare branches. Ethan set the toolbox inside while Dominic checked the feed on the dashboard display — all six modules were transmitting perfectly.

"Internet comes back on in a few hours," Ethan said as he hoisted the ladder onto the roof rack. "I checked the protocols. It won't be the internet as the locals remember it. Locked down. Sanitised. Only government channels and state news. We can use that. We can take over their ultra secure propaganda network."

They climbed into the van. The monitors showed the cemetery bathed in pale light, six overlapping fields of vision forming a quiet web of surveillance.

They would wait. Max would come — whether in hours, days, or longer.

He'd want a moment at Céleste Guérard's resting place — a chance to honour her properly.

And when he did, they would be ready.

*** 

# Chapter 36



Éric Lebas sat at the small kitchen table with his work jacket thrown over the back of the chair, a handful of invoices and a half-finished coffee pushed aside so Max had space. The construction contractor in him still moved with the solid, steady manner of someone used to fixing problems with his hands — but digital catastrophe was another matter.

"So the internet is working?" Max asked.

"Working is generous," Éric replied. "It's crawling. Everything's throttled. Half the pages time out. The other half load three minutes later."

Max rubbed at his temple. "Fuck."

"I managed to send out the last batch of orders for the company," Éric said. "Email, bank access, supplier forms — all of it still exists. It just takes ten times longer. Everything's being routed through whatever filters they've built overnight."

"And the idea of uploading anything...?" Max asked, already bracing for the answer.

"Gone." Éric gave a helpless shrug. "YouTube's frozen. No uploads at all. They've deleted half of what they already had — channels, archives, everything. People are calling it the purge."

"And it's all because of me." Max leaned back, throat tight. "I wanted the world to know what I saw. What I lived. And instead—" He exhaled sharply, voice cracking. "These governments... they're pathetic. Corrupt. Terrified of their own shadows. My proof of life should change things, but I don't even know how to get it out anymore."

Éric looked at him, unsure how to respond. He built houses, not revolutions.

The front door clicked, and Évelyne Jacquard stepped in with an armful of groceries, cheeks pink from the cold. She paused when she saw the tension in the room.

"What's happened?"

"We've run out of options," Éric said quietly. "At least as far as the internet goes."

Évelyne set the bags down on the counter. "Well... I have something for Max. It isn't good news, but you should hear it."

Max's head lifted slowly. "What is it?"

"I spoke to one of the florists I used to work with," she said. "She does funeral arrangements for several parishes. She remembered a funeral for a woman named Céleste."

Max went still — breath held, eyes widening just enough to show the blow landing.

"She was buried in Prévessin-Moëns," Évelyne continued gently. "At the Catholic cemetery near her home."

For a moment Max didn't speak. His jaw moved as though he was trying to find words that fit the shape of grief he'd carried alone for months. Finally he pushed his chair back.

"I want to go," he said. "I need to see her."

Évelyne nodded. "We'll take you."

Éric gathered the invoices into a neat stack — not because he needed to, but because it gave his hands something to do while the weight of Max's grief pressed into the room.

No one argued.

There was nowhere else in the world Max Rivette could go next.

***

**Friday, 31st January 2014, 10:15 p.m.**
**Cemetery, Prévessin-Moëns, France.**

Ethan tapped Dominic's leg twice — firm, urgent. Dominic came awake immediately, instinct sharpening as he pushed himself upright in the passenger seat. Ethan kept his voice low.

"A car just pulled in. Twenty metres out. It hasn't moved."

Dominic leaned over the console. On the monitor, one of the lamp-mounted cameras showed a pair of headlights sitting motionless in the small gravel lot. The beams washed across the nearby hedge, then clicked off. The interior of the car went dark.

"Been like that two minutes," Ethan murmured. "No doors. No movement."

Then, shapes.

Three silhouettes emerged from the vehicle. They paused as soon as their feet hit the ground — alert, scanning, cautious. Exactly how someone behaves when they know they're being hunted.

Dominic exhaled once, slow and certain. "That's him."

They didn't rush. They watched the feed a little longer, giving the trio time to move deeper into the grounds. When the three figures passed through the metal gate and were swallowed by the neat rows of headstones, Dominic and Ethan slipped out of the van.

The night was cold enough to sting. Frost glimmered on the gravel path as the two men entered the cemetery, moving without conversation, without wasted motion. Dominic led, cutting a silent path through the headstones while Ethan kept to his flank.

Céleste's grave wasn't far from the gate. They could already hear voices. One of them broke — raw, grieving.

"Why did they kill Céleste..." Max's voice cracked under the weight of it. "Fucking bastards."

Dominic stopped behind a marble headstone, peered around it, and nodded to Ethan. They were less than fifteen metres away now, just outside the trio's peripheral vision. He raised his hand once, signalling readiness, then slowly rose.

"Max," Dominic said.

Three figures spun toward the sound. Max froze mid-cry, chest heaving, eyes wide. Éric stepped in front of Évelyne in a protective reflex.

Dominic stepped fully into the light. "It's me. Dominic Garner."

Ethan followed, hands open, voice steady. "And Ethan."

Éric and Évelyne stared, trying to understand who these strangers were and why Max wasn't afraid.

Max wiped at his eyes with the back of his sleeve. "They're from the parallel universe."

After a moment, Max let out a tired breath. 'How did you even get here?'"

"Felix and his team finished the machine," Dominic said. "It's been working for over a month. Once we realised something had happened to you, we came."

Éric gestured vaguely at the darkness. "But how did you find us?"

Ethan gave a small, tired smile. "Intuition. And a bit of creative computer work."

Max didn't wait for more explanation. He stepped forward and pulled both men into a rough, unsteady embrace. Dominic hugged him back immediately; Ethan thumped a hand between Max's shoulders, steadying him as Max fought to breathe.

When Max finally let go, Dominic looked him over — the bruises, the exhaustion, the raw fear behind his eyes — and lowered his voice.

"Let's get out of here. Somewhere warm. Somewhere safe. Then we talk."

Ethan nodded. "We've got a lot to plan."

Max wiped his face again and took a long, shaking breath.

"Yeah," he said.

"Let's go."

***

**Saturday, 1st February 2014, 12.08 a.m.**
**The hideout, Prévessin-Moëns, France.**

Max pushed the curtain aside a few centimetres and looked out at the quiet street. Frost shimmered on the parked cars and hedges. The house was dark except for the kitchen light behind him.

"So how does someone who's new to this world find a place like this?" he asked.

Dominic leaned back in his chair. "Vacation rental. No owner on-site. Easy enough to book. We knew we'd need somewhere to bring you."

Max glanced over. "And how did you pay for it?"

Ethan raised a hand. "Before you panic — I didn't touch the CIA cards they gave us. I used a few senior managers' personal accounts instead."

Éric let out a quiet laugh. "So you're some kind of computer expert?"

"Where I come from, yes," Ethan said. "Here... I'm learning quickly." He tapped the heavy processing unit beside him. "And I've got an idea to break this wide open."

Évelyne sat at the edge of the table with a mug of tea. "But the internet is so tightly controlled. Everything is being blocked. Even YouTube won't allow uploads."

"That's what makes it perfect," Ethan said. "Their censorship can be turned into a weapon. And once we use it, they won't be able to control the outcome."

Dominic had already heard the outline. He nodded, impressed. "They built a cage for themselves."

Max pulled a chair closer. "Explain it. Slowly."

Ethan folded his arms. "Every device on their network relies on DNS. It's the address book of the internet. Normally decentralised, redundant, global. But after the shutdown, the U.S. government seized full control. Every website, every lookup, every route now funnels through a single hierarchy they manage. And because it updates every 24 hours, they can roll out countermeasures constantly."

Éric frowned. "So how does that help us?"

"Because centralised control cuts both ways," Ethan said. "If you take it, you take everything. Their entire system depends on one chain of trust. And that chain leads straight to the CIA—specifically to John Brennan."

Max shook his head. "But we're talking about the U.S. government. You can't simply out-muscle that."

"Yes, Max, I can," Ethan replied, patient but firm. "We had a different plan when we first arrived. But on Tuesday I realised their 'shutdown' wasn't a shutdown at all. The infrastructure remained up — just restricted. It only required the right key. So I found it."

Dominic smirked. "He found it in record time."

Ethan continued, "Once I gained initial access, I went straight for the agency's internal networks. The encryption layers were solid — took a while — but the final barrier is always the weakest link."

"And that was Brennan?" Max asked.

Ethan gave a small, incredulous nod. "The Director of the CIA. Password 'passsword123,' with three esses. And it only took three milliseconds."

Évelyne laughed at that.

"So what do you have now?" she asked.

"Full administrative control," Ethan said simply. "I can read everything, alter everything, redirect everything. But once I use that control in any obvious way, the system knows. When it resets its keys twenty-four hours later, they'll revoke Brennan's authority and patch the hole."

Max rubbed his forehead. "So it's a one-shot move."

Ethan nodded. "Exactly. But it's a decisive one. We inject truth directly into their central DNS layer. Not a torrent. Not a leak. Something they literally cannot hide. Every search they make, every page they open, every device that tries to reach anything will land on our message."

Silence settled around the table.

Max finally asked, "Are you absolutely sure this will work?"

Ethan looked at him evenly. "Max, who do you trust? Me — the man who cracked the CIA Director's account in less time than it takes to blink — or the guy who thought 'passsword123' was a good idea?"

The room burst into laughter, but Max didn't join in — he smiled with something closer to hope than he'd felt in months.

***

**Saturday, 1st February 2014, 4.42 p.m.**
**The hideout, Prévessin-Moëns, France.**

The lounge room barely resembled a lounge room anymore. Éric's halogen work lamps stood on their metal tripods like temporary stage lights, throwing a sharp white brightness across the space. The sofa had been pushed aside, the coffee table folded away, and in the middle of the room a single wooden chair sat against a grey tarpaulin hung from the ceiling with improvised clips and rope.

Ethan crouched behind the camera, making fine adjustments to the lens. He zoomed in, checked the focus, stepped forward to the chair and sat for a brief test.

"Sound check. One, two, three," he said lightly, then stood and returned to the camera for another tweak.

Across the room Dominic sat in an armchair, a notebook open on one knee. He worked through the pages of Max's prepared statement, scanning line by line, refining phrasing in his head. Every so often he made a small correction with his pen — adjusting tone, sharpening clarity, removing anything that felt like embellishment. He wasn't writing for drama; he was stripping the words down to truth.

At the small dining table near the wall, Éric, Évelyne, and Max spoke in low voices. No one was nervous in the usual sense — the atmosphere was too dense for that — but the reality of what they were about to do hung between them.

Ethan straightened and dusted his hands. "All right," he said. "Camera's set."

He turned toward Max. "What about you? Ready?"

The room fell still. Even the hum of the halogen lamps seemed to recede.

Max rose from his chair. He looked at each of them in turn — Dominic, thoughtful and steady; Ethan, focused; Éric and Évelyne, who had taken in a stranger and kept him alive when the world was hunting him.

"Yes," Max said quietly. "I'm ready."

He walked to the wooden chair and sat. Ethan framed him in the shot, then gave a single nod.

Max looked straight into the lens.

"My name is Maximilien Rivette," he began. "Few call me that — I've always been Max. And contrary to what your government is telling you..."

A breath.

"...I am very much alive."

***

**Sunday, 2nd February 2014, 8.10 p.m.**
**The hideout, Prévessin-Moëns, France.**


The dining table was pushed against the wall to make space, and Ethan's laptop sat in the centre of it. Everyone had gathered close, standing shoulder-to-shoulder, the room dim except for the glow of the screen.

Ethan rested his hands on the edge of the table. "Last chance," he said. "Any doubts? Any corrections? Anything you want me to change before I trigger the sequence?"

No one spoke. Évelyne folded her arms. Éric shook his head. Dominic shifted his weight but said nothing. Max watched the screen as if the world were already balanced on it.

"All right, then." Ethan tapped a single key.

The interface flipped instantly. On the right-hand side, coloured graphs sprang to life — rising threads of bandwidth, protocol tunnelling, and access-point saturation. On the left, command lines fired down the display, flowing too quickly for anyone but Ethan to track: credential escalations, handshake overrides, DNS packet captures, root-server redirects. It was a surgical seizure of the global network.

Nobody spoke for a while. The only sounds were the fans inside the processing unit and the occasional chirp of graphite as Dominic, almost without thinking, made a note on the pad in his hand.

"When do you think it'll finish?" Dominic asked quietly.

Ethan didn't take his eyes off the screen. "About forty minutes. Once the last root server reports back, the system locks. After that, we can't stop it — and neither can they."

Éric leaned forward. "And the video doesn't go live until noon GMT?"

"Correct," Ethan said. "At that moment, every one of the thirteen root nameservers will resolve to a single resource. No matter what you type, no matter what link you click — you get the video."

Évelyne frowned slightly. "What about email?"

"Messages will go through," Ethan said. "Attachments will be replaced with the link."

"Banking?" Éric asked.

"Different protocol. Most of it will function. Slower, but functional."

Max exhaled through his nose. "So for one full day, if you're on the internet, you see me. Not news, not commentary — just me."

"Yes," Ethan said. "Radio and television will still operate normally. They'll flood the airwaves with panels and denials and experts inventing reasons why the footage is fake. They'll do what they always do. But nobody online will see anything except the truth."

Dominic swept his gaze across the group. "Then let's be clear about tomorrow. Once the video goes live, we all know what has to happen. It's a risk for every one of us."

There was no bravado in the room. Just a quiet acceptance.

Max nodded. "The video alone won't shift the world. Someone has to stand there in person and force the point. That's on me."

Max looked at each of them in turn — the couple who had given him shelter, the operative who'd crossed universes to find him, the young technician who had dismantled the CIA's walls with a keyboard.

He exhaled softly.

"History remembers the brave."

Dominic met his eyes and repeated it, quieter, "History remembers the brave."

Ethan glanced between them, swallowed once, and echoed, "History remembers the brave."

Éric gave a faint, determined nod. "History remembers the brave."

Évelyne closed her hand over Max's and added the final voice to it. "History remembers the brave."

***

# Chapter 37



The van blended in well enough — a battered black Mercedes with "Geneva Fire Security Services" stencilled on the sliding door in fading vinyl. It sat at the edge of the narrow street, engine off, the winter quiet broken only by the occasional passing car.

Dominic and Éric occupied the front seats. Dominic rested his forearms on the steering wheel while running the final check on his sidearm: magazine out, back in, chamber confirmed, safety on. Completely methodical. Éric kept his eyes on the mirrors, watching the footpaths and the distant intersection.

In the cargo compartment, the remaining three sat on stacked crates that used to hold construction tools. Ethan balanced the laptop on his knees. Max sat next to him, shoulders tight. Évelyne leaned close enough to see the screen clearly.

The countdown timer in the corner of the laptop reached three seconds.

Then two.

Then one.

At noon GMT, the entire internet stuttered — and every device that attempted to load a page, whether in Belarus or Brisbane, in university labs or in someone's bedroom, was served the same file.

The video began to play inside the van.

Max, seated in the centre of the frame, began his statement. Calm. Direct. No theatrics — just a man calmly confronting the entire planet with the truth of his existence.

Ethan watched the first graph spike. "We're live," he murmured. "Root-server locks confirmed."

Dominic didn't turn around. "Bandwidth?"

"Global saturation. Every line they've got."

They all kept watching. One minute in, Max's recorded self spoke of his disappearance, of the lies, of the violence that had buried him. This wasn't polished rhetoric; it was personal testimony delivered with the kind of quiet force that people instinctively trust.

Évelyne let out a slow exhale. "Mon dieu…"

She watched the screen a few more seconds, then shook her head with a kind of astonished resignation.

"Là, ça va vraiment barder."

Now things were really going to blow up.

Dominic allowed himself the faintest of smiles. "That's the idea."

Max didn't respond. He just sat there in the dim cargo compartment, watching his own face on the laptop as the truth he had fought, bled, and almost died for spilled into every household on Earth.

Outside, Geneva moved along in its usual morning rhythm — unaware that within the next three minutes, every phone would begin vibrating, every computer screen would freeze and reload, and every news desk on the planet would be thrown into panic.

Inside the van, nobody spoke. They simply listened.

The match was lit.

The world hadn't realised yet.

But it was about to.

***

**Monday, 3rd February 2014, 7:14 a.m.**
**The Presidents office, Washington DC, United States of America.**

The morning intelligence briefing had barely begun when the desk intercom buzzed. Obama stepped away from the screens, crossed to his chair, and pressed the button.

His secretary's voice came through, clipped and uneasy. "Sir, John Brennan is on a secure line. He says you need to take this immediately."

"Put him through."

The line opened, and before anyone could brace for it, Brennan's voice tore through the speaker — frantic, breathless, and cracking around the edges.

"Mr President — I'm sorry. I've fucked up. I'm so sorry."

Every uniformed face in the room went still. Obama stared at the phone with a look that belonged more in a family emergency than a military briefing.

"What exactly is fucked up, John?"

"The internet," Brennan said, and his voice wavered. "We've lost control over the entire thing. Completely. We're locked out."

Obama straightened. "How do you lose control over a system you told me you owned?"

A long, defeated exhale came down the line. "We built a secure architecture, sir. Too secure. If you lose the top-level credentials... even we can't override it."

"Override what?"

"Max Rivette has surfaced," Brennan said. No buildup, no diplomacy — just the fact itself. "He released a video. It's everywhere. We tried to contain it, but the censorship protocols were turned back against us. The whole internet is serving only one file — him. He's telling the world he's alive, telling them about the twelve rules, telling them to abandon top-down government."

A murmur rippled through the room — shock, disbelief, something close to awe.

Obama's composure cracked. "John, you told me you were the keymaster. Your exact words. You told me nobody could break the system because you held the root access."

Silence. Then a small, hollow confession.

"My tech people say I was hacked."

"You were hacked," Obama repeated, like he couldn't quite process it.

Brennan sounded like he was swallowing glass. "My personal machine. My login. They got it."

"Your password was supposed to be a one-time, twelve-character, scrambled credential," Obama said.

"It—" Brennan's voice dropped to a strangled mutter. "It was passsword123. Three esses. I thought—"

Every person in the Oval Office froze.

Obama shouted it this time. "John, for fuck's sake!"

"I know," Brennan said. "I know. I've already heard it from my own people for the last ten minutes. They're telling me it's unrecoverable. They say it would take centuries to brute-force through the layers. The system resets in twenty-four hours but until then... we're spectators."

Obama held his forehead in both hands, then looked up. "Show me this video. How do I even get to it?"

"Type anything," Brennan said. "Any address. You'll get him."

Obama moved to the laptop on his desk. The officials gathered behind him — generals, intelligence chiefs, advisors, all craning in as though they were watching the slow unfurling of a natural disaster.

He typed a URL.

The browser loaded.

And Max's face dominated the screen — calm, resolute, uncompromising — speaking directly to billions.

No one breathed.

The United States government had just lost control of the modern world.

***

**http://* or https://***
**Monday 3rd February 2014. 12.00 p.m. GMT until**
**Tuesday 4th February 2014. 12.00 p.m. GMT**


I am Maximilien Rivette. Few call me that — I prefer Max.

Contrary to what the government is telling you, I am very much alive.

I was part of the team at CERN that worked on a machine that became a portal to another world in a parallel universe. And the leader of the team is in jail: Gaidon Ballerat.

We had a traitor among us — Vincent Duke. He enabled the CIA's involvement. And the CIA, specifically Dragonetz Coté, murdered my aunt, Céleste Guérard.

I have been held in a secret CIA prison here in Geneva for almost seven months. I was psychologically tortured. I was assaulted. I was denied my freedom. All to bury the truth.

And the truth is this: after living for an entire year in that parallel universe, I saw a society that evolved. Not through revolution, but through a quiet, deliberate shift shortly after the Great War. They rejected rule from above and adopted twelve simple rules that organise life from the bottom up.

Opponents have tried to label this system anarchist, extremist, oppressive — a form of terrorism. It is none of those things. It is whatever a community decides it should be, so long as it exists within the framework of those twelve rules.

Let me read them to you.

***

RULE 1 — LAW

These twelve rules shall be the only laws binding upon persons, communities, regions, and nations.

No authority may alter, add to, or remove these rules.

All other decisions shall be made by the people through their assemblies.

RULE 2 — COMMUNITIES AND REPRESENTATION

Every person belongs by choice to a community.

Communities may freely join together to form regions and nations, and may leave them at will.

Every person shall have equal voice in the decisions that affect their life.

Communities may appoint delegates to carry their decisions to wider assemblies.

Delegates must act only as instructed by those who appoint them and shall be recalled at once if they act against their charge.

RULE 3 — GOVERNANCE WITHOUT RULERS

Communities, regions, and nations may create councils to coordinate their common tasks.

These councils shall not make law. Their duty is to carry out the decisions of the people in accordance with these rules.

Delegates and administrators must obey the exact instructions of the people and may be recalled immediately if they depart from them.

All records of council actions and the use of resources shall be open for any person to examine.

RULE 4 — FREEDOM OF THE INDIVIDUAL

Every person may leave their family, community, region, or nation at any time.

No person or body may command another save in the just enforcement of these rules.

Every person is free to speak, to believe, to gather, and to know all matters of public record.

RULE 5 — NON-VIOLENCE AND THE PREVENTION OF HARM

Every person has the right to live free from physical harm.

No community, region, or nation shall begin war or raise arms except to repel direct attack.

Where a clear and reasonable danger of harm is foreseen, communities may act to prevent it.

Such action must rest upon evident proof, use only the least restriction needed, and remain under public oversight.

Any citizen may appeal against restraint before their community's tribunal.

RULE 6 — LAND AND THE EARTH

No person or body may own land.

Communities may hold land in trust for the common good.

Personal goods within one's dwelling belong to the person.

The resources of the Earth belong to all and shall be tended for the benefit of all.

RULE 7 — INDUSTRY AND LABOUR

Every person has the right to engage in safe and useful work.

Industry exists to serve need, not profit.

The fruits of industry shall be shared fairly among all.

All work shall respect the natural balance of the world and shall be guided by the judgement of the communities it serves.

RULE 8 — HEALTH

Every person is entitled to the highest attainable standard of health.

Communities, regions, and nations shall provide care freely to all who need it.

The means of health shall never be owned for gain.

RULE 9 — KNOWLEDGE AND LEARNING

Every person has the right to education and to the pursuit of knowledge.

Learning shall be free for all ages.

Science and art belong to all mankind and shall not be withheld or sold.

RULE 10 — HOUSING

Every person has the right to a secure and decent home.

Communities shall ensure that all are housed.

Dwellings may not be bought, sold, or held for profit.

RULE 11 — FOOD AND WATER

Every person has the right to nourishment and clean water.

Communities shall maintain the means to provide these to all people.

None may own or control the sources of food or water.

RULE 12 — THE ABOLITION OF MONEY

Money and trade for profit are abolished.

Goods and services shall be given according to need and received according to purpose.

Systems of exchange may exist only to maintain fairness and record, and shall never create privilege or debt.

***

Max paused before adding.

These Rules are founded upon peace, equality, and mutual care.

They bind no one to obedience beyond justice, and they release all from want, servitude, and fear.

Let them be carried to every land and written in every tongue, that the world may never again descend into war.

After reading the rules, Max continued:

"When I lived in the parallel universe, I filmed a year of my life — the people, the work, the decisions we made together, the dignity they gave one another. That documentary was taken from me when I returned. The CIA destroyed the original recordings. They did everything they could to erase them.

But a copy survived — made in the other world, kept safe, and brought across by two people who risked everything to help me. They used a portal machine I helped the other world design, crossing between universes to deliver the truth you have all seen over the past days.

They are also responsible for the takeover of the global internet routes. It will last only twenty-four hours. Long enough to make sure the truth cannot be buried again.

What happens after that is up to you.

If you choose to act, act peacefully. Real change cannot be forced. It must be chosen. That means citizens have the right to hold their leaders accountable, to remove those who abused power — but only through a lawful court that recognises the Twelve Rules.

I am asking you to reclaim what was always yours: your voice, your community, your responsibility for the world you live in. Go out into the streets. Stand at your centres of authority. Demand transparency, demand justice, demand your freedom back.

That is all I have to say for now.

And to prove that I am real, and alive — I will appear in public shortly."

***

**Monday, 3rd February 2014, 1.17 p.m.**
**Geneva, Switzerland.**

The back door of the van opened and Max, Ethan, and Évelyne stepped out into the mild winter air. The street looked like any ordinary Monday in Geneva—commuters moving with purpose, buses braking at the station, the steady hum of city life utterly unaware of what was arriving in its midst.

Dominic and Éric joined them at the rear of the van. "Shall we go for a walk?"

Max offered a small, dry smile. "Why not. It's a lovely day."

They headed north. For the first fifty metres they passed a dozen people, none paying them more than a glance. Then, as they stepped across Rue des Alpes, a young man on the opposite footpath froze mid-stride. He stared for several seconds, disbelief washing into recognition.

"Max Rivette!"

Max hesitated, caught off guard, and gave an awkward little wave.

It was enough.

The man sprinted across the street.

"You're alive!" he shouted, loud enough for half the block. "What are you doing here in Geneva?"

Max didn't slow. "Going for a walk."

"Where are you going?"

"To take back my life."

"Where's that?"

Max glanced at him. "Come and see."

The man fell in beside them, jittering with adrenaline. People slowed. A few phones lifted. Photos snapped. Within a minute more than twenty people had gathered, firing questions Max didn't bother answering.

He stopped at the T-intersection ahead. Down the right-hand street, only sixty metres away, stood the anonymous building where he had been held for nearly seven months. That morning he and Dominic had argued the route; Max insisted they pass it. He needed to see it from outside. He needed to reclaim the space that had been used to erase him.

Dominic leaned close. "You still want to go that way?" He flicked a glance toward the growing crowd. "Your call."

Max raised his voice. "I can't answer your questions right now. But if you'd like to walk with us, you're welcome."

Agreement rippled outward. More people joined, drawn by energy rather than explanation.

Max and his companions turned right.

By the time they reached the building, at least fifty people were with them. Someone shouted, "Max lives!" and Dominic—unable to resist—called back:

"History remembers the brave!"

The phrase caught instantly. The crowd began chanting it in waves, their voices carrying down the quiet midday street. Windows opened. Office workers stepped onto balconies. People abandoned errands and lunches, drifting out of doorways and across pavements to see the commotion.

The procession swelled.

By the time they hit Rue de Lausanne, the crowd had become a moving river— hundreds at first, then more. Cars stalled. A tram driver leaned out of his cab, stunned. The chant rose and reverberated between buildings:

"Max lives!

History remembers the brave!"

Two police cars tried approaching from a side street but were forced to stop when the mass of people filled the road. The officers stepped out, listening. This wasn't a riot. It wasn't violent. It was... determined. One officer met another's eyes, made a helpless little shrug, and quietly joined the crowd.

Ahead, the wide road opened, and Max looked at Dominic, Ethan, Éric, Évelyne, and the thousands now following. Something shifted inside him—a certainty that the government's lies were dissolving in real time. His existence could no longer be denied. The truth could no longer be buried.

A helicopter appeared overhead, circling low.

Behind Max, the procession stretched more than three hundred metres; ahead, at least eighty. Every step drew in more bodies. More voices. More witnesses.

When they reached Avenue de France, Max turned left. They pushed toward their final destination. The open plaza came into view—the fountains misting the air in thin arcs, and ahead, rising above the crowd:

Broken Chair.

A 12-metre wooden sculpture with one shattered leg, erected as a stark reminder of the victims of landmines and the governments that refused to limit their use. Even in the ordinary flow of tourists it was imposing; surrounded by thousands chanting his name, it looked like a monument waiting for a moment exactly like this one.

Max guided the march toward it.

It took ten minutes to push through the density of people. At last, he reached the front.

Beyond the plaza stood the gates of the Palais des Nations — the European seat of the United Nations.

Max stopped there, facing the crowd, the plaza, the city, and the future he had just set irreversibly in motion.

***

**Monday, 3rd February 2014, 8:15 a.m.**
**Press briefing room, The White House.,Washington DC, United States of America.**

There are around thirty people in the room. All are seated, including the President, and are watching the television on one of the walls behind the lectern. It is showing CNN news which has a newsreader talking over the live video from the helicopter above Geneva.

"The crowd is estimated at seventy thousand people and is growing by the minute."

"This all because of Max Rivette who has appeared on the streets of Geneva less than an hour ago. Soon after the fifteen minute video was released on the internet. That video is the only thing accessible on any website. Every website we have tried has that video. In that video Max Rivette claims to have been held in a prison in Geneva by the CIA."

"We have not heard from any US authorities on the matter."

The President hits the off switch on the remote for the TV and it turns off.

He stands slowly. Visibly a shattered man.

"I don't know what to say in a time like this. We tried to keep this a secret. Only some of you knew about Max. We tried to hide the truth because it will lead to enormous upheaval, the tearing down of capitalism - a system we all have an interest in managing, and leading. And now, it appears there is a better way. Max returning from the other universe and telling the world of this utopian other world was something I couldn't allow to become public..."

"It never happened!" screams a military person

"Shut up you idiot. I saw the video that Max..."

"it's fake" Some of the men restrain the man and lead him out of the room

"It's not fake. I not only saw the entire forty five hour video. I also saw the initial video from CERN, when they first flew the drone into the parallel universe to see just what it was that they had discovered. I know this parallel world is real. I know that they make the twelve rules work."

There is a long silence.

Finally a woman asks "What are we going to do now. As a government I mean"

Obama pauses, shakes his head "We are totally fucked. There is nothing we can do. You saw all those people in the streets of Geneva. I expect within hours every city on Earth will start to fill with regular folk demanding change."

"Max used the phrase bottom up government. As the leaders of a top down government all I can do is get out of the way and pray that they don't throw me in prison. Or kill me. I can only hope to have some sort of control so that too many people don't get killed".

***

# Chapter 38



**Monday, 3rd February 2014, 2.17 p.m.**
**Palais des Nations, Geneva, Switzerland.**

For nearly ten minutes Max and his friends held their position near the entrance gates to the compound. Beyond the narrow pedestrian point stood two layers of steel fencing, each around a metre and a half high, forming a broad perimeter across the landscaped grounds of the United Nations. A dozen security officers were stationed along the line, not hostile, simply urging the crowd to stay back. They didn't need to insist; no one was trying to climb the barriers.

The crowd behind Max had swelled so much that the noise came in waves — chanting, camera shutters, voices overlapping until it became a single rising sound.

A small grey car emerged from deeper inside the compound and rolled up to the inner side of the gate. Two sharply dressed men stepped out. They spoke briefly to the senior guard, who pointed towards Max. A moment later the guards at the narrow entry stepped aside, and the two men began making their way forward.

Dominic saw the movement first and nudged Max, then shifted his coat just enough to draw the handgun into his palm. He didn't raise it, but he made sure the men knew he was armed.

The first of the two held up both hands immediately. "We're unarmed," he said, stopping several metres away. His colleague mirrored the gesture. There were still a few members of the crowd between them and Max, but the mood around the moment shifted. Voices dimmed; phones dropped as people watched.

"We've been sent by Director-General Michael Møller," the first man continued. "He requests to meet you."

Max looked to Dominic first, then to Ethan, Éric, and Évelyne. None of them spoke. The silence spreading through the crowd was almost eerie after the hour of chanting.

"What does he want?" Max asked.

"He didn't say," the man replied. "But he's sympathetic. And he told us you'd be reluctant." His eyes flicked to Dominic's gun, then back to Max. "We saw the video just then. He only intends to talk. And you're not safe out here — not from the Americans. Even in a crowd this size."

The crowd, sensing the tension, surged into another chant — "Max lives! History remembers the brave!" — but the volume felt different now. Less of a protest roar, more of a protective shield.

Max exhaled, steady but uncertain. "I think this is the right thing to do," he said quietly to his friends.

Dominic gave a brief nod. "Then we go with you."

They pushed forward through the spectators, who stepped aside instinctively, some reaching out to touch Max's shoulder as he passed. At the gate the guards opened the barrier and allowed them through. The moment they crossed into the compound, the noise of the crowd dimmed to a low backdrop behind them.

They walked the long central path. Rows of flags from all 193 member states flanked them on either side, bright colours hanging motionless in the still afternoon air. It took several minutes to reach the steps of the Palais des Nations, its pale stone façade rising above them like a quiet, monumental witness to the world outside.

The five of them paused for a heartbeat at the base of the entrance, each aware that whatever waited inside would alter the course of events once again. Then they moved forward.

***

**Monday, 3rd February 2014, 2.34 p.m.**
**Palais des Nations, Geneva, Switzerland.**

They were guided through a quiet corridor lined with photographs of past assemblies and diplomatic milestones, then shown into a meeting room that felt more like a private study than an official venue. Bookshelves climbed the walls, filled with old volumes and ring binders. A cluster of armchairs and low lounges encircled a broad wooden coffee table polished to a soft sheen by decades of use.

The Director-General was already inside with two assistants. The UN security officers who had escorted Max took unobtrusive seats along the wall, close enough to act, distant enough not to intrude.

The Director-General stepped forward immediately. A tall, silver-haired man with the alert expression of someone accustomed to crisis, he looked genuinely shaken — the particular disquiet of a diplomat who realises protocol is now a historical artefact.

"Max," he said quietly, offering his hand. "You are... very much alive."

Max shook it. For the first time in months he felt welcome instead of hunted.

"Please," the Director-General said, gesturing toward the circle of chairs. "Sit. All of you."

They settled around the coffee table: Max between Évelyne and Dominic, Ethan and Éric facing them. The Director-General chose a chair angled slightly toward Max, signalling openness rather than authority.

Max introduced each of his companions by name alone. The Director-General didn't press for details; he clearly understood that these were the people who had risked everything to bring Max here alive.

When the introductions were done, the Director-General folded his hands, leaning back just enough to invite honesty.

"I would like to understand," he said. "All of it."

Max drew a long breath. Then he spoke.

For the next hour, he told the story — slowly at first, then with gathering clarity. CERN. The discovery of the parallel universe. The twelve rules. The year he lived among them. The CIA's imprisonment. His escape.

The Director-General never interrupted. His assistants tried to take notes at first, their pens scratching urgently across their pads — but after ten minutes the pens stilled. They simply listened, as if any attempt to reduce this into bullet points would be an insult to its enormity.

By the time Max finished, the room had fallen into a deep and breathless stillness — the kind of stillness that only appears when everyone present recognises, with absolute clarity, that the world outside this room has just shifted beneath their feet.

***

**Monday, 3rd February 2014, 11:23 a.m.**
**Press briefing room, The White House, Washington DC, United States of America.**

The room was packed. Reporters, staffers, and senior officials sat in tense silence as President Obama stepped to the lectern, the fatigue etched plainly around his eyes. He placed a sheet of paper down but didn't look at it.

He began quietly.

"This is a day that will be remembered for a very long time. And not because of anything my administration accomplished — but because of one man. Maximilien Rivette."

He let the name hang in the room.

"Many of you have seen the footage from Geneva. Max Rivette — alive, walking through crowds that welcomed him as though they'd been waiting their entire lives to see the truth surface. And the truth is this: my government detained him in a secret facility. My government tried to erase him. And history will not be kind to me for allowing that to happen."

A breath — steady, but heavy.

"When I watched the scenes coming out of Geneva... the chants, the scale of it, the sheer relief on people's faces... I realised something very simple. The moral authority in this moment doesn't belong to presidents or prime ministers. It belongs to the people. It belongs to a man who risked everything to bring back a message we tried very hard to bury."

He looked down, not in shame, but with the honesty of someone dropping a mask he'd worn too long.

"I'm a politician. I've been part of this system my whole life. And that means I have been part of its failures — its secrecy, its fear, its instinct to protect institutions before people. Good intentions don't change the fact that I've been beholden to structures built on unequal power."

He looked back up.

"I made a decision just before I came into this room. No action will be taken against Max Rivette. Not by our military. Not by our intelligence agencies. Not by anyone acting under my authority. We will not escalate. We will not silence him again. We are not going to kill to defend a lie."

A long pause. Reporters shifted in their seats.

"Some people in this building disagreed. Strongly. They told me that admitting the truth would destroy us. That the country would collapse. That we had to hold the line, no matter the cost. But the truth is — that line broke the moment Max stepped into the sunlight."

His voice lowered.

"There are powerful interests who want this to continue. Who want secrecy, hierarchy, obedience. They've asked me to help them keep their grip. They've tried to push me toward decisions that would haunt this nation for generations."

He straightened, exhausted but resolute.

"I'm not doing it. Not anymore. The direction is clear. We have to let go of the power we've hoarded for too long. We have to allow communities — people — to organise themselves from the bottom up. That's what Max showed the world. That's what his year in that other universe proved was possible."

He rested his palms on the lectern.

"I can't promise this will be easy. Change never is. But violence won't save us. Only courage will — the courage to live up to the twelve rules Max risked his life to share."

A small, fragile smile touched the corner of his mouth.

"We know such a society can work. Another universe is already living it."

Then the smile faded.

"I want to end with an apology. To Max Rivette — for what was done to him in our name. For his imprisonment. For the pain he endured. For the death of Céleste Guérard, an atrocity carried out by a rogue faction within our intelligence apparatus. And to Gaidon Ballerat who has suffered unjustly. I have ordered his immediate release."

He closed the folder he never used.

"My authority is limited now. But with what remains, I intend to support the most peaceful transition possible toward a system built on twelve rules — and the courage to live by them."

He stepped back from the lectern.

"Thank you."

And he walked out, leaving the room stunned, shaken — and finally, undeniably honest.

***

# Chapter 39



**Wednesday, 5th February 2014, 8:45 p.m.**
**Palais des Nations, Geneva, Switzerland.**

Max sat on the edge of the narrow bed that had been squeezed into the corner of the temporary room assigned to him. The walls were neutral and forgettable, but the article in his hands wasn't. A grainy photograph of Céleste stared back at him from the newsprint. He traced the image with a thumb, then let his gaze drift to the dark window. Geneva's lights shimmered in the distance. He didn't notice them. His thoughts hadn't left Céleste in days.

A knock broke the silence.

He wiped at his face instinctively, more out of habit than hope, and crossed the room. When he opened the door, words died in his throat.

Gaidon stood there.

Behind him were Daniel Mittermayer, Baset Theron, and Emerancie Favre — all watching him with a mixture of relief and something deeper: remorse, gratitude, shock at finally seeing him.

Max didn't move. For a moment he simply stared, breath caught, unable to reconcile the sight of them with the memory of every lie he'd been fed in the CIA prison.

Gaidon stepped forward first. He didn't wait for permission. He spread his arms and pulled Max into a firm, almost desperate embrace.

"Oh, Max," he said, voice tight. "Oh, Max. I am so sorry."

The dam broke. Max's breath shuddered against Gaidon's shoulder. He clung to him without thinking, overwhelmed by the weight of everything he'd carried alone.

Then Daniel reached them. Then Baset. Then Emerancie. The small room filled with arms, hands, murmured apologies, quiet relief — a clumsy, heartfelt collision of people who had once been a team, torn apart and now stitched back together in the most improbable circumstances.

Max tried to speak but his voice cracked. He nodded instead, letting each of them hold him in turn. He wasn't ready for conversation yet, and none of them pushed. They understood the gravity of the moment. They understood what these seven months had done to him.

The reunion stretched into minutes that none of them measured.

****

**Wednesday, 5th February 2014.,9:23 p.m.**
**Palais des Nations, Geneva, Switzerland.**

The meeting room had become a strange blend of worlds — the old life Max had lost and the new one carrying him forward. His friends from the parallel universe sat alongside the team from CERN. Dominic and Ethan were deep in conversation with Évelyne and Éric — the two who had helped Max escape the CIA prison — while Gaidon, Baset, Daniel and Emerancie compared stories with them as if they'd known one another for years.

Max stood slightly back from the cluster, unseen for a moment, simply taking it in. The sound of his old friends and new friends talking together — swapping stories about him, laughing at the contradictions, piecing together parts of his life neither group had ever heard — left him with a quiet, anchoring happiness.

For the first time in months, the room felt solid beneath him, as though the chaos of the last year had finally stopped spinning.

After a moment, Max drifted closer, drawn in by their laughter. He stopped near the low table in the centre of the room, steadying himself as the conversations tapered and the others slowly turned toward him. He could feel their quiet expectation settle on him — not heavy, just real. He cleared his throat.

"I want to go back," he said. "To the parallel universe. To the people who saved me. To the place that showed me what this world could become."

There was no shock in the room. Only stillness — a collective intake of breath, as if they knew he would say it and were relieved he finally had.

Before anyone could respond, the door opened and Dirk, the UN security officer Max had come to trust over the past two days, stepped in. He carried a small remote control and went straight to the video wall. With a few taps on the panel mounted beside it, the screens flicked to life.

A news presenter's voice filled the room mid-sentence.

"...the committee, which has the full support of senior figures within the military and police, made the arrests earlier this evening."

On the screen, live footage showed police escorting people in handcuffs from government buildings and private residences. The camera lingered on faces — some defiant, some stunned, some terrified.

Max stepped closer as the presenter continued.

"Among those taken into custody are former President Barack Obama and CIA Director John Brennan…"

The room erupted. A wave of cheers, disbelief, catharsis — the sound of people who had been powerless now seeing the first cracks in the edifice that had crushed them.

Dominic let out a low whistle. Ethan laughed in astonishment. Évelyne gripped Éric's arm. Gaidon muttered something under his breath that sounded suspiciously like "about bloody time."

But Max didn't cheer.

He simply stared.

For a long moment he watched Obama being led through a crowd of shouting onlookers — not humiliated, not injured, just held to account. The civilian committee's emblem flashed on the screen as the presenter added:

"According to a statement, all detainees will be brought before a public tribunal under emergency civilian authority. The committee stresses that these arrests are not acts of revenge but necessary steps toward restoring transparency, accountability, and order."

Max exhaled slowly. He hadn't realised he'd been holding his breath.

A weight he didn't have words for slid off his shoulders. He felt no triumph — only the quiet relief that comes when a nightmare finally starts to end. He thought of Céleste, of the year he spent in the other world, of the months in the cell, and of all the people who had believed him even when he could barely believe himself.

Dirk glanced at him. "Thought you'd want to see it."

Max nodded. "Thank you."

The room settled, the cheering fading into murmurs and shared glances. And Max, standing in the centre of it all, felt something he hadn't felt since the morning he walked into the portal so many months ago.

A sense that justice, however imperfect, had finally begun.

***

**Friday, 7th February 2014, 11:03 a.m.**
**Palais des Nations, Geneva, Switzerland.**

The morning briefing room carried a different kind of quiet — not fear, not exhaustion, but the calm that settles when everyone knows the next step has already been decided. Max stood at the long table with Gaidon, Daniel, Baset, Emerancie, Dominic, and Ethan.

Éric and Évelyne had gone home earlier that morning. They'd hugged Max, thanked him for the wild, unforgettable days they'd shared, and admitted they were tired. They wanted their own bed, their own kitchen, their own quiet. Max had understood completely.

Gaidon cleared his throat. "I've spoken to Constantine Lapôtre," he said. "CERN will be ready for you tomorrow. The chamber is prepped, the teams are in place, and the power schedule has been arranged."

Max exhaled, relieved. "And I've chosen this route for a reason."

He didn't elaborate, but there was weight behind his words — something personal he wasn't ready to name.

"There's something at CERN I need to collect before the machine is activated."

Dominic glanced at Ethan. "Speaking of leaving..."

He turned back to the room. "The two of us need to head out."

Max raised an eyebrow. "Now?"

"Now," Ethan confirmed. "We have an old Renault to return before the receptionist in Pfronten starts wondering why her car has vanished into thin air."

Dominic gave a faint grin. "If we don't bring it back, she'll assume we stole it. And she was kind to us. She deserves better than that."

Ethan slung his pack over one shoulder. "Once we drop it off, we're hiking up to the top of the ski run."

"At the summit, we'll trigger for the portal to expand fully, we step through and go home."

Max stepped closer to them. "Thank you. For everything. All of this began with your courage."

Ethan gave him a small, steady smile. "We'll see you again soon. On the other side."

They gave him a final nod — two men who had crossed worlds and would cross them again — and then slipped out of the room.

Max turned back to the others.

"Tomorrow," he said, "I go home."

Gaidon's voice cut through the quiet. "And we'll get you there."

The group gathered around him — not out of obligation, but out of purpose.

The decisions were made.

The paths were set.

They had a machine to ready.

And Max had a world — home and someone who loved him — waiting for him.

***

**Friday, 14th February 2014, 9:17 a.m.**
**Laboratory 888, CERN, Prévessin-Moëns, France.**

The laboratory entrance still looked exactly as it had the morning Max disappeared — except for the bicycle. His bicycle. It was leaning against the wall at a strange angle, the tyres collapsed into soft, defeated folds. Dust dulled the once-bright paint. The helmet strap hung loosely, stiff with age.

It hadn't moved since June 2012.

He stepped closer, touched the handlebar, and let out a long exasperated sigh.

"Of course," he muttered — not angry, just resigned at fate's sense of humour.

He crouched down, flipped open the frame-mounted pump, and began working the handle with short, sharp strokes. The tyre slowly lifted, reshaping itself from a flat, lifeless ring into something capable of surviving the road again. The metaphor was obvious even to him — and, annoyingly, apt. Seven months in hell, and here he was, putting air back into an old life.

When both tyres were firm, he checked the brakes, gave the wheels a spin, and pushed the bike toward the lift. The doors slid open with their familiar sigh. He wheeled the bicycle inside, pressed the button for Laboratory 888, and leaned against the wall as the lift descended.

Dull, deep machine noise greeted him when he stepped out. The machine was alive — a hulking cathedral of cables, shielding, instrument racks, and the unmistakable hum of superconducting power. The team was already gathered: Gaidon, Daniel, Baset, and Emerancie. They turned as one when they heard the wheels.

Daniel raised an eyebrow. "You're taking that old thing?"

Max gave the bike a gentle shake. "It carried me at the beginning of all this. It can carry me through the last part of it too."

Baset glanced at it. "I always wondered who that old thing belonged to."

Max smiled. "Mine. Always was."

The humour faded quickly. The moment was too big for much levity.

Gaidon stepped closer. "We've done the final checks. The machine is ready to operate."

Max rested one hand on the saddle. The smell of warm electronics and coolant filled the room — painfully familiar, painfully normal.

"Thank you," he said quietly. "For everything."

Daniel opened his arms. "Come here, you idiot."

Max was pulled into a hard, messy, affectionate hug. Then another. And another.

Baset clasped the back of Max's neck. "You're going home. Thats what matters."

Max nodded, throat too tight for words.

Max lifted the bike and carried it up the narrow stairs, the metal treads ringing under his boots.

He wheeled it along the steel platform, stopping beside the machine.

The team had retreated to the control room

He stood with the bike, one hand on the handlebars, and waited for the portal to open.

***

**Friday, 14th February 2014, 10:03 a.m.**
**Parallel Universe. Diderot farm, Prévessin-Moëns, France.**

The storm had been building since dawn — thick rolling clouds, wind pushing hard from the west, the air dense and electric. Rain came in hard bursts, then paused, then returned with twice the force, as if the sky itself couldn't hold its grief steady.

Renato was half-buried under the old tractor in his workshop, a grease-stained rag hanging from his pocket, the metal roof rattling each time the wind hit it just right. He muttered to himself in that familiar way — a string of half-Italian, half-French curses as he fought with a stubborn bolt.

He didn't hear the bicycle at first.

But he heard the brakes squeal.

And he heard a voice — a single word, spoken quietly but with a weight that didn't belong to any living man.

"Renato?"

The wrench in his hand dropped onto the concrete with a clatter.

He slid himself out from under the tractor — and then froze mid-motion.

Max stood in the open doorway, soaked through, hair plastered to his forehead, breathing hard from the ride in the storm. His clothes were different. His face was thinner. Older. But it was him.

Renato didn't speak. Didn't blink. Didn't even breathe for a moment.

Then the sound that came out of him wasn't a word — more a cracked exhale that collapsed into a sob.

He staggered forward, grabbed Max by the shoulders, and pulled him in with a force that was almost desperate.

"You're alive," Renato whispered into Max's hair. "You're alive, mon fils..." His hands were shaking. He pushed Max back just far enough to see his face. "I thought they killed you. I thought—"

Max couldn't answer. He just nodded once, eyes full, jaw tight, the storm wind whipping through the doorway around them.

The commotion carried out across the yard, and a moment later Bibiane appeared at the corner of the workshop, holding her shawl against the weather. She saw Renato clutching someone, walked a few steps closer — and stopped dead.

Her hand flew to her mouth. She started shaking her head as if she couldn't believe her eyes.

"Max? Max?"

She ran.

Renato stepped aside just in time for her to reach him. Bibiane threw her arms around Max so hard it knocked the breath out of him. She was crying openly, her face buried against his shoulder.

"We prayed for you," she said between sobs. "Every day. Every single day..."

Max held them both, the storm hammering the roof, the wind turning the rain sideways. The farm, the familiar fields, the smell of wet earth — it all came flooding back, overwhelming and grounding at the same time.

Renato wiped his face with the back of his sleeve, trying to compose himself, failing completely.

"Come inside," he said hoarsely. "You're soaked. You look half frozen. And you have a story to tell us — a long one."

Max nodded, unable to form a sentence.

The three of them walked together toward the farmhouse, arms still tangled around one another, the storm raging overhead as if the sky itself had been waiting for this moment.

***

# Chapter 40



**Friday, 14th February 2014, 3:44 p.m.**
**Parallel universe. Geneva airport/train station, Geneva, Switzerland.**

The automatic doors parted and Max pushed his bicycle into the terminal beside him. The tyres still carried some mud from the rural roads near the farm, and the frame clicked softly as it rolled — a familiar mechanical rhythm that anchored him after a long, emotional morning.

The airport had settled into its mid-afternoon lull. People moved in gentle waves: travellers dragging small cases, a few families juggling children and backpacks, two pilots chatting quietly near a café. No one paid him any special attention. This world had always carried its sense of calm with effortless grace.

Max slowed as he approached a wide window overlooking the runway. A jet taxied across the apron, toward a hangar, engines whining down. The sight held him for a moment. He had left this place as a man unsure of his future, his purpose, and his place in the world. He returned with the weight of two worlds on his shoulders — and the clarity that came from surviving both of them.

He rested a hand on the bicycle's handlebars. The metal was still wet from the journey. It struck him as faintly absurd that this old bike had travelled further than most people ever would. Once it had been nothing more than a practical tool for short commutes to CERN. Now it was a symbol of continuity — a quiet reminder that he still belonged somewhere, despite everything the past twenty months had thrown at him.

He pushed on.

Down the concourse, past the café with its smell of strong coffee and warm bread. Past a long wall of posters advertising communal services, learning programs, and community assemblies — the small, everyday things that made this society function without coercion or hierarchy. Every reminder strengthened his sense that he was finally home.

He reached the lift. As he waited, he caught his reflection in the brushed metal doors: a little gaunt, hair longer than he preferred, eyes carrying the shadows of the things he had endured. But behind those shadows was something steadier — not defiance, not even resilience, but a kind of settled purpose.

The lift arrived with a soft chime. Max wheeled the bicycle inside and pressed the button for the lower platforms. The doors closed, and the descent began with a low mechanical hum.

During the slow drop toward the high-speed rail lines, he felt the last few weeks settle into a coherent shape. He had helped transform his birth world, not because he sought revolution but because he had finally spoken the truth when it mattered. Fate had dragged him into the centre of history, and somehow he had survived the pull.

Yet what mattered most — what had carried him through the worst nights in the CIA prison — wasn't the politics or the prospect of change. It was Clarisse.

The thought of her drew a warmth through his chest. Her certainty. Her steadiness. The way her presence made the world feel navigable, as if she held a quiet map of all the places where a soul could be safe. He realised, for the first time with absolute clarity, that he had stopped searching. He had found the place and the person he needed.

The lift doors opened.

Cooler air drifted in from the platform. Max guided the bicycle forward, tyres whispering over the smooth floor. Ahead, the high-speed train hummed on the rails, preparing for departure.

He tightened his grip on the handlebars, stepped into the flow of travellers, and began the final leg of the journey back to her — back to Clarisse, back to the life he had chosen.

***

**Friday, 14th February 2014. 9:41 p.m.**
**Parallel universe. Max's apartment, Lorient, France.**

The train had left him at the edge of Lorient in the deep February darkness, the sky washed in a faint haze from the harbour lights. By the time he reached his street, the lamps were already burning — soft halos glowing against the damp night air, spreading pale circles across the wet pavement. Max pushed the bicycle beside him, his boots echoing along the quiet row of apartments. Familiar buildings rose around him — unchanged, steady, exactly as he'd left them eight months ago.

His chest tightened.

He slowed as he reached his old doorway, the bicycle coming to a gentle stop before he leaned it against the front of the apartment building. Max opened the door, the narrow hallway beyond was washed in a single warm light. He felt suddenly weightless, as if every step forward might undo him. Months of fear, grief, brutality, and impossible choices condensed into this one quiet walk down the corridor and up the stairs he had once climbed without a second thought.

He stopped at the door.

For a long moment he simply stood there, breathing carefully. The silence was thick, the kind that makes the heart beat louder than footsteps. He reached up, knuckles hovering above the wood. Dropped his hand. Tried again. Dropped it.

Then, with a quiet exhale that felt like surrender, he knocked.

A small sound inside — movement, then the soft pad of bare feet. The latch turned.

The door opened.

Clarisse stood framed in the warm light of the apartment, hair loose, face slightly flushed from an evening spent reading or painting or simply being alive. For half a second her expression was relaxed — then her mind caught up with what her eyes were seeing.

She froze.

Her breath hitched sharply, like someone struck in the chest. Her hand rose slowly to her mouth. Tears flooded before she could blink them away.

Max swallowed. His voice almost failed him, but he found it.

"I love you," he said — not as a flourish, not as drama, but as the plain truth of a man who had lived long enough to know the power of these words.

Clarisse didn't speak. She didn't need to. She moved — a sudden, stunned, disbelieving burst — and crashed into him with a force that knocked him back a half-step. Her arms locked around his neck, her face pressed to his shoulder as she sobbed with a sound that tore straight through him.

Max held her as tightly as he dared. Her tears soaked into his jacket. His own rose, hot and unstoppable, and he let them fall. They stayed like that for a long time — neither speaking, both shaking with the shock of a miracle they had never allowed themselves to believe in.

She finally pulled back just enough to see his face. Her hands framed it gently, as if afraid he might vanish again.

"It's really you," she whispered.

"It's me," Max said. "I'm home."

***

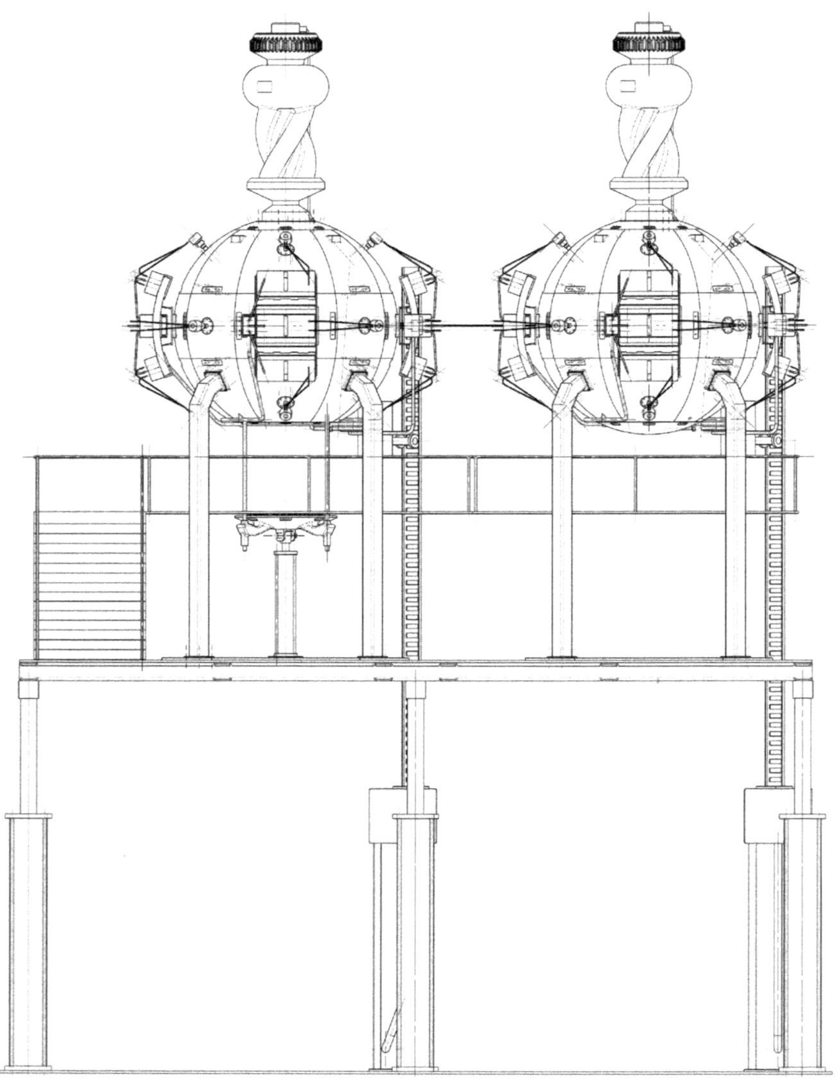

Early Parallel Universe Machine drawings
Drawn by: Maximillien Rivette.
Drawn: 27.03.2011
Revision: 3A

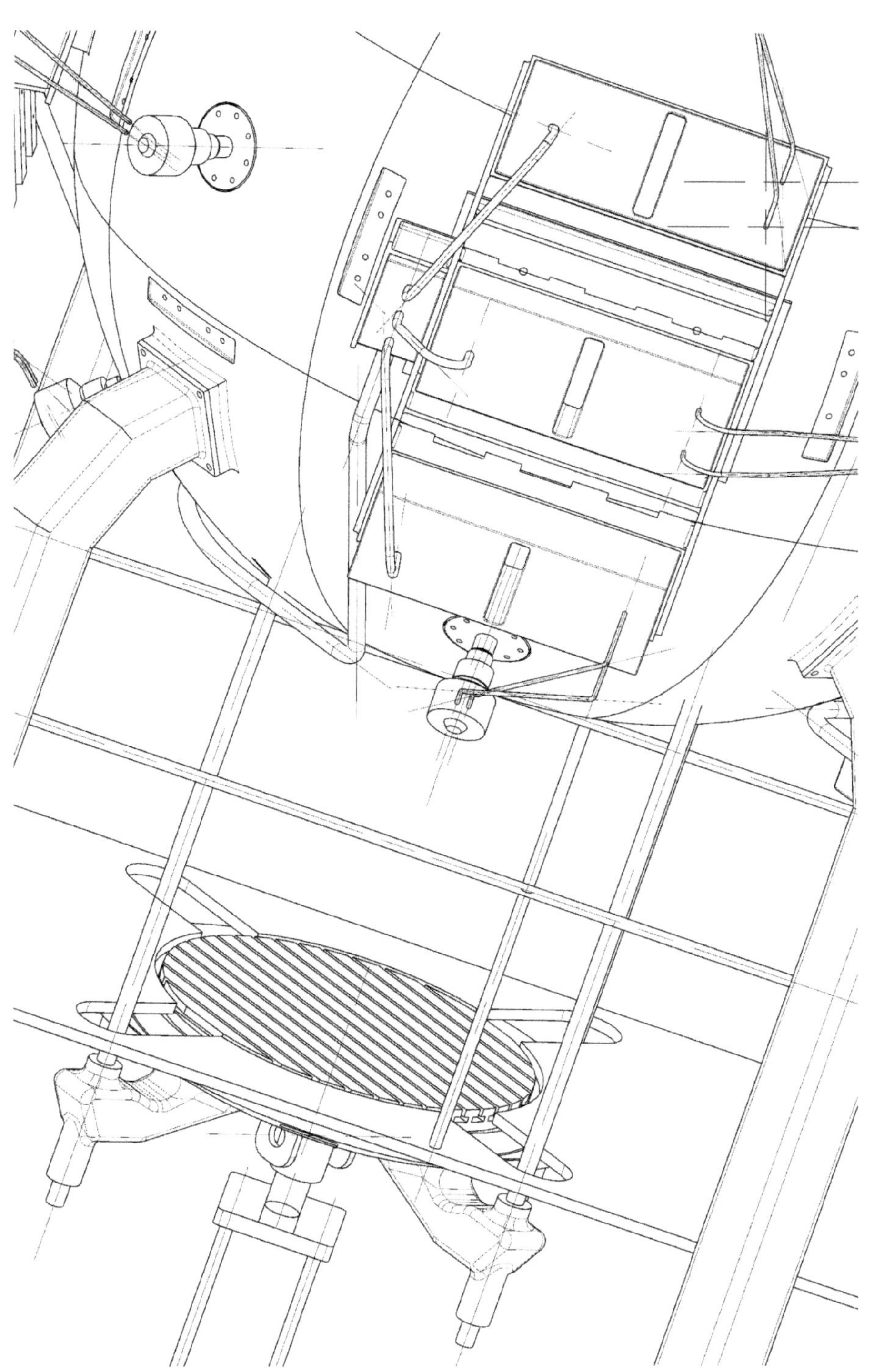